You c

———

Daughters of Courage

Margaret Dickinson

Daughters
of Courage

MACMILLAN

First published 2017 by Macmillan
an imprint of Pan Macmillan
20 New Wharf Road, London N1 9RR
Associated companies throughout the world
www.panmacmillan.com

ISBN 978-1-4472-9091-9

Copyright © Margaret Dickinson 2017

The right of Margaret Dickinson to be identified as the
author of this work has been asserted by her in accordance
with the Copyright, Designs and Patents Act 1988.

All rights reserved. No part of this publication may be reproduced,
stored in a retrieval system, or transmitted, in any form, or by any means
(electronic, mechanical, photocopying, recording or otherwise)
without the prior written permission of the publisher.

Pan Macmillan does not have any control over, or any responsibility for,
any author or third-party websites referred to in or on this book.

1 3 5 7 9 8 6 4 2

A CIP catalogue record for this book is available from the British Library.

Typeset by Palimpsest Book Production Limited, Falkirk, Stirlingshire
Printed and bound by CPI Group (UK) Ltd, Croydon, CR0 4YY

This book is sold subject to the condition that it shall not, by way of
trade or otherwise, be lent, hired out, or otherwise circulated without
the publisher's prior consent in any form of binding or cover other than
that in which it is published and without a similar condition including
this condition being imposed on the subsequent purchaser.

Visit **www.panmacmillan.com** to read more about all our books
and to buy them. You will also find features, author interviews and
news of any author events, and you can sign up for e-newsletters
so that you're always first to hear about our new releases.

*For Dennis
With All My Love*

ACKNOWLEDGEMENTS

My grateful thanks to Alison Duce, the Collections Manager at the Kelham Island Museum in Sheffield, for her valuable help and advice. And for his continuing support and encouragement my sincere thanks to Mike Hodgson, of Thorpe Camp Visitor Centre at Tattershall Thorpe, Lincolnshire, which is dedicated to the history of RAF Woodhall Spa and the squadrons that operated from the airfield during World War II. Thank you, too, to Steve Roberts of the Battle of Britain Memorial Flight reenactment group, whom I met at a 1940s weekend at Thorpe Camp. Our chat was extremely helpful – thank you.

A great many sources have been used in the research for this novel, but I must mention *Sheffield in the 1930s* by Peter Harvey (Sheaf Publishing Ltd in association with *The Star*, 1993).

Although in this book I have used real place names, streets and even actual buildings in both Sheffield and Ashford-in-the-Water, the characters and events in the story are entirely fictitious.

My love and thanks to my family and friends for their constant encouragement, especially those who read the script in the early stages; David Dickinson, Fred Hill and Pauline Griggs. And never forgetting my wonderful agent, Darley Anderson, and his team, and my editor, Trisha Jackson, and all the team at Pan Macmillan.

One

'What's up, Lizzie? You've got a face like a wet washday.'

With her hands on her hips, Emily faced the girl who'd just arrived at their place of work. Emily Trippet, tall and slim with blond hair and blue eyes, was already dressed in her workaday clothes; the buff-brat – a white, smock-like garment worn by all the buffer girls over a coarse dress – white cap and sturdy boots. Around her neck she'd tied a red scarf. She'd been about to cover herself with newspaper too to catch the worst of the oily sand that flew from the wheel as they buffed the cutlery, but now she paused. She could see that something was bothering Lizzie, her workmate and friend since Emily had first arrived in Sheffield five years earlier.

Their friendship had had its ups and downs through that time. They were both strong-minded, determined young women who'd recognized at first sight that they'd be either the best of friends or the worst of enemies and they'd been both at one time or another. But now they worked together, or rather Lizzie worked for Emily, for it was she who now ran the buffing

1

business above a grinders' workshop in Rockingham Street. It was known as Ryan's, which had been her maiden name, and Emily handled all the paperwork, visited their customers to collect and return work and was adept at finding new clients with her ready smile and honest approach, but she was not averse to donning the buffer girls' 'uniform' and lending a hand at a wheel when pressure of work demanded. And this morning they had to complete a big order, which would ensure all their wages for several weeks to come. Emily now employed four young women: Nell Geddis, who was readily acknowledged as the best buffer girl in the city, Ida Smithson, Flo Knight, who still acted as errand lass to them all, yet was learning the trade too in spare moments – and Lizzie Dugdale.

Emily was still waiting for an answer, but the girl glanced away to avoid meeting Emily's steady gaze. Lizzie bit her lip, still standing uncertainly just inside the door, almost as if she were unsure of her welcome this morning. Her blue eyes were fearful, her head bowed and her long black hair hid her lovely face. As she opened her mouth to speak, the door opened again with a flurry and Nell rushed in.

'Eeh, I'm sorry I'm late. I had to take Lucy to school this morning. It's her first day back after the summer holidays and poor little mite was frit to death and—' She stopped mid-sentence, suddenly becoming aware of the strange atmosphere in the workshop. She glanced worriedly from Emily to Lizzie and back again, raising her eyebrows in a question. With Nell's arrival, colour flooded Lizzie's pale face and she seemed even more ill at ease.

2

'What's up?' Nell repeated Emily's earlier question bluntly, but not unkindly. Nell had a strong face, which on a woman would be called handsome rather than beautiful, but nevertheless she was a striking-looking girl with a cloud of unruly, auburn curls that were already tucked firmly beneath her cap ready for work. She lived with her young daughter and elderly mother and worked hard to support the three of them.

Nell glanced at Emily who, still mystified, shrugged. Nell stepped closer to Lizzie and touched her arm. 'What is it, luv?'

After a moment's further hesitation, Lizzie whispered hoarsely, 'Mick's back.'

There was a pause before Emily said quietly, 'Is he now?'

Nell's mouth tightened. 'And has your mam marched him off to the police station by the scruff of his miserable neck like she threatened to?'

Lizzie shook her head. 'No. You – you know what mothers are like with their sons.'

Emily smiled wryly. Her younger brother Josh had always been their mother's favourite though Emily had never been jealous of him and loved him dearly. He had been the reason the family had come to Sheffield towards the end of 1920. Martha Ryan's ambitions for her son had known no bounds and she'd believed that the small cottage industry of candle-making, which had been in the Ryan family for at least four generations, was not good enough for Josh. The young man himself would have been content to stay in Ashford-in-the-Water, marry his

3

sweetheart, Amy, and continue with the family tradition, but Martha had squashed all his hopes and dreams. Underage at eighteen, he had not been able to marry without his parents' permission and Martha was the only one who could give that consent. Josh and Emily's father, Walter, had returned from the carnage of the Great War a broken man. He could no longer work nor, for a time, even speak. His days were spent sitting beside the kitchen range, plagued by fits of shaking caused by shell shock and exposure to gas attacks.

Now, as they waited for Lizzie to explain further, Emily was remembering the time they had arrived in the court off Garden Street, the kindness of Lizzie and her mother Bess, and, she had to admit, in the early days, even Mick had been good to them too. But it had been Lizzie's infatuation with Josh that had brought about an element of bitterness between the two families and when Josh, finding that Amy had borne his child, had returned to Ashford, things had got really nasty between the two families. Emily's memories were interrupted as Nell sniffed, marched towards her machine and snatched at the pile of newspaper with swift, angry movements. 'If he comes anywhere near me –' she glanced swiftly at Emily – 'us, then that's where he'll end up this time, I promise you. And as for Steve, well, when he hears that Mick's dared to show his face here again, I dread to think what might happen.'

Galvanized by Nell's remark, Lizzie hurried to her and grasped her arm, looking up into the other girl's face with pleading eyes. 'Please, Nell, don't tell Steve. I'm begging you. It'll cause such trouble.'

'You really expect me to say and do nothing when your precious brother trussed me an' Emily up like a pair of chickens and set fire to Mr Hawke's workshop with us still inside it? You think we're going to forgive *that*? He tried to kill us, Lizzie, and if it hadn't been for Mr Hawke's wonderful habit of losing his spectacles and coming back to look for them, we'd have been a pair of *fried* chickens.'

'I know, Nell, I know. But Mick's truly sorry and he – he's changed . . .'

Nell laughed wryly. 'If you think that, Lizzie Dugdale, then you're a fool.' Nell paused and seemed to be thinking. Slowly, she said, 'No, I won't tell Steve – not for your Mick's sake, but for Steve's – though I reckon he'll get to hear anyway.'

Steve Henderson was the leader of the biggest gang that plagued the city and the man whom Nell loved. He was the father of her six-year-old daughter Lucy, yet Nell was strongly determined that her daughter would not grow up in the shadow of a man who operated on the wrong side of the law. Years before, though Steve had wanted to marry her, she'd given him an ultimatum. 'You can see your child now and again. I'll not deny you – or her – that,' Nell had said, 'but you can't live with us and I certainly won't marry you unless you go straight.'

But it seemed that Steve did not love her enough to give up his criminal life and, though he saw his daughter regularly, breaking Nell's heart afresh every time he did so, and paid generously towards the little girl's keep, he was unwilling to give up his activities. He and one or two other rival gangs held the good people of the city to ransom. In the aftermath of the Great War, the city – like so many others – suffered from poor housing with rows of back-to-back dwellings with crowded, insanitary courts behind them, sharing one outside toilet. Unemployment was on the rise and even the brewers felt the drop in their sales. Families had no money to spend on beer. Yet, conversely, betting increased. Perhaps it was the thrill of the occasional win or a desperate attempt to forget their hardships for a few hours, but the likes of Steve Henderson and Mick Dugdale, who'd led a rival gang, had prospered from illegal gambling. Pitch and toss, playing with three coins being thrown into the air and bets being taken on how they would fall, was one of the easiest forms to organize. Sky Edge, a patch of wasteland with a high vantage point, had become one of the most popular places, which both Steve and Mick had used. The approach of the law could be seen easily by the lookouts posted to keep watch, the gamblers melting away and the three coins swiftly pocketed. But it was not the harmless game it might have seemed and now and then violent quarrels broke out if it was thought that a particular 'toss' had been unfairly executed. It was not, however, the only illegal enterprise of the gangs whose members often carried knives and razors; extortion, bare-knuckle fighting, pick pocketing and confrontations with innocent passers-by – all kinds of trickery were used. It was even rumoured that one gang ran a prostitution racket. The streets were no longer a safe place for law-abiding citizens. And, much to Nell's disgust, Steve seemed to be heavily involved.

And now Mick Dugdale, once Steve's friend and then his rival, was back and goodness only knew what would happen.

'Not a word to Ida or Flo,' Emily warned as they heard the girls' footsteps and laughter outside the door. 'I don't want them thinking we're all going up in smoke.'

Lizzie bit her lip but said no more as she pulled on her cap and moved towards her wheel. Once, Mick had been her friend and protector as well as her brother. He had seen that neither she nor their mother had gone short of anything, but they'd not realized that the money he splashed around freely had come from crime. They'd naively thought that he was a clever wheeler-dealer in the city. How wrong they had been and, now he was back, Lizzie was perhaps the most frightened of all of them. Since Mick's attempted act of revenge on Emily and Nell, because of what he saw as Josh's ill-treatment of his sister, Lizzie was no longer as vivacious and outgoing as she had been. Her mother, Bess, had been devastated when she'd learned the truth about her son and had buried herself away in the court behind Garden Street, venturing out very little. It was a subdued and unhappy household with just the two women and only Lizzie's wage to support them both. Despite his wicked ways, Mick was still her son and Bess mourned his loss, praying that somewhere he was still alive and well. Lizzie could still see the shock on her mother's face when he had walked in through the door the previous night; a look that had been swiftly followed by tears and hugs and, to Lizzie's amazement, there had been not a word of recrimination. But Lizzie was afraid. When Mick found out that she was still friends with Emily and Nell – was actually working with them – he would see it as a betrayal. His sister had thrown her lot in with the enemy.

As the door to the workshop opened and the other two girls came in, Nell, her even temper disturbed by the recent news, rounded on the young girl, Flo. 'You're late. You're supposed to be first here and to get everything set up. Where's me sand? Where's me pan of work? Time's money for me, y'know, Flo. It won't do.'

Flo, younger than the others, stood her ground. Hands on her hips, she said, 'Who's rattled your cage this mornin'? I got everything ready last night 'afore I left.' She waved her hand towards the bench near Nell. 'There's your sand and there's your work. The on'y thing I haven't got done yet is the fire, but Emily said she'd do it.' With one accord they all glanced towards the fire, which burned cheerfully in the grate. 'Ah, I see she has.' She smiled at Emily. 'Thanks, missus.'

Emily spoke quietly. 'Flo asked if she could be in a little later than usual this morning. She had to take her mother to the hospital.' She turned towards the girl. 'How is she, Flo?'

Anxiety flooded the girl's eyes and she bit her lip to stop it trembling. 'Not good, missus. She's had this pain for weeks now and no one seems to know what the matter is.'

'I'm sorry. Just let me know if you need any more time off. We'll cover for you.'

As she started up her machine, Nell sniffed her disapproval again, but this time, she said no more.

Two

As the girls turned off their machines that evening and were about to leave for home, they heard the sound of a child's voice echoing up the stairs from the grinders' workshop below. Nell's eyes widened with fear as she glanced at Emily.

'That's Lucy,' she whispered and, galvanized into action, she rushed towards the stairs. 'Lucy! What's the matter? What's happened? What are you doing here?'

Emily and the others followed her swiftly in time to see Nell reach the foot of the stairs and her young daughter rush towards her. She buried her face against her mother's skirt, not caring that she would be covered in the grime from Nell's working day.

'What is it? What's happened, luv? Is it Granny?'

'It's the girls at school. They locked me in the toilet at playtime and at dinner time and they wouldn't let me out.'

Nell squatted down in front of her and grasped the girl's shoulders. 'Have you been home to Granny? Does she know you've come here?'

With tears running down her face, Lucy shook her head. 'I came to find you, Mam.'

'You should have gone home first, Lucy, luv.' Nell's

voice was firm but kind. She could see her daughter was already distressed, but she had to instil obedience in her. 'Granny will be so worried that you're this late home from school.' She stood up and held out her hand. 'Come along, we must go straight home and then we'll sort those girls out.' Now a note of anger crept into her tone. No one, but no one, laid a finger on her girl.

'Is there anything we can do to help?' Emily asked.

Nell gave them all a quick smile. 'No, thanks, Emily. I'll sort it out.' She winked at her friends and added softly, 'Or her dad will.'

'Oo-er,' Flo said, making light of the matter, now that they could all see that Lucy was safe. 'I wouldn't be in their shoes when Steve Henderson goes knocking on a few doors.'

'I shan't involve him unless I have to,' Nell said. 'I think a quiet word from me will be enough.'

More than enough, I would think, Emily thought with amusement. Nell was a staunch friend, but even Emily admitted that she wouldn't like to get on Nell's 'wrong side'.

Outside their place of work in Rockingham Street, the girls separated and went their different ways home. Ida and Flo set off together, leaving Lizzie to walk to the court off Garden Street, while Emily, Nell and Lucy, who lived a distance away but only a few streets apart from each other, hurried to catch a tram or a bus that would take them nearer home.

Emily now lived in Carr Road. The house was in the centre of a terrace near the top of the road, two doors away from the pub on the corner. It had a living kitchen, a front parlour, three bedrooms and a small backyard. Having picked up some pork chops from the butcher on South Road, as soon as she arrived home, Emily removed her dirty working clothes and had a good wash, then began preparing the evening meal.

'I have to tell you something, Trip,' were Emily's first words to her husband, Thomas, when he arrived home, 'but before I do, I want you to promise that you won't do anything.'

Emily Ryan and Thomas Trippet – nicknamed Trip – had been friends from childhood and Emily had been in love with him forever. They had grown up together, roaming the hills and dales around Ashford-in-the-Water in Derbyshire where they'd lived. There'd been the four of them: Emily, her brother Josh, Trip, and Josh's childhood sweetheart, Amy Clark. Arthur Trippet had done his best to separate his son from what he considered 'unsuitable company' for his only child, who would one day inherit not only the biggest house in Ashford, but also his cutlery manufacturing business in Sheffield. Sending Trip to boarding school hadn't made any difference; the foursome still met in the school holidays. So then Arthur had decreed that Trip should 'learn the business from the bottom up' and had sent him to live and work in the city. But when the Ryan family moved there, Trip and Emily began walking out together. Incensed by the news, Arthur had uttered an ultimatum: give Emily up or be disowned. Trip had stood up to his father and, with his mother's help, had married Emily. It could have meant the loss of his inheritance, but never for one moment did Trip regret his decision. Emily was everything to him. However, following his father's serious stroke, Trip was back working at the factory alongside his half-brother, Richard, Arthur's illegitimate son by his mistress Belle Beauman. It was an arrangement that suited them all, even though it was somewhat unusual.

Now, Trip put his hands on his wife's shoulders and kissed her forehead. 'Ah, so you've heard too, have you? Mick's back.'

Emily looked up at him. 'How did you know?'

Trip laughed. 'The cutlers' grapevine has been hard at work. But I do have some good news.'

'Thank goodness for that,' Emily murmured.

'George Bayes is coming back to work.'

'Is he? That *is* good news.'

'He came to see me this morning. Since his wife died last year, he hasn't known what to do with himself. I thought he was going down on his knees at one point, but there was no need. I'm only too pleased to have him back. And so's Richard.'

George Bayes had worked at Trippets' factory for a long time and had been foreman there for several years, but about two years earlier he had given up his work to nurse his terminally ill wife.

'How old is Mr Bayes now?'

'A sprightly forty-nine, so he tells me.' A puzzled frown crossed Trip's forehead.

'What is it?' Emily, attune to his every look, asked softly. 'Are you worried about Mick and – and what he might do?'

Trip pulled a face. 'I suppose so. We'd better all

be on our guard, but it was something George said that set me wondering.'

Emily waited patiently as they sat down to their evening meal together. Trip picked up his knife and fork, but then hesitated, staring into the distance as if he was seeing not the food in front of him, but something quite different.

'He asked how my father was and I told him there was no change, but it was when he enquired after my mother that there was this look that came into his face. In fact, his whole demeanour changed.'

'How d'you mean?' When he didn't answer at once, Emily said, 'Don't let your meal go cold, Trip.'

Trip began to eat slowly, his mind obviously still elsewhere. Between mouthfuls, he said, 'His enquiry about Father was – well, just the sort of thing you'd expect him to ask. He's worked for the family firm for a long time and whilst I suspect he had disagreements with my father from time to time, I think he respected him. But it was when he asked about Mother that his genuine concern showed.'

'Your mother's a lovely woman. Everyone who meets her likes her, loves her even.'

Slowly, Trip turned to face her. 'That's it, Emily. You've hit the nail on the head.'

'I don't understand.'

'When George Bayes asked about her he didn't say "How's your mother?" or even "How's Mrs Trippet?"'

Emily frowned. 'I still don't see—'

'His words were "How's Constance?" He used her *Christian* name.'

14

Emily gasped in surprise and stared at Trip, her own meal forgotten too now. 'You mean – you think he's in love with your mother?'

'I don't know,' Trip said slowly, but then he grinned. 'Though I intend to find out. This calls for an excursion to Ashford on Sunday and when I casually bring into the conversation that George is coming back to work, I'll just watch Mother's face.'

Emily chuckled. 'Your mother won't give anything away, I can tell you that now.'

'We'll see, we'll see,' he murmured as, suddenly realizing he was quite hungry, he attacked his food with a great deal more interest. 'And besides,' he added, 'we really should warn Josh about Mick.'

Three

The following Sunday was bright and clear, but the country air was sharp. Autumn would soon be on its way, Emily thought, as she climbed into the sidecar attached to Trip's motorcycle. She glanced up at her husband. He really was a handsome man, she thought for the umpteenth time, with a smile that could melt hearts. He was tall with hair as black as a raven's feathers. The tiny lines around his warm, brown eyes crinkled when he laughed, which was often. He was kind and considerate and she loved him dearly.

'Hold on tight, Emily. We're off,' Trip said, as he started the engine and they weaved their way through the city streets and then roared up the hill towards Baslow and the place they still called home: Ashford-in-the-Water. It was a pretty village near Bakewell, set beside the meandering River Wye. At one end of the main street stood Trip's home, Riversdale House, whilst at the opposite end and just around the corner into Greaves Lane, was The Candle House, where Emily had lived for most of her life and where her parents now lived once more. Next door was the smithy where Josh lived with Amy, their two children and Amy's father, Bob Clark, the village blacksmith. But every working day, Josh walked the short distance to the front room of his parents' home where he had his candle-making business.

As they always did when they visited their families, they parked the motorcycle at Riversdale House and entered the building by the back door leading into the kitchen.

'Hello, Mrs Froggatt,' Trip said, putting his arms around the thick waist of the cook, whom he'd known since childhood. He planted a kiss on her red cheek and waltzed her round the kitchen table.

'Oh Master Thomas, you are a one,' she simpered. Pretending to be breathless but, in fact, enjoying every moment, she turned to Emily with a smile. 'Come along in, my dear. It's good to see you both. Everything all right, is it?'

Trip and Emily glanced at each other. They had decided to say nothing about Mick Dugdale's reappearance in the city to anyone apart from Josh and maybe Trip's mother.

'Everything's fine, Mrs Froggatt, thank you,' Emily said.

Then the cook stood with her hands on her hips and regarded them both. 'And when, might I ask, are you going to bring us some exciting news?'

Trip laughed loudly, perhaps to cover his embarrassment, though they both knew Mrs Froggatt's bluntness stemmed from her fondness for them both. 'All in good time.'

'Don't leave it too long, Master Thomas.' The cook wagged her finger at him. 'Trippets' needs an heir. It's not my business, of course, but I'd rather you didn't leave that to Master Richard.' She gave a disapproving sniff and then added hastily, 'Not that I've owt against the young man, mind. If your mother can accept the situation, then so can we. But I'd sooner like to think that *your* son will be at the helm in the next generation.'

'Richard's a nice young feller,' Trip said quietly.

'Aye, that's as may be, and I've nowt against him being in the business, but I wouldn't like to see the firm go down that line, if you see what I mean.'

'Oh I do, Cook, I do,' Trip said softly.

A less kind person would have taken umbrage at the cook's bluntness, giving vent to opinions that were none of her concern, but Mrs Froggatt had worked for the Trippets for many years and Trip was aware that she viewed the family as her own. He turned and held out his hand to Emily, knowing that the conversation would have touched a raw subject for her – for them both, if truth be told. They were both disappointed that Emily had not yet fallen pregnant and they, more than anyone, wanted the day to come when they could indeed bring exciting news to Ashford.

'Come, my love, we'll go and find Mother.'

'I'll send Polly up with coffee for three, then,' Mrs Froggatt said and waved them towards the door leading into the family's part of the house. 'And I'll make sure luncheon stretches to include two more.'

They found Constance in the morning room that looked out over the drive.

She laid aside her embroidery and rose from the window seat, holding her arms wide. 'I saw you arrive, my dears. How lovely to see you. Does Cook know you're here?'

Trip nodded and chuckled. 'And we've already been admonished for not bringing "exciting news", as she calls it. Mind you, we'd hardly be telling her first, now would we?'

Constance raised her eyebrows in a question, but Trip gave a slight shake of the head and she turned towards Emily to give her a warm hug of welcome.

'How's Father?' Trip asked, as they sat down to wait for the promised coffee to arrive.

Constance sighed. 'I think you'll see a change in him. I think he's deteriorating, I'm sad to say.'

Despite the fact that they had not married for love, Constance had been a dutiful wife and mother. Her only real sadness had been that she had been unable have a larger family. Two miscarriages after Thomas's birth had resulted in her husband being warned that if he wanted Constance's life not to be threatened, there should be no more children. After that, physical union between them had ceased and Constance had found out that Arthur had a mistress in the city.

Three years ago, Arthur Trippet had suffered a severe stroke, which had left him paralysed and unable to speak, necessitating a live-in nurse, Nurse Adams.

'He's losing weight and seems weaker,' Constance said.

'Does he still get up each day?'

'Oh yes. Nurse Adams and Kirkland make him.'

Kirkland had been the chauffeur and gardener for the Trippets for some years and now helped the nurse with the lifting of her patient from his bed to a chair each day.

'What does the doctor say? Has he called in a second opinion?'

'Yes, we had a specialist visit last week, but I'm afraid there's nothing that can be done. He won't improve any more.' Arthur had not left his bedroom since the day of his second stroke, even though Constance had tried to persuade him to use the bath chair she had acquired.

'The villagers have been very good,' she said, smiling, 'considering how he always treated them with disdain. The members of the Friendly Society visit him often, though I'm not quite sure how appreciative he is of their visits.'

Trip laughed. 'And are you still the leading light of that organization?'

Constance had built a life for herself in the village. She was well respected and liked by all who knew her and any one of them felt they could turn to her for help. There were only three women in the village, however, whom Constance would call her friends: Grace Partridge, whom she had come to know through the Friendly Society, and Martha and Amy Ryan, to whom she felt sort of related now that Emily and her son were married.

Constance chuckled at Trip's question. 'Now, now, Thomas, none of your sarcasm, if you please.'

'I wasn't being sarcastic, Mother. As if I would be. They're a great organization and do a lot to help their neighbours, but I also know that they regard you as their president, or whatever they call it.'

'We all work together,' Constance said modestly,

'and certainly they have all helped me over the last three years.'

There was a break in their conversation whilst Polly brought in the coffee and handed it round. When the maid had left the room, Trip asked, with deliberate casualness, 'Has George Bayes been to see him recently?'

Both Trip and Emily watched Constance's face carefully and later they were to agree that there had been a fleeting glimpse of something in her eyes at the mention of the man's name.

'Yes, he came once or twice in the first year, then not so often whilst his wife was so ill, but he called a couple of weeks ago.'

'He's coming back to work. Did you know?'

A smile flickered on Constance's mouth. 'Yes,' she murmured. 'It was my suggestion that he should speak to you. Since poor Muriel died, he's been feeling very lost. Times hangs heavy, as they say.'

'I'm glad you did, Mother. We've missed him and Richard can't wait for him to come back and help him with the admin side of things.'

'How is Richard? Are you getting on well with him?'

'Like the proverbial house on fire. He looks after all the paperwork – he's a very bright lad, actually – and I manage the factory side of things. It works very well.' Trip cast an amused glance at his mother. 'It was very astute of you to suggest such an arrangement.'

When he had disowned Thomas for a while over his refusal to abandon Emily, Arthur had installed his illegitimate son Richard into his firm and had made him his heir. But when Arthur had suffered the second and most severe stroke, it had been Constance who had come up with the idea to reinstate her own son and have the two young men become equal partners in the business.

'I'm only too pleased that it seems to have worked well. It might not have done.'

'True,' Trip agreed, 'but, luckily, it has.'

'He comes to dinner with us quite often,' Emily said, 'and we've even made him promise to come walking with us in the dales some time.'

'He's not too keen on that.' Trip laughed. 'I think he's a city lad at heart.'

At that moment, luncheon was announced and Trip decided to delay telling his mother about Mick Dugdale until they had eaten.

As they sat once more in the morning room after the meal, he said, 'Mother, I think there's something you should know, but please don't say anything to anyone else, though we do intend to warn Josh. We've heard that Mick Dugdale is back in the city.'

Constance nodded, understanding at once. Her glance went to Emily. 'Is he at home with Lizzie and their mother?'

Emily shook her head. 'He visited them briefly and then disappeared again, but we're pretty sure he's still in Sheffield.'

'And what is Lizzie's attitude?'

Emily wrinkled her forehead. 'Hard to say, really, but she knows that we won't tolerate her having

22

anything to do with him, if she wants to keep her job.'

'Just be careful, my dears, and remember the saying: "blood is thicker than water". And now,' she added, standing up, 'you'd better come up and see your father.'

Four

It was a great deal more difficult to get Josh on his own than it had been to speak to Constance privately. There was such a flurry of excitement in both households at their arrival.

'I *thought* I heard your motorcycle go past this morning,' Josh exclaimed, shaking Trip's hand and hugging his sister. 'How are you both? Oh, here's Harry to say "hello" to his favourite aunty and uncle.'

'We're his *only* aunty and uncle,' Emily laughed, picking up the four-year-old and dancing around the kitchen with him in her arms. 'How's my boy? My, you're getting heavy. And where's your little sister?'

'Upstairs having her afternoon nap in her cot.' The little boy was surprisingly articulate for his age. 'Have you seen Granny and Pap-pap?'

'Not yet. We've come to see you first, because you're the most important.'

The curly haired little boy beamed and wound his chubby arms around Emily's neck. Still with him in her arms, Emily turned to her brother. 'Josh, there's something—'

But she didn't get any further as the door opened and Amy came in. 'How lovely to see you. Come into the front room. Father's building up the fire.'

Still talking, Amy ushered them all through into the best parlour, which the family used all the time now, dispensing with the custom of have a front room that was only used on high days and holidays. As they entered the room, Bob turned to greet them with a smile.

Bob Clark was the village blacksmith and the family still lived in the house attached to his workplace. At forty-four, he was still fit and healthy with a strength belied by his slim stature. His family, friends and neighbours were everything to him. The only time he had ever felt the villagers' disapproval had been when he'd failed to volunteer in the Great War, but Amy had been more important to him; he couldn't risk leaving her an orphan, for his wife, Sarah, had died at Amy's birth and he'd loved and cared for his daughter ever since. And, to his mind too, his work was far more valuable to the local community than his becoming just one more casualty amongst the millions who'd been killed. Grace Partridge and her husband, Dan, had been Bob's staunch allies at that time, but it had not been until the local folk had seen poor Walter Ryan return from the war a broken man that they'd understood Bob's decision.

As Amy had grown, he'd watched with thankfulness in his heart as she and Josh Ryan had become close as children and he'd seen the love blossom between them. When Josh had been dragged away to the city by his ambitious mother, not knowing that he had left Amy pregnant, Bob had stood by his daughter and cared for her and the child. He remembered that time with mixed feelings. It had been troubling, of course, but, to his amazement, the villagers, led by Grace Partridge, had rallied round the young girl. Grace had helped to look after Amy from the time of her mother's death and, childless herself, had regarded Amy as the daughter she'd never had. Even more surprising had been Constance Trippet's understanding. Between them, Grace and Constance had ensured that Amy was never shunned or became the subject of village gossip. And when eventually Josh had found out about his son, he had left Sheffield and come back to Ashford. To the great delight of everyone, there had been a double wedding in the village church in April 1922 – Josh and Amy and Trip and Emily – and afterwards, Constance had held a joint reception at Riversdale House to which the whole village had been invited.

There had been only one person absent from the celebrations: Arthur Trippet.

Now, as they sat down together in the front room, the conversation revolved around family matters for the two hours they spent there and when Trip and Emily left to go next door to see Martha and Walter Ryan, they had still not had a chance to speak to Josh on his own.

As they walked the few paces to the back door of The Candle House, Trip whispered, 'I'll try to see him before we leave.'

The conversation within this household was very different from that next door. After courteous questions after everyone's health had been exchanged and the young couple had noticed that Walter had improved yet again since the last time they had seen him, Martha asked, 'And how is business, Thomas? Is the factory doing well?'

'I'm pleased to say it is, Mother-in-law.' Trip always gave Martha her full title – he felt it was what she expected – though he called Walter 'Dad', as Emily did. 'Despite the unsettled nature of the economy following the war, Emily's buffing business is going from strength to strength. She's thinking of taking on another premises and hiring more girls, aren't you, my love?'

'Are you really?'

Emily hid her smile at the surprise in Martha's tone. 'We are doing well, yes,' she said carefully, 'but it's a big step. There're the wages and increased overheads to think of. But, at the moment, we seem to have plenty of work coming in to cover it.'

'I've suggested that she takes a workshop at Trippets' – we've a space available, but because we're some distance from Rockingham Street, she feels it would be difficult to operate two premises.'

'Then she'll have to learn to drive and you'll have to buy her a little car, Trip, to travel between the two.'

It was the first time that Martha had ever taken an interest in Emily's achievements. In her mind, a woman's place was in the home and only a man should have a career. Emily gaped at her as, beside her, Trip said softly, 'D'you know, Mother-in-law, that's a very good idea.'

In his seat by the fire in the range, Walter smiled and nodded.

Five

When it was time for them to leave, Trip said, 'I'm just going out to check on the motorbike. I'll get Josh to give me a hand.'

He winked at Emily and she knew he was going to try to speak to Josh. She took her time in putting on her coat and tying a scarf around her head. Then she hugged her father and mother and went outside to see Trip and Josh standing together as if discussing the merits of Trip's motorcycle. They both turned as she approached and she could see by Josh's face that he had heard the news.

'You just take care of yourselves – both of you,' he warned, shaking Trip's hand and kissing Emily's cheek. 'Oh, and by the way, I have to come into the city next Friday for supplies. And would you believe, I've got an order from a shop there. I think it's one that's rented from your friend Nathan Hawke. Could I come early on Friday morning, Em, and then stay the night with you?'

Nathan Hawke had been one of the city's numerous 'little mesters', skilled, self-employed men, who had their own workshops and either worked alone or employed one or two men, usually carrying out certain processes of the cutlery trade for the larger firms. He'd had a workshop in Broad Lane and another in Rockingham Street and had been an enormous help to Emily since the day she had met him. In August 1921, Emily, Lizzie and Nell had been laid off from their employment at Waterfall's in Division Street. The three girls had decided to set up their own little buffing shop with, it had to be acknowledged, Mick Dugdale's help. It hadn't been until much later that Emily, innocent at that time of Mick's nefarious ways, had learned that he had threatened Nathan into assisting the girls. Only when Nathan got to know them properly and realized that they were ignorant of Mick's intimidation did it become a genuine pleasure for him to help them. When the friendship between Lizzie and Emily had soured over Josh, Emily had left. For a time, she had worked alone in the small workshop above Nathan's little mesters' premises in Broad Lane. But with Lizzie in charge, the Rockingham Street venture had failed and a desperate Nell had begged Emily to employ her. With Nathan's help, Emily had taken on both workshops and re-employed Nell and Ida, together with a young girl named Flo to work as errand lass for both premises. It had been Nathan's workshop in Broad Lane that a vengeful Mick had set on fire with Emily and Nell trapped inside. Emily and Nell had continued the business, now called Ryan's, in Rockingham Street. With Mick fleeing the city to escape the law and his mother and sister living in dire circumstances, Emily had taken pity on the girl, believing none of the catastrophes to be her fault, even though it had been her infatuation with Josh that had started the trouble. And so, Lizzie had returned to work with them, though the business from that time had become solely Emily's. With the loss of one of his premises, Nathan had decided to retire, but Emily still saw him often and would never cease to be grateful for his kindness to her.

'Bless him,' she said now to Josh. 'I expect he recommended you. He's been so good to our family. I haven't seen him lately. I must go and see if he's all right. And of course you can stay the night. It'll be lovely to have you, but you be careful too, Josh. If you were to run into you-know-who . . .'

'I will,' he said, as he helped her climb into the sidecar. 'Safe journey,' he mouthed now, as Trip struck up the noisy engine.

As they reached the top of the hill before descending into the city, it was already dusk. Conversation was impossible above the noise, but from time to time Trip glanced down at Emily, sitting beside him in the open-topped sidecar. He heard a rattle somewhere near his left foot and then a crack. At once he applied the brakes, but, to his horror, the sidecar suddenly broke away from the body of the motorcycle and veered to the left towards a ditch at the side of the road. He heard Emily scream, but there was nothing he could do as the sidecar landed with a bump in the shallow ditch. Trip came to a halt a little further on. He leapt off his machine, propped it on its stand and ran back towards Emily.

'Emily, Emily!' he shouted. Her head was resting against the grassy bank, her eyes were closed and she wasn't moving. He tugged at the sidecar, but it was wedged in the bottom of the narrow ditch. Then he tried to lift Emily out, but her unconscious body was too heavy for him to move. As he was struggling, the beam from the headlights of a car came over the crest of the hill and down towards him. Trip stood up and waved his arms. The car stopped and the driver turned off the engine. In the gathering gloom, Trip saw a tall, thin man unfold himself from behind the wheel.

'Want a hand, mate?'

'My wife's in the sidecar, but I can't move it.'

'Right. We'll lift it together.'

The two men straddled the ditch and hauled the sidecar up and set it on the side of the road.

'I'll hold it,' the stranger panted. 'You get her out.'

As Trip reached inside for her, Emily moaned and began to regain consciousness. 'What happened? Where am I?'

Trip felt a surge of relief.

'Wait a minute,' the stranger said. 'You ought to make sure nowt's broken before you move her.'

'My feet are wet,' Emily murmured. 'Why are my feet wet, Trip?'

Still steadying the sidecar, the man leaned towards Emily. 'Are you hurt, missus?'

Emily looked up at him and smiled stupidly. 'Hello. Who are you?'

'Your knight in shining armour, luv.' The man grinned. Now he was closer, Trip could see that he had curly fair hair and a strong, good-looking face, but the facts, for the moment, didn't really register in his concern for Emily. Only later was he to remember what their rescuer had looked like.

'I – don't think so. I've no pain.'

31

'And you can feel your feet?'

'Yes. They're cold and wet. What's happened, Trip?'

'The sidecar broke away from the bike. Now, I'm going to lift you out, my love, but tell me at once if anything hurts.'

Emily nodded.

Gently, Trip lifted her out and set her down on the bank above the ditch.

'Are you sure you're all right, Emily?'

'Yes, yes, I think so.' She put her hand to her head and felt a small lump. 'I think I must have bumped my head and passed out for a minute or two.'

'Let's get her in the back of my car,' the stranger said, 'and I'll take her t'Royal. You bring your bike, but I don't think we can do much about this –' he gestured towards the sidecar – 'till morning.'

Trip picked Emily up in his arms and placed her tenderly on the rear seat of the man's vehicle.

As the car set off and he returned to start up his motorcycle, he realized he still didn't know the name of their rescuer and by the time he arrived at the hospital, the young man had disappeared.

'Once he handed me over to a nurse, he was gone,' Emily explained. 'He seemed anxious to be off.'

'Maybe he doesn't like hospitals.' Trip smiled. Now he could see that Emily was unharmed, he could smile again. 'Lots of folk don't.'

It was very late when at last they arrived home from the hospital, Emily having been declared unhurt, if a little shaken. 'A day's rest and she'll be fine,' the sister in charge had said.

'Now, off to bed with you. I'll bring you up some cocoa and you have a day off tomorrow. I'll go to Rockingham Street in the morning and tell the girls what's happened.'

That night Trip lay with his arms around her as she slept against his shoulder. He sent up a prayer of thankfulness that she was unhurt and for the timely arrival of the unknown man. Trip shuddered to think what might have happened if he hadn't come along at that moment. Silently, he promised himself that Emily would not ride in the sidecar any more. The next day he would buy a motor car.

Emily returned to work on the Tuesday morning.

'A' you sure you should be here?' Nell asked. 'Trip came and told us what happened.' She grinned. 'If I didn't know better, I'd've thought you were just taking a Saint Monday.'

'Taking a Saint Monday' was a tradition, particularly in the cutlery industry, and was when workers did not go in to work. It was treated almost as another Saturday night with visits to the pub, playing cards or just drinking and talking. Most firms turned a blind eye, for their employees, many of whom were on piece work, always made up the time lost later in the week.

'I'm fine,' Emily said. 'I'm still a bit shaky, so I won't be working at the wheel today, but there are orders to take out and work to collect. A nice walk around town will do me good.'

'Take it steady. No rush.' Nell waved her hand as she returned to her wheel. Before she started the machine, she laughed, 'Trip told us a handsome young man stopped to help you.'

'Thank goodness he did,' Emily said. 'I might still have been sitting in the ditch, if he hadn't.'

By the end of the day, Emily felt quite well again and it was almost as if the incident hadn't happened, but when she arrived home it was to find a shiny new car sitting outside their house; a green, open-topped two-seater. Trip was standing proudly by it. He put his arm around her shoulders as they stood side by side to admire their new acquisition.

'Oh Trip, what have you done? Can we afford it?' Emily asked worriedly.

'I don't care whether we can or not. I'm not having you in danger like that again. I'll keep the bike to go to work on, but just for me. No more sidecar rides for you, my love,' he added firmly, tapping her nose with his finger. 'And the next thing is for both of us to learn to drive and I know the very person to teach us.'

'Who?'

'Kirkland, of course. I'm sure Mother would let him come into the city once a week to give us lessons and then you can think seriously about setting up another workshop in Trippets' premises.'

That night their tender lovemaking was even more special. Trip knew Emily could have been badly injured or even killed. His thankfulness that she had escaped unscathed and his gratitude to the 'Good Samaritan' were boundless.

Six

'I don't know about you lot, but I've had enough for today,' Emily said on the Thursday evening when they'd all worked later than usual. Already it was seven o'clock. She stepped back from her wheel and shook the black dust from her apron. 'Nights are pulling in now we're in September. It seems to get dark quicker here than in the country, but maybe that's just my imagination. Anyway, I don't fancy staying too late and having to walk home in the pitch-black.' She left the words unspoken but they all knew what she meant: not now Mick Dugdale might be roaming the city streets.

The machines slowed.

'Just let me finish these spoons and I'm right with you,' Nell said, as the other girls tidied up their workbenches and collected their belongings from the little room at the rear of the workshop. They clattered down the stairs, walked through the workspace where a grinder, Phil Latham, had his little mester's business on the ground floor, and out into the damp, early evening air. There were just Nell and Emily left and they exchanged a glance, remembering the time when they had been working late together and Mick Dugdale had found them.

'You go, Emily,' Nell said. 'I can lock up.'

'No, I'll wait for you. You've nearly finished. Besides, we ought to stay together as much as possible just now.'

Nell pulled a wry face, understanding at once.

Emily watched her friend at work, as fascinated as ever to see the shining spoons emerge from Nell's skilful hands. Nell Geddis had taught Emily the buffing work when they had both worked for Waterfall's, but it had been Emily who had had the courage to keep the modest business going even after Mick's murderous attempts. Now, she was the buffer missus in charge of four girls and it might soon be more, if their reputation continued to spread. Word travelled fast on the 'cutlers' grapevine' as Emily laughingly called it. Recently, she'd hardly needed to go out looking for work; it came to them and she was spending more and more time at the wheel instead of taking care of the administrative side of the business. The paperwork piled up and she often took it home at weekends to catch up.

'You're working too hard,' Trip told her constantly. 'We should be getting out into the countryside or to see our folks on a Sunday, Emily.' But he was proud of her achievements and his admonishments were only gentle ones.

As Nell finished the final spoon, they heard a voice calling from below. A woman's frightened voice. 'Nell – Nell, are you there?'

Nell's eyes widened as she stared at Emily for a brief moment. 'That's me mam. Whatever—?'

Nell hurried to the stairs and almost fell down

them in her haste. Emily followed, anxious too. Dora Geddis rarely ventured from her home; her legs were bad and walking very far was painful. It must be something very serious to have caused the woman to travel all the way to Rockingham Street from their home.

'Mam –' Nell had reached her. 'What is it? What's happened?'

'It's Lucy. She's not come home from school.'

'Not come home!' Nell repeated. 'But it's gone seven. She should have been home three hours ago. The little tyke!'

'Oh Nell –' Tears flowed down Dora Geddis's wrinkled cheeks. 'I didn't know what to do. I went to the school, but they said she'd left at the usual time with all the other children. Wherever can she be? She's always been such a good girl – never caused me a minute's worry before . . .' Dora hesitated and added, 'Well, only that one time last week when she was being bullied and came here to find you. Nell, you don't think those awful girls have locked her in somewhere, do you?'

Despite her anxiety, Nell laughed grimly. 'Not after I'd finished with them; they wouldn't dare.'

'Could she be playing out somewhere or have gone to a friend's house,' Emily put in tentatively, 'and lost track of the time?'

Nell shook her head. 'No. She might play out later, but she knows now that she must go straight home to Mam first. Last week – when she came here – was the first time she'd ever done such a thing, wasn't it, Mam?'

37

Dora nodded.

Nell bit her lip, her eyes anxious, but then there was a sudden spark of anger. 'If she hasn't . . .' The words and her tone implied that Lucy would be in big trouble if she had been disobedient.

'Do you think those bullies *have* waylaid her?' Emily suggested. 'Maybe it isn't her fault.'

'If they have, I wouldn't be in their shoes when I catch up with them again.'

'Should we go to the police?' Dora asked hesitantly.

Nell glanced at her briefly and then looked away. 'No,' she said firmly, 'but I know who I can ask.'

Dora gave a soft sigh and nodded. 'Aye, you're right, Nell. He'd be the one to help us, though—'

Nell touched her mother's arm. 'It's all right, Mam. Steve knows what the score is.'

Catching on, Emily said, 'Steve? Steve Henderson?'

Even amidst her anxiety, Nell smiled wryly. 'He is Lucy's dad, Emily. You know that. And if anyone knows what's going on in this city, then it's Steve.'

Emily forbore to say what she was thinking. *Of course he does, because he's behind most of what happens – the criminal activities, that is.* But she said nothing. Nell would sup with the Devil if it meant finding Lucy quickly and Emily, for one, couldn't blame her. Emily and Trip longed to have children and though it hadn't happened yet, she could imagine a mother's fear only too well. And she could come close; if something like this were to happen to Harry, her little nephew, whom she adored . . .

Steve Henderson, the leader of the largest gang in the city, was Mick Dugdale's sworn enemy. Once they had been friends, but then their two gangs had opposed each other until the day that Mick had been forced to flee the city after his attempt on Nell's and Emily's lives. Rumour had it that he now had a jagged scar down the left-hand side of his face; a parting gift from Steve. With their leader gone, the Dugdale gang had fallen apart and its members had joined other mobs, one or two even gravitating towards Steve. But now, Mick was back . . .

'Nell,' Emily said swiftly, 'do you think Mick might have something to do with this?'

Nell stared at her in horror before whispering, 'Oh my God, Emily. Don't say that. *Please* don't say that.'

Emily gripped her arm. 'Come on, we'd best get moving. Do you know how to get hold of Steve?' Whilst Emily wouldn't normally have been party to using a gang member instead of the police, sadly, on this occasion – if her supposition was right – she had to admit that Steve was probably the best person to help.

Nell nodded.

'Then you go and find him and I'll take your mother home—'

'No – no,' Dora protested. 'You go with Nell. I'll be all right. Just – just find her.' The woman dissolved into tears again.

Swiftly, they left the premises and Emily locked the door. Dora started to walk slowly home but Nell and Emily were running up the street, then twisting and turning through the back alleys, with Emily clinging on to the back of Nell's skirt.

'I hope you know where we're going, Nell,' she panted, 'because I'm completely lost.'

'I know this city like the back of me hand. Don't worry, just hang on to me.'

After what seemed an age, Nell slowed her pace and then paused outside the passageway between two terraced houses.

'This is it. Come on.' She led the way into the darkness of the passage, lifted the latch on the back gate and they stepped into a surprisingly tidy backyard. Emily was not sure what she had expected the yard of the house where a notorious gang leader lived to look like, but it was not this. In the evening light, she made out the shapes. In one corner stood the usual outhouses – the privy and washhouse. To one side of the yard, she saw a raised bed, planted with herbs and flowers and wondered whether a woman lived here too, who used herbs in her cooking and decorated the house with flowers? Despite what Nell had always believed – that Steve wanted to marry her – had he grown tired of waiting and found himself a wife?

Nell was knocking loudly on the back door, the sound echoing across the row of backyards. After a moment, the door was flung open and a tall, broad-shouldered young man stood there.

'Nell!' His surprise was obvious. 'Come in.' Then he spotted Emily standing in the shadows behind her. 'Both of you.'

As they moved into the light of the kitchen, Emily was surprised to see that Steve Henderson was fair-haired with a firm chin and the bluest eyes she had ever seen. He was very good-looking and, like his backyard, nothing like the gangster type Emily had expected to see.

'Oh my goodness,' she said. 'It's you!'

Now, for the first time, for his attention had been wholly on Nell, he looked at Emily. 'Ah yes, my damsel in distress. Fancy seeing you again.'

He said no more for the moment as his attention went back to Nell's obvious distress. 'What is it? What's wrong?'

'Lucy!' Nell gasped, her hand to her chest as if she had a violent pain there. 'She's gone.'

'Gone? What d'you mean, "gone"?'

Nell swayed and her face turned deathly white. Steve took hold of her and lowered her into a chair, bending over her solicitously. Nell closed her eyes and leaned back, fear and exhaustion taking its toll. Swiftly, Emily took up the explanation. 'Lucy didn't go home from school as she always does. Nell's mam came to our workshop just as we were leaving.'

'Good Lord! The old girl must have been worried, if she walked all that way. She hardly ever goes out, does she?'

It seemed Steve knew all about his 'family'. Even though they didn't live together – would never do so until Steve changed his disreputable ways – Emily knew that Nell allowed him to see Lucy as often as he wished.

'He's her dad,' Nell had explained simply. 'And whilst I don't want her knowing what he does – not yet anyway, though I expect as she gets older she'll find out – I wouldn't keep her from seeing him. She loves him to bits and he's so good with her. If only . . .'

41

And now they were here to ask for his help in finding his daughter.

Seeing that Nell's colour was coming back, Steve straightened up and went towards the hob. Deftly, he made tea for them all. Watching him, Emily could sense that he was efficient in the kitchen. Perhaps he did live alone.

As they sat around the table, he said, 'Could she have gone to a friend's house? Have you checked with the school and all her friends?'

Shakily, Nell said, 'Mam went to the school first, but they said she'd left at the usual time with all the other children, and no, we haven't been round her friends. I – I came straight to you. I couldn't think what else to do.'

Go to the police, Emily wanted to shout, but she kept silent. She knew it was not what Nell – and certainly not what Steve – would want. But the police force would have the resources. They could have policemen searching the streets within minutes, couldn't they?

Steve took hold of Nell's hand. 'You did t'right thing.' He spoke with the Sheffield dialect; he was clean-shaven, his hair neatly trimmed and he was dressed in well-cut clothes. It was another surprise and Emily realized that she had been unfair in having a picture of an ugly, scruffy thug in her mind. The sound of his voice dragged Emily back to listen to what he was saying. 'I'll get t'lads out looking and get in touch with t'other leaders too.'

Nell gasped and stared at him. 'Of the other gangs in the city, you mean?'

Steve nodded.

'But – but – they're your sworn enemies, aren't they?'

Steve laughed. 'Most of the time, yes, if we tread on each other's toes or try to take over someone else's patch, but when it's something like this, especially when the safety of a child is involved, then we're just one big happy family.' There was irony in his tone and yet truth in what he said. Emily had heard that even the old lags in prison hated any crime that involved harming a child and those inmates convicted of such heinous acts were given a tough time inside. It seemed that there really was some kind of 'honour amongst thieves'. And it looked as if Steve was about to prove that there was the same code on the outside too.

'Emily had an idea,' Nell said. 'I hope she's not right, but . . .'

Steve glanced towards Emily as she said, 'You know that Mick Dugdale is back, don't you?'

Steve nodded and though his blue eyes were fastened intently on her face and he let her continue, she could already read in his expression that his mind was leaping forward and coming to the same thought.

'Do you think he could have taken her?'

Steve's face was thunderous. 'Quite possibly. And if he has . . .' He left the words hanging, but the dire threat was there.

Nell leaned forward and clasped Steve's hands tightly in her own. 'Don't start a street war, Steve. Please. Just get Lucy back safe and sound.'

'I will. I promise you I will, Nell.' Now they were

gazing at each other, drinking in the sight of each other, united in the greatest fear that any parent can know. 'You go home, Nell, and stay with the old girl. Leave it to me.'

They all stood up and, briefly, Steve held Nell in his arms, laying his cheek against her hair. 'I'll find her, Nell.'

Nell buried her face against his chest. After a moment, she drew back and turned to leave. Pausing a moment near the open door, Steve held out his hand to Emily. 'I'm pleased to meet you properly this time, Emily, though I'm sorry it's in such circumstances. You've been good to my Nell and I never forget a kindness.' His face darkened for a moment. 'In the same way, I never forget someone who crosses me.'

Emily felt her hand enclosed gently in his warm grasp. She looked up into his face. 'What can we do to help? Is there anything Trip can do?'

Steve nodded. 'Yes, he can get the cutlers' grapevine into action. Get the word out amongst his own employees and news will soon spread to other factories in the city.'

'I will. I'll tell him the moment I get home.'

Steve was still holding her hand and now his own pressed it more tightly. 'Just one thing, Emily. No police.'

She stared at him for a long moment before saying, 'I can't promise on Trip's behalf, Steve, but I'll do my best to dissuade him. I give you my word on that.'

Steve nodded. 'So be it.'

'The main thing is that we find Lucy – however it's done.'

She could see the struggle in his face, but then he nodded and murmured, 'You're right, of course.'

For the safe return of his missing daughter, Steve was even prepared to take the risk of giving up his own freedom.

Seven

Outside Steve's home, the two young women parted to go their separate ways home. Nell lived on Walkley Street, which ran at right angles to Cromwell Street, where Steve lived. Emily and Trip now lived on Carr Road, a long street just around the corner from Trippets' factory and, to Emily's surprise, it was only a few streets away from where they were standing. In the five years she had lived in Sheffield, Emily had come to know the city's streets well, though she kept to the main thoroughfares, not tempted to take short cuts through the dark and dangerous back alleys. Those, through which Nell had led her earlier, she did not know, and she'd been unaware until this moment of exactly where they were. Now she knew her way home. As she stepped into their home by the back door, the smell of liver and onions being fried met her. Although her belly rumbled with hunger, she didn't feel like eating.

'I thought you'd soon be home, so I started tea.' Trip was not the kind of man who expected his wife to do everything about the home and work long hours too.

She closed the door behind her and leaned against

it for a moment, breathless from having hurried home. 'Trip – we've got trouble.'

He glanced up from cooking the liver. 'At the workshop? What's happened? Someone got collared?' It was the word used in the trade when someone got caught in a machine and was injured.

Emily shook her head. 'No. It's Lucy. She's missing.'

Trip took the pan off the heat and set it aside, all thoughts of eating forgotten.

He crossed the room, took her hands and led her to a chair near the warmth from the range. 'Tell me.'

Swiftly, she explained, ending, 'We went to see Steve Henderson. Would you believe it, Trip, it was Steve who stopped that night and helped you pull me out of the ditch.'

'No wonder he didn't hang around the hospital. Go on.'

'Nell and Steve are both adamant that we shouldn't go to the police.'

Trip was tight-lipped. 'I can understand why, but I think they're wrong.'

'They've asked if you could get all your workers out looking and they think word will spread to all the other workers in the cutlery industry and possibly beyond. We'd have a veritable army out there looking for her. And if Mick Dugdale has got her . . .' Her voice tailed away and she shuddered.

Trip leapt up, galvanized into action. 'I've thought of an idea that might alert the police without anyone actually going to them.'

'Trip, what are you going to do?'

'Best you don't know. Just trust me.'

Briefly he hugged her and then he pulled on a thick, warm coat. 'Get yourself something to eat and then you go round to Nell's. It's getting late, I know, but I'm sure she and her mother could do with your company. They must be half out of their minds with worry. Will you be all right?'

'Of course I will, and I'll go and tell Ida – and Flo too. The more people who know, the better.'

Trip gave her a brief peck on the cheek and went out into the night to help search for a lost little girl. Outside, he paused a moment, debating whether or not what he was about to do was the right thing. Then, with a dismissive shrug towards his own conscience, he set off on his motorcycle towards the home of Eddie Crossland, the foreman at the small cutlery manufacturing business in Division Street, Waterfall's, where Nell, Lizzie and Emily had all worked a few years earlier. Eddie was a good friend of George Bayes and, even more importantly at this moment, he had a nephew in the police force.

When the front door opened and the burly man saw who was standing on his doorstep, there was no mistaking the surprise in his tone.

'Nah then, Mr Trippet, whatever brings you to my door this late?'

Trip held out his hand. 'Thomas, please, Mr Crossland, or even Trip.'

Eddie grasped Trip's hand in a warm clasp. 'Then it's Eddie, Trip. Come in, come in and tell me what's to do. Millie'll mek you a cuppa. Have you eaten?'

'To tell you the truth, no.'

'Then you shall have one of my sister's apple pasties. Freshly baked this morning.'

He ushered Trip into the kitchen where Eddie's sister, Millie, was busily clearing away the remnants of their evening meal. She greeted Trip and then bustled about pouring him a cup of tea and placing an apple pasty on a plate. Trip had known that Eddie and his sister now lived together. Millie had never married and although Eddie had been married briefly, his wife had died a few years earlier.

'You get that down you, Trip, whilst you tell me what's to do.'

'You remember Nell Geddis, don't you?'

'Of course I do. Go on.'

'Did you know she had a little girl, Lucy? She'll be about six now.'

Quietly, Millie Crossland sat down beside them to listen.

'Aye, I had heard and rumour has it,' Eddie said, 'that Steve Henderson is the father.'

Trip bit into the pasty and for a moment savoured the tangy taste of apple. He nodded. 'It's true, but Nell won't marry him until he gives up his life of crime.'

'Good for her.'

'And had you also heard that Mick Dugdale is back in town?'

Eddie's face hardened. 'Aye, I had,' he said shortly, but Trip did not ask from whom he'd heard. He hoped it was his nephew, but he didn't want the policeman's name to come into the conversation. He wanted to drop a hint and then leave it to Eddie

Crossland to do whatever he thought best. That way Trip would not be directly involved in the police being informed.

He came to the real reason for his visit. 'Lucy didn't arrive home from school at the usual time and that's not like her. We're afraid that Mick might have taken her. No doubt he still holds a grudge against Steve and possibly Nell too.'

Beside him, Millie gave a little cry, covered her mouth with trembling fingers and gazed at her brother with wide, fearful eyes.

Eddie nodded. 'Someone who's seen him says he has a nasty scar down the left side of his face. They reckon Steve Henderson gave him that just before he disappeared. So, yes, he'll be bearing a grudge orreight.'

Tears flowed down Millie's face. 'Oh, that poor little mite. What will he do to her?'

The two men exchanged a grim glance.

'I just wondered if you could alert your workforce, Eddie? I'm on my way to see George and to get all our employees out on the streets.'

'I'll send word. It'll soon ripple around. A lot of our workers live close to each other and they know folk from other factories too. And we should get word out amongst the little mesters.'

Trip rose. 'Nathan Hawke would be the best man to do that. As soon as I've seen George, I'll go and tell Mr Hawke.' He turned towards Miss Crossland. 'Thank you for the tea and the pasty. That'll keep me going nicely.'

He left quickly before Eddie might think of his nephew and mention his name, but Trip hoped he'd planted the seed in the man's mind. He would have been gratified if he could have heard the conversation between Eddie and his sister only moments after the door had closed behind him.

'I'd best go and see our Joe.'

'Do you think you should?' Millie asked worriedly. 'Steve Henderson wouldn't want the police involved, Eddie. I don't want him coming after you.'

Despite the seriousness of the moment, Eddie chuckled. 'That's why Trip came here. Don't you see? He knows I can get a discreet word through to the police without it being official. He's a bright young feller, that. What he doesn't realize – none of them do – is that the police are about far more than just catching criminals. They'll put aside their differences with Steve Henderson to help find his daughter. Her safety and well-being are paramount. Now, lass, let me get off and see if our Joe's at home.'

Half an hour later, Eddie was standing in his nephew's home facing his young wife, Betty.

'He's not here, Uncle Eddie. There's a flap on. It seems a little girl's gone missing and—'

'Do you know her name?'

'Lucy something, I think. One of his snouts, as he calls his informers, slipped a note through our door about an hour ago. It said a little girl had been *taken*. That's what made Joe rush off.'

'My word, news does travel fast.'

Betty nodded and pursed her lips. 'It was very courageous of whoever it was to come to our home, but even the criminal world doesn't like this sort of thing, Uncle Eddie.'

51

'Did the note say who'd got her?'

Betty shook her head.

'Well, you tell our Joe as soon as you can that Lucy is Nell Geddis's little girl and Steve Henderson is her dad.'

Betty's eyes widened. 'Oh my!'

'And,' Eddie went on grimly, 'we're afraid that it might be Mick Dugdale who's taken her.'

He needed to say no more to the policeman's wife; she understood only too well.

Eight

At the same moment that Eddie was leaving his nephew's home, Trip was knocking on George Bayes's door. After a similar conversation with Trippets' foreman, who at once set out to alert as many of their workforce as he could, Trip headed for Nathan Hawke's home.

'Why, Trip, come in, come in,' Nathan greeted him on opening the door. 'It's good to see you, but is something wrong? You're rather late for a social call.'

'No social call, I'm afraid, Mr Hawke. And yes, something is very wrong.' Swiftly, he explained and the older man's face darkened. 'I had heard on the grapevine that Mick was back, but not this latest news. Oh dear, this is dreadful. What can I do to help?'

'Can you get word out amongst all the little mesters?'

'Of course.' He reached for his jacket and cap from the back of the door. 'I'll start at once. Now, where did I put my spectacles?'

Trip rode through the dark streets towards Walkley Street, going over in his mind if there was anything else he could do, anyone else he could ask for help. He could, of course, approach the other owners of the various factories in the city, but he believed – and rightly so – that word would spread from worker to worker and very soon most of the city would be alerted. He hoped, too, that Eddie Crossland had thought to get in touch with his nephew.

And then he remembered Richard. It was only fair that he informed his own half-brother of what was happening. If Trippets' workers were out all night searching, there wouldn't be many turning up for work in the morning, except perhaps to collect their pay, as it would be Friday. So he turned off his route to Nell's home and headed instead for the street where Richard now lived with his mother, Belle Beauman.

As he pulled his motorbike onto its stand and removed his helmet, he was again thinking of the past and of the peculiar circumstances that had brought Richard and himself to be partners in Trippets'. Now Trip knew the full story, he would never cease to marvel at the satisfactory outcome of what could have been a sorry tale. And it was due mainly to his mother's amazingly generous spirit. Years earlier, when Constance had suffered two miscarriages and had been advised that she should not endanger her life by bearing more children, Arthur had taken a mistress. Constance had made it her business to find out about the former music-hall dancer, Belle Beauman, whom Arthur had set up in a modest terraced house. Much to his annoyance, Belle had fallen pregnant and he had insisted that she have an abortion. After several months away from her and believing she had complied with his wishes, Arthur resumed his visits to her. What he did not know – though Constance had made it her business to find out – was that Belle had not been able to bring herself to abort her baby and so her son, Richard, had been raised in secret. It wasn't until Arthur had disowned Trip over his son's desire to marry Emily Ryan that he found out that he had another son, albeit an illegitimate one. By this time Richard was fifteen and, more out of spite than anything, Arthur had taken the boy into his business, promising to make him his heir. Shortly afterwards, Arthur had two strokes, the second of which incapacitated him. Constance then showed her true mettle. Not being a jealous woman, she had engineered that her own son be reinstated in the family firm and that the two young men should become equal partners. Now, they worked together harmoniously and liked and respected each other enormously. Constance's benevolent understanding had not ended there; since her husband's incapacity she had invited Belle and Richard to visit Riversdale often to see Arthur. And now Richard lived openly with his mother instead of with the foster parents with whom she'd placed him as a baby.

As the door was opened by a maid, light flooded into the street.

'Oh Mr Trippet, what brings you here? Mrs Beauman and Mr Richard are at dinner. Should I—?'

'I'm sorry, but I must speak with Mr Richard. Please inform him I am here.'

'Of course, sir. Please step inside.'

Only moments later, Richard was hurrying into the hallway. 'Trip, my dear fellow. What is it? Is it Father?'

Trip shook his head and explained as the young man listened with growing horror. The two half-brothers were uncannily alike; they had the same black hair and brown eyes, which crinkled when they smiled or laughed.

'I'll come at once,' Richard said.

'But you're dining . . .'

'No matter. This is more important. I bet you haven't eaten, have you? Can we get you something?'

Trip shook his head. 'No, but thank you.'

'I must just tell Mother. Please come in.'

They went into the dining room. Belle was still a pretty woman, a brunette with a shapely figure and mischievous eyes. But now her eyes were frightened and Trip guessed she was thinking that his sudden appearance meant something dreadful had happened to Arthur.

'It's not Father,' he said quickly and told her of Lucy's disappearance.

'I'm going out to help. Don't wait up . . .' Richard kissed Belle's forehead as she rose from her place and held out her hands towards them. She was trembling as she said, 'Take care, both of you.'

Outside, Trip said, 'I've told everyone I can think of except the other owners of factories in the city.'

'I'll see to that. If you can take me to our factory, I can send word out from there. I have names and addresses for most of our competitors in the files.' Richard worked in the offices of Trippets'.

'I've seen George. I think he's gone there already.' George Bayes had been Richard's mentor and now he was back working alongside him.

'Good, then we'll work through them together. Can you take me there on your bike? It'd be quicker than me walking.'

'I could . . .' Trip said doubtfully. 'But there isn't a proper pillion seat and no footrests. I don't want another accident.'

'I'll perch on that luggage rack at the back and if you drive slowly, I'll just stick my legs out so my feet don't get caught. Come on. We must think of that poor little girl . . .'

They arrived at Trippets' factory in Creswick Street without incident and having deposited Richard at the gates, Trip roared off towards Nell's house, anxious to hear if there had been any news.

He found Nell and her mother in a dreadful state, with Emily just as worried but trying to keep calm. She had been making endless cups of tea, and whilst neither Nell nor her mother seemed to want to drink them, it gave Emily something to do. Trip, however, was glad of the steaming mug of tea she gave him as he told them what he'd done, glossing over his visit to Eddie Crossland's home. 'I can't think what else to do, can you?'

'It's the waiting about that's so hard,' Emily said. 'If only we could go out searching too.'

Nell's head snapped up as another idea came to her. 'Has anyone thought to go and see Lizzie and her mother? You know what she said the day she told us he was back.'

Emily stared at her and murmured, 'That Mrs Dugdale won't turn him in now, though she threatened to when . . .' She waved her hand and they all knew she was referring to the time of the fire. 'But she might change her mind if she realizes he might be involved in this.'

Trip got up at once. 'You're right, Nell. Anything's worth a try. They just might know something.'

'But will they tell us?' Nell asked flatly.

Trip's face was grim as he said, 'We won't know that unless we ask. I'll go at once.'

'They might listen to me – or Nell – better than you, Trip,' Emily said.

Mrs Geddis seemed to have recovered a little, though she was still desperately anxious and feeling that this was all her fault. 'I should have met her from school,' she kept murmuring to herself. 'I shouldn't have let a little lass like that walk home on her own.' Listening to their conversation, she said now, 'You go, all three of you. I'll be all right and I'll be here if . . .' Her voice faded away and her head dropped.

Nell patted her mother's shoulder, but could not bring herself to speak.

Nine

As the three of them set off together, they were heartened to see that the streets were alive with men and boys. The front door of every house was being knocked on, every backyard and alleyway searched and the more householders realized what was happening, the more folk came onto the streets, even women and girls now. One or two recognized Nell as she walked along and, without preamble, asked, 'Any news?' When she shook her head, they touched her arm in sympathy and hurried on.

'The police must have heard. Look,' Trip said, nodding towards two constables walking down the road, stopping every now and then to speak to the searchers.

Seeing them, Nell suddenly veered off to her right. 'This is a short cut to Garden Street. Come on.'

Trip took hold of Emily's hand and whispered, 'I don't think it is, but we'd better follow her. Mind your footing.'

At last they arrived in the court where Emily had once lived with her parents and her brother.

'Which house are they living in now?' Trip asked, glancing round the gloomy court.

'Number four. Where we used to live . . .' Emily

pulled Trip after her, but Nell was already hammering on the door of the Dugdales' home.

'Where is he? Come on out, Mick Dugdale, if you're there. I want a word with you.'

Other doors opened at the sound of the commotion, but it wasn't until Lizzie, with frightened eyes, opened their door that Nell ceased her shouting.

'Where is he? Where's Mick?'

'He's not here. What d'you want him for anyway?'

Nell pushed past her and stepped into the kitchen. Bess, rotund and red-faced from the heat of her oven, straightened up from the range.

'Whatever's the matter?'

Nell stood with her hands on her hips, her eyes spitting fire. 'Don't tell me you don't know. That you haven't heard. The whole city must know by now. My Lucy's gone missing.'

'Aw lass, I'm sorry to hear that. And you want our Mick to help, is that it?'

Nell glared at her. Was the woman stupid or just blind to her son's character? Hadn't what he'd done in the past told even his mother that he was a bad 'un through and through?

Nell stepped closer, menacingly. 'Yes, I do want his help – but not the way you mean. I think he's got her. I think he's taken her in revenge.'

'Oh no, no.' Bess shook her head vehemently. 'Our Mick wouldn't do that. He'd never harm a child . . .'

'Your precious Mick would do anything – *anything* – to get back at Steve.' She flung her arm out towards Emily and Trip who had followed her in. 'And the rest of us.'

Now she whirled around to face Lizzie. 'D'you know anything? Have you seen him?'

Lizzie's eyes filled with tears. 'How can you think that of me, Nell? I'm your friend . . .'

'That wasn't always the case, was it, Lizzie? You were almost as vengeful as your brother against Emily – and me. It was only when he scarpered and left you and your mam to fend for yourselves that you came crawling back begging forgiveness because you needed a job.'

Lizzie's face turned white.

'Just a minute, Nell . . .' Now Bess waded in to defend her daughter. 'Lizzie was hurt by the way Josh Ryan treated her. He let her think they were walking out and then he just dumped her and went back to his sweetheart in Ashford. And then, after he'd gone and Emily set up on her own against Lizzie's buffing business – which, let me remind you, our Mick had helped the three of you set up in the first place – of course she was resentful.'

'Mam, leave it – please. It was me that was in the wrong. I know that now. Emily had tried to warn me all along, but I was so obsessed with Josh, I just didn't listen.' She turned to face Nell and Emily. 'After Mick left and you forgave me and took me back to work with you, I gave you my word that it was all over, that there was no bitterness on my part. And that's still the truth. I told you at once when Mick came back, and yes, at first he did come here, but he went again and we haven't seen him since. I swear to you that we don't know where he is and I certainly don't know anything about Lucy.'

61

For a long moment, both Emily and Nell stared at Lizzie. They exchanged a glance and then Nell nodded and said flatly, 'I believe you, Lizzie. I'm sorry, Mrs Dugdale, but I'm out of me mind with worry.'

'Sit down, luv. You too, Trip. I'll make tea and we'll have a think.'

As the atmosphere in the room changed and they sat down together to drink tea, Bess said, 'You really think Mick might have taken her?'

'I'm sorry,' Nell said hoarsely, 'but yes, I do.' She paused and asked hesitantly, 'Has he got a nasty scar down one side of his face?'

Mother and daughter exchanged a glance and then nodded.

'Rumour has it that Steve did that to him. Now, if that's true, Mick isn't going to forget – or forgive – that in a hurry, now is he?' More calmly now, but still desperate with worry, Nell added, 'Is there any-where you can think of where he might be? Where he could have taken her?'

'What about his mates?' Emily put in.

'Mates?' Lizzie scoffed. 'He hasn't any left now.' She gestured towards Nell. 'Once he'd left, his so-called mates defected. Some of 'em joined your Steve – even his best friends, Pete and Gary.'

'So – you've really no idea?'

They both shook their heads.

There was no point in staying and as they walked out of the court together, Emily said, 'D'you reckon they're telling the truth?'

'I don't know,' Nell said grimly, 'but I know one

thing: if I ever find out Lizzie's been lying to us, I'll be asking you to sack her.'

'You wouldn't need to ask, Nell.'

At the end of the road, they separated from Trip as he set off to join in the search. Back at Nell's home, there was still no news.

'You ought to go home, Emily,' Nell said in the early hours of what was now the following morning. 'Get some rest. You'll have to go into work in the morning. Ida and Flo can't cope on their own, only I won't be in.'

Emily touched her friend's shoulder. 'You take as long as you need. Everyone will understand.'

Nell looked at her with red, swollen eyes, her voice quavering. 'You – you do think they *will* find her, don't you?'

'Of course I do,' Emily declared stoutly, trying to instil into her tone as much confidence as she could muster. 'You've got to believe, Nell.'

She kissed her friend and hurried home. She would snatch a couple of hours' sleep – if she could – and then go to the workshop. It was Friday; Ida and Flo would need their wages. Whatever was happening, life had to go on.

Trip wasn't at home and she hadn't expected him to be there. He would stay out on the streets for as long as it took to find Lucy.

Surprisingly, Emily fell into an exhausted sleep fully dressed and was roused only when there was a loud knocking on the door. Her heart leapt and she scrambled out of bed, threw a shawl around her shoulders and hurried downstairs to open the door.

'Josh!' she said, staring at him in surprise.

'Hello, Em. Don't tell me you'd forgotten I was coming today?'

'Oh Josh!' Tears swam in her eyes as she pulled him inside and flung herself against him, bursting into noisy sobs. The anxiety and trying to keep strong for Nell's sake finally overwhelmed her and the sight of her brother released the floodgates.

'Hey, what's all this? Whatever's wrong?'

He held her at arm's length and looked down into her troubled face.

'It's Lucy.'

'Nell's kiddie?'

Emily nodded. 'She's missing. She didn't come home from school last night. We've got the whole city out looking for her.'

Josh frowned. 'But there's more to it than that, isn't there? I know you so well, Em. I can see it in your eyes.'

'We – we think Mick Dugdale might have taken her.'

At the time of the fire, none of their family in Ashford had known about it and neither of their parents knew anything about it even now, but weeks later, Emily had confided in her brother, swearing him to secrecy. So, now, he understood their fears.

'Come on, sit down. Have you had any breakfast?'

'I couldn't eat a thing.'

'You must. You won't be any help to anyone if

you don't keep your strength up. What about Trip? Is he here?'

Emily shook her head. 'Still out looking, I expect. He's not been home all night. I should get to work. Ida and Flo will want to know what's happening and besides, it's payday. I must—'

'I'm sure they'll manage for another day or two in the circumstances. And anyone waiting for their work to be done will understand why it's late when they know the reason. And if, as you say, half the city are out looking for Lucy, there won't be much work done today anywhere. They'll all be taking a Saint Friday.'

Josh pushed her gently into a chair at the kitchen table, found cereal and milk and made tea. 'There. Go on – eat it, Em, there's a good girl.'

Emily tried, forcing the food down her throat, whilst Josh sat drinking tea and tapping his fingers idly on the table. He was deep in thought.

At last, when he had seen that Emily had managed to eat about half the bowlful, he asked, 'Has anyone come up with an idea of where he might be hiding her? That's if he has got her.'

Emily shook her head.

'D'you think he might have taken her out of the city?'

Emily stared at him. 'It's possible, I suppose. But where?'

Josh's mouth was a tight line. 'Em – I don't think you knew about this at the time. But before I left Sheffield to go back to Amy, I got involved in some of Mick's scams.'

Emily nodded, but said nothing.

'We used to go up to Sky Edge to run his pitch and toss games.'

Emily said quietly, 'I knew about the gambling. Go on.'

'Then there was the night we went out into the countryside to watch bare-knuckle boxing. It was the night that I came in very late and you told me about Mam hiding our letters from Amy. And then, the next day, I went back to Ashford and found that Amy was pregnant with my child.'

'So, finding out about Amy and going back to her saved your bacon from Mick, did it?'

'Yes, but that wasn't the reason I went back. You know that.'

'So why are you telling me all this now?'

Before Josh could continue, there was a rattle at the back door and Trip staggered in. Emily rose at once and went to him, putting her arms about him and leading him to a chair. He was exhausted, his face was white and his eyes were wide with tiredness.

Josh made more tea and pushed a bowl of cereal in front of him. 'Eat,' he commanded and, automatically, Trip obeyed.

Emily sat down again and said. 'There's no news, I take it.'

His mouth full, Trip shook his head. 'There are hundreds of folks out looking. We must have scoured the city twice over, but we just don't know where to look next.' He laughed wryly. 'If it wasn't so serious, it'd be comical to see the police and Steve and his gang members working in cahoots. It's as if they've called an unspoken truce. Though all bets will be off once she's found.' He stopped and forbore to add: '*If* she's found'.

'Talking of bets . . .' Swiftly, Josh repeated what he had been in the process of telling Emily when Trip had arrived home and continued, 'We went out of town in a car Pete had "borrowed". He set fire to it on the way back and we ran the last few miles home. Anyway, that's another story. What I wanted to tell you about is the old barn in the middle of nowhere that Mick used for the boxing match. I just wondered . . .'

'If he might have taken her out there?'

Josh nodded, but then pulled a face. 'Mind you, it was really Steve's place. Him and his gang were waiting for us when we came out and warned Mick off from using it again. It nearly came to fisticuffs.'

Trip was thoughtful. 'I don't know if Mick would take Steve's daughter to a place that was her dad's stamping ground, though it's probably the sort of twisted thing he would do. Hiding her in plain sight, so to speak. No one would think of looking for her there for that very reason.'

'It's worth a look, isn't it?'

'Of course. We'll go at once. That's if you can remember where the barn was.'

'I know we set off up the Baslow Road and just seemed to keep going. Maybe I'll recognize it as we go.'

'I presume you came in my mother's car. I saw it outside when I came home and thought she was here.'

Josh nodded. 'Your mother's very good to us, Trip, in all sorts of ways.'

Trip smiled weakly. In normal circumstances, it would have been a huge grin, but today no one felt like smiling. 'I've bought a car now,' he murmured, 'but neither of us have had time to learn to drive it yet.'

'Well, I can drive. Mr Kirkland taught me. Come on, then, let's get going,' Josh said, getting up.

'Just hang on a minute whilst I have a quick wash,' Emily said.

'I don't think you should come, darling. If Mick's there . . .'

'Yes, I should. Lucy doesn't know either of you all that well. If she is there, she'll be even more frightened than she already is, poor mite. I *must* come. Please, Trip.'

'All right,' Trip agreed reluctantly, 'but you must promise me you'll stay well back till we see what's what.'

'That's if we can find the place.'

Ten

Ten minutes later, after Emily had splashed her face hurriedly, they were in Constance's little car, with Emily squashed into the narrow space at the back, and heading out of the city.

'We ought to have told someone where we're going,' Emily shouted above the noise of the engine. 'We ought to have some sort of back up.'

As they chugged up the hill, they saw several men going from house to house, knocking on doors and talking to the occupants.

'Looks as if the search is still going on round here,' Josh remarked. 'Do you want to stop and tell someone where we're going?'

'Trip – I think we should.'

'Pull over, Josh, and I'll speak to one of them . . . Oh, there's Ben. He works in our grinding shop . . .'

Almost before the vehicle stopped, Trip leapt out and ran towards one of the men, who was just about to approach another house.

'Ben – Ben, wait a minute. I need a word.'

'Why, Mr Trippet. What is it? Has t'little lass been found?'

'Sorry, no, but my brother-in-law, Josh, has thought

69

of a place out in the country where Mick might have taken her.'

'Want me to come along?'

Trip hesitated. It was a tempting offer; Ben was tall, broad shouldered and strong. 'I wish you could, but I don't think we can fit you in the car.'

Ben looked at it for a moment and then said, 'I could ride on that there luggage thing at the back, if he drives steady.'

'Are you sure?'

'If Mick Dugdale's there, you're going to need a bit of brawn. Meaning no disrespect, sir.'

'None taken, Ben. Come along, we'll see what we can do.'

'Wait a minute, I'll just tell my mate what's happening, so he can finish off this row of houses.'

When Emily and Josh heard what was proposed, Emily said at once, 'Oh no you don't, Ben. Trip and I can squeeze in the back and you sit beside Josh.' She clambered out. 'You get in, Trip, and I'll sit on your knee. No arguing.'

And no one did. They set off again, Constance's little car struggling up the hills with the extra weight.

'Where are we headed?'

'Out of town somewhere up the Baslow Road, where Mick Dugdale used to run bare-knuckle fights,' Josh explained. 'Trouble is, I only went there the once and I'm not sure if I can remember where it is exactly.'

Beside him, Ben chuckled. 'But I can. I know it well, though I thought it was Steve's hideout. But don't you tell my missus. She'll box my ears.' The image of a little woman, however fiery, boxing the ears of the big man brought a smile to all of them.

'It was Steve's place – still is, probably,' Josh said. 'That's why we thought Mick might take her there – a place no one would think of looking.'

They travelled a few miles in silence until Ben said suddenly, 'I reckon it's round this next corner. Turn left down a narrow lane and then . . . Aye, there it is, down the slope of that field on the left.' The car jolted down the rough track. 'Pull up here, Josh, on t'side of t'road. We don't want the sound of the car to alert him if he is there.'

They left the car on the grass verge and walked into the field and down the slope.

'You stay back, Emily.' But Emily shook her head and walked on. 'If Lucy is here, Trip, I need to be with you.'

Trip sighed, but said no more. Silent now, they tiptoed towards the barn door and listened. Josh tried the door, but it was locked. Quietly, he said, 'I'm going to walk round the back. If Mick is here, he will have parked his vehicle out of sight from the road. That's what he did before.'

Ben nodded in agreement. 'You go with him, Trip – just in case. I'll stay here with your missus.'

A few minutes later Trip and Josh returned, shaking their heads. 'Nothing round there and no way in, either. I don't think he's here.'

'Let's just hope the lass is.'

Ben rattled the door. 'Thank goodness t'isn't a solid barn door. This won't take much breaking down. Not for me, but a little lass'd never open it.'

Emily sniffed. 'He's good at locking folks in places,' she murmured. Thank goodness he hadn't set fire to this one, if Lucy was here.

Ben smashed a hole in the flimsy timber of the door and tore away the panels, making a hole big enough for them all to step through. Inside, the barn was dark and gloomy and it took a moment for their eyes to become accustomed to the dimness. They listened for a moment, but there was no sound.

'Lucy, are you here? Don't be frightened, darling. It's Aunty Emily.'

They listened again and heard a scuffle and then whimpering.

'Lucy – is that you? Where are you? We can't see—'

'Up there.' Josh pointed. 'In the hayloft. But there's no ladder.'

'Yes, there is. Over there by the wall,' Trip said. 'Help me carry it, Josh.'

Together the two men fetched the ladder and leaned it up against the edge of the hayloft. 'I'll go up,' Trip said. 'She knows me.'

As he stepped onto the floor of the loft and looked around him, he saw the figure of a small girl huddled in the far corner with a gag over her mouth and a rope around her wrist, tethering her to an iron ring in the wall. He hurried across and squatted down in front of her. 'It's all right, Lucy. We'll take you home to your mam. Don't cry, sweetheart. You're safe now.'

He slid the gag from her mouth, so that it lay loosely around her neck. At once, her sobs were louder. Speaking reassuringly to her, he struggled to untie the thick rope. 'We'll soon have you out of here.'

Her wrists were red and raw where she'd struggled against the bonds. At last she was free and she threw herself against Trip, clinging to him and weeping loudly.

'There, there,' he tried to comfort her as he picked her up and carried her to the top of the ladder. He set her down, but she was unsteady, her legs weak from being forced to sit for several hours.

'Josh,' Trip shouted down, 'can you come up the ladder and help her down?'

'S'all right, Mr Trippet,' Ben shouted before Josh could make a move. 'I can carry her down.' Without waiting for a reply, he started up the ladder. Stepping onto the floor of the loft, he said, 'Now, me little lass, you've got to be very brave, 'cos we've got to get you down from here. Can you climb onto my back, put your arms around my neck and hang on very tightly?' He squatted down and Lucy did as he asked.

'Now, you must hold on tight, lass. Can you do that?'

Trip watched anxiously. If the girl were to let go halfway down the ladder . . . 'Wait a minute, Ben. Let's use that rope to tie her on. It'll be safer.'

He fetched the rope and looped it around her back and under her arms and then under Ben's arms, tying it in front of the man's chest. 'There, that should do it.'

As Ben stepped carefully onto the top of the ladder and turned round to begin his descent, Lucy found herself dangling in mid-air. Sobbing with fear now, she almost throttled Ben, her arms clinging tightly around his neck. But the big man did not complain. He could put up with a few moments' discomfort if it got this little girl to safety. After what seemed like an agonizingly long time, his foot touched the ground and eager hands untied the rope around his chest and Lucy was lifted from his back. She clung to Emily and sobbed against her shoulder. Emily held her tightly and tried to soothe her wails.

As soon as Trip had climbed down the ladder, he said, 'Come on, let's get out of here before—'

He hadn't finished speaking before they heard a noise at the broken doorway. They turned to see Mick Dugdale climbing though the hole. He straightened up and faced them, grinning.

'Well, well, well, four rats in my trap. Emily and even Josh. What a catch!'

Ben took a step towards him, his fists clenched, but Trip caught his arm and said quietly, 'No, Ben. He's got a gun.'

Eleven

Bravely, Emily stepped forward. 'Mick, don't be a fool. Put the gun down and let us go.'

'I would be a fool if I did that, pretty Emily. When I have at least two of the people I want revenge on – three, if you count the girl.' He waved his gun towards Lucy.

'Are you still resentful on Lizzie's behalf? Because you needn't be. She's back with us, working with us. Surely — ?'

'Not working *with* you, working *for* you. There's a big difference. You're forgetting that it was me who set you up in your first business, when you and Lizzie were partners, but he –' Mick gestured towards Josh – 'had to go and spoil it all by running back to his slut in the country and leaving my poor sister heart-broken. You really think I'm ever going to forgive *that*?'

'She's not heartbroken. I doubt she ever was. Besides, she's walking out with Billy Nicholson now.'

'Huh! That milksop! That'll not last, 'cos I won't let it. He's not good enough for her.' He glanced again at Josh. 'I thought you were. I liked you, Josh. You were even part of my gang for a while, weren't you?'

Emily gasped and glanced behind her at Josh, who'd turned red. She'd known he'd been involved with Mick's gambling, but she'd not realized he'd been regarded as part of the Dugdale gang.

Noticing, Mick smirked. 'Oh dear! Am I letting out secrets? Didn't your big sister know?'

Josh squared his shoulders. 'I was never really part of your gang. I got pulled in with you for a while, I admit that.'

Mick's lip curled. 'And then you ran away like the scaredy cat you really are. I reckon our Lizzie had a lucky escape. Your slut's welcome to you.' He turned back as if tired of going over old ground yet again. He fingered the jagged scar on his left cheek. His present quarrel was with Steve Henderson. Lucy's father.

'Hand the girl over and the rest of you can scarper.'

The four adults all spoke at once as they ranged themselves in front of the young girl.

'Not likely.' 'You'll have to get past all four of us before that.' 'Let us go, Mick –' this was from Emily – 'your only hope is if you go, and go now.'

'Oh aye, and how long before you send the coppers after me, eh?'

Emily shrugged. 'Do you see any coppers with us? We've no means of getting word to them and by the time we get back to Sheffield, you can be long gone.'

For a brief moment, Mick actually seemed to be considering her suggestion, but then his face hardened. 'How do I know it's not some sort of trick? For all I know, you might have told the coppers where you were coming. They might be on their way here right now.'

Trip stepped forward to stand beside Emily, saying with a forced smile, 'You're right there, Mick. We might easily have done.' *How I wish we had*, he thought to himself.

Almost, as if by wishing it so, there was a noise outside the barn door.

''Ere, what's going on?' a deep, angry voice said. 'Who's wrecked my barn door?'

At the noise, Mick whirled around, his gun pointing towards the hole in the door. Beyond it, they could all see the burly figure of a man already tugging at the splintered timbers.

Trip turned towards Ben and Josh and hissed, 'Quick, let's rush him. Emily, you and Lucy get down on the floor.'

'Who's in there?' The man on the other side of the door was shouting now and turning a key in the lock. Mick raised his gun and pointed it towards the door, waiting for it to swing open, waiting to get a good target . . .

Trip, Josh and Ben launched themselves at Mick, knocking him to the ground. Trip scrabbled to get hold of the gun, but Mick pulled the trigger and the gun discharged, echoing through the barn.

'Bloody 'ell!' They heard the man's expletive and saw him disappear from view at the same moment as Ben stamped on Mick's wrist. The gun fell from his grasp and Ben scooped it up. 'Now t'boot's on t'other foot, ain't it, mate?'

Mick sat up nursing his wrist and wincing with pain. 'I reckon you've broken it.'

'Don't worry, mate. They'll fix it in t'prison hospital.'

Trip bent and helped Emily and Lucy up. 'We'd better go and see what's happened to the man outside. I hope he's not hurt.'

Trip opened the damaged door now that it had been unlocked, but it almost fell off its hinges. He stepped outside to see the man standing close to the barn wall. He was holding a shotgun and he levelled it at Trip.

'Stay where you are, else I'll shoot. This is my land and I'm within my rights. You're trespassing.'

Trip put his hands up. 'Let me explain, but first, are you hurt?'

The farmer shook his head. 'No, you missed me, but *I'll* not miss, if you cause me any trouble now. Thank goodness I was rabbiting and had my gun with me.'

'I need you to call the police. Thanks to your timely arrival, we have the gunman under control. We have his gun.'

The man blinked and was obviously mystified. 'You'd better tell me exactly what's going on.'

Swiftly, Trip explained everything. 'But we've got Mick Dugdale's gun now and—'

'Mick Dugdale – that scoundrel! I thought he'd scarpered a while back.' Trip must have looked surprised, for the man gave a short laugh and said, 'Oh aye, we might live out in the middle of nowhere in your eyes, but we know what goes on in the city.

I've a brother who lives there. We hear the gossip and we know all about t'gangs. And I'd heard about t'little lass going missing. T'lad, who fetches t'milk, told us early this morning. That's why I came up here. Thought I'd better take a look, just in case, like.' He nodded towards the barn and raised his gun again. 'You sure you've got him safe?'

Trip glanced behind him to see Josh tying Mick's hands behind his back. Mick was yowling. 'Me wrist's broken, I tell you. Have a heart!'

'Like the "heart" you had when you abducted a six-year-old lass?' Josh gave a final yank to the knot and Mick cried out again.

'What are we going to do with him?' Trip asked for suggestions. 'We can't get us all in the car to go back to the city and we should get Lucy home to her mam as quickly as possible and get the word out she's been found.'

'If one of you fellers will stay with me,' the farmer put in, 'we can keep him locked up until the police get here.'

Mick turned white. 'Not the coppers. Please not the coppers. I'll hang for sure.'

Trip squatted down in front of him. 'Just tell me, Mick, why we should have an ounce of sympathy for you after everything you've done?'

He shook his head and whispered, 'Think of Lizzie – of me mam.'

'What we ought to do,' Trip said, as he stood up again, 'is to tell Steve where you are. We'll let him decide.'

79

Mick gave a groan and fell back, his eyes closed. 'Then I'm a goner anyway,' he muttered.

'I don't think we should do that, Trip,' Emily said worriedly. 'Steve will kill him and then he'd end up at the end of a rope too. This has gone on long enough. It's time we took a stand on the side of the law. If you don't go to the police when we get back, then I will.'

Twelve

The news that the missing child had been found safe and well spread through the city like a tidal wave, bringing relief to everyone and welcome rest for the searchers. But the feeling was soon superseded by anger; anger that anyone in their wonderful city could do such a thing. Rumour soon spread that it was the revenge of one gang leader against another.

'They'll have to be stopped. Someone ought to do something,' was the general consensus of opinion. But who?

The 'who' stood in the small back kitchen of their terraced house with her hands on her hips and faced her husband. 'Are you with me on this, Trip – or against me?'

Trip gazed at the face of his lovely wife, her eyes icy with ill-concealed fury. 'It's one thing to attempt to kill Nell and me, but quite another to frighten an innocent child. God only knows what he might have done if we hadn't found her when we did.'

'Thanks to your Josh,' Trip murmured.

'Well, yes,' Emily agreed reluctantly. 'There is that.' She'd known a little of her brother's involvement with Mick Dugdale and his gang during the time he'd lived with his family in Sheffield, but not just how deeply he'd been sucked in. If she'd known at the time, she'd have had something to say, but back then she'd been rather naive and trusting. Now, she knew better.

'What will Nell say if you go to the police?'

'As long as I don't mention Steve – and I won't, because, luckily, he wasn't involved except in searching for her – then I don't think she'll say anything.' Emily bit her lip. 'I wish Steve would give it all up. I mean, he doesn't *look* like a gangster. And his home was quite a surprise.'

Trip chuckled. 'What does a gangster look like, love? A crooked nose and a scarred face?

'Like Mick Dugdale, you mean?' she laughed wryly. 'I suppose that's how I would think of one, but Steve is very good-looking. But of course you know that. No wonder Nell loves him.'

'She must be very strong-willed to hold out against marrying him.'

'She is.'

'Good for her, I say, but that doesn't answer my question. I still don't think she'll be very happy with you if you go to the police.'

Emily's chin went up defiantly. 'Then that's a risk I'll have to take, because if Ben and that farmer are still holding him, the longer we leave it, the more chance he has of escaping – again!'

Trip rose slowly. 'Then I'll come with you.'

'So you do agree that it's the right thing to do?'

'Certainly, but it's not necessarily the *best* thing in the circumstances. Anyway, we'd better go, if we're going. Ben'll want to be getting home. We can't leave him out there any longer than necessary.'

The police acted swiftly, as soon as Emily reported to them where Mick was being held. When she arrived at work, Emily was surprised to see Nell there. She told her at once what she and Trip had done. Nell nodded and turned away, but not before Emily had seen the determined set of her chin. Emily touched her arm. 'We didn't mention Steve. We kept him out of it, Nell. All we told them was that we'd found where Mick had taken her, but you'd better tell Steve that because it's likely the police will keep an eye on the barn now.'

Nell nodded, but still did not say anything.

'I'm sorry,' Emily said and she was. 'But we couldn't let him go, now could we?'

This time Nell shook her head, picked up a bunch of spoons and a handful of sand and moved towards her buffing wheel. The conversation – such as it was – was over. Emily watched her colleague and friend as she began her work but this morning, Nell was not singing at her wheel. Emily sighed and moved away. Despite what Steve Henderson was, she had seen another side to him now; the one Nell loved.

That evening as they were finishing their meal, a knock came at their front door and Emily opened it to see the tall, dark figure of a police sergeant.

'Come in. Would you like a cup of tea?'

'That'd be most welcome, missus. Ta.'

As he removed his helmet and followed Emily into

their living room, Trip got up from his chair in front of the range and held out his hand. 'Sergeant Crossland, isn't it?'

'It is, sir, yes. I just thought I should come and tell you, so you're on your guard, like.'

Emily and Trip glanced at each other and then turned back to Joe Crossland.

'Unfortunately,' Joe ran his tongue around his lips, 'we got there too late. He'd given Ben and the farmer, Mr Portas, the slip. I'm sorry to say that Mick Dugdale is at large again.'

'What!' Trip and Emily exclaimed together.

'How could that have happened? They were guarding him with guns.'

Emily covered her mouth fearfully with shaking fingers. 'He's not got a gun, has he?'

'No, no,' Joe Crossland said swiftly. 'He didn't manage that, thank goodness.'

'How did he get away from them?' Trip asked.

'They took him to the farm and he expressed a need to visit the privy. It's an outside one at Mr Portas's farm, down the little garden at the back of the house. Well, Ben and the farmer stood by the back door chatting. When they realized he'd been gone a long time, they went to investigate and there he was – gone.'

'But – how! I mean they must have kept watch on the privy, mustn't they?'

Joe shrugged. 'They must have taken their eyes off it and it would only take a second or two for him to slip out and round the back into the bushes and then away across the fields. I don't think either of them realized just what a slippery character he is.'

'Didn't they go after him? They must have known roughly what direction he'd gone in.'

'Oh aye, but unfortunately, there's woodland not far from the farmhouse and once he got into it, there was no hope of finding him.'

'What about a dog? Hasn't the farmer got a sheepdog?'

'He *had*, but the poor old thing died about a month ago. He's got a young puppy, but it needs training. At the moment, Mr Portas said, he's less than useless.'

'D'you think Mick'll come back to the city?'

'Not if he's any sense. I reckon he'll lose himself in the Smoke. Mind you, if he's bent on revenge, there's no knowing what he might do.' He cleared his throat. 'We're gearing ourselves up for street fights. All leave's been cancelled. I'd warn all your family, friends and work colleagues to stay off the streets at night, just till we get this lot sorted out.'

'Will you, though? It's been going on a long time now.'

Joe grinned. 'Aye it has, far too long. Maybe the general public don't know, but in May our Chief Constable set up what he calls a Special Duties Squad to deal with the gangs. You mark my words. We'll soon have our city out of the clutches of these gangsters once and for all. You'll see.'

As Trip saw him to the door, he murmured, 'I hope you're right, sergeant.'

Word spread once more through the city that

law-abiding folk should keep to their homes after dark.

'It's like being under a curfew,' Trip grumbled. 'I hardly dare walk up the road to the pub on the corner.'

'It's only for a while,' Emily said, 'but I've warned Nell. I hope she manages to convince Steve that he should stay out of trouble.'

Thirteen

Emily would not have been so hopeful if she had witnessed the scene between Nell and Steve. Nell faced him boldly in his own home. 'If you start a street war, you'll be arrested.'

Steve's eyes sparked defiance. 'You really think I'm going to let him get away with kidnapping my daughter and terrifying you?'

'The police will find him. He'll get his punishment.'

'Huh! I wouldn't like my life to depend on it.'

'Your life might very well depend on it, Steve,' Nell said, softly, and tears filled her eyes. That, more than anything, almost undid Steve's resolve to avenge himself on Mick Dugdale. Nell rarely cried and to see her close to tears moved him more than he'd ever thought possible.

But still, it was not enough. Three nights after Lucy had been found, Steve and three of his gang members marched into the court off Garden Street armed with cricket bats and knives. They paused briefly outside the house where Steve knew Lizzie and her mother lived.

'Now, no hurting the women, you understand. It's him we're after, not them.'

'What if they won't tell us where he is?'

'Leave that to me,' Steve said grimly as he tried the door. As they had expected, it was locked but it didn't take many minutes for the door to be smashed and entry gained. As Steve was about to step inside, a shout from behind them made him turn back briefly.

'Oi, what d'you think you're doin'?'

Several doors in the buildings surrounding the court had opened and people were peering out to see what else was happening in the Dugdale home, but only one dared to run towards them. Two of Steve's mates turned to face him, their bats raised.

'S'all right,' Steve said. 'It's only Billy. He lives in the house on the corner. Just hold on to him, but don't hurt him. He's not one of Mick's.'

As two of his cohorts grabbed Billy and held him firmly, Steve turned away again and stepped through the splintered door to see the two women cowering in the far corner of the kitchen.

'Don't be frightened, Lizzie, nor you, Mrs Dugdale. We won't hurt you.'

'You've hurt my door, though, you young tear-away,' Bess said bravely, whilst Lizzie tried to shush her.

Despite the seriousness of his mission, Steve smiled. It had been a long time since anyone had referred to him by such a mild adjective. The names people called him these days were a lot stronger.

'I'm sorry about that, Mrs Dugdale, but we're here to find Mick.'

'He's not here,' Lizzie said, her voice high-pitched with terror. 'I swear he's not.'

Quietly, Steve turned to the third member of his followers and nodded his head towards the stairs. 'Just take a look up there, Pete. No more damage, mind. Not this time. And don't forget to look in the loft, if there is one.'

Outside the door, Billy had managed to pull himself free and he launched himself through the gap. 'Don't you touch Lizzie, Steve, else I'll bloody well kill you.'

'Calm down, Billy, there's a good lad. I've no quarrel with them.' His expression hardened. 'But I have with Mick. He's going to pay for what he did to my daughter. He frightened her and her mother and I don't take kindly to that.'

'Just let me go to Lizzie,' Billy said.

After a moment's thought, Steve nodded and Billy went at once to Lizzie and put his arm around her. Lizzie clung to him, her dark eyes still wide and fearful.

A few moments elapsed whilst they listened to Pete banging about upstairs, but there was no sound of anything breaking. Then he came clattering down the stairs. 'He's not here. I checked t'loft an' all. There's no sign he's even been here.'

'He hasn't, Steve,' Lizzie said. 'Honest. He came that one time when he first came back to Sheffield, but we've not seen him since.'

'Do you know where he is, though?'

Both women shook their heads vigorously.

'They wouldn't tell you if they did, Steve,' Pete said.

'As a matter of fact, young man,' Bess said sternly, though she wiped a tear away from her eye, 'no, I wouldn't tell you lot, you're right there, but I would take him by the scruff of his miserable neck to the police station. I threatened it last time, but when he turned up . . .' She turned her gaze to Steve as if appealing for understanding. 'I was that glad to see him safe and sound that I forgot me vow. But not any more. He's overstepped the mark this time. And even though he's me own flesh an' blood –' her voice broke a little – 'I won't stand by him no more.'

For a moment, Steve stared at her and then slowly he nodded and said quietly, 'I believe you, Mrs Dugdale.'

But as he turned to leave, Bess caught hold of his arm. 'Please, Steve, if you find him, don't – don't kill him. Please. Give him a good hiding, if you must, but then hand him in to the police. I know it's not what he deserves, but – but – he's my lad.' Now the tears flowed as Bess broke down and wept. 'He's my son.'

Steve hesitated and then he put his arms around the woman and held her. He was realizing that she must feel for Mick exactly what he felt for Lucy. Though he wanted revenge on Mick, wanted to rid the earth of a piece of scum, in that moment he realized he would be no better – *was* no better – than Mick Dugdale.

'I'll not kill him, Mrs Dugdale. I promised Nell that, but he might get a good thrashing and run out of town, 'cos we don't involve the police. You know that.'

Against his chest, Bess nodded. 'I know,' she whispered. 'I know.'

The four gang members disappeared as quickly as they had arrived, leaving the two women trembling and a grim-faced Billy muttering, 'I should have done more. I should have . . .'

Billy was tall, with short, wiry red hair, strong, broad shoulders and, usually, a warm smile. But, at the moment, he was not smiling.

'Don't blame yourself, Billy lad. No one's a match for them four. Not even you. I just shudder to think what will happen when they find Mick.'

'*If* they find him, Mam,' Lizzie said. 'If he's any sense, he'll be long gone.'

When Lizzie didn't arrive at work at the usual time the following morning, Emily was worried, especially when Nell avoided meeting her gaze, leaned into her machine and refused to say a word.

Emily sighed. She was due to go out that day to deliver and collect new work so she resolved to call round to the court in Garden Street where she had once lived to see if Lizzie was ill. But she did not tell Nell what she intended to do.

The day was bright though cold for September, but Emily enjoyed the walk, striding along, her head held high and her lovely face and trim figure attracting admiring glances from menfolk and envy from women. With the finished work delivered, she decided to visit Lizzie before she collected any more.

The court was little changed; it was still dank and dreary and the constant tapping from the file-maker's workshop in one corner still rang out. Emily approached number four, the house which the Ryan family had moved into five years earlier and where the Dugdales now lived.

As she hesitated outside the door, Emily's mind flew back to the time she had lived there, first with her family and then, for a few months, with Trip after they'd married. She remembered with a shudder coming home one evening to find the house had been trashed, their belongings smashed or torn and scattered everywhere. They'd moved out at once and stayed with Nathan Hawke for a while until they'd been able to move into a house some distance away. Both Trip and Emily believed that Mick Dugdale had been behind the ransacking of their home in Court 8. And then there had been the dreadful fire at Nathan Hawke's workshop in Broad Lane, endangering Emily and Nell. In retaliation, street fighting between Mick Dugdale's gang and Steve Henderson's had broken out. The Dugdales' house had been trashed, Emily believed, by Steve Henderson's gang and it seemed as if the warfare would continue. But then Mick had disappeared from the city for almost three years. With his recent return, she feared all the old trouble would flare up once more. Taking a deep breath, Emily knocked on the door that had been repaired with boards since Steve's assault on it and waited until it opened tentatively and Lizzie's white face appeared. Seeing who it was, her eyes filled with tears. 'Oh Emily, come in, but please excuse the mess. We – we've been attacked again.'

'Lizzie, no! Are you hurt?' As Emily stepped through the door into the kitchen she saw the devastation.

Broken crockery littered the floor, a stew was spilt and furniture smashed.

'It's the same upstairs. Only the beds were left untouched. Mam's lying down. She's heartbroken. This is the second time it's happened, Emily. When's it going to stop?'

Emily put her arm around her friend's shoulders, saying gently, 'When Mick stops making trouble, love.'

Lizzie's tears flowed afresh. 'But we've had nothing to do with that. I swear we haven't, but Steve and his gang came here looking for Mick last night . . .'

'Steve did this?' Emily was shocked.

'No, no. He didn't – he didn't touch anything except the door – but another gang – one of the new ones – came soon after he'd left. They were only boys trying to muscle in on the act and thinking themselves big men. We were no match for them, Emily. Billy tried to stop them and got a cut lip for his trouble.'

Emily stared at her in horror. 'You mean you were here when it happened?'

Lizzie nodded.

'Did they hurt you or your mam?'

'No, they didn't touch us. Just – just our things.' She waved her arm to indicate the destruction.

'Right,' Emily said, taking off her coat and hat and hanging them on the peg on the wall. 'Let's get this place cleaned up. You light a fire in the grate and get the kettle boiling. In fact, run across to Rosa Jacklin's and see if she'll make a cup of tea for us.'

'I – daren't. No one's speaking to us in the yard.

Mam's been sacked from her job at Mr Farrell's . . .'
Lizzie nodded towards the file-maker's workshop.

'What about Billy, surely he's standing by you?'

Lizzie smiled weakly. 'Oh yes,' she said, with a
hint of irony in her tone, 'there's always Billy.'

Billy Nicholson, who lived with his mother in the
house in the opposite corner, had been in love with
Lizzie for years. Even when she had become infatuated with Josh, he had waited in the wings. Now, it
seemed, he had his chance.

'What about his mother? Is she still the buffer
missus at Waterfall's?' Ruth Nicholson had been the
first person to give Emily a job in the buffing shop
at the small cutlery firm.

'She's all right, but I think she'd sooner Billy didn't
have anything to do with us – with me.'

'Billy will never desert you, Lizzie. He loves you,'
Emily said simply. 'Will Billy or his mam be at home
now? I could ask them, if you'd rather.'

Lizzie shook her head. 'No, they'll be at work.
I'm sorry I didn't come in today . . .' She gestured
helplessly towards the wreckage and her shoulders
sagged as if, this time, she was utterly defeated.

'Have you any idea at all where Mick's gone?'

'No, none, and we don't want to. That's why
Mam's so upset. It's not just this, it's that we both
realize it's over now. Really over. He's gone for good.
We – we'll never see him again.' Her voice broke and
she sobbed against Emily's shoulder. 'I know he was
a bad 'un, Emily, but he was Mam's son and my
brother.'

'I know, I know.' Emily patted her shoulder and

then said briskly, 'Right, let's get on with clearing this lot up.'

The rest of the morning was spent cleaning and tidying up as best they could. At Emily's request, Rosa Jacklin made tea for them all, though Emily thought she was a little reluctant.

'I hardly dare let my kids play in the yard in case *he*'s about,' she muttered, when Emily visited her.

'I think they're safe enough now, Rosa. Mick's gone and I don't think anyone will bother Mrs Dugdale and Lizzie any more.'

Rosa was a young mother of two girls and had been widowed by the Great War. Life was enough of a struggle without the added anxiety of trouble in the court. Now, she sniffed in disbelief at Emily's words but said no more as she readied a tray with three cups of tea on it.

As Emily took it from her, Rosa said hesitantly, 'Tell them if they need owt, they can come across. I'll not see them in trouble. Times were when the Dugdales were good to me and mine. Even Mick. And despite what's happened recently, I never forget a kindness.'

'I'll tell them, Rosa, and thanks.'

Later that morning, Bess appeared downstairs. Emily was shocked by the change in the woman. When they'd first arrived in the court, Bess Dugdale had been a rotund, bustling woman with a beaming smile who'd always been ready to help her neighbours. She had been the first to greet the Ryan family and she and Lizzie had cleaned the house through in preparation for the newcomers' arrival. Now, though still plump, her eyes were red-rimmed from lack of sleep and, no doubt, from copious tears too.

'Here, sit down, Mrs Dugdale. This chair's all right to sit on. Lizzie's got the fire going and I've fetched some meat from the butcher's and vegetables from the greengrocer's. We've put a new pan of stew on and potatoes are baking in the oven. You'll soon have a nice hot meal. You'll feel better then.'

Bess sank into the chair near the range. 'I don't reckon I'll ever feel better, Emily luv. This has broken me.'

'Now look,' Emily bent towards her, 'you just listen to me. It's time we put all this behind us. I can sympathize with you about your son. It must be devastating for both of you, but let's be honest about this. Mick's brought this on himself. None of this recent trouble would have happened if he'd stayed away and built a life for himself somewhere else, but now . . .'

'We'll never see him again. My boy – he's a wanted man now. He'll never come back home, will he?'

'Never's a long time, Mrs Dugdale, and perhaps he'll write to you and let you know he's all right.'

Bess shook her head and said bitterly, 'I doubt it. In the last two years he's been gone, never a word.'

'Then I'm sorry – truly I am – but you and Lizzie must try to pick up the pieces of your own lives. We'll help Lizzie.'

Bess looked up at Emily. 'You mean – you mean – you'll still keep Lizzie on? I thought – we thought – you'd want her to leave.'

'No, we believe Lizzie when she says she's had nothing to do with Mick taking Lucy.'

'Even Nell?' Bess whispered.

'Yes, even Nell. So . . .' Emily straightened up. 'You come back to work whenever you're ready, Lizzie. But please don't leave it too long. We've a lot of work on and more coming in every day. In fact, I'd better be on my way now. I've one or two more calls to make.'

As she left the house, the two young women hugged each other. 'I'll be back tomorrow,' Lizzie promised. 'But will you check with Nell? If she doesn't want me back then . . .'

'I'll talk to her, I promise.'

Fourteen

Emily was late getting back to the workshop and Nell was on the point of leaving. The other two girls had gone already.

'I know you want to get home, but can you spare me five minutes?'

Nell laughed. 'Just so long as you don't expect me to start on that lot tonight.' She nodded towards the heavy basket of unfinished cutlery, which Emily was carrying and took it from her. 'My, this is heavy. However have you managed to carry all this?'

'I'm developing muscles I didn't know I had!'

'The sooner you learn to drive that nice little car your lovely husband has bought you, the better. And talking of that, have you thought any more about taking Trip up on his offer for you to rent another workshop in his factory?'

'Yes, I have. I think we have enough work coming in from regular customers now to warrant it.'

'Are you sure it will continue to come in, though, Emily? And does Trip want a long lease?' Despite Nell's lack of a formal education she was streetwise.

Emily shook her head. 'No. We've already talked about it and he's said he'll charge us rent month by month.'

'You're very lucky. Most folks would want at least a year or two, if not more.'

'What do you think I married him for?' Emily said flippantly, but Nell was deadly serious as she said, 'Don't give me that, Emily Trippet. You married him because you're besotted with him.'

Emily laughed. 'You're right, of course.'

'Anyway, I'd best be getting home.' Nell moved towards the door, the discussion over as far as she was concerned. 'I'm still a bit worried about Lucy.'

'Is she still having trouble with those girls at school?'

Nell laughed wryly. 'No chance. I saw their mothers. They won't be bothering her again. No, she's still a bit fearful when she walks home from school. That's when Mick picked her up, you know. Mind you, it's made the little tyke come home at the proper time. No more wandering about the streets.'

'Just one more thing . . .' Emily said hastily and went on to tell Nell about her visit to the Dugdales' home and all that had happened, ending, 'You are all right about Lizzie still working for us, aren't you?'

Nell's mouth tightened as she considered for a moment, whilst Emily held her breath.

'As long as you're sure – *we*'re sure – that she's telling us the truth.'

'If we find out she's not, Nell, she's out. I promise you that.'

Nell nodded. 'All right, then. Let's see how it goes, shall we?'

* * *

Lizzie returned to the workshop the following morning, quiet and subdued. She was nothing like the bubbly, outgoing girl she'd been when Emily had first met her, but she was pleased to see that the other girls, taking their lead from Nell, greeted her in a friendly manner. Emily sighed. She hoped that time would heal all the hurt but she feared it would take a long while.

That same night, it seemed that Emily's tentative hopes for an end to all the animosity were even further away than she'd thought.

Street fighting broke out and for the next five weeks, mayhem reigned in the city. Steve Henderson's mob had been established the longest, but younger youths now formed their own gangs and rampaged through the streets, threatening the citizens. There were even a couple of fights up on Sky Edge over the betting, and threats towards men leaving their work on pay day escalated. In a time of hardship, this extra fear brought many citizens to the edge of despair.

But no one could find Mick Dugdale.

Bess was relieved and prayed each night that her son had gone and would have the sense now to stay away. She mourned his loss and when Emily visited one evening, she was in a nostalgic mood.

'He was a lovely little lad, you know, Emily. You wouldn't have ever thought he'd've turned out the way he has. I don't know where I've gone wrong, really I don't. Of course, maybe not having a father might have been one reason, but my dad – when he was alive, bless him – was like a father to both of them.'

'I remember Granddad,' Lizzie put in, handing round cups of tea and sitting down to join in the reminiscing. 'He was a lovely old boy. Mr Hawke always reminds me a bit of him.'

'He was very good to us when I was left a widow. Him and me mam both were. I wish now I'd never named Mick after his granddad. He'd be devastated to see what his grandson has become. He'd be so ashamed.'

'But I thought Granddad's name was Lionel? Not Michael.'

'No, no, not his Christian name. I didn't like the name Lionel, so I used the surname – Hartley – as Mick's second name.'

'And I'm called after Grannie, am I?'

'Yes, Elizabeth. You and me are both named after her.'

'I have to say that Mick was good to us when we first came to the city,' Emily said. 'You all were, but I didn't realize at the time that he was threatening poor Mr Hawke into helping us to set up in business. If I *had* known . . .'

Bess gave a deep sigh. 'Aye well, I'm not so sure that folks believe me an' Lizzie when we say we were in complete ignorance about his carryings on. People just saw all the goodies he brought us and thought we were all in on it. Eee, I was that naive.'

'Me too,' Lizzie murmured. 'I thought he was just sticking up for his sister.'

The mention of Nathan Hawke had reminded

Emily that she had not visited him recently and, silently, she resolved to call to see him on her way home.

'I should be going,' she said, standing up. 'Are you sure you're both all right?'

When the two women nodded, Emily added, 'Be sure to let me know if there's anything you need. Anything at all. I'll see you at work tomorrow, Lizzie.'

Emily walked swiftly through the dusk, being careful to keep to the main streets. When she knocked on Nathan's door, she was not surprised to see him peer out of the window first to see who was standing there.

'Emily, my dear girl, come in, come in,' he said, throwing the door wide open. 'What are you doing out in the dark?' He peered behind her. 'Isn't Trip with you?'

'No, I'm fine, Mr Hawke.' She chuckled as he led her through to his kitchen and saw her seated in his own chair by the range. 'I happen to be on good terms with the most notorious gang leader in the city. Strangely, I'm not afraid to be out on my own at night, though I have to admit, Trip doesn't like it.'

'Quite right too.'

'I'm sorry it's been a while since I called to see you. How are you?'

He waved aside her apology. 'You've had a lot on your mind, my dear. And I'm fine, except for this wretched arthritis that's getting worse by the day. I can still get about, you know, but I'm so slow these days, it's frustrating.'

Emily repeated what she had said to Bess and

Lizzie. 'You must let me know if there's anything you need. Promise me?'

Nathan smiled and nodded. 'I will. Thank you. Now, tell me how are things with the business? Are you still managing to find enough work to keep all your employees busy?'

They chatted for a while longer, but after she had been there about half an hour, he said, 'Much as I love your visits, Emily, I really think you should be getting home. Trip will be worried. But before you go, I have some news. The workshop in Broad Lane has been rebuilt since the fire and is ready for rental again. I don't know if you'd want to work there again after what happened to you and Nell. It must have terrifying memories for both of you. But if you wanted to rent it again, it's yours.'

Emily's eyes gleamed and her mind worked quickly. 'I'd love to rent it. May I have a few days to talk it over with Trip? We had been talking about me taking a workshop in his factory, but to have the one in Broad Lane again would be ideal.'

'Of course. No hurry. It's been long enough getting rebuilt,' he added wryly.

'Thank you for offering it to me.'

Nathan smiled at her. 'There's no one else I'd rather have as my tenant.'

Not wanting to cause him anxiety, she got up to leave. 'I'll come again soon – in daylight,' she teased. 'Or bring my own bodyguard.'

He laughed. 'You do that. I'd like to see Trip too.'

Fifteen

'So, what do you think?' Emily put the same question to Nell and Lizzie that she'd asked Trip the evening before.

'Have we enough work to run two workshops again?' Nell asked, whilst Lizzie remained silent.

'I think so. If I tell Mr Hawke that we'll take it on a month's trial and tell any girls we hire the same, that'll give us time to see if we can drum up enough business.'

'You mean if *you* can,' Nell laughed, but, after a moment, she asked more seriously, 'What did Trip say?'

'It was he who suggested taking it for a month to start with.'

'Mm, clever chap, your Trip.' She paused for a moment, 'If we've got that safeguard of being able to give it up after a month if it doesn't work, then I say yes.' She turned to look at Lizzie. There was still a bit of resentment on Nell's side towards Lizzie, but she was trying hard to overcome it. 'What d'you think, Lizzie?'

For a moment Lizzie looked startled that her opinion should be sought, but then she smiled weakly and said, 'I think it's a great idea.'

'Mr Hawke wondered if we'd not want to work there,' Emily murmured.

Nell gave an explosive snort. 'We've got a bit more about us than that, Emily Trippet. It certainly won't bother me.'

Emily chuckled. 'That's what I thought you'd say. Right, we'll give it a try. Do you know any good buffer girls who might want to come and work for us?'

'We'll ask around and let you know.'

The following morning, Nell had three names for Emily. 'They're three sisters. Surname's Frith. Their mam was a buffer girl and they've followed the family tradition. Dorothy – she's twenty-three, Hilda, twenty-one, and Winifred. She's just turned sixteen and has no experience. I thought she'd do as an errand girl. Flo ought not to be doing that now. She's experienced enough to become a full-time buffer girl and be put on piece work.'

The life of an errand lass was not easy. She fetched and carried for all the buffer girls so that all their time could be spent at their wheels. The girls were paid piece rates for the work they did and so time was money to them. It was still the way Emily operated her business. A young girl, usually straight from school, was employed as an errand lass. She would arrive in the workshop before the buffer girls, light the fire, boil the kettle, dish out the oily sand to each place and when the workers arrived she would give out the work under the buffer missus's direction. Throughout the day, she mashed tea and made sure that their food was ready on time. She even went shopping for them so that they could spend longer hours at their work. She cut out a supply of brown paper aprons and in spare moments – though there weren't many in the life of an errand lass – the young girl would watch the experienced buffer girls and learn the trade. When she was old enough and had learned enough to 'go on the side', she would perhaps start with 'heeling and pipping', buffing the ends of the handles and then progress to being a 'rougher', taking the dents and marks out of spoons and forks. As she improved, her place would be taken by another school leaver and so the process of training a new buffer girl would begin again.

'Would this girl – Winifred – be able to handle the two workshops as errand girl like Flo used to do when we had both?'

'They don't live too far away from Broad Lane. Not as near as Flo, admittedly, but we can ask them. Anyway, Emily, they're all coming in to see you this morning. I hope that's all right.'

'Of course it is.'

'By the way, I saw Jane Arnold, who used to work for us, and I asked her if she was interested, but she's happy where she's working now.'

The three girls presented themselves later that morning and were happy with the offer that Emily made them, even though there was the fear of being unemployed after a month. Dorothy, the eldest, seemed to be the spokeswoman for all of them.

'We hate it where we are, missus. The workshop's badly run. The missus there likes a drop of the hard stuff and half the time the work's not given out. We lose money because we have to stop and collect our own. If you take us on, missus, we'll work hard for you. Me an' Hilda are good buffer girls, though not,' she added with a smile, 'as good as Nell Geddis. Her name's legendary in Sheffield. And young Winifred's eager to learn. She'll do what you're asking. Look after both workshops. They're only just round the corner from each other and me an' Hilda will come in early and help her out if she needs it. And we wouldn't expect extra pay for doing that, missus. It'd be just to help our sister out.'

Emily smiled; she liked these girls. 'I would hope to give Winifred a little more than the normal errand lass's pay as she'd be looking after two workshops. And, if all goes well, I'd still like her to train to be a buffer girl.'

'That's very good of you, missus.'

'Then we'll give you all a month's trial, if you're willing. And if I can get the work in and you all prove satisfactory, we'll make your positions permanent.'

'You can't say fairer than that, missus. Thank you. When can we start?'

'I presume you'd better give a week's notice and, besides, I need to get the refurbished workshop fitted with machinery.'

Nell, who'd made no secret of the fact that she was eavesdropping, asked, 'Are we to have both floors now, Emily, or is Mr Hawke coming back to work?'

'He's retired, Nell, so, yes, if we want them, we

can have both floors but he's also agreed that I can sublet one of the floors if I want to. We might be able to use both. The area there is not as big as this one and we can't expand here with Phil Latham still the tenant on the ground floor with his grinders' workshop.'

Nell nodded. 'We'll see how it goes, then. See you next week, girls.'

'There was a chorus of "Thank you, Nell".'

On the following Monday, Emily arrived early at the workshop in Broad Lane to greet her new employees and set them to work. Nathan Hawke was standing in front of the double doors, a huge grin on his face.

'I thought I'd come and hand you the keys personally. And look, I have a little surprise for you.' He moved to the side and Emily saw the large, newly painted white lettering RYAN'S on the doors.

'Oh Mr Hawke, how kind of you. But we're only on a month's trial. What if it doesn't work out?'

Nathan chuckled and waved his hand dismissively. 'I'll believe that when I see it happen, Emily Trippet. I have every faith in you, my dear.'

It was the beginning of December before the citizens began to feel safe once more. Word was spreading that there was now a special squad of police being trained to deal with the thugs, but still women and children were fearful of going out after dark. There was no news of Mick Dugdale and now, even Steve Henderson seemed to have disappeared too, though his gang still operated the pitch and toss games and the bare-knuckle fights, though they had found a different venue to the farmer's barn.

'Is Steve all right? Have you heard from him?' Emily whispered so that Lizzie would not overhear. Emily had organized her two workshops so that Nell, Ida, Lizzie and Flo stayed in Rockingham Street. They worked so well together that it would have been foolish to break up their team. She employed the three new girls in the small workshop in Broad Street with Winifred running between the two to act as errand girl. Far from feeling as if she was being put on, the young girl thrived on the hard work. 'It's nice,' she said shyly, when Emily asked her if she was coping. 'I work with me sisters in t'other place and then I get to see what Nell and the others are doing.'

Now Nell gazed at Emily for a moment before saying hesitantly, 'Can I trust you?'

'Of course you can.'

Nell glanced over her shoulder to make sure the other three girls could not hear. 'There's something you ought to know, but please don't tell the others, especially not Lizzie.'

'What is it, Nell?'

Nell ran her tongue over her lips. 'Steve's staying with me at the moment. Just until the heat's off. You won't say anything to anyone, will you?'

'Of course not, but do be careful, Nell.'

'I just wish I knew if the police are actually looking for him. I know there's a warrant out for Mick's arrest, but I don't know about Steve.'

'Would you like me to try to find out?'

'If – if you could without stirring up more trouble. I just need to know.'

'I'll ask Trip to talk to Joe Crossland. They meet in the pub at the top of our street sometimes. He goes there with his uncle. You remember Eddie Crossland, don't you, from Waterfall's?' Nell nodded. 'Joe'd be off duty, so it'd be unofficial.' Emily stopped short of telling Nell how Trip had gone to see Eddie at the time of Lucy's disappearance. The less she knew about that, the better.

As it turned out, though, Trip didn't need to ask the policeman directly. On the Saturday night following Emily's discussion with Nell, the three men happened to meet up in the pub.

'Good to see you, Joe. Getting your time off again now, are you?' Trip greeted the police sergeant, keeping the conversation light.

'Aye, thank God. Been a tough time, but t'chief reckons he's getting top side of it, though I'm not so sure. There's still a lot of bother from the gangs.'

'Anyone in custody?'

Joe shook his head. 'Only one or two we could catch. And of course Mick Dugdale's slipped the net again. Let's hope he stays away this time.'

Joe glanced at Trip, who was studying his glass of beer intently. Lowering his voice he leaned towards Trip and murmured, 'We're not looking for anyone else now. There are one or two – no names, no pack drill –' he tapped the side of his nose – 'who we know were gangsters, but we've insufficient evidence against them and those we have got in custody are keeping quiet.' He gave a wry laugh. '*Very* quiet. Evidently, they know what's good for them. They're taking the fall for one or two of their associates, if you get my meaning.'

Trip nodded. He asked no further questions; there was no need. He believed that Joe had deliberately passed on this information so that word could be passed to Steve. It was more than likely – particularly since Lucy's abduction – that more people than they realized now knew about Steve Henderson's connection to the little girl and her mother.

'How about a game of darts, Joe? You up for that?' Trip said, as the two men smiled at each other and exchanged an unspoken pact.

'Aye, let's have a team competition. Uncle Eddie loves his darts and if I know owd John in the corner over there, he never passes up the chance to play.'

It was late when Trip staggered home, but luckily he only had a few yards to go to reach his own front door and he knew there would be no trouble from his wife when he told her the news.

The next day, as they finished work, Emily said, 'Nell, could you stay behind for a few moments? I won't keep you long.'

It was not unusual for Emily to consult Nell on matters of business so the other girls thought nothing of it. They left calling out a cheery 'goodnight'. Only Lizzie was still subdued after the recent trouble. She and her mother Bess still had no idea where Mick had gone and they both realized that if he was caught, it would mean a long jail sentence for him.

As the three girls clattered down the stairs and paused for a few moments to flirt with the grinders in the workshop below, Emily said in a low voice, 'I think it's going to be all right, Nell.' And she recounted what Trip had told her the previous night, ending, 'They're not looking for Steve.'

Nell bit her lip. 'How can you be sure? Maybe this copper you're so friendly with was just telling Trip that to flush Steve out.'

'Maybe, but I don't think so.'

Nell was thoughtful before murmuring, 'Thanks anyway, Emily. And please thank Trip too, won't you? I'll tell Steve what you've said.'

'If there's any way we can help you, Nell, you let us know, won't you?'

Nell touched Emily's hand in a gesture of gratitude and nodded, but she could not speak for the lump in her throat. Nell was usually so strong, so feisty, but her daughter's abduction and her fears for the man she loved had shaken her badly.

Three days later, Trip had a surprise visitor at Trippets' factory. As the man walked through the workshops, several heads turned and the news was spread by mouthing the words and being lip-read by fellow workers. Before the visitor even reached the offices, Trip knew of his arrival and so he was waiting with his office door open when the man arrived in the corridor.

Trip held out his hand. 'Steve Henderson, I believe. We haven't met officially, but it was you who rescued us the night my sidecar decided to take a detour off

the road. Do come in. Patricia –' he called to one of
the women typists in the next office – 'can you rustle
up some tea for us, please?' Ushering Steve into his
office and indicating a chair for him to sit, Trip added,
'How can I help you?'

His unexpected visitor came at once to the point.
'If I were to decide to go straight, Trip,' Steve's mouth
twisted with wry humour, 'would you help me find
a job?'

Trip stared at him solemnly for a few moments.
'If you were to give me your word that you really
meant it and that it's not a way into my factory to
carry on your betting scams and so on, then, yes, I'd
be willing to give you a trial, though it would depend
on how good your work is, like anyone else.'

'When I first left school, I was an apprentice
grinder. I didn't finish my training.' He laughed
shortly. 'I found other ways to make money – a lot
more money – but I didn't dislike the work then and
I think I was quite good at it. Anyway, you ask
George Bayes. He'll remember me.'

'You mean, you worked at Trippets'?'

Steve nodded. 'For two years.'

'Well, I'll be damned.'

'No, Trip,' Steve said seriously. 'It'll be me who's
damned if I don't change my ways. It's high time I
looked after my family properly and there's only one
way Nell will let me do that.'

'And that's the only reason you want to give up
a life of crime?'

'If I'm honest,' Steve added and Trip managed to
keep a straight face, 'there is another reason. The

113

police are gearing up to rid the city of the gangs and I reckon they'll do it, an' all. But if they catch up with me, Trip, it'd be prison for a long time. Nell would never marry me then and I wouldn't see my girl grow up. So, you see, I really am serious. Please believe me.'

Trip looked deep into the man's eyes. After a moment's deliberate pause he held out his hand. 'I do believe you, Steve, and I'll do what I can to help you. And the sooner the better, I take it?'

'Oh yes.' Steve's words were heartfelt as they shook hands.

'Now,' Trip said, 'let's have that tea and then we'll go and find George Bayes.'

Twenty minutes later, they were talking to George.

'You were always a good worker, Steve, I'll give you that, but we'd have to start you at the bottom again. It's a while since you worked here, though I reckon you'd move up pretty quickly. It'd soon come back to you. Aye, Master Thomas –' the two half-brothers, who both had the surname Trippet now, were always referred to as Master Thomas or Master Richard to save confusion – 'I'd be willing to take him on a month's trial, if you're agreeable.'

'I am and there's something else you could help me with too, Steve, if you'd be willing. Emily's taken on Mr Hawke's rebuilt workshop again, so she will be needing to get further afield to fetch and carry work. After our accident with the sidecar, I bought her a car. Obviously, Mr Kirkland, who's been giving us both driving lessons, can't be here all the time, so until she's safe to go out on her own, I wonder if we might call on you to help out when necessary?'

Steve nodded. 'I'd be glad to.'

'Then organize your work schedule with Mr Bayes and Master Richard.' Trip put his hand on Steve's shoulder and dropped his voice so that only he and George Bayes could hear. 'And what about you and Nell?'

'I've got to prove myself to her first – to you all, really, haven't I? But I'm hopeful that she'll agree to marry me one day.'

When Steve left the factory half an hour later, he felt as if he were walking on air. For the first time in several years – more than he cared to think about now – he felt he could walk freely and without fear through the streets. He'd been a bad lad – he knew that – and he'd been a fool too. Nell would have married him years earlier if only he'd not led a life of crime. He'd been extraordinarily lucky never to have been arrested and he knew he owed a debt of gratitude to those who had been caught and had kept their mouths shut. He promised himself that he would see that their wives and families were all right whilst they served their sentences, but that would be as far as it went. He no longer wanted to live 'on the wrong side of the law'.

He couldn't wait to get home and tell Nell the good news. He'd soon have her singing at her buffing machine once more. And, if she agreed, they'd have the best Christmas ever as a real family for the first time.

Sixteen

In the second week of December, Emily said, 'Trip – I have some news.'

'Good or bad?' Trip was wary. There had been so much troubling news recently, he was beginning to think there wasn't any other kind.

Emily chuckled. 'I'm hoping you'll think it's good news.' She paused, and then added impishly, 'You're going to be a dad.'

He stared at her for a moment then crossed the space between them and folded her into his arms. 'My darling, it's wonderful news.' And then, as if he couldn't quite believe it, added hesitantly, 'Are you sure?'

'I saw the doctor this morning and he confirmed it.'

They leaned back from each other, though Trip still held her tenderly in his embrace. She reached up and touched his cheek. 'I can't promise, of course, but I hope it's a boy for you.'

Trip shook his head. 'Oh no,' he said firmly, 'I hope it's a girl as beautiful as you.'

'Don't you want a son to carry on the family business?'

He didn't answer her but instead said, 'When are you due?'

'Early June, the doctor thinks.'

'June! That's only six months away. Why didn't you tell me before now?'

Emily chuckled. 'To be honest, Trip, I didn't know. I've been feeling so well. None of this morning sickness everyone talks about – nothing. It wasn't until about a week ago when the waistband on one of my favourite skirts suddenly seemed too tight that I realized I'd put on weight. And, there are other signs too – women's, um, problems. You know?'

Trip blinked, nodded and hastily changed the subject. 'We'll have to start thinking of names. And we must go to Ashford on Sunday and tell the parents. Thank goodness we've got a car now. It certainly wouldn't have been good for you to travel in the sidecar.'

'Darling, I'm not ill, just pregnant. Please don't start treating me like porcelain.'

'You're more precious to me than any porcelain.' For a moment, his face was bleak. 'And I don't want you to go through what my poor mother endured.'

They were both silent for a moment, thinking of Constance Trippet. It had been a great sadness to her that she'd been advised to have no more children after Trip's birth.

Softly, Emily said, 'We'll give her a barrow-load of grandchildren and I expect – if it is a boy – you'll want to call him after your father.'

'Not likely,' Trip said with asperity.

Emily leaned back again to look up at him. 'Really? After you, then?'

Trip shook his head again. 'No, the little chap should have his own name. Besides –' he grinned suddenly – 'you can't call a girl "Thomas".'

Emily blinked. 'Oh! Oh, all right.' She chuckled. 'Then you'd better get your thinking cap on.'

Early on the Sunday morning, they set off to Ashford-in-the-Water.

'I wonder how we'll find Father,' Trip said as he drove. He was now a very competent driver.

'About the same, I should think,' Emily said.

'We'll see your parents first,' Trip said, 'and then go to Riversdale for luncheon.'

Emily smiled softly to herself. Her kindly, ever-thoughtful husband was making the suggestion so that feeding two extra mouths would not put a strain on the Ryans' resources. They were acutely aware that Josh's candle-making business was in decline with modern inventions taking the place of candles. Bob Clark was still a fit and healthy forty-four-year-old, but he could not do the volume of blacksmithing work that he had done as a much younger man.

When they pulled up outside the smithy, Josh opened the front door. 'I thought I heard a car. I hoped it was you two. Come in, come in. We're just about to eat. Mam and Dad are here too, so I'm sure Amy can stretch—'

'That'd be lovely, but we're expected at Riversdale House for lunch,' Trip said blandly.

'Well, you must come one Sunday and eat with us. I insist,' Josh added firmly. 'Just let us know when you're coming, that's all.'

'We will,' Emily said, kissing her brother fondly on the cheek. 'How's everyone?'

'Fine. Blooming, in fact.' Josh's grin spread across his face. 'Amy's expecting again and it seems to suit her.'

Emily glanced at Trip and they both burst out laughing. Josh blushed, not guessing at the real reason for their amusement. 'I expect you think it's a bit quick after Sarah, but—'

Emily leaned against Josh, 'No, no, it's not that. We've come to tell you the same thing.'

'What?' Josh glanced from one to the other. 'You mean, you're . . . ?'

'Yes, I am.'

'Now, this does call for a celebration.' Josh held open the door and ushered them through to the kitchen, calling, 'Look who's here and they've got something to tell us.'

The Ryan family and Bob Clark always had Sunday dinner together in one of their houses. Today, it was Amy's turn to cook for all of them. Emily found herself blushing as she stepped into Amy's hot kitchen. All eyes were turned towards her.

'Is something wrong?' Martha said at once. 'We've been reading in the papers about the trouble you've been having in the city with these wretched gangs. Are your businesses affected?'

Trip put his arm around Emily's shoulders. 'That all seems to be settling down now, thank goodness.

119

No, our news is much better than that.' He glanced at Amy. 'It seems there are to be two new additions to the family around the same time.'

There was a stunned silence and then everyone started speaking at once.

'Oh Emily, how lovely. When are you due?'

'And about time too, I say,' Josh said.

In a chair near the range, with Harry on his knee, Walter smiled and nodded his delight.

'What about your business, Emily? Who'll run that?' Since the early days when Emily had never figured in Martha's ambitions – all her hopes and dreams had been centred on Josh – her ever-growing interest in Emily's success never ceased to amaze her daughter.

But today, the talk was of babies, of names and of what the sex might be. 'Yours must be a boy, Emily,' Martha declared firmly, 'to carry on the Trippet name. Your mother will be delighted, Thomas. Have you told her yet?'

'No, we called here first, but we're on our way there to have lunch with her.'

'I should warn you, Thomas,' Martha said, 'that your father has had another little stroke this week – on Friday it was. He's rallied again, but it's left its mark.' Martha cleaned at Riversdale House on two days a week and often knew the news from there before anyone else, although she was careful never to spread it around the village. Her place in the community since their return from the city was better than it had ever been and she didn't want to jeopardize that by gossiping about the Trippet family.

'I see.' His mother hadn't sent word that anything was seriously wrong. Trip wondered why. Waving 'goodbye' to the Ryan and Clark families, they set off to drive the short distance past the church to the ivy-clad house standing in its own grounds beside the river. Driving round to the courtyard at the rear of the house they entered by the kitchen door. Mrs Froggatt, the cook, beamed a welcome and Polly scuttled upstairs at once to tell Constance that they had arrived.

The cook had worked for the Trippet family since before the war. Once, there had been a full staff of servants at Riversdale House, but now only a cook, a kitchen maid, a housemaid and Kirkland, the chauffeur-cum-gardener, looked after the family and the house. Only Mrs Froggatt and Polly, the housemaid, lived in, as did Nurse Adams, who cared for Arthur Trippet. Ginny, the kitchen maid, came in daily and Kirkland lived with his wife on the other side of the village.

'Luncheon will be in half an hour, Master Thomas.' Mrs Froggatt's face sobered as she added, 'Perhaps you'd like to see your father first.'

'How is he?' Trip asked, not wanting to reveal that Martha had already told them about the latest episode.

Mrs Froggatt shrugged, but seemed to presume that Trip and Emily already knew the latest news. 'Doctor says he'll be all right, but I think you'll see a change in him.'

'We'll go through,' Trip said, taking Emily's hand as Polly returned to tell them that the mistress was in the morning room.

'My dears, what a lovely surprise.' Constance rose

from her seat in the window and stretched her arms wide to embrace them in turn.

'What's been happening?' Trip asked. 'Mrs Froggatt implied that Father's not been too well.'

'He had a very minor stroke on Friday.'

'You should have sent word, Mother,' Trip said gently.

'I would have done, had it been any worse, but Doctor Unwin has told us that he's likely to have small ones every so often and, in themselves, they're nothing to worry about.' She hesitated.

'I feel a "but" coming,' Trip prompted softly.

Constance smiled faintly. 'But – he said that the more he has, the worse they may become. We should be prepared for that.'

'I see. Is he all right for us to visit him?'

'Of course. It would be best if you went up now, before luncheon. It takes Nurse Adams a long time to feed him and then he has a nap.'

Trip held out his hand to her. 'We'd like you to come up with us, Mother. We have something to tell you both.'

For a brief moment Constance looked anxious as she glanced at each of them in turn, but then she nodded and led the way upstairs.

After the usual greeting, Trip said, 'Mother – Father – we have some happy news to tell you. Emily is expecting a baby.'

'Oh, my dears!' Constance clapped her hands and tears filled her eyes. She rarely allowed her emotions to show, but the thought of becoming a grandmother had filled her waking thoughts ever since her son and

Emily had been married. Her joy in her son had been boundless, but the sorrow that she had been unable to have a larger family still haunted her. She hugged first Emily and then Trip. Even Arthur managed a lopsided smile, though Trip was concerned to see that his father seemed thinner, his eyes dark ringed and his cheeks hollow. However slight the doctor had said the most recent stroke was, it had definitely left its mark. But, much to Trip's relief, his father could still understand what was being said to him.

Over luncheon, Constance talked so animatedly about the expected arrival that she could hardly eat her meal.

'I don't mind what it is – I expect you don't either – as long as it's fit and healthy. My dear Emily, you must take good care of yourself and please, please let me know if there's anything you need.'

'I'll make sure she doesn't overdo it,' Trip said and added proudly, 'though there's no way I'm going to even *try* to stop my wife carrying on with her growing business empire.'

Seventeen

The weather for December was cold and Trip promised Emily, 'As long as it doesn't snow, we'll go to Ashford for Christmas. We'll stay at Riversdale House but see your family often.'

It was a happy time for them all. At Constance's invitation, the whole family assembled at Riversdale House after lunch to open their Christmas gifts. Trip and Emily had bought a self-assembly model aeroplane for Harry and the afternoon of Christmas Day was spent with the four men – Bob, Walter, Josh and Trip – poring over the instructions whilst Harry waited impatiently for the model to be ready for him to play with. When it was complete, he ran around making engine noises as if it were flying.

On Boxing Day, the weather turned a little milder. In the afternoon, Trip and Emily walked up to Monsal Head, one of their favourite places, taking Harry with them.

'Are you sure you can walk that far, Emily?' Trip asked anxiously. 'I don't want you to overdo it. You were busy all morning helping your mother prepare lunch for us all.'

'I'll be fine,' Emily reassured him. 'As long as I take it steadily, the exercise will do me good.'

'We'll take you for a ride on the train in the summer, Harry,' Trip promised, as he pointed to the viaduct over the river in the dale far below them. 'We'll be coming over to Ashford quite often. We're going to have a little boy or girl soon and your Granny and Grandpa Ryan will want to see him or her as often as we can come over.'

Harry nodded. 'I know. Mummy told me and she's going to have another baby too. I hope it's a little boy this time for me to play with. Sarah always wants to play with *dolls* and she's got two more this Christmas.' The little boy grimaced, but he was laughing as he said it.

'But you got a lovely train set and the model aeroplane and both your granddads will play with those with you. Besides,' Emily laughed, 'it'll be a little while before the new baby's big enough to play with you, won't it?'

Harry was a sunny-natured child and they knew his complaints about his younger sister didn't go deep. They'd witnessed for themselves how gentle and patient he was with her and how he often forfeited his own playing time to amuse her.

'Now, we'd better be getting back. We're having tea with you at your house, aren't we?'

As they turned to go, they noticed that Harry was dragging his heels. Then Trip realized just how far the four-year-old had walked.

'Would you like a piggy-back, Harry?' He squatted down, whilst Emily helped the boy to climb onto his back.

The three of them set off down the hill towards the smithy.

'I'm ready for my tea, aren't you, Harry?'

Emily laughed. 'You can't possibly be hungry after that huge lunch.'

Trip laughed. 'Oh, but I can.'

Amy and Emily were keeping well in their pregnancies. Later that evening, when the children were in bed, they found a few moments to be alone. Emily was keen to ask her sister-in-law's advice.

Amy laughed. 'The menfolk worry about us doing too much, especially my father.'

Emily pulled a face. 'And Trip's mother, too. But they mean well.'

'No doubt, and both of them have cause for concern – we know that. My dad's bound to be anxious when I'm pregnant. But how can I slow up with three menfolk and a little one to look after? And I can't see you taking it easy either.'

Emily touched Amy's hand. 'Harry's such a loveable little boy. He's very like Josh, isn't he? His eyes are hazel, just like his dad's.'

'But his hair's fair like mine. He's the perfect mixture of both of us.'

'And Sarah's a pretty little thing, but she's quiet and shy, isn't she? Trip says he wants a girl, but I hope it's a boy.'

'I have relatively easy childbirths, unlike my poor mother. I hope it will be as good for you.'

Emily pulled a face. 'I have no idea what to expect.' So, for the next hour the two young women talked about childbirth and caring for a baby. Far from worrying Emily, she ended the conversation by saying, 'D'you know, Amy, I can't wait now?'

Solemnly, Amy said, 'There's nothing – absolutely nothing – so wonderful as holding your baby in your arms.'

The New Year of 1926 started well, but by March there was industrial unrest.

'I think there's going to be real trouble soon,' Trip said dolefully one evening when Richard had been invited to dinner.

Emily, though heavily pregnant now, was as energetic as ever. As she served the food and then sat down herself, she said, 'What sort of trouble, Trip? Street fights again, d'you mean? Gang warfare is still rife, I hear.'

'I know. I thought, with Mick Dugdale gone and now we've taken Steve Henderson off the streets and made an honest workman of him, the rest of them would lose heart. However, it seems the youths are taking over. Mind you, there's talk of someone being brought in to sort these gangs out. But no, it's more serious even than that in a way. There's unrest amongst the miners and I think it will have a knock-on effect throughout the country.'

'I thought that had all been settled last year when the Government granted a subsidy to the mining industry,' Richard commented. 'And didn't a Royal Commission undertake an inquiry?'

Trip nodded, his face grim. 'Yes, and that report has just been published this month. Unfortunately, it recommends that the subsidy be withdrawn and that miners' wages should be reduced and that they should work longer hours too.'

Emily frowned. 'But why would a miners' dispute affect us?'

'Because I think it's so fundamental that workers everywhere will unite behind them.'

'So you think it's going to affect the cutlery industry too?' Richard said quietly. The two young men glanced at each other. Though half-brothers, they were remarkably alike in appearance, and the more she got to know Richard, the more Emily could see that they were alike in other ways too. They were both kindly men and good employers. They were thoughtful regarding the welfare of their workers.

Trip's forebodings were well founded. In April the miners were subjected to new conditions – a cut in wages and longer hours. The workers were given until the beginning of May to accept the terms or risk being locked out of their place of work.

'That's so unfair,' Emily said, rattling the newspaper in her frustration.

Trip agreed with her. 'But the miners are fighting back. They've adopted a slogan. "Not a penny off the pay, not a minute on the day." But I fear the whole country's going to come to a standstill if other trades follow suit in support.' He glanced anxiously at Emily and she could read just what was running through his mind.

She patted his cheek and joked, 'I don't expect it will affect midwives or hospitals.'

'There's no knowing,' he said gloomily. 'All our workforce are threatening to join in and goodness only knows how long it might last if there's a nation-wide stoppage. What about your girls?'

'I expect they'll carry on.'

'They might not be able to, if they get threatened.'

'Threatened? You're not serious?'

'I'm afraid I am. They'll likely have picket lines and anyone trying to get into work will be called a blackleg or scab or worse.'

'But we're self-employed. We—'

'*You* are, but not the others. You employ them. They're workers, just like all Trippets' employees.'

'Oh.' Now Emily had no reply. She was thoughtful for a moment before saying quietly, 'I'll have a talk with them tomorrow.'

The following morning, Emily broached the sensitive subject with all the girls. 'I don't want you to run the gauntlet of picket lines. You must stay at home out of danger, if it comes to it.'

Nell pulled a face. 'I'm not frightened of that, but to be honest, we haven't got a lot of work in at the moment. I don't think we will have until all this trouble is over.'

Lizzie gave a wry laugh. 'Or we might have a helluva lot more if the factories are all shut down.'

'We'll just have to see what happens. In the mean-time, we'll just carry on as normal – as far as we can.'

'When are you due?' Lizzie asked quietly.

'About the first week in June,' Emily said.

'You're looking well – blooming, as they say – but you ought to take it a bit steadier these last few weeks. Have you got a midwife organized?'

'No, Trip wants me to go into the hospital. I think he's over-anxious because of what happened to his mother.'

'That's understandable,' Lizzie murmured, and then smiled. 'So, just take care of yourself, Emily, for all our sakes – but especially for your baby's.'

Emily nodded, unable to speak for the sudden lump in her throat.

Eighteen

On Saturday, 1 May, the miners went on strike and the Trades Union Congress called for a nationwide General Strike in sympathy, which began at midnight on Monday, 3 May.

After the first few days, when all their workers had joined in the protest, Trip told Emily dolefully, 'It's turning into a class war.'

'What d'you mean?'

'The middle classes – the white-collar workers – they're driving buses and lorries with essential food supplies. Even trains. Some of the university students are treating it like a holiday from their studies. I just wonder if they realize the seriousness of it all.'

'So you mean they're acting against the workers?'

'Of course they are. If supplies get through and the general public don't feel the pinch, the strikers won't be able to prove their point.'

Despite the gravity of their conversation, Emily couldn't help smiling impishly at him. 'You're middle class. Aren't you going to help them?'

'No, I am not. I want *all* workers to have a decent day's pay for a good day's work. Don't you?'

'Of course, but I'm working class. You aren't.'

Trip was forced to laugh. 'Emily Trippet . . .' He

touched her face tenderly. 'You're not any class. You're a woman of great courage and tenacity, with a big heart. You're a one-off. Don't ever change, will you?'

'Oh Trip,' she put her arms around him and snuggled her face to his chest, 'you say the nicest things.'

On the morning of Tuesday, 11 May, Emily awoke with sharp contractions in her lower abdomen. She washed and dressed quietly, made herself a poached egg on toast and checked that she had everything ready in her suitcase before she gently woke Trip.

'Why didn't you wake me earlier?' he said, scrambling hastily out of bed and pulling on his clothes. His hair tousled, his chin with the shadow of dark stubble, he began firing questions: 'Is everything ready? Have you had something to eat? We'd better go now. It's earlier than you said, Emily. Is everything all right?'

'Trip darling, calm down. The contractions aren't that regular yet. No need to panic. You get something to eat too.'

'I couldn't eat a thing.'

'Yes, you can and you must. It might be a long day.'

For a brief moment, he stared at her and then put his arms around her. 'How are you so relaxed?'

'I need to be and so do you. Now, get washed and shaved and have your breakfast, even if it's only a slice of toast and a cup of tea this morning. And then we'll go.'

Twenty minutes later, they were ready to leave.

'You sit in the back, Emily. It'll be more comfortable. I'll put your case in the luggage box.' Only the previous week, Constance had insisted on buying them a second car. 'You'll need a bigger car now your family is expanding,' she'd said happily. 'But Emily should keep her two-seater for her business. You're both competent drivers now, so please let me do this, Thomas. Call it an early present for my grandchild.' So now Trip drove a four-seater Morris Oxford 'bullnose' car with a roomy back seat ready for a baby to travel in style.

By the time they left, it was mid-morning and the route to the hospital was thronging with strikers intent on stopping all vehicles, wherever they were going. As they surrounded the car, banging on the roof and the bonnet, Trip tried to plead with them. 'Please – let us through. We're going to the hospital. My wife's in labour.'

But above the hullabaloo, no one was listening – or they didn't want to.

'Trip, the pains are getting worse and – and closer together. We have to get going.'

He tried revving his engine, but the strikers merely surrounded the car, jumping on the bonnet and bouncing it.

Emily bit her lips to stop herself from crying out as a wave of pain washed through her. When they were losing hope of ever being able to move, a tall, fair-haired man shouldered his way through the crowd and opened the door on the driver's side.

'What's up, Trip?'

'Steve – oh thank goodness. Can you get us through

this lot? Emily's gone into labour. We're on our way to the hospital.'

Steve cast a worried glance at Emily now stretched out on the back seat. At once, he straightened up and began shouting, but no one was listening to him either. Then he grabbed one or two men by the arm and shouted at them. 'Make a way through for this car. There's a woman in the back about to give birth.'

Several appeared to listen to him and tried to clear a path for the vehicle, but there were just too many people. Now, Emily could not hold back her cries.

'Trip, my waters have broken. There's a towel in my suitcase. Can you get it for me?'

Trip got out of the car and fought his way to the rear of the vehicle, pushed and jostled as he went. Strangely, the crowd was not hostile; the atmosphere was almost like the streets on New Year's Eve or on Armistice night, but only the men nearest to the car realized what was happening. Now, they tried to help.

'I'll find a policemen or an ambulance,' someone said.

'They'll not get through any more than we can,' Trip muttered, climbing into the back of the car. 'Oh Emily . . .' He was close to tears, but through her pain, Emily managed to smile. She eased herself up a little and drew her knees towards her chest, opening them so that if the baby wanted to come, it would have a clear way.

'We're going to make a bit of a mess on the seat, Trip.'

Trip made a peculiar sound, something between a

laugh and a sob. At that moment, Steve poked his head into the car. 'Can I help? I've seen a birth before. When me mam had her last, I was ten and it came so quick, it arrived before the midwife could get there.'

'Then you'd better get in here instead of me,' Trip said.

'No, mate, you stay with Emily. I'll just be on hand if you need anything.'

Steve knelt on the driver's seat, watching anxiously as Emily panted and then pushed when she felt a contraction. 'That's it, Em,' Steve murmured, 'push when you feel the pain and then pant in between.'

Emily almost laughed aloud. Steve was using Josh's pet name for her and it brought her brother closer.

Word seemed to be getting around the crowd now and a way through was being made for them.

'You stay in the back with her, Trip,' Steve said, 'I'll drive.'

'No, no,' Emily shouted, 'Don't go, Steve. It's – it's coming. I'm sure it's – aaahh . . .'

With one final wave of pain and a gigantic push, she felt the baby leave her body. At once there was a cry, a loud protest at arriving in the world in such an undignified manner.

'It's a boy. Trip, mate, it's a boy!' Gently, Steve reached over and took hold of the slippery infant and laid him on Emily's breast. 'We ought to cut the cord. Have you got a knife?'

Trip wriggled in the cramped space to fish a penknife – a Trippet penknife – out of his pocket.

'It's brand new, so it'll be clean. I only picked it up yesterday.'

Steve chuckled. 'You must have known . . .'

Whilst Steve dealt, surprisingly deftly, with the business of cutting the cord, Trip said, 'We ought to wrap him in something.'

He scrambled out of the car and took off his shirt. Then, leaning back in, he laid it gently over the baby.

Steve too removed his shirt and laid it across Emily's knees. 'To preserve your modesty whilst we get you to the hospital.'

Emily, tired but elated, giggled. 'It's a bit late for that, but thanks, Steve.'

It was a wonderful moment for them all. Despite the circumstances, Amy had been absolutely right. It was the best moment of Emily's life. It even eclipsed her wonderful wedding day, though she would never tell Trip that.

The journey to the hospital was now concluded in surprisingly quick time as word spread and the crowd parted. On their arrival, Steve dashed into the hospital and soon nurses and doctors surrounded the car. Before long, Emily and her baby boy were safely within the labour ward and Trip and Steve were able to breathe a sigh of relief.

Trip put his hand on Steve's shoulder and said, 'I don't know how to thank you, Steve. What would have happened if you hadn't been there, I don't know. And, by the way, remind me to buy you a new shirt.'

'All in a day's work.' Steve grinned. 'You've got a son, Trip. What are you going to call him?'

Trip blinked. 'I don't know, but I reckon "Steve" will have to be in there somewhere, don't you?'

'Well, well,' the young man said softly and his eyes were suspiciously wet. 'Who'd have thought it. Thomas Trippet naming his son after me. Wait till I tell Nell. She'll never believe it. Perhaps now, she'll agree to us getting married.'

Nineteen

Nell did agree. She was proud of Steve now, not only for what he had done to help Emily and Trip, but also the way in which he was trying to turn his life around. And to confirm her belief in him, word came in a roundabout way through Eddie Crossland that the police were definitely no longer interested in Steve Henderson. It seemed that they, too, had heard that he was making a valiant effort to go straight and they wanted to help him do so. The former gangland leader was an example to other gangs and they hoped that if word spread amongst the city's underworld that reformed characters would no longer be pursued, then there might be a few more who would decide that the time had come for them to give up their life of crime. But there was another – even more pressing – reason why the gangs who still roamed the streets, threatening the citizens and running their various criminal enterprises, might have cause to rethink their lives: the appointment of Captain Sillitoe to the post of Chief Constable. He had taken up his new post at the beginning of May and had vowed to smash the gangs once and for all.

'Have you heard about him?' Steve asked Trip,

when they met in the pub for a celebratory drink before going home.

'Yes, on the grapevine. I have to say, Steve, I hope he does it.'

Steve laughed wryly. 'You'll be surprised to hear me say it, Trip, but so do I. Oh, I've been a bad lad in my time, but I was never so vicious as the gangs of youngsters we've got now. I never really hurt anyone. Well, maybe just one person. Mick Dugdale. I gave him something to remember me by, but he deserved it.'

Trip was silent. He didn't condone violence at all, yet he could understand Steve's reaction to what Mick had done to his family.

'Let's just hope he stays away for good now.'

'Amen to that, Trip. And here's to your son.' They drank to the baby's health and as Steve put his glass down, he added, 'I expect you haven't heard, but the TUC has called off the General Strike. We'll all be back at work tomorrow morning. Don't forget to tell Emily when you see her tonight. And tell her, Nell will look after things at work until she's back.'

'I thought you said you didn't want to name him after someone else,' Emily said, smiling, when, on his visit that evening, Trip suggested that they should name their son after their rescuer.

Trip pulled a wry face. 'What I meant was I didn't want generations of Arthurs or Walters or even Thomases, and I'm only suggesting it should be a second name, just by way of recognition of what

Steve did. I'm not into "Big Steve" and "Little Steve" either.'

Emily nodded soberly. 'I agree. So, what do you think? I've thought of two: Andrew or Lewis.'

'I like them both, but I think I prefer Lewis. Lewis Steven Trippet. What do you think?'

'Perfect,' Emily said. 'Just like he is.'

'By the way,' Trip said as an afterthought, 'the General Strike is over but the miners are fighting on.'

Emily sighed. 'Well, I hope they win. If it goes on for long, we'd better start thinking about setting up some soup kitchens or something.'

Trip smiled to himself. That was Emily; despite the traumatic events of the day, she still had thoughts for others who might be facing hard times.

There was a steady stream of visitors once Emily arrived home from hospital. Constance, bringing Martha with her, was the first to arrive. She stood over the cot gazing down at the infant, who looked up at her with blue eyes and waved his small fists. 'I have a grandson,' she murmured, as if she couldn't quite believe it. For Martha, of course, the feeling was not so new, but the boy's arrival was still a cause for joy and Martha had begun planning his future already.

'There, Thomas, you have a son and heir to your family firm.'

Trip smiled and nodded, but said nothing. He didn't want to shatter Martha's dreams, but he was very much afraid that if the unrest amongst the workers escalated, there might not be much of a future for his son at Trippets'.

'As long as he's healthy and happy,' Constance murmured softly, 'that's all I ask for him.'

When it came to choosing godparents, Emily and Trip found themselves with a dilemma. 'We've got to have Josh and we ought to include Richard, but what about Steve? We can't leave him out after everything.'

'There's no restriction on the number you can have, is there?'

Emily shook her head. 'I don't think so. The usual is two godfathers and one godmother for a boy and two godmothers and one godfather for a girl.'

'Then we'll just ask whoever we want. We must ask Amy, of course.'

'And I'd like to ask Nell.'

'What about Lizzie?'

Emily sighed. 'I know – there's her too. I don't want to hurt anyone's feelings.'

'I tell you what. Why don't we stick to the usual number? We'll have Josh and Steve and Amy. There, how does that sound?'

'All right, but what about Richard?'

Trip chuckled. 'I'll tell him he's top of the list for the next one.'

'And I'll tell Nell and Lizzie the same, because if it's a girl, that'd be just right.'

Trip took her hand and kissed it. 'You're a very brave woman to even think of having more babies after what happened.'

Emily laughed. 'Actually, despite the circumstances, it was a lot easier than I thought. The pain was bad, of course, but it didn't last long. The nurses at the hospital told me that, for a first baby, he came surprisingly quickly.'

'We're very lucky,' Trip said, his voice husky as he thought how very different the outcome might have been.

Although Emily didn't return to work for a few weeks, she organized the setting up of two soup kitchens in a local school and the distribution of free bread to help the miners' families. The citizens rallied round and the miners continued their battle.

Lewis was christened in Ashford's church on a warm August morning in a double celebration with Josh and Amy's second son, Philip, who had been born only a week after Lewis.

The whole family was invited to Riversdale House for luncheon following the service and, although he was still confined to his bed, Arthur was able to hold his grandson in his arms and, with a lopsided smile, nod his delight to Trip and Emily.

Belle and Richard had been invited to join the gathering and, after lunch, they spent a little time with Arthur in his room.

Martha and the rest of the Ryan family left soon after luncheon.

'Walter's a little tired,' Martha explained. 'It's been an exciting day for him. Two grandsons christened on the same day. Who'd have thought it?'

And so Trip and Emily were left in the sitting room with Constance nursing her newly baptized grandson.

Conversationally, she said, 'George came to see Arthur the other day.' With her gaze never leaving

Lewis's face, she did not see Trip and Emily exchange a quick glance. Carefully, and making no comment on his mother's use of the factory foreman's Christian name, Trip said, 'That was nice of him. I think they always got on pretty well.'

Constance gave a low chuckle. 'As well as anyone could get along with your father.'

Trip and Emily smiled weakly, but made no comment. Arthur Trippet had been a difficult man to live with and to work for, but it didn't seem right to be speaking ill of the man lying incapacitated upstairs, closer to death than he was to life.

There was a long silence, the only sound the baby's snuffling in his sleep as he lay contentedly in his grandmother's arms.

At last, Constance said quietly, 'I have known George a long time – longer, in fact, than I have known your father. We grew up together in Over Haddon. We were –' she paused a moment as if searching for the right word – 'good friends, but both our parents thought the friendship unsuitable. My father was a landowner – I think you know that – and held great sway in the district, whilst George's father was the village wheelwright and blacksmith. To put it bluntly, my father was a snob, though of course I didn't realize it at the time. I was just a young girl being obedient to her father's wishes. He introduced me to Arthur and, well, you can guess the rest.'

She was silent again and neither Trip nor Emily felt able to probe any further. But the conversation left them wondering . . .

*   *   *

Although Steve had moved into the house Nell and Lucy shared with Dora Geddis, there was still no sign of a date for their marriage being fixed, but Emily was heartened to hear Nell singing at her wheel once more. Emily had returned to work only four weeks after Lewis's birth, taking him in a baby basket beside her on the seat of her car everywhere she went. Trip insisted that she have some help in the house so they employed Flo's younger sister, Daisy, to clean and wash and iron for them, though Emily made sure she was home by five o'clock every night to cook dinner for Trip herself. Far from being over-tired, Emily seemed invigorated by the arrival of their son. Lewis was a happy and contented child and, in the evenings, they both enjoyed 'family time'; bathing and feeding their son and putting him to bed. Although Trip was happy to be involved, he flatly refused to change nappies!

'I don't know what I'd do if he was a fractious baby,' Emily commented more than once to Trip. 'According to Josh's last letter, Philip rarely sleeps through the night and is a difficult baby.'

'We ought to go to see them all on Sunday.'

'Yes, let's, but on Saturday morning, there are a couple of people I want to take Lewis to see.'

'Oh? Who?'

'Mr Hawke, for one and –' She paused before adding, 'Mrs Dugdale. They've both seen him before, of course, but I want to keep in regular contact with them both.'

Trip paused for a moment and then he nodded, 'Yes, I agree. Mr Hawke has been extraordinarily good to you over the years and as regards Mrs Dugdale, it's time to build a few bridges. Resentment and ill-feeling have gone on long enough. How is Lizzie, by the way?'

'A bit quiet. Subdued, you'd say. Nothing like the bubbly, vivacious girl I first met when we arrived in Sheffield.' She sighed. 'It's sad really.'

'All because of her devil of a brother.'

'I know, and we all thought he was so kind and helpful – and clever.'

'He was clever all right, but, unfortunately, he put his ingenuity on the wrong side of the law. I wonder what became of him? Has Lizzie ever said that they've heard from him?'

Emily shook her head. 'Even if they had, I don't think she'd tell us, do you?'

'Probably not.'

Twenty

The buffing work had dropped off a little and so Emily's girls did not now work at weekends. Early on the Saturday following her conversation with Trip, Emily called first at Nathan Hawke's terraced house.

'What a grand little chap,' Nathan said, gazing down at the child. 'I'm sure he's grown since I last saw him.'

'They alter almost daily at this age.'

'It was a great sadness to my wife and me that we never had children. They'd be a great comfort to me now, I'm sure. That's as long as—'

Emily looked at him questioningly and with a wry smile, Nathan added, 'As long as they hadn't turned out like Mick Dugdale.'

'I'm going to see Mrs Dugdale when I leave. Lewis'll be wanting a feed by then.'

'Well, you can—' Nathan stopped in embarrassment. 'Of course, I understand.' Much to Emily's amusement the man was blushing.

To cover his confusion, Nathan turned to a safer topic. 'How's business?'

Emily grimaced. 'A little quiet, but we are keeping our heads above water – just.'

'You're still managing to run both workshops?'

'Yes, though I haven't used the first floor in the Broad Lane premises yet.'

'And the three sisters you set on to work there – they're proving satisfactory?'

'Very. They're excellent workers and you should see Winifred actually running between the two work-shops acting as errand lass for everyone.'

'And Trip?'

'The same, really. Just holding on.'

'I hope it doesn't get any worse.' He smiled at her. 'I hear you've been very active in providing food for the miners' families.'

Emily looked up at him, but she could read nothing in the expression on his face. 'Do – do you approve?' she asked tentatively.

'Wholeheartedly, my dear. I might have been classed as an employer in a small way, but I've always thought of myself as a worker. I've never forgotten my roots. I've just been lucky, that's all.'

'You've worked hard for everything you've got.'

'So have you, Emily,' he murmured. And, he thought to himself, she had a good heart. She hadn't forgotten where she'd come from either.

As Lewis began to stir, Emily picked up the large wicker basket she used to carry her baby. 'I expect he's getting hungry. We'll be off. But don't be a stranger to us, Mr Hawke. Come for dinner one evening. How about next Saturday? I'll ask Richard to come too.'

Nathan's face brightened. 'I'd like that. Thank you.'

*   *   *

By the time Emily had parked the car in Garden Street and walked into Court 8, Lewis was whimpering. Lizzie opened the door. 'Is something wrong?'

'No, I just thought that it was high time your mam saw Lewis again.'

Lizzie blinked and then smiled uncertainly as she murmured, 'How thoughtful of you. She's been bombarding me with questions. Come in, do.'

Emily stepped straight into the kitchen. 'Hello, Mrs Dugdale. How are you?' It was an unnecessary question really. Since Mick's disappearance, in her distress, Bess had lost weight and was now was half the size she'd once been; her clothes hung loosely on her, her face was gaunt and her eyes were dark-rimmed. She looked as if she hadn't slept properly for weeks. But, as she looked down at Lewis, she smiled. 'Aw, Emily, he's such a bonny little chap. Come in and sit by the fire.'

'He's ready for a feed. Would you mind if I . . . ?'

'Of *course* not.' Her smile faded as she added quietly, 'There're no men likely to come in now.'

Emily settled herself beside the fire in the shining, black-leaded range in the very spot where her father had spent his days during the two years that they had lived here. She glanced round the kitchen; it was much as she remembered it. On one side of the range were some built-in cupboards from floor to ceiling. On the other side was a cast-iron copper, set in brickwork over a fire grate. Next to that was a stone sink with cupboards beneath it. Her mind flew back to the day when the Ryan family had first stepped into the house. Then, Bess had welcomed them and shown them round, telling them everything they needed to know about this new and strange world they had come to. Now, the rest of her family were back in Ashford, but Emily had returned to the city to make her life there with Trip.

Never one to shy away from a difficult subject, Emily asked, 'Have you heard anything from Mick?' Now that she had a child herself, she understood a mother's heartache a little better.

Bess glanced away, but shook her head and murmured huskily, 'Not a word. We don't know if he's alive or – or . . .' She bit her lip and couldn't continue.

'We think he might have gone to London,' Lizzie said. 'You know, lost himself in the big city. We don't want him to come back here, but Mam just wants to know if he's all right.'

'Whatever he's done,' Bess said, tentatively, 'he's still my boy.' Tears filled her eyes.

'I know,' Emily said, as her own son nuzzled her breast and fed hungrily. She tried to imagine how she would feel if, in the years ahead, she was to be faced with the same anxiety and disappointment in Lewis.

Bess raised her head and met Emily's gaze. 'I was so proud of him, Emily, back then. I thought he was so clever with his wheeling and dealing. Oh, if I'd stopped to think about it, I would have realized that maybe now and again his dealings were a little bit – well, shady, but I never dreamed he was running a gang and was involved in extortion and threatening folks.'

Emily could see that the thoughts were haunting her. 'It wasn't your fault – or Lizzie's. You must both try to move on and to build your lives without him because – I'm sorry to say it for your sakes – but I don't think he will come back here. He's still a wanted man.'

Bess nodded. 'I know I should try – for Lizzie's sake – but it's so hard.'

'I can understand that.' Emily paused. 'Are you working again?'

Bess shook her head. 'Mr Farrell sacked me when he heard that Mick had taken little Lucy. Hardly anyone in the court is speaking to me – to us.'

From being the mainstay of the court, Bess was now ostracized by the people she had once helped so readily.

'Is there any other work you can do, other than file-making?'

Bess shook her head. 'Cleaning, washing, cooking, I suppose. That's all I've ever done.'

'Then I have a suggestion to make.' Emily smiled. She had discussed the idea with Trip over breakfast and though he had been thoughtful for a few moments, in the end he'd agreed.

'Would you like to come and be our housekeeper? You know that Flo's sister's been helping out, but she's only a young girl and she wants to find work in a shop. You could do so much more for us than she can, Mrs Dugdale. I daren't leave Lewis with her for a moment. Not because I don't trust her,' she added hastily, 'but because she has no experience of babies. But I'd happily leave him in your care.'

Bess gaped at her. 'You'd – you'd do that for me? For us? After all that's happened?'

Emily shrugged. 'Like I said, none of it was your fault. Everyone knows that.'

With some of her old vigour, Bess snorted derisively. 'They don't seem to think so round here.'

'Then why don't you move?'

'I would, if I could find somewhere we could afford, but with only Lizzie's wage . . . Don't get me wrong, Emily. You're very generous with what you pay her, but with me not able to find work anywhere, it comes very heavy on Lizzie.'

'There's a very nice little house not far from us on Cromwell Street which has come up for rent. It's within easy walking distance for you – only about five streets away. You'd have further to go to work, Lizzie, but I can give you a lift most days,' she added, glancing at her. Then she turned back to Bess. 'I can speak to the owner, if you'd like, and see if he's willing to let it to you.'

'Do you know him? And would he accept us when he knows who we are?' Her voice fell away.

Emily was smiling. 'Oh, I think so. It's where Steve used to live. It's his house, but now, of course, he's moved in with Nell.'

Bess's mouth fell open. 'You – you really think he'd let us have it? The mother and sister of his arch-enemy?'

Emily smiled and, with unusual conceit, said, 'I think so – if *I* ask him.'

151

Twenty-One

Steve was quick to give his agreement. 'We're all trying to make a fresh start. Your Trip has been more than good to me – you all have – and I'll set the rent at a modest amount. One they'll be able to afford. Only one thing, I don't want *him* back there.'

Emily shook her head. 'I agree with you and, whilst poor Mrs Dugdale is heartbroken, they don't want him back either. They want to try to move on and, like you say, build a new life and moving house will help.'

'And Mrs Dugdale is going to look after Lewis, is she?'

'Not all the time. The best way she can help me is to keep things right in the house. I can then concentrate on my son and the business.'

Steve nodded. 'It sounds the best for everyone, though I don't know what Billy Nicholson'll say. I think things were progressing nicely between him and Lizzie – according to what Nell says, but if she moves away from the Court . . .'

Emily grinned. 'Then he'll have to invest in a bicycle.'

Steve threw back his head and laughed loudly.

'D'you know something, Emily Trippet, you have an answer for everything.'

The following Sunday, with the help of Trip, Steve and even Billy, Bess and Lizzie moved into the terraced house only five streets away from Carr Road. Bess was ecstatic with her new home. 'I've never had a backyard and a proper bathroom indoors.'

'The privy's still outside down the yard,' Lizzie pointed out.

'Best place for it,' Bess said tartly, 'but to think I don't have to stand at the kitchen sink no more to get washed.' She shook her head in wonderment. 'And *three* bedrooms. One each for us, Lizzie, and a small one if Emily ever wants us to have the little feller to stay here overnight.'

'It's not much bigger than a cupboard, Mam, but, yes, you're right. It's a lovely little house. We'll be happy here.' Lizzie put her arms round her mother's shoulders and leaned her cheek against Bess's hair. 'I know it's hard, Mam, but we've got to move on. I hope he's all right – I wouldn't wish him any harm – but we've got our lives to live.'

Bess nodded, but she could not speak for the huge lump in her throat. She hoped Lizzie would be able to 'move on', as she put it. She was young and had her whole life in front of her, but Bess doubted she herself would ever be able to do so. Mick, for all his badness, was still her little boy. But silently she resolved to put on a brave face and, who knew, maybe some time in the future her act of coming to terms with it all might become a reality. She was determined to try. So many people were trying to help her and Lizzie – people she wouldn't have expected to do so – and now it was up to her. Their moving to a lovely little house, into which the sun shone over the rooftops every morning, and Bess's new job, were all thanks to Emily. She would spend the rest of her life, she promised herself, trying to repay that kindness.

Billy did indeed acquire a bicycle and he became a frequent visitor to the Dugdales' new home.

'Are you really walking out with him, Lizzie?' Nell asked bluntly, as was her way. 'Don't keep the poor lad dangling any longer. He's loved you for years, you know.'

Lizzie sighed. 'I know and I'm very fond of him, it's just that –' She paused and bit her lip.

'It's not the grand passion that all us girls dream about, eh?'

Lizzie nodded. 'Not like Emily and Trip or you and Steve. D'you know, your eyes light up the minute they walk into a room? That's the sort of love I want. I thought I'd found it with – with Josh Ryan, but . . .'

'Lizzie luv, he was never yours. You know that, if you're honest, and Emily tried to warn you from the start, didn't she?'

Lizzie nodded again. 'I know. I was a fool and I'm glad for him he's happy.' She smiled. 'He's got three children now, and he's as happy as a pig in muck, to use her phrase.'

'But what about Billy?' Nell persisted.

'I'd miss him if he wasn't there any more,' Lizzie murmured.

'There are different kinds of love, you know. They're not always the stomach-churning kind. And he's filled out lately,' Nell said gently. 'He's not a skinny youth any more.'

Lizzie did give a great deal of thought to her relationship with Billy and realized that her life would indeed be empty without him. She hadn't been thinking straight, what with being infatuated with Josh and then finding out that her brother, whom she loved dearly, was not what she thought he was, had hurt and disillusioned her. And she'd grown up with Billy, played in the street with him and seen him grow from being a scruffy little urchin into a man; a kind and caring one at that. So, when Billy at last plucked up the courage to ask her straight out to be his girl, Lizzie was able to smile and say 'yes'.

'Thank goodness for that,' Nell said. 'Now perhaps we can all get on with what work we've still got.'

One evening in late September, when the weather had turned decidedly autumnal, Emily was sitting contentedly by the range in the kitchen, giving Lewis his evening feed, when the back door burst open and Trip almost fell through it. He slammed it behind him, making the baby jump and begin to whimper.

'I'm sorry, Emily, but I've had news from home. Father's had another very serious stroke. He's not expected to last the night. I must go at once.'

'Oh Trip, I'm so sorry. Shall we come too? He might want to see Lewis before . . .'

Trip hesitated and murmured, 'Yes, you're right. I hadn't thought of that. And I think I should pick up Belle and Richard too, don't you?'

'Yes, I do. Just run round to Mrs Dugdale and tell her what's happening while I get Lewis ready. She'll see to everything here for us. And ask Lizzie to take a message to Nell to keep the soup kitchens going as well as things at work.'

'Right – yes. I'll do that.' Trip seemed uncharacteristically flustered. He went out again and was gone for about half an hour, so that by the time he returned both Emily and the baby were ready and waiting.

She sat beside him in the front seat of his car with Lewis on her lap as they drove to the street where Belle still lived in the modest terraced house, which Arthur Trippet had bought for her many years earlier.

There was silence in the car as the four adults and the child travelled through the deepening dusk towards Ashford. No one knew what to say and when they arrived at Riversdale House, Belle and Richard hung back, as if they weren't really sure of their welcome at such a time. But they need not have worried, Constance held out her arms to Belle and ushered her into the sitting room. 'I'm so glad Thomas thought to bring both of you. I should have suggested it myself, but I wasn't thinking straight.'

'How – how is he?'

'Not good, my dear.' Constance still held Belle's hand. 'You must be prepared for the worst. The doctor is still here with him, and Nurse Adams too, of course. We can go up, though perhaps not all at once.'

'Thomas, Emily and the baby should go up first. Richard and I will wait.'

Constance nodded. 'Very well, then.'

As they entered the bedroom, Emily held on tightly to Lewis, hoping he would not cry. But the sight of the man in the bed was a shock. From the big, blustering man Arthur Trippet had once been, he had shrunk to a thin, pathetic figure. He lay, propped up on pillows, his eyes closed, his breathing shallow.

'Father?' Trip approached the bedside.

Arthur's eyelids flickered at the sound of his son's voice and, it seemed with a supreme effort, he opened them. Trip took hold of his wrinkled hand and said softly, 'We've brought your grandson to see you.'

Emily moved towards the bedside and propped the baby in front of him. Arthur's eyes focussed on the child and there seemed to be a ghost of a smile. His hand trembled as if he was trying to reach out to Lewis, but the effort was too much and he closed his eyes with a sigh. The baby began to whimper and Emily picked him up, put him against her shoulder and walked to the far side of the room, patting his back to soothe him.

They stayed in the bedroom for ten minutes and then returned downstairs to allow Belle and Richard some time with Arthur. They, too, only stayed about ten minutes and when they returned downstairs Belle was in tears.

Constance put her arms around her. 'There, there, my dear. Don't grieve. He's had a good life and you were a big part of that life.' She smiled gently as she said candidly, 'I think you brought him far more joy than ever I did.'

Belle wept against her shoulder. It was a strange situation that was not lost on any of them; the mistress being comforted by the wife.

'I can't believe how kind you've been to me and to Richard too,' Belle sobbed. 'You're an amazing woman. Thank you.'

They all sat down and Polly brought in tea.

Just under an hour later, the doctor entered the sitting room to say that Arthur had passed away quite peacefully. 'I think, once he had seen you all, he just let go.'

Belle looked towards Constance and bit her lip. It was obvious there was something she wanted to say.

'What is it, my dear?' Constance said gently.

'May I – may I sit with him for a while?'

'Of course. Do you want to be on your own?'

'If – if you don't mind?'

Constance nodded. No doubt there were things Belle wanted to whisper to him that she didn't want anyone else to hear. She was not even asking to take Richard with her. Constance didn't really feel the need to sit beside him again. She had spent many hours at his bedside since his first incapacitating stroke, talking and reading to him. She had done her duty by her husband and had done it well.

Twenty-Two

The funeral, held in Ashford's church a week later, was not as well attended as might have been supposed for a man of Arthur's standing. A few owners of factories in the city came to the village, but, though respected, Arthur had not been well liked. He had been seen as a ruthless man who, at one time, had even disowned his own son because Thomas would not bend to his father's will. They had been reconciled later, but the older man's action had not been forgotten. Several villagers attended, but not all by any means. He had never made himself part of the community.

'Now, if it had been Mrs Trippet,' they murmured to one another, 'that'd've been a different matter. Church'd've been packed.'

Trip led his mother behind the coffin, followed by Belle and Richard. The Ryan family brought up the rear with George Bayes walking at the very back. The service and the burial in the windy churchyard were both brief and the mourners returned to a buffet at Riversdale House.

'Constance, my dear, I'm sorry for your loss.' George, a plate of food in one hand and a glass in the other, found her standing a little apart from the others.

Constance smiled. 'Thank you, George. And I never really said how sorry I was to hear of Muriel's death. It must have been a very hard time for you.'

'You sent a sweet letter, Constance. I appreciated it.'

Their eyes met and held. There was so much to say, but now was neither the time nor the place.

Life settled back into a routine, but now there were other worries, which filled everyone's minds. The miners' strike continued and Emily did her best to help where she could. Miners' wives now manned the kitchens, which Emily had set up, but it broke her heart to see the white-faced, thin little children with hardly the energy to play, and to watch the miners roaming the streets in search of some kind of paid work.

'How long can they go on?' she asked Trip, but he had no answer.

In November, the strike came to an end, but sadly it was not a victory for the miners, who were forced to accept longer working hours and a cut in their wages.

'It's diabolical,' Emily stormed. 'I wish we could employ them all.'

Christmas and New Year celebrations were a little subdued that year because of Arthur's death, but Emily, Trip and Lewis spent the holiday in Ashford as usual. The small children, not quite understanding, were as lively and as boisterous as ever. Arthur had been ill for a long time and had been unable to take an active part in the life at Riversdale or in the

160

running of the factory that had been his. Now that ownership had truly passed to Trip and Richard.

'But where it's all going to go, I don't know,' Trip said.

'Things'll get better soon, I'm sure,' Emily said, trying to cheer him. Though he said very little, she wondered if his father's death had affected Trip more than he cared to admit. Perhaps he was feeling guilty because they had not enjoyed a better relationship. But Arthur Trippet had been an overbearing, dictatorial man. It had been hard for anyone to feel close to him. Perhaps the only person who ever had was Belle Beauman. This year, however, Belle and Richard declined the invitation to Riversdale for Christmas.

'I can understand why,' said Constance as she read Belle's letter. 'Coming here would be difficult so soon after his death and she doesn't want to put a damper on the festivities, because,' she went on firmly, 'we must keep going as normal for the children's sake.'

And it was the children who did indeed keep things going. Harry, important in his role as the eldest in the family, kept Sarah amused and even helped out with the two growing babies. At seven months, both Lewis and Philip were sitting up and taking notice of everything that went on around them. Lewis was the more placid of the two and would stare in amazement at his cousin when Philip was fractious.

'Just look at them,' Emily laughed. 'I hope they'll grow up to be friends, Amy, being the same age.'

'Of course they will. When they get older, Lewis must come and stay with us in the school holidays.'

'And yours, too, must come to the city.'

Amy laughed. 'I wouldn't inflict all three on you at once, but maybe Harry could come in a few years.'

'It's a promise.'

'Mother, whatever are you doing here?'

On a warm spring day in April, Constance stood uncertainly in the doorway to Trip's office in the factory.

'I – er – thought I'd just take a drive into the city.'

'Come in – come in and sit down.' Trip placed a chair in front of his desk and as Constance sat down, he perched on the corner of the desk. 'Has Kirkland brought you?'

Constance's eyes twinkled merrily. 'No. I've sold my little car and bought myself a brand new one, Thomas.'

'What about Father's Rolls? Didn't you want to drive that?'

Constance waved away his suggestion. 'Far too big and ostentatious for me. I'm not sure what to do with it, really. Do you want it, Thomas?'

'Heavens, no! I feel the same as you about it.'

'I thought I should be more adventurous and be courageous enough to drive anywhere I want to go,' Constance went on. 'And I wanted to come here.'

The corner of Trip's mouth twitched with amusement. He could understand his mother wanting to visit her family – especially her grandson, on whom she doted – but why, exactly, had she come to the factory?

It was over six months since his father's funeral and he was pleased to see that his mother was picking up the pieces of her own life. Arthur had been ill for so long that it was far from being disrespectful to him that she should cast off her mourning clothes and move on.

'I thought perhaps you could come to lunch with me and then later I'll visit Belle and, perhaps, I could see Lewis too, when Emily gets home.'

'I can hardly believe he'll be a year old next month. He crawls everywhere like lightning and even tries to pull himself up to stand.' Trip couldn't hide the pride at every milestone in his little son's life. 'Emily leaves him some days with Mrs Dugdale and he's started on solids. You could call at her house to see him, if you like, then you won't be so late setting off back home. You know where she lives, don't you?'

Constance nodded. 'All right. I'll do that. I'll visit Belle another time and spend more time with my grandson.' There was still a note of joy in her tone every time she uttered the word 'grandson'.

'How are all the Ryan family? Have you seen them lately? We must really come over to Ashford very soon.'

'They're all well, but now I'll let you get on,' Constance said, standing up. 'Shall I pick you up about twelve-thirty?'

'That'd be perfect.'

As she stood up, she said casually, 'Is George in his office? I'd just like to say "hello".'

'I think so. I'll show you . . .'

'It's all right. I know the way.'

As she left the room, Trip stared after her thoughtfully.

* * *

'Constance, my dear.' George Bayes stood up from behind his desk and came towards her with his hands outstretched as they always were whenever they met.

'I – I'm not sure I should have come,' she said. Constance was usually a confident, self-possessed woman, but at this moment she was strangely hesitant and unsure of herself.

'Why ever not?' George said blandly and added, with a conspiratorial wink, 'I presume you've come to see your son – or even Richard.'

Constance laughed and relaxed a little, but she was still aware of her hands clasped in his. If anyone should come into the room suddenly and see them . . .

Gently, George led her to a chair. 'How are you now, my dear? I haven't seen you since Arthur's funeral. I've been thinking about you though, but I thought it wouldn't be –' he paused, as if searching for the appropriate word – 'seemly to be seen visiting you so soon.' Still holding her hands, he sat down on a chair facing her and leaned forwards. 'But I've been thinking of you. *How* I've been thinking of you.'

'Have you, George?' she murmured, her gaze fastened onto his. Then she took a deep breath and said boldly, 'And I've been thinking about you too. We're both alone now and – I mean . . .' All at once the uncertainty was back.

'You're wondering if we could recapture those heady days of our youth, aren't you? Before our parents stepped in and told both of us we weren't suitable for each other.'

Not trusting herself to speak, Constance nodded.

'You know, I could understand your father being against any kind of a match – he being a wealthy landowner with you as his only heir – but what I couldn't understand was my father's attitude. He was even more set against our friendship – and it was only a friendship then, wasn't it? – than your father.'

'My father was a strict disciplinarian and vengeful, too, if things didn't go his way,' Constance said. 'I've no doubt that if – if things had gone further between us, he would have stopped it somehow. And I think he would have destroyed your father and his business in the process, just to get his revenge.'

George's father had been blacksmith and wheelwright in the village where Constance's father had owned much of the surrounding farmland. Alfie Bayes had been dependent for his livelihood on the goodwill of such an important man in the district. If Mr Vincent, Constance's father, had taken against him and forbidden any of his tenant farmers to patronize Alfie Bayes's smithy, the man would have faced ruin.

'What if we'd eloped?' George said, with a roguish twinkle in his eyes.

'I was only fifteen. You'd have been in serious trouble and I'm not sure it would have been legal anyway – not even at Gretna Green.'

'But it would be now,' George murmured and then he squeezed her hands. 'Let's do it now, Constance. Let's elope.'

'What?' Constance stared at him and laughed nervously. 'George, I . . .'

'My dear, you must know how I adored you then and I love you still. Always have and always will.'

'But you – you married, you . . .'

'Yes, I did, and I was very fond of Muriel. She was a good wife and would have been a good mother to our children if we had been so blessed, but we weren't. I did my duty by her. I left work to nurse her in her final illness, but I have to admit to you – and only to you – that I was never able to love her in the same way that I loved you.'

Slowly, Constance murmured, 'I never really questioned my feelings. All I know is that I missed you dreadfully when my father banned me from seeing you any more and then, of course, when he introduced Arthur to me and told me – yes, told me – that he was the man I was to marry, well, I just went along with it. You just didn't disobey your father, did you? And in the early days, Arthur was very attentive, showering me with flowers and chocolates. And champagne on my birthday. I suppose at seventeen, as I was by then, I was swept along in the romance of it all.'

'But now we're both on our own with no one to tell us what we should – or shouldn't – do let's put all that behind us, Constance, and make up for lost time. My dear, will you marry me or am I still so far beneath you that . . . ?'

Constance hushed him and laid her finger gently against his lips. 'Don't you dare say such things, George Bayes. And, yes, of course I want to marry you. But do you think now is still a little soon after . . . ?'

'Perhaps it is, so we'll keep it our secret for now, though perhaps you should tell Thomas.'

'I'm taking him to lunch today. Should I . . . ?'

George grinned. 'The sooner the better, as far as I'm concerned. But you are sure, Constance, aren't you? I mean, I can't keep you in the manner you've been used to. There's the problem of where we would live, for a start . . .'

Constance chuckled. Though she felt a little guilty, she couldn't remember the last time she'd felt so happy. Perhaps not since the birth of her son and, of course, it went without saying, her adorable grandson. 'Now, don't start getting cold feet, George. No problem is insurmountable when two people love each other.'

As they rose together, he took her in his arms and kissed her.

'I'll talk to Thomas this very day,' she promised.

As she left the factory, Constance felt she was walking on air. Suddenly, life seemed very good.

Twenty-Three

As they sat down to lunch in the restaurant, which Trip had recommended, he said, 'This is very nice, Mother. Is there any particular reason?'

Constance glanced at him and smiled. 'It's funny you should ask that. There wasn't when I arrived this morning, but there is now.'

'Oh,' Trip said, trying to keep the smile from his own face as he spread his napkin on his knee and took the menu from the waiter's hand. 'Let's order first and then you can tell me.'

They studied the menu and placed their orders for drinks, starters and main courses. As the waiter gave a little bow towards them and then moved away, Trip said, 'Fire away, Mother.'

'I think I told you not long ago how George and I knew one another when we were youngsters.'

'You did. Go on.'

'We were very good friends. Very – close, and if it hadn't been for the disapproval of both our fathers, I think things might have developed even then into something more than just friendship. In fact, I know they would have. But I was only fifteen when my father banned me from seeing George. As I grew older and one or two suitors came knocking at the door, my father chose Arthur Trippet as the man I should marry. He saw in him an entrepreneurial streak and thought that the money and lands, which I would one day inherit, would be used wisely. Being so young, I didn't have the courage to disobey him and by that time, I knew that George's father was also firmly set against our – friendship. You see my father would have ruined Alfie Bayes, if he'd been so minded. And believe me, he would have been.'

She was quiet for a moment, as if thinking back down the years, perhaps thinking about 'what might have been'. Trip too remained silent, waiting until she felt like continuing. He was desperately sorry for his mother, who had been dominated all her life by ruthlessly ambitious men. He certainly knew from experience how callous his own father had been when he did not get his own way. Now, he was learning that poor Constance had been ruled by two of them. He hoped that what she was about to tell him would lead to a much happier life for her.

She was playing nervously with the cutlery on the table and avoiding looking into his eyes. 'This morning, George asked me to marry him and I've – I've agreed.' She chuckled suddenly and was like a girl again. 'George suggested that we should elope, but I wanted to tell you. I need to have your approval, Thomas.' Now she looked up at him to meet his gaze and her eyes were pleading.

Trip reached across the table. 'My darling Mother, of course you have it. George is a lovely man and if he's the one to make you happy, then I'm all for it.' He leaned across the table and lowered his voice.

'But would you really like to elope? Run away together and come back married or do you want a big village wedding?'

'It'd be exciting, wouldn't it?' Her eyes shone at the thought. 'But no, in the circumstances, I don't think either of us would want a lot of fuss and tongues wagging.'

'Then do it, Mother. I'll tell Emily, of course, but we won't tell anyone else.'

'Really? Do you think I – we – should?'

Trip chuckled. 'I really do, Mother. I think it would be perfect.' He paused and then asked, 'Have you thought about where you would live though, because I don't think George would be happy living in Riversdale House, do you?'

Constance laughed, throwing her head back and not caring who heard her. 'He mentioned the same thing and I told him that nothing was insurmountable when two people loved each other. Just like when you and Emily were married. We had problems then, didn't we?'

'But you were on our side, Mother,' he said softly, remembering how she had sided with the young couple against her husband and had even held the reception for the double wedding between Trip and Emily and Josh and Amy at Riversdale House. The whole village had attended and the only person missing had been Arthur Trippet. 'And now I'm on yours. And I know Emily will be too. You and George do whatever you want to do and you have my blessing. I just want – more than anything – to see you happy.'

*   *   *

Emily was thrilled when Trip told her that evening. 'How romantic!'

'But we're not to say a word to anyone. I think for two pins they'd have gone without even telling us.'

Emily laughed. 'That's what they should have done, but I expect she didn't want to risk upsetting you.'

Trip wrinkled his forehead thoughtfully. 'I really can't think of anything that my mother could possibly do that would upset me.'

Emily put her arms around him and laid her cheek against his chest, listening for a moment to the rhythmic beat of his heart. 'You're a wonderful son, Trip, husband and now a father too. Don't ever change, will you?'

His arms tightened about her as he bent to kiss her.

'How do you like my new hairstyle, Trip? It's all the rage. It's called a shingle.'

Emily had had her blond hair cut short at the back and there were waves and curls framing her face.

'I like it. It's very pretty, but then,' he said, kissing the tip of her nose, 'you always look pretty.'

'And I treated myself to a new suit. I have to look smart when I'm visiting customers.'

Emily held up a gold-coloured skirt and matching jacket trimmed with a black fur collar and cuffs.

'And a cloche hat to go with it.'

'Very nice,' Trip approved. 'You'll have your customers falling over themselves to give you orders. I'll take you to Ashford on Sunday and show you off, though,' he added, with a chuckle, 'I doubt my mother or yours will take much notice of you when Lewis is around.'

When they pulled up outside the blacksmith's house on the Sunday afternoon, Harry ran out and hurled himself at them. 'Uncle Trip! Aunty Emily! Did you see the papers? Have you heard the news? Isn't it thrilling?'

Alighting from the car, Trip picked him up and swung him round. 'What's all the excitement about?'

'Last weekend Charles Lindbergh flew across the Atlantic from New York to Paris. Imagine that, Uncle Trip, three thousand six hundred miles non-stop. Granddad Walter is going to help me make a model of his aircraft. It's called *Spirit of St Louis*.' The little boy pronounced the name 'Lewis'. 'And it's a Ryan NYP monoplane. Fancy him calling his plane after me and Lewis. He must know I like planes. Does Lewis like planes, Uncle Trip?'

'He's too young yet, old chap, but I expect he will when he's older.'

Emily climbed out of the car carrying Lewis and laughed. 'He will if he's around you for long, won't he, Harry?'

'Yes,' Harry said solemnly. 'I suppose he is a bit little yet, isn't he? He's like our Phil. Does Lewis cry much? Phil's *always* crying. Mummy says he's a whiny baby. Is Lewis walking yet?'

On and on the little boy chattered, the questions tumbling out, but Emily answered them patiently.

'No, we're lucky, Lewis doesn't cry much and he's not quite walking yet, but he pulls himself up.'

At that point, Amy came out of the front door, drying her hands on a towel. 'Come in, come in.' Her smile was as warm as ever, but Emily thought she looked thinner and tired. There were dark shadows beneath her eyes. 'Are you staying for tea, Emily?'

'A cup of tea would be lovely, but we're due at Riversdale a little later.' Emily forbore to say 'for dinner', not wishing to sound too grand to her sister-in-law.

For some reason, which Emily couldn't quite understand, the visit to both the smithy and to her parents' home was strained. After a cup of tea with Amy, Josh and their children they went next door to visit Emily's parents, but Walter, in his chair by the fire, seemed ill-at-ease and her mother was tight-lipped, hardly able to bring herself to offer them refreshment.

'I suppose you'll want a cup of tea and cake to go with it?' Martha's offer was grudging and Emily said swiftly, 'No, no, Mam. We've just had one with Josh and Amy.'

Martha sniffed and muttered, 'As if they haven't got enough mouths to feed.'

By the time they left, Emily couldn't help but feel relief. As she kissed her father's cheek, he grasped her hand and held onto it for a few moments and, although she knew that now he could speak again, he said nothing to her.

When they arrived home in Sheffield later that

evening after dinner with Constance at Riversdale, Emily said, 'What on earth do you think was wrong with my family? They all seemed – oh, I don't know – odd, somehow.'

'I wondered if there'd been a big row. You could've cut the atmosphere with one of our penknives.'

'I'm used to my mother's moods, but Dad seemed upset. That's what worried me the most.'

'Josh didn't seem himself, I have to say.'

'If it hadn't been for Harry's excited chatter, I'd have felt distinctly unwelcome.'

'My mother made up for it though, didn't she? You'd think no one else in the whole world had a grandson.'

'Oh, they haven't,' Emily teased. 'Believe me, they haven't.'

In late September, the villagers of Ashford-in-the-Water were agog when the news finally reached them that Constance Trippet had married again.

'And to the foreman of her late husband's factory. Would you believe it?'

'Has it been going on a while, d'you think?'

Shoulders were shrugged at the question, but there was one person, a stalwart of the village, who defended Constance. 'Mrs Trippet's a lady,' Grace Partridge told anyone willing to listen. 'She would never do anything untoward, and besides, her husband was little more than a vegetable for the past four or five years. And before that, well –' she wriggled her shoulders – 'we all know now what he was up to, don't we? Producing an illegitimate son out

174

of the woodwork *and* making the boy his heir when he fell out with young Thomas for a while. If you ask me,' Grace didn't care if they were asking her opinion or not, they were going to hear it anyway, 'that poor woman has put up with a lot over the years. She's been very forbearing. She deserves whatever happiness she can find, and if she can find it with George Bayes, then good luck to her, I say.'

And with those few, well-chosen words, Grace Partridge silenced the gossiping tongues. Constance was well liked and respected in the village. There was hardly a soul in the community that she hadn't helped in one way or another at some time.

'George Bayes is a good man,' Josh said, as he shook Trip's hand on their first visit home after the news had broken. 'I'm sure they'll be happy. Where are they going to live, d'you know? And is he giving up work at the factory?'

Trip laughed. 'I don't know anything yet, but we're hoping to find out a little more this afternoon after we've had luncheon with you.'

Josh's face clouded. 'You're welcome, of course, you know that, but it might not be quite what you're used to. Things are tough at the moment. The candle-making business is dying, Trip, and I'm not sure what to do. I've asked about finding work on the local farms, but no one will take me on.' He ran his fingers through his hair. 'Mr Clark's doing all right, but we can't expect him to keep all of us. I've even tried my hand at blacksmithing, but I'm useless at it.'

'Then we won't stay—'

'Oh, you must. Amy would be mortified if she thought I had breathed a word to you. Please don't say anything to her or to my mam. They're both very proud women.' He sighed. 'I catch me mam looking at me sometimes as if to say, you should have stayed in the city.'

Trip shook his head. 'It's no better there, Josh. Unemployment is still quite high. The papers say it's about one million nationally and the north, with its industries, is harder hit than the south.'

Josh blew out his cheeks. 'Then I wouldn't have been any better there, then?'

'No,' Trip said firmly. 'Believe me, you wouldn't.'

At lunch, which the Ryans still called dinner, both Trip and Emily noticed the meagre portions of meat. They were all gathered around the table in Amy's best parlour and Emily saw that both Amy and Martha went without meat. She said nothing and dared not even glance at Trip.

'How are things in the city?' Martha asked.

'Difficult,' Trip said. 'And, sadly, I can see them getting worse before they get better. The decision to return to the gold standard, which has meant an over-valuation of Sterling, has made exports more expensive and therefore our coal and steel exports have become less competitive and consequently—'

'Oh Trip,' Emily cut in, trying desperately to steer the conversation away from such matters. 'It's way over my head.'

Trip laughed. 'It wouldn't be, if you were interested and set your mind to understanding it. You're an intelligent woman, Emily.'

'All I care about is having enough customers to keep my employees occupied so that I can pay them a decent living wage at the end of the week.'

'But don't you see . . . ?'

'I understand what you mean, Trip,' Josh said quietly. 'And I expect we're still in debt – as a nation – for the war.'

'Exactly! And the export industries are talking about lowering workers' wages in an effort to cut production costs.'

'That could cause another strike, if they do,' Bob murmured.

'Well, I'm not lowering my girls' wages,' Emily said, firmly. 'We'll keep going somehow.'

'I think the larger factories in the cutlery industry are turning to the little mesters and little missuses even more than before because they can't afford to pay men to work full time. Placing work with out-workers is more economical.'

'Work's still coming to me,' Bob Clark ventured. 'Though I've noticed a slight drop off in business. I think some farmers are trying to do their own repairs instead of paying a blacksmith. I must admit, I'm finding it harder to cope in my advancing years.' He smiled ruefully. He was still a very strong, active man, but his work was hard, physical graft. 'Anyway, we're managing.'

Martha sniffed. 'Josh isn't,' she said bluntly. 'His business is all but dead. He'll have to find some other work soon.' She glanced at Trip. 'Could you find him something, Thomas? He is your brother-in-law now.'

Before Trip could answer, Josh's head shot up and

he exclaimed, 'Mam! Don't put Trip in such an awkward position. You've just heard what he said. Things are as bad there too. Living in the country, we can still get food direct from the farmers. City folk can't do that.'

'You wouldn't really want to come back to the city, Josh, would you?' Emily asked.

Amy was quiet, but her face was bleak. She didn't want to lose her husband to the city for a second time. Now, she had three young children . . .

To her relief, Josh was adamant as he said, 'No, I wouldn't. I know you've taken to it, Em, but city life's not for me and I certainly wouldn't take my family there.'

Martha stood up and began to collect the plates, crashing them together with quick, angry movements. 'Well, you'd better think of something soon, Josh, else we'll all starve. Looks like I'm even going to lose my little cleaning job at Riversdale House now that Mrs Trippet – I mean, Mrs Bayes – has got herself married again. I expect they'll be leaving. They won't want to live *there*, will they?' It was more of a statement than a question directed at Trip as she turned away and marched out of the room carrying the stack of dirty plates.

Twenty-Four

A little later, as they were about to leave Josh's home to visit Constance and George at Riversdale House, Amy said, 'You can leave Lewis with us, if you like. If – if you want to talk to your mam, Trip.'

'Heavens!' Trip laughed. 'It's a kind offer, Amy, but I wouldn't dare walk into that house without her grandson in my arms.' He kissed the young woman's cheek and whispered, 'Don't worry, love. Things will work out, I'm sure.'

Amy smiled weakly, but stood to wave them off as they climbed into the car to drive the short distance to Trip's former home.

Constance and George were seated in the window of the morning room overlooking the driveway, watching for their arrival. Trip parked the car in front of the house and, by the time they were climbing out, Constance was at the front door.

'Here he is. My little man,' she cried, reaching for Lewis. 'Come in, come in. We'll go into the sitting room.'

George was hovering in the hallway. Trip shook his hand. 'Good to see you. Did you have a lovely time? All go well, did it?'

George looked a trifle embarrassed, a little out of

179

place, but Trip's warm handshake and Emily's kiss on his cheek seemed to relax him as he followed them through to the sitting room where, already, Constance was nursing her grandson. George was smiling as he answered Trip's questions. 'We went all the way to Gretna Green. We did it properly and then we had a week touring the southern part of Scotland. We got up as far as the Trossachs and Loch Lomond. Beautiful countryside up there.' He chuckled. 'Nearly as nice as Derbyshire.'

They sat down together as they exchanged news.

'Hasn't Lewis grown?' Constance said, carrying him around the room to show him the pictures on the wall and ornaments in the glass cabinet and then setting him on the floor to watch him walking. 'Such a big boy now, aren't you? I can't believe how he's grown since we last saw him.'

'They alter so quickly when they're little, don't they? We've seen a huge difference in little Phil today. They played quite nicely together today, didn't they, Trip?'

Trip laughed. 'With Harry acting as referee – yes.'

There was a pause before Trip asked, 'Well, you two, what are your plans? Where are you going to live, for one thing, and, for another, are you coming back to work, George?'

The older couple, the love shining from their faces, glanced at each other as Constance said softly, 'We have talked about it, of course. We both feel we need to move out of this house and buy a home together. But, as for continuing work, that must be George's decision.'

180

'I'd like to stay on, Master Thomas . . .'

Trip chuckled. 'I think "Thomas" or even "Trip" would be all right now, don't you?'

George laughed and continued. 'I'm well aware of the difference in our stations in life . . .' he nodded briefly towards Constance, who murmured, 'Oh George . . .', but he only shrugged and went on, 'There's no getting away from it and we'd be foolish to try to pretend it doesn't exist. So, I'd be happier working and contributing something to our living expenses.'

Constance glanced at her son and smiled. 'Very different to your father's attitude, isn't it? He actually married me for my money and made no secret of the fact. And now, George doesn't really want to touch a penny of it.'

'Well, I, for one, admire that,' Trip said, 'but I think you should both regard yourselves as equal partners.' He glanced at Emily. 'That's what we do. We pull together. Whatever we have is *ours*, not mine or hers. And we've made it all legal. We've both made wills so that Lewis is protected and any more children we might have too.'

'Very sensible,' Constance said quietly, her gaze still on her grandson. She couldn't take her eyes off the little chap.

'So,' Trip pressed on, 'where were you thinking of living?'

'Probably on the outskirts of Sheffield. There are some lovely areas not too far from Creswick Street.'

'I could bike in or—' George began and Constance added, 'Or use my car.'

'And what would you do with this place?'

Constance wrinkled her forehead. 'There are several things we could do with it. We could sell it, but I am reluctant to do that. I don't really want to sever my ties completely with the village. We could keep it and all of us –' she waved her hands to encompass Trip, Emily and Lewis – 'could use it as a weekend retreat and for longer holidays in the summer. That way, I could keep the staff on to look after it for us. There's only Mrs Froggatt, the two maids and Kirkland. Nurse Adams has gone now, of course. Or –' she paused for a moment – 'we could rent it out, but if we did that, we wouldn't be able to use it ourselves and I couldn't be sure tenants would keep the staff on. The girls would find other employment easily enough, but I'm not sure about Mrs Froggatt and Kirkland.'

'There is another way, Mother,' Trip said softly.

'Is there? I believed I'd thought of all the options. What is it, Thomas?'

'You could turn it into a high-class hotel with a superb restaurant offering meals to non-residents too. That way you could keep on all the present staff and probably employ more. You – and us – could no doubt still come and stay here if we wanted to. This area is very popular with visitors; beautiful scenery, wonderful walks and so many places of interest to visit.'

Constance stared at her son and then said, 'Now, that *is* a good idea, Thomas.' She turned towards her husband and asked, 'What do you think, George? And don't say it has nothing to do with you, because it has.'

George smiled. 'I think it's an excellent suggestion, but there's a lot to go into. And I think you'd have to employ a manager and, yes, you would need more staff. If you were thinking of keeping Mrs Froggatt on as cook, she would need help. You can't expect one person to cook around the clock. And this sort of hotel would need to offer full board and half-board, too, as well as catering – as Thomas suggests – for casual diners. And there'd have to be a bar, so you'd need to be licensed. You'd need cleaners, waiters and probably a hall porter.'

'And I've got just the people to fill some of those positions,' Trip put in, glancing at Emily. 'Josh's candle-making business is just about on its last legs. He'd be glad of any kind of work you could find him and Martha is already worrying that your marriage will mean the end of her cleaning job here. And although Amy has three children to care for, she might even be glad to train as a waitress and work one or two evenings a week. There's always Bob to keep an eye on the children.'

Constance laughed, picked up Lewis and tossed him high in the air. The little boy squealed with delight. 'Do you know, Lewis Trippet, I think your grandmother is going into the hotel business?' She sat down and set him on her lap as she said, more seriously, 'I think we can do better than that. Do you think Josh might like to train to be the manager, Emily? And I think your mother – and perhaps Grace Partridge – could help out as cooks. Or do we have to call them "chefs" in a hotel?'

They talked for a long time, mulling over the ideas,

each of them coming up with suggestions, and the more they talked, the more enthused they all became. They had tea together – Lewis sitting in the brand-new high chair Constance had bought for him – and then it was time to leave.

'Don't say a word about this to anyone yet,' Constance warned. 'We'll look into it thoroughly and find out what it entails before we announce our intentions to the world. But we'll both see you later this week. We'll be coming house hunting in Sheffield and George will be back at work tomorrow morning. He can use my car to travel to and fro until we find a house there. Oh, it's all so exciting!'

'Do you know,' Trip said, as they drove back to the city, 'I don't think I've ever seen my mother looking quite so happy?'

Seated beside him with Lewis on her knee, Emily chuckled. 'Only the first time she laid eyes on her grandson.'

Trip laughed with her. 'Ah, yes. Nothing will ever surpass that moment.'

Twenty-Five

Events moved very swiftly once the decision had been made. Constance and George found a house the following week in the Walkley district of Sheffield, which wasn't too far from Trippets' works. Because Constance had no property to sell first, the purchase was concluded in record time. With the help of both her son and George, Constance found out everything they needed to know about turning Riversdale House into a hotel. She made copious lists of all that needed to be done, the authorities she needed to consult, any licences and insurances that needed to be applied for, and she sought the help of other hoteliers for guidance and warnings of any pitfalls she might encounter. Surprisingly, even the local hotels were helpful. 'There's room for us all, Mrs Trippet,' the managers said. 'In fact, we recommend each other if we're full. Business is still good for us – for which we're thankful – despite the tough times the country is going through.'

'I did wonder about the common sense in opening up a new business just now, but you've made me feel more hopeful.'

By Christmas everything was in place for Constance to make an announcement about what she intended to do.

'I want to tell family, friends and my staff myself before they hear it from anywhere else. Rumours are bound to start since I've been talking to the other hotel managers in the area. So,' Constance said to Emily, when they were back in the city after spending Christmas at Riversdale as usual, 'are you going to tell your family what I hope will be good news for them to start 1928?'

'Oh no,' Emily said swiftly. 'You should do it.'

'Very well, then, if you're sure. I intend to go home – oh dear, I mustn't call it home any more, must I? My home is here in Sheffield with George and so much nearer to you three too.' She clapped her hands. She and George had moved into their house just before Christmas and were well settled. Constance already employed a cook and housemaid. But far from being daunted by this, George was pleased. The difference in their former lifestyles would always be there, but Constance was such a down-to-earth woman with no airs and graces and her son was obviously happy to see his mother so content, that George ceased to worry. He cycled to work or, if Constance did not need her car, he used it to drive to the factory. And he even tried to get used to having his meals cooked and his clothes washed and ironed by employees. He even no longer had to make his own bed. It was all very new to George, but he was married to the woman he had loved secretly for most of his life, and a few changes in his lifestyle were easily surmountable.

'Emily thinks I should be the one to tell them all in Ashford,' Constance said, as she and George sat down to dinner one evening during the first week in January. 'Shall we go at the weekend and tell everyone?'

'I think you should go on your own, my love,' he said.

Her face fell. 'Really? Why?'

'Because this is something in which I really have no part and I think it would be so much nicer for them to hear it from you personally.'

'But I *want* you to be involved, George. You know I do.'

'I know, and I love you for it, but the folks there hardly know me. When we were young together –' they smiled across the table at each other at the shared memories – 'it was in Over Haddon – not Ashford. That was your life with Arthur and Thomas and your village friends – not me. I'm always there for you to talk to and to be of practical help if I'm needed, but this is your venture, yours and Thomas's. Our life – yours and mine – is here in our new home together.'

Constance didn't quite understand, yet she respected his feelings. After a moment's pause, she nodded and said, though with some reluctance, 'Very well, then. But will you do something for me?'

'If I can, you know I will.'

'I'll be going backwards and forwards between here and Ashford, at least until things get settled, so will you buy yourself a little car to go to work in? I can't bear to think of you cycling in all weathers in winter.' She was careful to phrase her words so that he should not feel she was suggesting that she should buy him a car. But George knew her so well that he chuckled and played along with her. 'Very well, my love. I will promise you that.'

Despite wishing that George had agreed to come with her, Constance set out the following morning with mounting excitement. It had been over two months since she had moved to Sheffield, but during that time she had kept Riversdale just as it was until the final decisions had been made about its future. But now, she was ready to reveal her plans to Mrs Froggatt and the rest of her staff.

'I knew something was going on when all them builders kept arriving to measure up the rooms,' Mrs Froggatt said. 'I thought you'd sold the place and it was the new people. I've had young Polly in tears for days because she thought her job was going. And me, well, I thought I was heading for the workhouse. Who'd want to employ me at my age?'

'I would,' Constance said firmly. 'I want you to be head cook.'

'Me!' Now Mrs Froggatt was startled. 'Oh now, I don't know about that, Mrs Trippet – I mean, Mrs Bayes – I'm a good, plain cook – I know that – but I can't do fancy dishes that hotel guests would want.'

'Why not?'

The cook gaped at her. 'Er – um – well . . .' Mrs Froggatt fell silent; she could not actually think of a reply.

'I don't intend that you should do it alone. I'm suggesting that I employ Martha Ryan and Grace Partridge on a rota system, but they would work under your direction. And I'm also employing Josh as hotel manager. With a little training, I think he'll do very nicely.'

Now Mrs Froggatt sat down with a bump. 'Well, I never did,' was all she could manage to say.

'And now, where are Polly and Kirkland? They are to have employment here too – if they want it, of course.'

'They'll want it, madam.' Mrs Froggatt wiped her eyes with the corner of her white apron. 'You're an angel, that's what you are.'

'I'm sure, in my time,' Constance laughed, 'I've been described as many things, but I don't think "an angel" has been one of them.'

But Elsie Froggatt said solemnly, 'Oh you have, madam, and on more than one occasion too, I can assure you. I don't think you quite realize how well loved you are in this village.'

Constance felt humbled suddenly. 'I just hope no one's going to be put out by my new enterprise.'

Elsie shook her head. 'I shouldn't think so, for a minute. It'll create more jobs and more business for the village. They'd be foolish if they are, that's all I can say.'

'And you'd be quite happy to work with Martha Ryan and Grace?'

Mrs Froggatt's eyes twinkled. 'Just so long as they know who's in charge.'

Constance chuckled. 'I'll make sure they do.'

After she'd spoken to Polly, who shed tears of relief against her shoulder and to Kirkland, who turned bright red and pumped her hand up and down in gratitude, Constance walked down the street to the smithy and The Candle House standing side by side on Greaves Lane.

The smithy was silent and the doors were closed, and when she peered through the front window of the house next door, she couldn't see Josh sitting at his workbench.

'Mm, looks like I'm here not a moment too soon,' Constance murmured as she knocked on the door of the blacksmith's home and waited until a white-faced Amy appeared. From behind her, Constance could hear a child wailing.

'Please come in, Mrs Bayes. You'll have to excuse us . . .' She led the way through to the back room. As she opened the door it seemed to Constance as if a sea of faces with huge, almost pleading eyes met her. She stepped inside to see Bob Clark sitting beside the fire. On the opposite side of the hearth sat Walter Ryan. Martha was seated at the table with Amy's youngest child on her lap – the baby that was about the same age as Lewis. Now, what was his name? Philip. That was it. It wouldn't do to forget the little chap's name. As she smiled at the child lying in Martha's arms, she could see that he was thinner than her own grandson and listless. He whimpered feebly. Beside her stood the little girl, resting her head on her grandmother's shoulder. Harry was sitting on the hearthrug, playing lethargically with his model aeroplane. He didn't even glance up when Constance entered the room. She was shocked; he'd always been such a warm, friendly child, but today there was no welcoming smile.

'Please sit down,' Amy said. 'May we offer you a cup of tea, Mrs Bayes?'

As she took the seat on the opposite side of the table to Martha and withdrew her gloves, Constance felt the strained atmosphere within the room.

'It's about all we can offer you, Mrs Bayes . . .' Martha began, to be gently reminded by Constance that they now called each other by their Christian names. 'I'm sorry to say you find us in straitened circumstances. How Josh thought he could ever support all of us with his little candle-making business, I don't know. And that's all but gone now. We should never have come back here. I should never have agreed to it. I should have *made* him stay in the city.'

'Where is Josh?' Constance asked, looking round.

'Out trying to find work, but I don't hold out much hope,' Martha answered. 'He's only covering the same ground he's been over before.'

Constance glanced at Walter, who seemed to shrink further into his chair with every word Martha uttered. Even Bob Clark sat with his head in his hands and poor Amy was obviously ill at ease.

'I'm sorry if I've called at an inconvenient time, but it is Josh I really wanted a word with, as well as you, Martha, and possibly Amy too.'

She glanced across at Bob Clark, wondering how she could help him. Perhaps Kirkland would need some help. There would be a lot of work for a man to do at the hotel, perhaps too much for one. She pursed her lips thoughtfully, whilst the occupants of the small room seemed to be waiting for her to speak.

She turned her head and smiled at Amy. 'Do you think Josh will be back soon?'

Amy shook her head. 'Not until dark, Mrs Bayes. He'll not give up before then.'

'Oh dear, I must be leaving earlier than that. I don't like driving at night.'

There were a few moments' silence and then, as if to give the lie to Amy's words, the back door opened and Josh came in stamping his feet angrily on the doormat. 'Buggers won't even give me the time of day, let alone a job.'

Amy flew to his side.

'Josh, shush. We have a visitor. Mind your language.'

Josh looked up and noticed Constance for the first time. At once, he was contrite. He'd always liked Trip's mother and he had reason to be very grateful to her. He would never forget that at their double wedding with Emily and Trip, she had paid for everything. His beloved Amy had had a beautiful wedding day, thanks to this woman.

He pulled the cap from his head and said at once, 'I'm sorry, Mrs Bayes, but I've had a hell of a day.'

'I can see that, Josh, but sit down and listen to what I have to say. Amy, I think you should give Josh that cup of tea you offered me. He looks as if he needs it far more than I do.'

Twenty-Six

When he was settled and they were all listening, Constance took a deep breath.

'Of course you all know that since my marriage to George Bayes, I have moved to live on the outskirts of Sheffield. The question was, what to do with Riversdale House.' She paused a moment, but no one spoke. 'I've decided to turn it into a hotel and I'll be wanting quite a lot more staff and, in particular, a trustworthy manager to run it. Josh,' she said, addressing him directly, 'how would you like to train to be the manager of my hotel?'

He stared at her. 'But – but I don't know anything about running a hotel.'

Constance smiled at him as she said softly, 'That's why I said "train". I'd pay for any courses you need to go on. Please say "yes".'

'Of course he'll do it,' Martha said, before Josh could even form a reply. 'It'd be a marvellous opportunity for you, Josh. Who knows where it might lead.'

'I wouldn't want it to lead anywhere else, Mam,' Josh said quietly. But his gaze was still fixed on Constance's face as he added, 'But are you sure I could do it?'

'Yes, I am,' Constance answered firmly and mentally crossed her fingers in the hope that her confidence wasn't misplaced.

'Then I'd be glad to accept. And thank you. When do you want me to start?'

'Straight away. Tomorrow morning. I'll be back and we'll meet at the house and discuss plans.' Then Constance turned to Bob Clark. 'I just wondered if you have any spare time, Mr Clark, and whether you'd like to help Kirkland? There's a lot to be done.'

Bob looked up, his gentle smile spreading across his face. Their gaze met and held and Constance could see that the wise man knew exactly what she was doing and why she was doing it. She knew that the difficult times had hit this family hard and she was – very tactfully – trying to help them by making out that it was she who needed their help and not the other way round. What a remarkable woman she was, Bob was thinking – and not for the first time in his life. He would never forget the time that Josh had moved to Sheffield at his mother's behest, it had to be said, leaving Amy pregnant. The lad hadn't known at the time and when he had found out nearly two years later, he'd come back at once and married her. But when the village learned of Amy's shame, it had been Constance Trippet and Grace Partridge who had stilled the wagging tongues. Martha Ryan had always been an ambitious woman for her son, but she was right about one thing; the candle-making business was no longer supporting them all. And his blacksmithing wasn't in such demand as it had once been.

'I'd be glad to help you out, Mrs Bayes, in any way

I can,' he said quietly, but his gratitude was in his eyes. Seeing it, she nodded and then turned to Martha.

'Now, Martha. I have appointed Mrs Froggatt as Head Cook, but she'll need help. She can't work around the clock and we must offer full board and half-board. So, I'm proposing that you and Grace Partridge, if she's willing, should be relief cooks when Mrs Froggatt has her days off.'

Now it was Martha's turn to look bewildered and a little flustered. 'I don't know if I could, Mrs Bayes.'

Constance smiled. 'That's exactly what Mrs Froggatt said, but I think you could all learn together. Now, what do you say?'

'I say, thank you, Mrs Bayes. I'd be delighted.'

'Good,' Constance said, promising herself that she would watch out so that Martha didn't try to interfere with Josh's running of the place.

'And now you, Amy. I know you must have your hands full with looking after all the family, but if you wanted to be a part-time housemaid or waitress to help out especially at busy times, you let me know.'

Amy, quite dumbstruck by all that had happened in the last few moments, nodded and murmured huskily, 'I will, Mrs Tr— Mrs Bayes. And – thank you. Thank you so much.'

Constance stood up. 'And now I must be going. I want to have a word with Grace, if she's in, and then I must be getting home.'

Within minutes of being invited into Grace Partridge's house, Constance was sitting at her kitchen table, drinking tea and eating a scone with cream and jam.

'That'll keep you going till you get home, Constance. Now,' Grace went on, sitting down on the opposite side of the table with her own cup of tea, 'tell me all the news. Did you have a lovely wedding and honeymoon? Where did you go?'

Constance chuckled. 'We went to Gretna Green and then toured Scotland.'

'And your new home in the city? Are you happy there?'

'Gloriously!' was all Constance needed to say for Grace could see the happiness shining out of her eyes.

'What's happening to the house here?' she asked but by the time Constance had finished outlining all her plans, Grace clapped her hands, exclaiming, 'What a perfectly wonderful idea, and, yes, I'd love to be a cook alongside Elsie and Martha. We get on so much better since the Ryans have come back here. She's not so unhealthily ambitious for poor Josh.'

Constance laughed. 'You might find that rears its ugly head again, now that I've appointed him manager.'

Grace pulled a face. 'We'll keep her in her place and see that she doesn't try to interfere with Josh.'

'I'm relieved to hear you say that, Grace. It was worrying me a little, I must admit.'

'I'm delighted to hear your plans. I've been very worried about that family for a while now. It'll be a marvellous opportunity for Josh, but d'you think you'll get guests at the hotel, then? I mean, there are quite a few hotels and guest houses around here already.'

'I can't be sure – how can anyone – we'll just have to wait and see. I can but try.'

To everyone's surprise, Martha Ryan fitted into the kitchen arrangement of the new hotel very well. She never went into the main part of the building, never interfered with Josh or the other staff, and she was amenable to everything that Elsie Froggatt asked of her. The three women got on very well, sitting together to plan meals and learning to cook new dishes that would be suitable for a high-class hotel. Best of all, both Martha and Grace willingly accepted Elsie Froggatt's leadership. Everyone was so relieved to have work and this was an exciting new venture for them all.

Bob Clark began helping Kirkland, but he too was sensible enough to let the other man take the lead and tell him each day what needed doing and Bob was never too proud to do whatever was asked of him.

Josh, after a few nervous days, took to his new job like the ducks took to the river near Sheep Wash Bridge, as the locals were fond of saying. He was never too proud to learn and he visited the other hotels in the district seeking – and receiving – their generous advice.

On the day that Riversdale Hotel opened for business, Josh was at the front door, dressed in his black morning suit, to welcome the first guests. Behind him stood Clive, the new restaurant manager and Jimmy, the hall porter, who was a young lad from the village. In the kitchen, Elsie Froggatt and her new kitchen maid, Ginny, prepared their first evening meal for six guests to be served by the restaurant manager and Polly in her waitress's black uniform and white cap and apron.

'D'you know, George?' Constance said, when she arrived home late on that first evening, 'I really think it's going to work.'

George nodded and smiled. 'I'm glad.'

Over the next few months, the hotel prospered steadily and in the city Trip and Emily, with careful management, kept all their employees fully occupied. Ever the optimist, Emily said, 'I think things are improving, Trip.'

Trip smiled, but said nothing. Emily was happy and busy. Lewis was growing into a healthy, active little boy and the Ryans were content. So why did he have this premonition that their present stability was only fleeting? He didn't want to worry Emily, but he had the awful feeling that something was going to happen that was outside their control; something that would affect all their lives.

Twenty-Seven

Life continued in Sheffield and Ashford for all of them. Riversdale Hotel was doing modestly well as the word spread that it offered a comfortable stay and good food in beautiful surroundings. In the city, business was difficult and unemployment figures were still rising. 'Let's hope the building of the new City Hall will create some employment. They're hoping to start work on it at long last and it's going to be built of Darley Dale stone.' Trip smiled at his wife. 'You'll be able to look at it and be reminded of home.' Darley Dale was only a few miles from Ashford. 'We all need something to give us a boost and inspire some confidence. How are things with you, Emily?'

'We're holding our own at the moment, though I still haven't felt able to open up the first floor work-shop in Broad Lane. What about you?'

His expression sobered. 'I haven't laid anyone off yet, but I feel it's coming close. I'll hate doing it, but I might have no choice. The orders just aren't coming in any more.'

'Don't worry, Trip. I'm sure things will pick up soon.'

Sadly, Emily's optimism was unfounded.

* * *

'Have you heard the news?' Trip called out the moment he arrived home one evening in late October the following year. 'There's been a crash on Wall Street in the States.'

Emily blinked. 'I don't understand what you mean. What sort of a crash?'

'The New York Stock Exchange. Billions have been lost and Wall Street is in a panic. People are facing ruin. There have already been suicides because of it.'

Emily stared at him, wide-eyed. 'How dreadful! Will it affect the ordinary man in the street?'

'Of course. Firms will collapse and thousands of jobs will be lost. We have close ties with the US. It'll be a downward spiral. Orders will decline, so businesses will struggle to survive. Then they'll lay off employees and so orders will decline even more. Unemployment will rocket and folks will be plunged into poverty.' He threw the newspaper onto the table in disgust. 'What on earth is going to happen now, I just don't know. We've struggled through the twenties and now it looks as if things are just going to get worse.'

'You mean it'll affect us?'

'There could be a global slump.'

They stared at each other solemnly, feeling the responsibility for their employees weighing heavily upon their shoulders.

'So much of our own business rests on exports now,' Trip said.

'And just as I thought things were starting to get better,' Emily murmured. Their businesses, if not exactly growing over the last two years, had held their own, but this latest news could threaten everything they held dear.

That evening, after a dinner that they hardly touched, Emily and Trip sat together and read the day's newspapers. As it began to grow dark, a soft knock came at their front door and Trip opened it to find both his mother and George standing there.

'I know we're too late for Lewis's bedtime, but we just wanted to know if you've read the news.'

Trip opened the door wider. 'Come in. Yes, we were just reading the papers.'

He ushered them into the front room and poured a drink for each of them.

'I presume it might affect Trippets', but what about you, Emily?' George said. 'Perhaps the smaller businesses, such as your buffing workshops, can survive.'

'I really don't know yet. The only thing that seems to be happening so far is that we're getting more work, not less.'

'I think,' Trip said, as he handed round the drinks, 'as firms find it harder and harder to keep men in full employment, they'll lay them off and then, if work does come in, they'll farm it out to little mesters or buffing businesses like Emily's. Do you think it will affect the hotel?'

'Most of our clientele are in the wealthier class, but of course, if they lose a lot of money on the stock exchange, we might start to suffer.'

'How is Josh doing?' Emily asked.

Constance smiled. 'Wonderfully. He's taken to it as if he was born to the trade. And your mother and Grace work very well under Mrs Froggatt's direction.'

'Mam doesn't try to interfere with Josh, does she?'

Constance shook her head. 'Not at all and, I have to admit, Emily, I am quite surprised.'

Emily laughed. 'So am I! What about Amy?'

'She helps out when she can, but, of course, she's busy with the little ones and there's your father and her own to care for too, but what she does in the home releases both Josh and Martha to work at Riversdale.'

'And does Mr Clark work for you too, Mother?' Trip asked.

'Only part-time. His smithing business is picking up a little, I think.' Her eyes twinkled as she added, 'Some of the farmers tried to save money by doing their own repairs, but found it wasn't as easy as they had thought, so they're drifting back to patronize the village blacksmith again.'

'So, all's well in the countryside, is it?'

'For the moment, but we're not complacent. This latest disturbing news will eventually affect everyone.'

Twenty-Eight

The news about the state of the economy was gloomier each day and by the beginning of the following year, 1930, it was feared that there would be a world-wide slump. Trip's worst forebodings were coming true.

'I don't know if we're going to survive,' he said anxiously as he scoured the newspaper's headlines one morning in late February. 'I'm having to lay off employees now. One or two might set up on their own account, like Steve, but not all of them can.'

'How's Steve coping?' Emily asked.

'Quite well, I think. How're things with you?'

'Not too bad. I think it's because we're relatively small that we're surviving. For the moment, any-way. I'm looking to take on another one or two more workers. Preferably a man, who can do the jobs that traditionally buffer girls don't do.'

Trip sighed. 'Sadly, the men I'm laying off don't fit the bill. Pity.'

'Let me know if you hear of anyone. Nell learned a lot of the different processes during the war when the men were away. Without her skills, I don't think I'd ever have got Ryan's off the ground.'

Trip smiled and put his arm around her. 'But you

did. You're doing well and there're not many that can say that these days.'

Emily chuckled. 'My mam always had a saying, "It's an ill wind that blows nobody any good."'

'She's right. Even in hard times – and we are facing tough times now – there're always folks who can survive – even prosper.' He laughed and hugged her to him. 'Thank goodness I'm married to one.'

At that moment, a piping voice called from upstairs, 'Mamma.'

'That's his lordship wanting his breakfast. I'll get him dressed and take him to Mrs Dugdale's.'

'I tell you what, Mrs Trippet, ask her if she can have Lewis tonight. Let's forget our worries just for one night. I'm taking you out. Be ready for six o'clock.'

'Oh, I love it when you're masterful, Trip,' she teased, but she did not argue with his plans. Evenings out with her husband were a rare treat.

Over their breakfast that same morning, Constance looked across the table at George. 'What is it, my dear? Something's troubling you. Is it the news?'

George lowered his newspaper and sighed heavily. 'Yes and no. Things are getting very difficult at work. Thomas probably won't tell you it all, but he's had to lay off three more employees. The only good thing about it is that it releases another workshop and I think one or two of the men concerned are going to rent it at a modest amount and set up as little mesters.'

'I see.' Constance bit her lip, unsure whether or not she should voice what was in her mind. She composed the wording before she said, 'Is there still plenty of work for you to do there?'

'Nothing that Richard couldn't manage perfectly well on his own. Factory office workers – necessary though they are in any organization – don't actually produce anything saleable. If clerical staff can be cut, it will mean a considerable saving for the company that is already beginning to struggle.' George chuckled, his mood lightened. 'You know, my love, I can see right through you. You'll be suggesting next that you need my help with the hotel.'

Constance raised her eyebrow quizzically. 'As a matter of fact, I do. I think I need more staff, but I'm not sure.'

'Haven't you noticed a downturn in bookings over these last few months?'

Constance shook her head. 'Surprisingly, no. We were fully booked at Christmas and even now – in February – the hotel is half full.' She chuckled. 'I think people like to see Derbyshire in the snow.'

'So, what have you got lined up for me to do? Hall porter? Carry your bags, m'lady?' He pretended to doff his cap.

'It'd be fun, wouldn't it? And with me as a chambermaid? No, seriously, I didn't realize there'd be so much paperwork – there's more and more – and no one there is expert at that.'

'Mm.' George was thoughtful. 'I could help out with that, of course, and now I've got my little car, I could easily travel to Ashford, even if you didn't need to go.'

Constance leaned forward. 'But it would be so nice to run it *together*, my love.'

'I thought Josh was Manager?'

'I don't mean the day-to-day running of it, but the administrative side; we could do that, couldn't we?'

'You'd like that?'

'Yes, I would. I really would.'

'Then I'll talk to Thomas and Richard.'

'Here's my little man,' Bess said, reaching to take the little boy's hand as Emily and Lewis arrived at her home.

'Do you think he could stay the night, Mrs Dugdale? I've brought his suitcase.'

Bess's smile widened. 'Of course he can. Any time, Emily, you know that. But can you come in for a moment? There's someone I want you to see.'

Emily felt her heart give a leap in her chest. Surely, Mick hadn't come back? But when she entered Bess's kitchen it was to see Ruth Nicholson, Billy's mother, sitting by the fire in the range, her hands outstretched towards its warmth.

When the Ryan family had first arrived in the city and moved into the court off Garden Street, Ruth had lived there too. She still did, as far as Emily knew. Ruth's story was a sad one. She had lost her husband and two sons to the war and now there was only her son Billy left. He'd been too young to be conscripted. Ruth had been the buffer missus at Waterfall's in charge of twenty or so buffer girls. Then she'd been plump and round-faced, yet her smile had never reached her eyes, which held a deep sorrow. It had been Ruth Nicholson who'd given Emily her first job in the cutlery industry as an errand lass. As Emily sat down opposite Ruth, she realized just how much she owed this woman. But for her giving Emily the opportunity, she might still be employed in some menial job. Emily knew that she owed her present good fortune to Ruth and she was shocked to see the change in her. Now she was thin and gaunt. She walked over to Ruth and knelt by her chair, taking her hands in her own.

'What is it, missus?' Emily still called her by the name all the girls had used, even though she was one herself now and had her own business, which Ruth had never had. Beneath Emily's touch, Ruth's hands trembled and tears welled in her eyes. 'I've lost me job and so has Billy.'

Emily gasped. 'No! Has – has Waterfall's closed?' If it had, she was surprised that neither she nor Trip had heard, but Ruth was shaking her head.

'No, but they're cutting down and laying folks off. They think they can manage without a buffer missus. They seem to regard my job as non-productive and therefore not actually making them any money.'

Emily snorted derisively. 'I think they'll soon find that production will drop if there's no one in charge of twenty or so girls. For one thing, I bet there'll soon be arguments about who's doing what.'

Ruth smiled wanly and nodded. 'I tried to argue that very point, but they weren't listening – or didn't want to. Besides, they've laid off nearly half the girls too. There're only about twelve left.'

'And what about Billy? He works as a male buffer, doesn't he?'

'Yes, they've laid him off because they can train the women to do his job and pay them less.'

'Ah, I see.'

Emily's legs were getting cramped with kneeling, so she gave Ruth's hands a pat and sat back in the other chair. For several minutes, she was thoughtful, gazing unseeingly out of the window on to the street. She watched one or two passers-by, all of them looking as if they had the weight of the world's problems on their shoulders. They probably felt as if they had; this Depression was affecting everyone.

'Right,' Emily said, coming to a decision. She wished she could talk it over with Trip first and maybe with Nell too, but she couldn't leave the missus looking like she did. Although Emily had a shrewd business head and was quite capable of making tough decisions when necessary, she had a gentler side to her nature and seeing Ruth like this tore at her heartstrings. 'We need another buffer, possibly two. If Billy would be willing to come and work for me and do all the processes that men do, we could take on some work that, at the moment, I'm having to turn away. Nell's very good, but she just can't cope with the volume of work I could have if I had a male worker. And if Billy would train the other girls to do some of the processes that they can't do yet – even better.'

'Oh Emily.' Tears now flowed down Ruth's cheeks. 'Do you mean it?'

Before she could answer, Bess, who had been eavesdropping on the conversation, stepped closer. 'I'll tell you summat, Ruth luv, me an' this lass have had our ups and downs in the past – mostly because of that son of mine, I have to say – but she's been the saving of me and my Lizzie. And she'll not say owt she doesn't mean.'

Ruth leaned across and now it was she who grasped Emily's hands. 'Thank you, thank you.'

'We'd better ask Billy, though, hadn't we?' Emily laughed. 'He might not want to be the only man in a workshop of women.'

Again, it was Bess who spoke up. 'He'll leap at the chance if he's any sense. What man wouldn't? Besides, he'll be working alongside Lizzie, won't he?'

'Are they still walking out together? Lizzie doesn't say much.'

'Oh yes, have been for a while. Billy's loved her since he was a young lad,' Ruth said quietly.

'Aye, well, Lizzie's come to her senses now,' Bess put in. No more was said, but they were all remembering Lizzie's infatuation with Josh and the trouble it had caused.

'Now, what about you, missus?' Emily said. She wasn't done yet.

'Me? You don't want a buffer missus any more than Waterfall's.' She paused and stared at Emily before adding tentatively, 'Do you?'

'Not as such,' Emily said slowly. 'Nell is in charge of the workshop in Rockingham Street and I oversee the one in Broad Lane, leaving Dorothy Frith in charge if I'm out. That's where I'd like Billy to work, if he's agreeable. There's another workshop there on the first floor that I haven't used yet. But, if Billy would come, we could open it up. But I was just wondering . . .'

Ruth took the words from her mouth, 'If I would go back to being a buffer girl? I would, Emily; it's not pride, but I'm so out of touch with the work. It's years since I—'

But Emily was shaking her head. 'No, not that.' She laughed. 'To be honest, I didn't know you'd ever been a buffer girl, but I suppose it stands to reason that you were once. No, I have something else in mind.' She paused for a moment, marshalling her thoughts before she spoke again. The other two women waited patiently, whilst Lewis wriggled on Bess's lap. He wanted to play on the floor with his toys. The talk amongst the three women was boring and he didn't like it when no one was paying attention to him. He was growing more like his father every day, with dark hair and brown eyes and a cheeky grin that melted hearts.

'I think you could help me fetching and delivering work. That would release me to keep up with the paperwork, which seems to increase by the day and will increase even more if I expand. Maybe I shouldn't even be thinking of taking on more staff in the current economic climate, but I believe we have to keep trying. I don't suppose you can drive, can you?'

Ruth shook her head. 'No, I can't. At least . . .' She hesitated and bit her lip. She glanced at Bess, who nodded, 'You can tell Emily, Ruth. She probably knows anyway from when she lived in the court.'

Ruth took a deep breath. 'We don't make a song and dance about it, but Eddie Crossland and me have been keeping company for several years. He was friends with all of us in the court, wasn't he, Bess? But I was heartbroken when I lost my hubby and then my two boys too. I – I don't know what I'd've done if it hadn't been for Eddie's friendship keeping me sane. I had to keep going for Billy's sake, but it was hard. We were just friends at first, but as time went on . . .' Her voice trailed away and Emily filled in the rest in her mind.

'You don't need to justify yourself to me, missus. I can only guess what you must have gone through. It was bad enough what happened to my poor dad in the war, but at least he came back.'

Ruth nodded. 'I remember seeing him in the court. Poor man.' She paused a moment and then went on more strongly. 'What I was going to say was that perhaps Eddie would teach me. I know he can drive, but he doesn't own a car. But I don't understand. Why do you want me to be able to drive?'

'Because', Bess interrupted in her excitement, 'you can take out the work and fetch it in in Emily's little car. Is that right, Emily?'

'Exactly right.'

Ruth was thoughtful for a moment. 'Do – do you think I could do it?'

Emily chuckled. 'I wouldn't have asked you if I didn't.'

'There is something else, Emily, that I might be able to help you with.'

'What's that?'

'I know an awful lot of Waterfall's customers. They've known me over the years and they trust me.

211

I don't want to sound conceited, but I think some of them – perhaps several of them – would – er – follow me.'

Emily stared at her for a moment before she began to laugh, leaning back helplessly in the chair. 'Now, wouldn't that just serve Waterfall's right for having sacked you and Billy? There's just one thing, though,' she said, as she sat up again and wiped her eyes. 'We don't want it to rebound on Mr Crossland. He still works for them, doesn't he?'

'I don't think it would affect him. He's in charge of the manufacturing side. Besides, they'd be idiots if they got rid of Eddie. He virtually runs the place and whilst they've been laying a few men off, old man Waterfall won't want to get his hands dirty and as for that son of his, he's less than useless. What'll happen to the business when the old man goes, I don't know.'

The two women stared across the hearth at each other whilst Bess, impatient as ever, said, 'So, Ruth, what d'you say?'

Softly Ruth said, 'I say, God bless you, Emily Trippet, and when can we start?'

Over their meal that evening in a fancy restaurant, Emily told Trip what had happened that day.

'That's a great idea, darling.' Emily was relieved to hear that he approved, but he had a cautionary note to add. 'So long as you've the work still coming in to support two more workers and opening up another workshop.'

'I have at the moment and Ruth will bring more.

212

I'm sure of it. Like I told her, I've had to turn some work away that Nell couldn't cope with.'

'Good, but now . . .' Trip grinned as he stood up and held out his hand to her, 'I have a surprise for you. We're going to the pictures.'

It wasn't until they were seated in the Cinema House and were watching the opening titles to a film called *Climbing the Golden Stairs* that Emily understood Trip's excitement.

'Oh my!' she exclaimed, as a gasp of surprise rippled through the whole audience. 'They're talking. The actors are *talking*!'

'It's the first talkie to come to this cinema,' Trip whispered. 'I thought you'd like it.'

They watched the whole film, entranced by the new invention that brought not only moving pictures but sound too.

'That was amazing,' Emily said, as they left the cinema and heard the animated chatter around them. 'We must invite Harry to come and stay with us in the school holidays. He'd love that.'

Twenty-Nine

A feeling of despondency pervaded the city, as indeed it did the whole country. By 1930, the city was rumoured to have 43,000 people out of work. And yet there were pockets of hope and one was the name of Emily Trippet and her business, Ryan's. In a few weeks, Eddie had taught Ruth to drive and it was now she who drove Emily's little car around the city picking up work and delivering the finished articles. And, as Ruth had predicted, several of the manufacturers who'd known and respected her for years now brought their business to Ryan's.

'Waterfall's are going into receivership,' Ruth told Emily one Monday morning in early April.

'What'll happen to Mr Crossland?' Emily asked Ruth.

'He's worried, I know that. He doesn't think he'll find other employment at his age.'

Emily frowned thoughtfully. 'I'll talk to Trip. We'll see what we can do.'

'We wouldn't expect you to *make* a job for him, Emily. Times are tough for you, too.'

Emily patted Ruth's shoulder. 'Leave it with me, but don't say a word to Eddie yet. I don't want to get his hopes up.'

'Funnily enough,' Trip said, when Emily told him of the recent developments that evening over dinner. Lewis was in bed and sound asleep and the two of them had time to talk. 'I've had two young chaps give their notice in today. Two brothers. They've decided to emigrate – Australia, I think. Or Canada. I'm not sure which, but wherever it is, they think their prospects will be better there. They've no ties here. They're not married and their parents both died in the influenza epidemic in 1919. So, they can take the chance. But what I mean is, it leaves me suddenly short. Whereas I might have been relieved to see one less, two leaves me in a bit of a pickle, so yes, perhaps Eddie could help us out. But it would mean working at a grinding machine. Do you know what his skills were before he became a foreman? And besides, perhaps he wouldn't take kindly to such a demotion.'

Emily shook her head. 'I'll ask Ruth tomorrow.'

'This must be my lucky day,' Eddie said, as he shook Trip's hand warmly two days after Emily's conversation with her husband. 'I was a grinder for ten years, Mr Trippet, before Henry Waterfall made me foreman. I don't reckon it'd take me long to hone my skills.'

'But it'd be a step down for you, Eddie – and please call me Trip.'

'I'm not a proud man, Trip. None of us can afford to be these days. I'm just grateful you're offering me work. That's if you are.'

'Of course I am, but have you got to work any notice?'

'Not really. The old man says he's got to close the doors in a month, but he's told all of us that if we can find work, we can leave whenever we want. D'you know, Trip, he's not been an easy man to work for, but I really feel sorry for him now. The factory has been his life. He worked his way up from the bottom, took it over, and now he's going to have to close it down. Sad, isn't it?'

'It is,' Trip said soberly, silently praying that the same would not happen to his family's business.

And so, once again, it was the Trippet family to the rescue. Trip had inherited his mother's generous nature and Emily's shrewd business brain was coupled with an innate kindness. Together, the two worked hard, yet they were ever watchful to see that family, friends and all those around them were cared for. And they were rewarded by loyalty and hard work from their employees. Despite the hard times, because they were all in it together, there grew up a kind of camaraderie. They all watched out for each other. Bess continued to care for Lewis and plans had been made so that when he started school the following year, Emily would take him in the morning and Bess would fetch him home each afternoon. And even Lizzie regained some of her old bubbly, outgoing nature. The memory of her nefarious brother and all the trouble he had caused was dimming for all of them with the passage of time.

'It's high time Lewis had a baby brother or sister,' she teased and Emily retorted by saying, 'And it's high time you put poor Billy out of his misery and named the day.'

Since Billy had begun working at Ryan's, it was not only obvious that he adored Lizzie, but also that she too was growing fonder of him. Now, she actually blushed. He was constantly finding some excuse to trot between the two workshops to see Lizzie. 'We have talked about getting married, but it doesn't seem right to have a big fancy wedding when there're folks on the breadline.' She sighed. 'But I do so want to get married in white, Emily.'

'Of course you do. Every girl wants a special day – a day to remember for the rest of her life.' Emily narrowed her eyes thoughtfully, but for the moment, she said no more.

The following Saturday afternoon, Trip drove them to Ashford-in-the-Water. It was Easter weekend and they were all to stay at the Riversdale Hotel. There would be plenty of willing hands to care for Lewis, and Trip and Emily could take some long walks around their old haunts.

'We don't see half enough of our little grandson,' Martha said. 'You leave him with us for the afternoon on Sunday. Walter will love it and Harry's so good with little ones.' She laughed. 'He's had plenty of practice.'

Since Josh had given up the candle-making business for good, the front room at The Candle House, which no doubt would always bear that name, had been turned into a front parlour for Martha. On that Sunday afternoon, the floor was strewn with toys and the youngsters played noisy games of Snakes and Ladders, Ludo and even draughts. Harry, a sturdy boy of nine with fair curly hair and hazel eyes, was in charge. He marshalled his younger sister and brother with a firm but gentle hand, whilst Lewis leaned against Walter's knee watching the other children longingly as if he wanted to join in.

'D'you know how to play these games, little feller?' Walter asked him and when Lewis shook his head, his grandfather suggested, 'Why don't you and me do this wooden jigsaw, eh? It's one your mummy had when she was a little girl.'

'But I want to play with them. I'll be a good boy. I'll do what Harry tells me.'

'He'll be all right, Grandpa,' Harry said. 'We'll play Snakes and Ladders now. That's a bit easier. Move over, Sarah, and let Lewis sit between you and me and we'll teach him how to play.'

Sarah, at nearly six, was a slim, shy child, with fair hair and delicate features like her mother, Amy.

Seeing them happily settled, Emily and Trip turned to go. 'It's a shame Josh and Amy can't join us. We're going to walk up to Monsal Head.'

'Josh has a busy weekend,' Martha said, not even trying to hide the pride in her tone. 'With you all there too, I think the hotel is full. I'm on duty tonight to cook the evening meal and Amy will be waiting on the diners. Bob and your dad look after the children. It's all worked out very nicely . . .' She glanced at Trip and had the grace to add, 'Thanks to your mother.'

As they left the cottage and walked hand in hand up the hill towards Monsal Head, Emily said, 'Trip, I've been thinking . . .'

Trip pretended to groan. 'Oh dear, that sounds ominous. When you've been "thinking", it usually means you have plans to expand – again!' He was teasing her, yet there was no hiding the pride in his tone. 'Go on,' he added with an exaggerated sigh. 'Tell me.'

Emily laughed, lifting her face to the sun, exhilarated by the wind in her hair and a precious few hours alone with Trip. 'No, nothing like that. Not this time,' she joked in return, 'though I'm making no promises on that front.'

Trip chuckled but said no more as he waited for her to explain.

'It's about Lizzie and Billy . . .' she began and went on to recount her conversation with her friend ending, 'I was wondering – if you've no objection – if I could ask your mother if she would hold a reception at Riversdale? They could be married in Ashford's church.'

'I think it's a splendid idea, but what about all her family and friends from Sheffield? Would they want to come all the way out here to attend the wedding?'

'I don't think either of them have much family and, as for their friends, we could hire a charabanc to bring them all here.'

'You have been thinking it all out, haven't you?'

'Mm.'

'I'm sure Mother would agree. In fact, I think

she'd think it would be a wonderful way to advertise the hotel as a wedding venue.'

'Oh, it would, it would. I hadn't thought of that. How clever you are, Trip.'

They continued discussing the idea as they climbed steadily but when they reached the top and stood on the edge of Monsal Head looking out over the breathtaking view, they fell silent, drinking in the panorama before them. Far below them the River Wye curved through the dale, with one or two houses scattered along its banks. Then it disappeared between the hills. To their left was the viaduct that carried the railway that ran from Rowsley through to Buxton.

'You know,' Trip said at last, 'I never realize until I'm actually standing here again, just how much I miss this place.'

'I know,' Emily said, her voice a little shaky. 'I love the city life – I really do – probably more than you do, but this is still the place I consider my home – my roots.'

Trip put his arm around her shoulder. 'Do you think Mrs Dugdale could manage to look after another little one?'

Emily twisted her head to look up at him. 'Another? Why, do you know someone who is looking for a childminder?'

Trip turned and smiled down at her, a roguish twinkle in his eyes. 'Sort of. Darling, I think we should have another baby. But only if you're agreeable, of course, Mrs Trippet.'

Emily gasped, startled for a moment, then she

wound her arms around his waist and rested her cheek against his chest. 'I'd love to have another baby, Trip,' she said softly, 'and this time, it'll be a girl for you.'

Thirty

Constance was enchanted by the idea of holding a wedding reception at the hotel for Lizzie and Billy and even agreed with her son's proposal.

'In which case,' she said firmly, 'I suggest we offer Billy and Lizzie a very special price, explaining, of course, that we're doing it because we want to *use* the occasion to promote the hotel as a wedding reception venue.' She gave a huge wink as she added, 'That way they won't feel embarrassed.'

Later that afternoon, the five of them – Constance, George, Josh, Emily and Trip – were in the small room in the hotel set aside as the office.

'I'll hire a professional photographer,' Constance went on. 'There'll be photographs for them, of course, of their big day, but I'll see that he takes some that we can use for promotion. Now, you must tell them they'll need a special licence, unless one of them can come and live here for the required number of weeks before the wedding. I'm not sure how long it is. I'll check with the vicar, if you like, to see what they need to do.'

'Whoa, whoa, steady on, Mother,' Trip laughed. 'We haven't even asked them yet. They might not want to get married away from the city.'

'Ah – I hadn't thought of that. Sorry, I was getting a bit carried away.'

Emily turned to her brother. 'Are you all right with this, Josh?'

'I am if Lizzie is,' he said. 'I'm delighted she's realized just how much Billy loves her. I hope she truly loves him, though.'

There was a moment's silence before Constance said, 'You think they might refuse because it's Josh who's the manager here? That he'll be the one organizing their reception?'

'I could keep out of the way, if necessary,' Josh offered. 'Once everything's in place, I needn't even be here on the day itself, if my presence is likely to cause any awkwardness.'

'And there's Amy too. She's so good at waitressing; she'd be a natural choice to have on duty on such an occasion.'

'I'll talk to Lizzie – explain everything to her and see what she says,' Emily promised.

Lizzie was overwhelmed by the offer. 'How kind of Mrs Bayes. Oh Emily, I never thought –' she shook her head in wonderment – 'that you and your family would be so good to me, not after everything that's happened. You've already saved Mam and me from starvation and now this.'

Emily laughed as she hugged her. 'I think you're exaggerating a bit.'

'No, I'm not.' Lizzie was serious. 'You could have made life very difficult for both of us after what Mick did. You're a very generous-hearted woman, Emily. How can I ever thank you?'

'By being happy, Lizzie dear, that's how. And whilst we're talking about the past, I'll never forget the way you helped my family when we arrived in the city. But for you – and your mother – I don't know how we'd have managed. Even Mick – in the early days – was generous.'

'But none of us realized his generosity came from his criminal activities. Even Mam and me didn't guess. How blind we were!'

Emily had always secretly wondered whether Bess Dugdale and Lizzie had truly not known that Mick had been a leader of one of Sheffield's notorious gangs or whether they had chosen to ignore it whilst the goodies kept coming their way. And a few generous gifts had come the way of the Ryan family too at that time, she had to admit, but back then, Emily had been a naïve country mouse lost in the big city. But she wasn't any more. Now she understood urban life, but still loved it anyway. And Bess and her daughter had been punished enough for something that had never really been their fault. Lizzie's only mistake had been to imagine herself in love with Josh and let her resentment fester when Josh had gone back to Amy. It was then, seeing his sister's unhappiness, that Mick had decided to try to wreak revenge. But Mick was gone now, fleeing from a vengeful Steve Henderson. She hoped he would never come back, though she felt for her friends. Mick was still Bess's son and Lizzie's brother. A mother herself now as well as a sister, Emily could understand their heartache.

'Just one more thing – are you going to be all right

around Josh and Amy? Josh runs Mrs Bayes's hotel now.'

Lizzie bit her lip. 'If I'm honest, I don't know how I'm going to feel when I see him again, but I promise you I won't make trouble. It's obvious that it was always Amy he loved. He's happy with her and their children. I swear I won't do anything to spoil that. And besides –' she forced a smile onto her mouth – 'Billy loves me devotedly and I wouldn't hurt him either. He's been the only one to stand by me through all the trouble – apart from you and Nell. The name of Dugdale is mud in this city now. No one else will touch me with a barge pole.'

'Oh, Lizzie,' Emily said, hugging her again, 'it'll all come right. You'll see.'

It wasn't until much later that Emily realized that Lizzie had not actually said that she loved Billy.

Lizzie and Billy's marriage was a pretty village July wedding attended by their friends and a few relatives. Nell and Steve came, bringing Lucy. Ruth Nicholson arrived wearing a smart fashionable outfit with a brand new hat on which she'd spent a week's wages in honour of her son's wedding.

'She's made that dress herself,' Bess whispered to Emily as they waited in the church for the arrival of Lizzie on the arm of the man who was to give her away. 'Isn't she clever?'

Having no father or brother either now, the choice of who should give Lizzie away had presented a difficulty until Nell had said bluntly, standing with her hands on her hips, 'Steve'll do it, if I ask him.'

'Would he?' Lizzie had said tentatively.

'It's high time the hatchet was well and truly buried,' Nell had laughed wryly, 'and, preferably, not in someone's head.'

'Only thing is, I think Billy was going to ask Steve to be his best man.'

'Ah, I didn't know that.'

'There's Trip,' Emily had suggested, 'but I tell you what, why don't you ask Mr Hawke? He's not been well lately and I think his trouble is loneliness. I think it would cheer him up no end.'

Lizzie's face had brightened. 'Now, that is a good idea.' But then her expression had sobered. 'Unless he can't abide the name of Dugdale.'

'I don't think Mr Hawke is the sort to bear a grudge against you, Lizzie. Besides, he can always refuse, but you won't know until you ask him.'

Nathan Hawke had been delighted to have been asked to give the bride away. 'I'll be able to imagine, just for a day, that I'm walking my daughter down the aisle.' The poignancy of his word brought tears to Emily's eyes. 'And I'll be happy to escort Mrs Dugdale to the reception too, if she doesn't mind.'

Bess didn't mind. In fact, as all the guests from the city piled into the charabanc to take them to Ashford, Nathan and Bess sat together, causing more than a few nudges and winks.

It was a happy day apart from a brief moment of awkwardness when Lizzie and Billy arrived at the hotel to be welcomed by Josh, smartly dressed in his morning suit for the occasion. But Josh had decided exactly how he would play this. He stepped forward, shook hands with the nervous groom and kissed the bride on the cheek without a trace of embarrassment. Then he introduced his staff – including Amy – one by one and then led the couple into the bar area where champagne was being served.

After the sumptuous meal, a witty and humorous speech from Nathan Hawke and a nervous reply from Billy, the guests mingled together, renewing old acquaintances or meeting new people. The photographer whom Constance had hired took numerous pictures both inside the hotel and outside on the lawn, whilst the children played around them.

'What say you we go for a walk?' Harry whispered to Lucy. At nine he considered himself far too old now to be playing childish games of tag and he was sure this pretty girl, who must be at least two years older than him, felt the same. 'Only as far as the bridge. We can ask my gran if she's anything we can feed the ducks with. But let's not tell the others. They'll all want to come and I don't fancy being held responsible for anyone falling in the water. My little brother's a nightmare and Lewis isn't much better.'

'Which one's your gran?'

Harry grinned. 'She's in the kitchen. She cooked the dinner.'

Lucy gasped and stared wide-eyed at him. 'Your gran cooked all that wonderful food? I've never tasted anything like that in my life. I don't think I'll need to eat for a week.'

Harry basked in the reflected glory being heaped on Martha Ryan, but was honest enough to say, 'She didn't do it all on her own. Mrs Froggatt's in charge here and Mrs Partridge helped out too, but they're all great cooks.'

He led Lucy through to the kitchens and introduced her.

'Hello, Lucy,' Martha said. 'Now, you two be careful. Mind you tell your mams where you're going. And don't let Lucy get that pretty dress all mucky, our Harry.'

'I won't, Gran.'

Armed with food for the ducks, the pair set off down the drive and out of the gate. Walking a few yards to the right, they were soon standing on Sheep Wash Bridge and staring down into the waters of the River Wye. The ducks gathered beneath them, pecking each other and darting for the food as it was thrown.

'It's lovely here. You are lucky to live in the country-side,' Lucy said shyly.

Harry shrugged, looking around him and trying to see the village through the eyes of a stranger.

'It's so dirty and smelly in the city,' Lucy said, closing her eyes and lifting her face to the sun. She breathed in deeply. 'It's so *fresh* here. I bet your mam's washing isn't covered with smuts every week.'

Harry laughed. 'No, I have to admit, it isn't.' He paused and then added, 'I don't know if I'd like to live there all the time, but I would like to see the city. My aunty Emily loves it there.'

'Why don't you ask her if you could come and stay with her in the school holidays and then I could show you around?'

'Would you? Wouldn't your mates tease you, being seen about with a boy?' Lucy looked at him. With his fair curly hair, hazel eyes and his skin lightly tanned through being out of doors a lot of the time, she thought him the handsomest boy she'd ever seen. No, her friends would not tease her; they'd be envious. And even if they did, she really wouldn't care. She shook her head. 'But what about you? Wouldn't you get made fun of for going around with a *girl*?'

Harry grinned. 'Nah, they'd be jealous.'

By the time Harry had shown her more of the village and they'd returned to the celebrations, they were firm friends and when Lucy had to leave with her parents, Harry wangled himself an invitation to spend a week of his summer holidays with Emily and Trip. As the charabanc rattled down the village street, Harry was the last one watching it disappear around the corner.

Thirty-One

Two weeks after Lizzie's wedding, Emily said, 'You're looking a bit peaky, Nell. Is everything all right?'

'I reckon I'm pregnant.'

'Nell, that's wonderful.' She paused. Nell didn't seem enthusiastic.

'Is it? If I can't work, Steve's money's not going to be enough to keep five of us.'

'Mm.' Emily was thoughtful. There was no easier job that Emily could give Nell. She couldn't drive, nor were her educational skills sufficient to use her on the administrative side.

'Look, leave that with me. I've got an idea I've been mulling over for a while now, but I need to talk to Trip.'

'I don't want charity,' Nell snapped. 'I don't want you *creating* a job for me.'

'I wouldn't do that.'

'Yes, you would. You have done. What about Ruth Nicholson? And Bess Dugdale, if it comes to that. And I'm not sure that Trip didn't find a job for Steve. Though,' she added grudgingly, 'I suppose I should be grateful for that.'

Emily hid her smile. She admired Nell's prickly pride, though it was difficult to handle at times. With deliberate mildness, she said, 'Steve's now renting a workshop – you know that. He's his own boss and, as for Ruth, she's doing a valuable job that releases me to do other things. *And* she's brought us a lot of new customers through her old contacts, so no, Nell, I wasn't being philanthropic when I offered her a job.'

Nell put her hands on her hips and glared at Emily. 'I might agree with you if I knew what you were talking about.'

Emily turned away. She hadn't meant to embarrass Nell by using big words and to try to explain now would only make matters worse. Living with Trip had extended Emily's vocabulary, but she must guard against appearing to talk down to her friends; that would never do.

But Nell wasn't done yet. 'And don't go telling anyone else about me until I'm sure. I haven't told Steve or me mam yet.'

Emily glanced back. 'Steve'll be pleased, won't he?'

But Nell only shrugged, picked up a handful of spoons and leaned into her machine. Their conversation was at an end.

'Trip,' Emily began as they finished their evening meal and cleared away the dishes together. 'Have you got any workshops at the factory that are still empty?'

'Just one, but it's quite small. That's why I've been unable to let it. It's not really big enough even for a little mester, who might want to employ one or two men. I thought a while back that you might take it, but then Mr Hawke's Broad Lane workshop was usable again and it made more sense for you to take that one. Why?' He smiled tenderly. 'Has my ambitious wife come up with yet another idea to extend her enterprise?'

Emily giggled. 'Maybe, but first you must promise me that you'll keep a secret. Nell would have my guts for garters if she found out I'd told anyone – even you.'

'Wives shouldn't keep secrets from their husbands,' Trip said, pretending loftiness, then he laughed and added, 'Do tell.'

'Nell thinks she's pregnant.'

'That's great news. I bet Steve's thrilled, isn't he?'

'That's the point. He doesn't know yet.'

Trip stared at her. 'Why ever not? I hope you wouldn't keep it from me – not again – even if you weren't absolutely sure. You wouldn't, would you?'

Emily wound her arms around his waist and leaned her head against his chest. 'Of course not. It'll happen if it's meant to.'

He kissed her forehead. 'It's not for want of trying, is it? So, what's this about a workshop?'

'I've had an idea I've been thinking about for a while now, but when Nell told me her news this morning, things seemed to slot into place. But she was defensive when she thought that I might be trying to *find* her an easier job.' Emily went on to repeat her conversation with Nell.

'Mm. I see. Well, I don't really, because you haven't told me what your idea is yet.'

'With the high unemployment in the city, there are a lot of girls and young women who might want to learn a new skill. I thought I could set up a small workshop to train a new generation of buffer girls.'

Trip frowned. 'But will they be wanted? I mean, even once they're trained, there might not be work for them.'

'Things'll get better. It might take a while, but the Depression can't last for ever.'

Trip sighed heavily. 'I wish I had your optimism.'

'So, you don't think it's a good idea?'

'I think it's a wonderful idea. I'm just not sure it would lead to employment for them, that's all. You might be getting their hopes up for nothing. But I presume, despite what she said, you *are* thinking of Nell.'

'Yes, but don't tell her, whatever you do.'

'But she's your best worker.'

'True, but I'm not thinking of her doing nothing. She'd still be able to do some buffing, just not all the time.'

'She'll see through you. She's as sharp as the knives she polishes.'

Emily laughed wryly. 'I know and that's why I've got to go about this very carefully. Anyway, I'll come and look at your vacant workshop tomorrow.'

'This is a perfect size, Trip,' Emily exclaimed, clapping her hands as she stood in the middle of the workshop in Trippets' factory and turned full circle to take in everything about the room. 'Can I have it and if so, what rent would you charge?'

'Ah, now let me see.' Trip stroked his chin, pretending to be mulling the matter over. 'Tell you what,

I'll do what Nathan Hawke did in the early days. Rent free for a month until you get going and then a minimum rent. You won't actually be producing work here that will bring money in, will you?'

'I could charge a fee for their training, I suppose.'

Trip shook his head. 'They wouldn't be able to afford it.' He paused, then added, 'Do you intend to pay them?'

'Not until they can produce work that's saleable.'

'You're a hard woman, Mrs Trippet.'

'It's business,' Emily retorted.

Trip chuckled. 'I don't think Nell will see it that way.'

'I knew it,' Nell exploded when Emily had patiently explained her idea. 'You're trying to find me easier work.'

'How do you make that out? I'll still expect you to do some work, but most of the time – especially at the start – you'll be training the girls.'

Nell nodded. 'And I suppose you'll be arranging for me to sit down while I do that, won't you?'

Emily shrugged. 'You could, if you wanted to.'

'Well, I won't.' She paused and then added, 'Why do you want to get rid of me, Emily? I'm your best buffer. You've said that yourself.'

'Of course I don't want to get rid of you,' Emily countered. 'I just thought, with all the unemployment just now, offering training to a few would be helping. I know it's only in a small way but, surely, anything's better than nothing. Don't tell me you don't know of girls or young women who are desperate for work?'

Nell wriggled her shoulders, then sighed. 'I can't deny that. I've had three girls ask me recently if they could come here as errand lasses and learn the trade. They know how it works, see.'

'With my idea there'd be no need for them to work as an errand lass first. But talking of errand lasses, how's Winifred shaping up?'

'Orreight. I've tried her out on a wheel in the dinner break and, yes, I think she'll do well. Her sisters have been giving her a bit of tuition in their own time, too.'

'There you are, then. We do need proper training for young girls. They can't all be errand lasses and learn that way. So, what's it to be, then?'

Nell turned away towards her machine. 'I'll give it some thought and let you know tomorrow.'

Thirty-Two

'I told Steve and me mam last night about – about – well, you know.'

'And were they pleased?'

Nell smiled, suddenly strangely self-conscious. 'Steve's happy as a pig in muck, as you say, though I'm not so sure about me mam. She's not good on her legs at all now. Lucy's growing up and is a real help about the house, but I don't think mam could cope with a baby now.'

'Baby?' Lizzie's sharp ears had overheard. 'Who's having a baby? Is it you, Emily?'

Emily didn't answer so Nell was forced to say, 'No. It's me.'

Lizzie's face was a picture and then she flung her arms around Nell. 'How lovely.' She drew back and stared into Nell's face. 'What is it? Aren't you happy about it? Oh, Nell, there's nothing wrong with you or the baby, is there?'

'No, it's just that I can't afford not to work and Mam's not as young as she was. She'll never cope with a young baby.'

'But *my* mam could. She's never been so fit since we moved – thanks to Emily.'

Nell shot a look at Emily, but said nothing.

'And she loves looking after little ones. She's hanging her hat up for Emily to get cracking and have another one and as for me, you should hear her going on at Billy. It gets quite embarrassing at times. You'd think no one in the world had ever had a grandchild before.'

Since their marriage, Billy had moved in with Lizzie and her mother in Cromwell Street, though he had been reluctant to leave his mother alone in the court off Garden Street. But it seemed Ruth was quite content. 'Eddie comes round almost every night. I'm not lonely, I promise you, and you're better off with Bess. It's a nice house she's got.' There'd been a wistful note in her tone and silently Billy wished that Eddie Crossland would get on with it and propose to Ruth. That way she, too, could leave the back-street court.

'So, think about it, Nell. When you have the baby, you could pay my mam a bit to look after it. Is that what you and Emily have been whispering about?'

'Sort of,' Emily said carefully.

Nell sighed. 'You'd better tell her. She's got ears like an elephant when it comes to secrets. In fact, you'd better tell all of 'em.'

Machines slowed and Ida and Flo joined them. Their faces were solemn, as if they were expecting bad news. There was so much of it just now in their city, where work was concerned. But as Emily explained swiftly, their expressions lightened. 'If Nell does go to Creswick Street, can you carry on teaching Winifred between you?'

The three women glanced at each other and then chorused, 'Yes.'

'You'd be daft not to take up Emily's offer, Nell,' Lizzie added bluntly.

'But I don't need mollycoddling. I worked up to the very last day when I had Lucy.'

Lizzie laughed. 'She did. Her waters broke as she was standing at her machine. We had a right job to get her home.'

Nell had the grace to smile wryly. 'All right, then, Emily, you win.'

Emily touched her arm. 'It's not a case of winning, Nell. This is something I want to do and you're the best person to help me.'

And if, at the same time, it eased Nell's workload over the next few weeks and months, then that would be a bonus. But Emily kept these thoughts to herself. She'd got Nell's agreement and – for the moment – that was all she wanted.

During the August school holidays, Harry came to stay. Two days after his arrival, Nell and Lucy arrived at Emily's door early one evening. 'We've come to take Harry to the pictures,' Nell said. 'There's a Laurel and Hardy on at the Palace in Union Street. We thought he'd love that.'

'He would,' Emily said, but added doubtfully, 'What's the rest of the programme, though? Is it suitable for a nine-year-old?'

'Oh phooey, Emily, don't be such a sobersides. I know the manager there. He'll let us in.'

'That's not what I'm worried about, Nell. It's what Amy and Josh would say if I let him see something – well, inappropriate when he's in my care.'

Nell grinned. 'You can put all the blame on me. If I don't tell you about the other film or films, you can't be held responsible, can you?'

'You're impossible, Nell,' Emily laughed. 'All right, then.' She turned and called him. 'You've got visitors, Harry, and they've come to take you to the cinema.'

'Lucy!' The boy's pleasure at the sight of the friend he had made in Ashford was plain for them all to see. Politely, he added, 'And Aunty Nell.'

'We need a gentleman to escort us, you see,' Nell's eyes twinkled. 'And we thought of you.'

'May I go, Aunty Emily?'

'Yes, of course.'

As they walked away, with Harry between them, Emily heard Lucy say, 'Get ready for a surprise, Harry. It's quite a shock when you hear the talkies for the first time, but it's a nice surprise.'

Emily shook her head, a little unsure as to whether she had done the right thing. But she needn't have worried. When Harry returned later, he was vague about the other films he had seen, and their story line, but he enthused about the Laurel and Hardy and recounted all their antics in detail. Emily was forced to wonder if Nell had primed him to say little about the other films on the programme.

'Did you have a good time, Harry?' Trip asked.

'It was great, Uncle Trip.'

'We have another treat for you. Next week, Amy Johnson's new Gipsy Moth aeroplane is on display at Coles in town. We'll take you to see it, if you'd like,' Trip told him.

239

The boy's eyes shone. 'Oh Uncle Trip, that would be wonderful. Thank you, thank you, *thank you.*'

Trip laughed and ruffled his hair. At nine, Harry was growing into a very handsome boy and a nice one too. He was well mannered and patient with his younger cousin, Lewis. No doubt it had to do with having a younger sister and brother.

'Wait until you hear what else we've got lined up for you,' Emily said, laughing at the boy's delight. 'If you can stay long enough, we'll take you to Sheffield's Aviation Week. It starts at the beginning of September.'

Harry's face fell. 'I have to go back to school then.'

'I'll write to your mam and dad and see if they'll let you stay.'

Josh wrote back at once to say, 'I'm sure the head teacher won't mind for once. After all, it could be regarded as educational!'

It was a merry family party that set out on Saturday, 23 August. Harry could hardly contain his excitement at seeing the famous Amy Johnson's plane close to and Lewis, infected by his cousin's enthusiasm, kept asking questions non-stop.

'Is it a real moth, Daddy?'

'No, no, Lewis. It's just the name of a make of aeroplane.'

'Is it going to fly today?'

'I don't think so. It's just for everyone to look at.'

They queued to see the aircraft and it took them over an hour to reach the display. Harry stood in awe. 'It's so big, isn't it?' he whispered.

'We'll have to move on. I'm sorry, Harry, but other people are waiting to see it too. You know how long we had to wait.'

But Harry dragged his feet, his gaze still on the aeroplane until at last he had to leave.

'I'll buy you a photograph of it,' Trip promised. 'I'm sure there will be some on sale. You can keep it as a memento of your visit. And in a few days' time we'll be going to the air show. That's something to look forward to, isn't it?'

'Yes, Uncle Trip,' Harry said dutifully, but they could see he was bitterly disappointed not to be allowed to stay longer, just drinking in the sight of the Gipsy Moth.

At the beginning of September, Harry's excitement rose again at the promised visit to the air show at Coal Aston, several miles south of the city. Trip drove them all there and paid the admission fee.

'I see they're offering flights,' Trip said quietly to Emily. 'What do you think? Would Josh or Amy mind if I took him up, d'you think?'

'No, but just you and Harry go. I think Lewis is a bit too young. He might be airsick.'

'Right.' He touched Harry's shoulder. 'Come on, Harry, let's go flying.'

The boy looked up with wide eyes. 'Really, Uncle Trip?'

'Yes, really.'

Emily watched them go. Inside, she was a little fearful. She didn't think Amy would be too happy, though she believed that Josh would have agreed. A little while later, she watched as the little plane lifted into the air. She watched it climb into the clouds and bank away to fly over the city. In the plane, Harry twisted and turned in his seat to get the best view.

'Uncle Trip, it's fantastic. Look, we're above the clouds. They really do look like cotton wool, don't they? And everything's so tiny on the ground. The people look like ants. I can't even see Aunty Emily and Lewis now. Oh, it's wonderful. When I'm older, I'm going to learn to fly.'

Trip nodded. He was feeling a little queasy. Obviously, flying wasn't for him, but there was no way he was going to admit it. Back on the ground, he walked unsteadily towards Emily and Lewis. Emily convulsed with laughter. 'You look positively *green*, Trip. Was it that bad?'

'Not really, but I'm obviously not cut out for flying, whereas Harry is. Now, let's go and watch the stunt flying, shall we?'

'I could eat a hot dog,' Emily said mischievously. 'How about you, Trip?'

Trip heaved, turned away and ran across the field, whilst Emily bent double with laughter.

'Aunty Emily, you're cruel,' Harry said, but he was laughing too.

'Come on, boys,' Emily said, wiping the tears of laughter from her eyes. 'I'll buy us a hot dog each. I really don't think Uncle Trip wants one, do you?'

They found a good vantage point to watch the stunt displays and Trip joined them, looking sheepish.

'Sorry, Trip,' Emily said, still hardly able to keep

the laughter from her voice. 'I've been scolded by my nephew for being cruel.'

'Thanks, old chap,' Trip said and winked at Harry. He was looking much better now. 'Tell you what, I'll pay for a second trip for you, but this time your aunty is going with you.'

At once Emily's merriment died. 'Oh, I don't think . . .'

'Please, Aunty Emily. It's great. You'll love it.'

'All right, you're on,' she said.

'Can't I go up, Mummy?' Lewis begged, but Emily was firm. 'No, you're too young. But in a few years' time, when Harry's older, he'll take you up. Now then, let's watch the rest of the display and then we'll go and pay for another flight.'

To everyone's surprise, not least her own, Emily loved the flight and was as thrilled as Harry when they landed. Trip had the good grace to laugh wryly. 'Serves me right for trying to get my own back.'

He linked arms with his wife and together they walked back to where they had left the car, with the two boys chattering excitedly about everything they had seen that day. Harry just couldn't stop talking about the two flights he'd had.

'You know, Trip,' Emily said thoughtfully, 'I think Harry is born to fly.'

Thirty-Three

When word got around that Emily was setting up a small workshop to train buffer girls, there was a steady stream of unemployed girls and women seeking her out.

'I can only take about six to start with,' Emily explained, her heartstrings tugged by the wan faces and desperation in their eyes, but she interviewed each one who came, listened carefully and made her choice not with her heart but with her head.

'That's five I've chosen,' she told Nell as the door closed behind the last one late in the afternoon. 'I can only take one more.'

'Do you remember Jane Arnold, who worked for us as an errand lass for a while years ago?'

'I do. In fact, you mentioned her when I was looking for buffer girls before but you said she was happy where she was then. Why?'

Nell bit her lip. 'Well, she's not now. She's hit hard times. *Very* hard times. Steve saw her out on the streets last night. He thought she was – you know –' she waved her hand – 'touting for business.'

Emily stared at her in horror. 'Oh no – no! We must do something to help her, Nell. Where did Steve see her?'

'I don't know, but I'll ask him.'

Emily thought quickly. 'I must find her,' she murmured. 'I'll go out tonight looking for her.'

'Not on your own, you won't,' Nell said quickly. 'I'll tell Steve to come round to yours tonight. He'll go with you.'

As they locked up the premises and turned for home, Nell laughed as she murmured, 'And you're trying to tell me you're not being – what was that big word you used – philanthropic?'

Emily smiled and punched her lightly on the arm. 'Of course I'm not. Jane was shaping up to be a good little buffer girl. You told me yourself. Remember?'

'She was. I'll not deny that, but I still think you're—'

'Go on with you, Nell Geddis. Get yourself home and put your feet up.'

Nell was still chuckling as she disappeared into the night.

'Hello, Steve,' Trip greeted him, when he answered the back door. 'What are you doing here? Not trouble at work, is it?'

Steve shook his head. 'Nell asked me to come round and go with Emily.'

Trip was mystified. 'Go with Emily? Where?'

'Er—' Steve hesitated, not wanting to let Emily down.

'Come in and we'll sort it out,' Trip said. 'There's obviously something my dear wife hasn't told me.

Emily –' he raised his voice – 'Steve's come to take you out – somewhere.'

As he ushered Steve into the kitchen, Emily was just finishing helping Lewis into his pyjamas. 'Hello, Steve. Would you like a cuppa before we go?'

'Er – yes. That would be nice.' Steve felt ill-at-ease. It was clear that Emily had not told Trip what was happening. He didn't want to end up in the middle of a row between husband and wife. But he need not have worried; Emily and Trip rarely had a cross word, never mind anything that could be called a full-scale row. Her next words explained everything.

'Trip's only just got in from work, Steve. I haven't had time to tell him. In fact, you tell him while I take Lewis up. Trip, your dinner's in the oven and perhaps you could make Steve a cup of tea.'

Whilst Trip ate and they both drank tea, Steve told him about seeing Jane. As he laid his knife and fork down side by side, Trip said, 'Emily's quite right. We can't stand by and let that happen, but she's wrong about one thing. She's not going out to look for her, not even with you, Steve. No offence, mate.'

'None taken.' Steve shook his head. He was relieved. He hadn't liked the idea of taking Emily to the place frequented by prostitutes.

'I'll go with you.'

'Oh, I don't think . . .'

'I'm not going to let you go on your own, Steve, so you can forget that idea.'

Steve smiled wryly. 'I'm known down there. Some of my former – er – colleagues run the girls, if you know what I mean.'

'They're pimps?'

Steve flinched, but was forced to nod.

'Then all the more reason why you shouldn't go alone. They might not take too kindly to us lifting one of their girls off the streets.'

Steve stared at him for a moment and then looked away.

'What? What have I said?'

'They'll not harm me, Trip. It was me who handed them their – um – business when I decided to go straight.'

'Ah, I see.' Trip said no more. He hadn't known that running a prostitution racket had been one of Steve's enterprises. But then, he thought, the gangs back then had been involved in all sorts of immoral dealings. As Emily came back into the room, he stood up and told her what had been decided.

'Bring her back here if you find her, Trip. We'll feed her and she can stay here until we get a doctor to check her out. Then I'll see about setting her on with the rest of the girls.'

As they turned to leave, Steve said quietly. 'I can't thank you enough for what you're doing to help Nell.'

Emily smiled. 'Nonsense, I'm helping myself set up another string to my bow.'

Steve grinned as he pulled on his cap. 'And if you think anyone's going to believe that, then you're not the clever woman I thought you were, Emily Trippet.'

'There she is.' Steve gripped Trip's arm. 'Look, over there.'

Trip looked to where Steve was pointing and saw a girl talking to a man, who seemed to be gesticulating angrily. Then they saw him grab hold of her arm and try to drag her towards a dark alleyway.

'Looks like she's got trouble. Come on.'

The two hurried across the road.

'Hello, Jane,' Steve said. 'This punter causing you bother, is he?'

The girl turned frightened eyes towards them, but before she could speak, the man butted in, 'Sling yer hook, the pair of you. She's mine. I've paid good money and now she's refusing to do what I want.'

'Then I will pay you twice whatever you gave her for you to let her go.'

'Want her for yerselves, do yer? A threesome, is it? Well, she won't do it. She's picky, this one.' But he let go of Jane's arm and held out his hand. 'Go on, then. Let's see yer money.'

As Steve stepped into the light cast by a nearby window, the man's expression changed in a flash. 'Oh Gawd, it's you, Mr Henderson. I'm sorry, I didn't know she was one of your girls. I wouldn't have treated her rough if I'd known . . .'

'She isn't one of mine. I'm not in that game any more. Here, take this and scarper.' Steve thrust a handful of notes into the man's hand.

'So, you do want her for yerselves . . .'

Suddenly, Steve's hand shot out and he gripped the man by the throat. 'No, we don't. We're taking her off the streets, that's what we're doing.'

''Er pimp won't like it.'

248

'Her pimp – whoever he is – will have me to answer to. See? Now, clear off.'

As the man stumbled away clutching the money, Steve turned to the trembling girl. 'Come on, luv. We mean you no harm. We're taking you home to Mrs Trippet. She's got a job for you.'

Bewildered, Jane walked between them.

'By the way, who is your pimp?' Steve asked quietly.

'Pete something. I don't know his surname, but he used to be mates with Mick Dugdale years back.'

'Ah yes, I knew him. He latched onto me for a while, so don't you worry your head any more. I'll deal with him. Now, let's get you home.'

Thirty-Four

By the time the three of them arrived back in Carr Road, Emily had already made up a bed in the tiny spare room and dragged the tin bath from the wash-house into the kitchen in front of the range.

'Hello, Jane. Come in. See, I've got you some supper ready. After you've eaten, we'll banish Trip upstairs and you can have a nice bath and wash your hair. Then it's off to bed with you.'

'I'll be off, then, Emily,' Steve said and nodded towards Trip. 'See you in the morning.'

Emily gave him a beaming smile. 'Thanks, Steve.'

As he was about to leave, Jane caught hold of his arm. 'Thank you, Mr Henderson, for what you did. I'll never forget it.'

Steve patted her hand. 'Don't you worry any more, luv. I'll square it with Pete. He'll not bother you again.'

'Maybe you'd better give him this.' Jane pulled some coins from her pocket.

Steve glanced down at the money lying in the palm of her hand. There was a strange mixture of emotions on his face as if, for the first time, he was realizing just what he had once put girls like Jane through. Huskily, he said, 'You keep it, luv. You've more than

250

earned it.' Then he turned abruptly to leave, closing the door quietly behind him. For a moment Jane stood, her head bowed, her face flushing with shame until Emily touched her arm and said gently, 'Come on, love, sit down and eat your supper.'

Later, Emily helped the girl to bathe and wash her hair, soaping her back and cutting her toenails for her.

'Why are you being so kind to me, Mrs Trippet? I'm a fallen woman. My family have disowned me – all except me mam and she's heartbroken.'

'I can't help all the girls in the city who've had to do what you've done – I only wish I could – but I can help you. Now, there's just one thing – I want you to allow my doctor to check you out tomorrow.'

Jane hung her head again. 'I can't afford—'

'I'll pay him,' Emily cut in. 'You don't need to worry about that. Now, sit on the hearthrug and I'll dry your hair.'

Emily had put a hot brick in the bed and, as she snuggled into the warmth and her head touched the pillow, Jane was asleep. Emily stood looking down at her and her heart twisted with pity. Poor girl, she thought, and felt a stab of guilt that she could not help all the young girls who had been forced into such a life. She sighed as she closed the door quietly and, having checked on Lewis, went to her own bedroom. Trip was still awake. 'Everything all right?'

'For the moment. I just hope that the doctor doesn't find anything nasty tomorrow, but I'll face that if I have to.'

Jane had been lucky; her few weeks on the streets

had not left her with a horrible disease and Emily was happy to take her to the workshop in Creswick Street and introduce her to the other girls who had signed up to train as buffer girls.

'But first you must go home and see your mother.'

Jane's eyes widened in fright. 'I can't – I daren't. If me dad's there, he'll kill me.'

'Then I will come with you and explain what you'll be doing from now on. Where have you been living?'

'With – with another girl who's a . . .' Jane faltered and bit her lip.

'You must fetch your things from there and move back home.'

'They won't have me. Me dad turned me out.'

'I'll talk to him,' Emily said, with far more confidence than she was feeling inside.

'Do you want me to come with you?' Trip asked when Emily told him what was happening, but she shook her head. 'I don't think so. I can handle Mr Arnold.'

Trip chuckled. 'I don't doubt it for a minute.'

That evening, they set out to Jane's home. When they knocked at the door, the girl was close to tears and trembling. The door was opened by a burly man who towered over them both.

'Oh, it's you, is it? I told you not to come here again. And who's this? Another dirty little tart? Well, you can clear off, the pair of you.'

'Mr Arnold, I'm Emily Trippet. Jane used to work for me some time ago and—'

The man was staring at her. 'Trippet? From Trippets' in Creswick Street?'

'Sort of. That's my husband. But I am about to set up a workshop to train girls and women who are out of work and would like to learn the buffing trade. Jane was shaping up nicely when she worked for me before, so she's an obvious choice to finish her training.'

The man's mouth fell open. 'But – but . . .' he blustered. 'Don't you know what she's been doing? What she's become?'

'I know all about it, and that's why I want to help her now. She's to leave that life behind – and she will. That's a condition of me taking her on.'

Percy Arnold was mystified. He couldn't understand Emily's altruistic motives. His eyes narrowed. 'What's in it for you, eh?'

'I'll get a well-trained buffer girl. Actually – hopefully – I'll get six of them.'

'And can you find them jobs afterwards?'

'That I can't promise at the moment, but at least with a trade at their fingertips – literally – they'll have a better chance of finding work even in these difficult times.'

His eyes swivelled to his daughter, but there was still disgust in his expression.

'If you still don't want me back,' Jane began hesitantly, 'then I'll—'

'I don't,' he said harshly, 'but I've no doubt yer mam will.' He raised his voice and half turned to shout over his shoulder. 'Gladys, there's someone to see yer.'

'What's all the shouting about, Percy? I—' A small, busy little woman, drying her hands on a towel, appeared behind him and peered around his bulk which was still filling the doorway. Her eyes widened and her mouth rounded into an 'Oh' of surprise.

'It seems yer slut of a daughter has decided to mend 'er ways and has come crawling back hopin' we'll be killing the fatted calf for 'er. I can't say I'm pleased about it, Gladys. What me work mates'll say, I daren't think. But if it's what you want, then I'll not go against you. You've been a good wife to me and a good mother. T'ain't your fault what she's done, I know that.'

Gladys Arnold was still staring at her daughter and then she became aware of Emily standing quietly beside her. Her hand flew to cover her mouth. 'Oh Mrs Trippet, whatever—?'

Swiftly, Jane said, 'Mam, it's all thanks to Mrs Trippet. She's offered me work – well, more training – to be a buffer girl.'

Gladys seemed to recover from the shock of seeing her daughter and now she reached out and grasped Jane's arm and pulled her into the house. 'Come inside, quick. Both of you. I don't want the neighbours . . .'

Percy stood aside and allowed them to enter. As they moved into the kitchen, Jane said, 'I'm so sorry, Mam, that I shamed you, but I couldn't find work. And with Dad getting finished at the steelworks—'

'Oh, so it's all my fault, is it? I've worked nigh on thirty years at that place and they out me without a backward glance. That's gratitude for you.'

254

'What is your trade, Mr Arnold?' Emily asked him, trying to divert the attention from Jane.

He laughed ruefully, 'Well, it ain't buffing, missus.'

Emily smiled. 'No, I realize that, but Trip – my husband – and I keep our ear to the ground where work in the city is concerned. I just thought that if we heard of anything going – what sort of thing would you be willing to do?'

'Owt, missus. I'd do owt to be working again.' Now his tone was fervent and Emily realized that here was a proud, working man who had taken a series of hard knocks and disappointments recently.

'If we hear of anything, we'll be sure to tell Jane. That's if . . .' She paused. It still hadn't finally been decided whether or not the girl was going to be allowed home.

Percy and Gladys exchanged a glance and when he gave a brief nod, the woman turned to her daughter and said, 'You can come back, lass, but no more shenanigans, else out you go. You hear me.'

'Yes, Mam,' Jane said meekly and then fell, weeping, into her mother's arms.

Emily patted her shoulder as she turned to leave. 'If you want any help with fetching your things from where you were living, Jane, let me know. I don't want you to face trouble.'

'I'll go with her,' Percy said. 'If she's given her word that there'll be no more of – of *that*, then we'll say no more about it. We're a good family, missus, and we'll stand by her now. All of us, though I may have a bit of bother with her two brothers.'

As he showed Emily to the door, he held out his

hand. 'I don't know how to thank you, missus.' He lowered his voice. 'Only thing now is, is she – you know – all right?'

Emily lowered her voice. 'I took her to my doctor this morning. Everything's fine.'

A look of relief and gratitude flooded the big man's face and he clasped Emily's hand in his huge paw as he added huskily, 'Thank you, missus. I don't know how I'll ever be able to repay you.'

'No repayment necessary. Just forgive her, Mr Arnold, that's all I ask.'

When Jane presented herself at the newly formed training workshop in Trippets' factory the following morning, there was a bit of whispering and nudging amongst the other five girls, but Nell, who knew all about Jane, soon took charge.

'You six are all here because the missus knows you've all been through a tough time one way or another, but she believes you will be good workers.' Her steely glance raked them all in turn. 'Don't let her – or me – down, because there're plenty of lasses out there –' she waved her arm as if to encompass the whole city – 'would give their eye-teeth for a place here and a chance to learn a skill, so think on. Don't be late in a mornin', work hard and we promise you that you'll be the best little buffer girls in the city. Orreight?'

'Yes, missus.'

'I'm not the missus here in this workshop; Mrs Trippet is. You just call me "Nell". Now, let's get you started.'

256

Seeing that Nell had everything under control, Emily called in at her other workshops. Lizzie was now in charge in Rockingham Street over the other two women, while the Broad Lane premises remained untouched by the changes. Ruth still worked between the two, collecting and delivering around the city.

'So, how's it working out?' Trip asked Emily that evening.

'Early days yet,' Emily said cautiously, 'but I think they'll be all right.'

'And Jane's parents have taken her back?'

'Yes. It was touch and go at first. I really thought her father was going to refuse. But he deferred to his wife and she, of course, welcomed her back with open arms.'

'Why "of course"?'

'She's her mother, isn't she?' was all Emily needed to say.

Thirty-Five

'I really should go and see Mr Hawke. Mrs Dugdale told me she'd seen him recently and he's not looking too well. And it's ages since I saw him,' Emily told Trip.

'Why don't you take Lewis to see him one afternoon? I'm sure he'd love to see the little chap.'

So, on the next Saturday afternoon, Emily took the lively four-year-old in his red pushchair along the streets to the small terraced house where Nathan Hawke lived. He was a long time answering her knock and Emily was startled by the change in him. His shoulders were rounded in a stoop and he shuffled his feet. He had lost weight and his clothes hung loosely on him, but his smile was as welcoming as ever.

'My dear young lady, how lovely to see you and you've brought young Master Trippet to see me too. Come in, come in. Now, let's see what I can find for you to play with, young man. My, how he's grown. Is he ready to start school yet, Emily?'

'Well ready,' Emily said, with feeling. 'Poor Mrs Dugdale has quite a task to keep him occupied all day long. He's as bright as a button and active with it.'

He led the way to the kitchen and whilst the surfaces were a little cluttered, Emily was relieved to see that everywhere was clean and there was evidence of meals having been cooked recently.

'How are you, Mr Hawke?'

'Quite well, thank you,' he said, as he bent to place a box of assorted buttons on the hearth. At once, Lewis tipped them out onto the rug and began to sort them into neat piles. 'And you?' Nathan went on. 'Tell me all about yourself and your family. How's business? I expect things are difficult.'

Emily wasn't sure that his answer about his own health had been entirely truthful, but he seemed cheerful enough and his interest was as keen as ever. Whilst Lewis played happily, Emily told him about her latest venture.

'The buffing business is holding its own – just, though Trip has had to lay off some of his workers or turn part of the factory into individual workshops for rental.'

Nathan nodded. 'That's always been done.' He smiled. 'Long live the little mesters, eh?' Having been one himself for all of his working life, Nathan had an empathy with the self-employed craftsmen.

'And Nell's to have another child, you say?'

'Yes, it's due some time in February.'

'And you?' he asked gently.

Emily couldn't stop the smile fading from her face. 'We'd like another one, but it doesn't seem to be happening.'

'Maybe you're working too hard.' He laughed

wryly. 'But I don't suppose it's any good me asking you to slow down, is it?'

'Not a scrap.'

When he'd waved his visitors goodbye and closed the door behind them, Nathan returned to his chair beside the range. He sank into it with a sigh and sat for a long time deep in thought. Emily's visit had reminded him what an enterprising, yet kindly, young woman she was. She was tough and determined and yet that strength was tempered by an innate kindness for others. He'd always known she would be successful and go far and she was certainly on her way. And perhaps, now, there was something he could do to help.

When he'd been diagnosed with the malignant growth that was likely to take his life within months, he had not known how to dispose of his assets and time was running out for him to make a will. He was a widower with no children, indeed no close relatives at all, but today had given him an idea. He'd always thought that Emily was just the sort of daughter he would have liked to have had, had he been so blessed and now, hearing of her altruistic ventures, he knew what he could do. He would make an appointment to see his solicitor that very day.

'What is it, Nell? What's the matter?'

Nell had stepped back from the machine where she was showing one of the trainees how to do the roughing and was clutching at her stomach and bending over.

'Pains, Emily. I reckon I'm starting.'

'Oh, my goodness. Here, sit down.' Emily grabbed a nearby chair and pushed it behind Nell. 'Jane, send for an ambulance . . .'

'No, no need for that. Just get Steve, if you can.'

'Yes, fetch Steve. You know where his workshop is, don't you?'

Jane ran and within minutes Steve was hurrying into the workshop.

'Take my car – it's in the yard,' Emily said. 'Get her to the hospital.'

Steve grinned. 'Aye, we don't want another back-of-the car job.'

Nell was gripping Emily's hand. 'Come with me, Emily. I'm not good at this sort of thing.'

Despite the urgency of the situation, Emily smiled. To hear strong, feisty Nell admitting to a weakness surprised her. 'Of course I'll come. You'll be fine. Now, can you stand up?'

With Steve and Emily on either side of her, Nell struggled to her feet and the three of them lurched out of the building to Emily's car. As Steve drove through the streets, Emily said, 'It's a lot quieter than last time, Steve.'

'Thank goodness. I still don't know how you coped with all that, Em.'

She laughed. 'It was a case of having to. Lewis wasn't going to wait.'

Nell let out a deep groan. 'I don't reckon this one is either. How much further – ow!'

'We're here,' Steve said, as he drove up to the door of the hospital and jerked to a halt. He switched off the engine and leapt out of the car. 'I'll find a nurse. Hang on, Nell luv.'

Two nurses and a porter hurried out and whisked Nell away, leaving Steve and Emily to catch their breath.

'My, that was a close shave,' he murmured, running his hand through his hair. 'Now, the awful waiting begins.'

But the wait wasn't very long. Within twenty minutes a nurse came to tell Steve that he had a healthy baby boy. 'You can see them for a few minutes. I'll come back and fetch you when we're ready. Just the husband, mind,' she added, casting an apologetic glance at Emily. 'You can come back in visiting hours.'

Emily hugged the bemused new father as he murmured, 'A boy, oh Em, it's a boy. Now, I really must mend my ways.'

'You already have, Steve. We're all so proud of you.'

'Perhaps Nell will marry me now. What d'you think, Em?'

'I'm sure she will. If you ask her.'

'I will. I'll do it today. Now. When I see my son, I'll ask her.'

Emily waited patiently for him to return and when he did he was grinning. 'He's a grand little chap, Em. And big. I don't know how she did it.'

'And did she say "yes"?'

'Eh?' For a moment, Steve looked blank and then his grin widened even more.

'She did, but she told me to tell you we don't want no fancy wedding. She knows what you're like. We'll just slip away and do it quietly when she's well enough.'

Emily was disappointed at not being able to organize another village wedding at Ashford but she understood when Steve added softly, 'In the circumstances, Em, it'd be for the best. We don't want to draw attention to ourselves. 'Specially me, and with two illegitimate children, Nell doesn't either.'

'Ah, now in a way that's where you're wrong, because if I'm not mistaken,' Emily said, tucking her arm through his as they walked out of the hospital, 'when the parents marry, it legitimizes their children.'

'Does it really? I'd not heard that.'

'There was an Act passed four or five years ago and I read up about it because of Harry.'

'I hope you're right. That'll please Nell no end. But she still won't want a big wedding, Em. You do understand, don't you?'

Emily sighed. 'I suppose so.'

Only a month later, there were just a few guests at the marriage of Nell and Steve, held in a small church near to their home; Dora Geddis, Nell's mother, who gave her away, Trip, who acted as Steve's Best Man and Lucy, who was bridesmaid. Emily held the baby boy, now named Simon, in her arms. He slept through the ceremony, unaware of the proceedings. 'But I want him there,' Nell had insisted. 'I want to be able to tell him when he's older that he was there.'

The only other two present were Lizzie and her mother, Bess. Lewis spent the day with Constance and George.

'I know you didn't want a fuss, Nell,' Emily said after the ceremony, 'but I've laid on a wedding breakfast in the pub at the top of our road. It's in the back room, and Tom has said we can go in the back way, if you don't want to be seen going through the bar.'

Nell was smiling. 'It's all right, Emily. I don't mind that. I just didn't want a huge white wedding like you gave Lizzie. That's all. The pub'll suit us fine.'

Emily breathed a sigh of relief. She'd been worried that Nell, who could be very prickly if something didn't suit her, would have refused to come. But it was a happy little party that set off for the pub and Nell and Steve walked proudly through the bar, to be cheered by the lunchtime regulars there.

It was a happy ending to what had been a long and difficult time for Nell, and Emily wished with all her heart that her friend would now have the happiness she deserved.

As they walked the short distance to their home afterwards, Emily said, 'It gives you a good feeling, doesn't it, Trip, to see something turn out right for once? I hope this is a sign of better things to come.'

'On a personal level, Emily, I hope so too, but things are getting even more serious on the economic front since the Wall Street crash.'

Emily hugged his arm to her side. 'Let's not worry about that just now. We've had a lovely day.'

But when they arrived at their front door, Constance opened it. Her face was solemn.

'My dears, I'm so sorry to be the bearer of bad news on a day of rejoicing.'

'What is it, Mother?'

Before she could answer, Emily looked around wildly. 'Lewis? Where's Lewis?'

Constance touched her arm and said swiftly, 'He's fine. He's in bed. No, we've just heard that Nathan Hawke has died.'

The news of Nathan's death came as a shock. Emily wept against Trip's shoulder.

'I should have realized the last time I went to see him. He looked so much thinner and slower in his movements. I feel so guilty that I didn't visit him more often, that I didn't do anything to care for him.'

'I'm sure he neither expected it nor thought any less of you,' he comforted her.

When the letter from Nathan's solicitors arrived two days later, Trip said, 'There you are, I was right. He wouldn't have done this if he'd felt the slightest resentment.'

Emily took the letter from Trip's hands and read it with growing disbelief. Then she looked up at her husband with tears in her eyes. 'He's left me everything. His house, his workshops and his two retail shops in the city centre. And just over a thousand pounds in the bank. Trip, it's a fortune. I can't believe it. I don't deserve it.'

'Yes, you do. Have you read the last paragraph?'

When she seemed overcome with emotion, Trip gently eased the letter from her fingers and read it aloud:

'"*Mr Hawke has made you his sole heir because he was very fond of you as a person and because he admired your work ethic and your philanthropic nature to help those less fortunate than yourself. He firmly believed that his considerable wealth will be in safe hands and wisely used not only to build your own business but, along the way, to help the people of the city he loved so much and which had given him his livelihood."* And then it lists the details of his estate. His two workshops – the one in Broad Lane, which he had rebuilt after the fire and you now rent from him; the Rockingham Street workshop, which you also currently rent – two small retail shops in the city centre; his house and one thousand, four hundred and fifty pounds, ten shillings and sixpence. Isn't that wonderful, Emily?'

'I can't believe it,' she whispered again. After a few moments, she wiped her eyes and said more strongly, 'But what do you think he wants me to do?'

'Nothing – other than what you're already doing.'

'But – but everything I've done has been for my own benefit – for our benefit – not for the whole city.'

'I think you're wrong about that. Maybe you think it's only in a small way, but you've supported your friends, forgiven Lizzie for the past, helped Nell in so many ways and, in this latest venture, you've even rescued a young lass from a life on the streets. And the soup kitchens you helped to set up during the miners' strike – don't forget those. I presume you told him all about it?'

'Only as a topic of conversation. He always wanted to know what I was doing.' She lifted her shoulders. 'So I told him, but I didn't mean it to sound as if I was – conceited.'

'He wouldn't have thought that, not for a moment. He liked you and he liked what you were doing. If it'd make you feel better, go and see his solicitor and find out if Mr Hawke mentioned anything particular that he'd like you to do. Other than that, just accept it and be very grateful.'

'Oh, I am, I am, and I will put it all to good use. Every penny of it.'

'I don't think he meant you to *give* it away, though, if that's what you're thinking. I think he meant you to use it to enhance your business and in so doing provide work for others. Just giving money to the poor doesn't actually help them in the long term. It just makes them more dependent, but to provide them with the opportunity to earn their own living gives them back their pride and makes them useful members of the community. And now, you can do that.'

'Yes, yes, you're right, Trip. I see that. You're very wise.'

He laughed aloud. 'Maybe, but the wisest thing I ever did was to marry you, Emily Trippet. And now, my love,' his mirth subsided as he added seriously, 'sadly, you have a funeral to arrange.'

Thirty-Six

It wasn't until the funeral service in the church nearest to Nathan's home that Emily and Trip realized just how well known – and how well liked – he had been. Scores of people attended; men and women from all walks of life.

'He was good to me.'

'Mr Hawke helped me when I was at the lowest point in my life.'

'He helped my family when me dad didn't come back from the war.'

'He gave me a job when I came out of prison. I promised him then that I'd go straight – and I have.'

On and on the comments and tributes went. Rumours were circulating about the terms of his will and many looked at Emily with fresh eyes. They'd heard about what she – in her small way – was trying to do. She, in turn, was full of ideas to extend her own business and at the same time create employment for others.

Over the weeks and months that followed, Emily expanded her training plans and created six more places. The first six were now ready to work on their own and bring in money and so twelve girls were recruited.

'That workshop isn't big enough now, Trip. What shall I do?'

'Couldn't you make better use of the workshop in Broad Lane? Billy's working on his own on the upper floor. That seems a waste of space.'

But Emily shook her head. 'I don't want to alter the lay-out there. The girls go to him when he teaches them the different processes they don't already know. No, I need another workshop.'

'I haven't a spare area you could use, but I've heard that there's a workshop in Rockingham Street – not far from yours – that's come up for rent or for sale. Why not take a look at it?'

'Will you come with me?'

'Of course. When shall we go?'

Emily laughed. 'Right now.'

The workshop was larger than the one three doors away that she now owned and the twelve trainee girls would fit in easily. And there was space upstairs for expansion, if needed in the future.

'But what about the one at your factory, Trip? I don't want to leave you with a vacant space.'

'Why not keep the six girls, who are ready to work on their own, there – as fully fledged buffer girls, maybe with Jane in charge – and set this one up as the training workshop?'

'That's a good idea.'

'You could afford to buy it with the money Nathan Hawke left you.'

Emily shook her head. 'No, I want to keep that behind me. There'll be a lot of expense fitting this place out . . .' She shuddered as she glanced around the dusty workshop. 'And cleaning it, to say nothing of all the machinery we'll need.'

Trip chuckled. 'Why not set the new girls you choose as trainees to clean the place up first. That'll sort out any idle ones for you.'

'Very true,' Emily said seriously. She knew Trip was half-joking, but his idea was a good one. 'And I'll set on another errand lass for Creswick Street. The training workshop doesn't need one; the trainees must fetch and carry for themselves. That way it teaches them how to treat an errand lass in the future. If they've done the work, they appreciate what a young lass has to cope with.'

Emily would then have four workshops running: the original two and now the premises within Trip's factory would also become a buffing workshop, whilst the newly acquired one would be the training room.

'I think Jane has a younger sister, who's just about to leave school. I'll see if she's interested in becoming an errand lass. I'd like to help that family a little more if I can.'

'Has the father found work yet, d'you know?'

Emily shook her head.

'I wonder if he'd be willing to retrain. I'm in need of a spring knife cutter.'

Soberly, Emily said, 'I think the poor man would do anything to be working again.'

'I'll have a word with Richard.'

As they turned to leave the workshop, Trip said, 'Emily, there's just one other thing that Richard and I have been talking about. We'd like you to consider becoming an equal partner in Trippets'.'

'Really? Wouldn't that make it rather unfair on Richard? Husband and wife are bound to stick together if there is ever any disagreement.'

Trip threw back his head and laughed aloud. 'Do you really think we don't know you well enough to know that you'd always voice your own opinion – that'd you'd never just side with me because I'm your husband? *I* know that and Richard knows it too. So, what do you say?'

Emily was silent for a moment, her mind working furiously. At last she said slowly, 'I suppose you and Richard would want to be partners in my enterprises too, would you?'

To her surprise Trip shook his head. 'No, we wouldn't. We both feel those are yours and yours alone. You're building these workshops up from nothing and we don't want to take anything away from you, but our thinking is that with you as an equal partner it will safeguard the future for Lewis and for any children that Richard might have. If something happened to one of us, we know how fair-minded you are. You'd see that both sides were treated equally.'

Emily shrugged. 'If that's what you've both agreed, then yes, I'd be happy to do that.' She giggled and eyed her husband saucily. 'As just a sleeping partner, I presume?'

Trip took her in his arms and kissed her soundly.

As the 1930s progressed, the economic situation showed no sign of easing and overshadowed everyone's life, so much so that often happenings abroad failed to be noticed. Unemployment rose and, in Sheffield, it reached sixty thousand. Any job that was advertised attracted many applicants. There were pockets of cheer, though, which for a few hours could take the citizens away from their anxieties. The coming of the 'talkies', as everyone called them, meant that new cinemas had opened, often converted from theatres.

But Trip remained interested in international affairs too, especially in Europe.

'Have you seen this?' he said as he opened the daily newspaper on 30 January 1933. 'There seems to be a lot of unrest in Germany. Hindenburg has appointed this feller Hitler as Chancellor.'

'Really? But I thought it was only last year that he rejected him.'

'He did. As recently as November, on the grounds that he thought this man's cabinet would develop into a party dictatorship.'

'What's made him change his mind?'

'I really don't know. I expect he was put under pressure of some sort and, besides, he's an old man. He's eighty-five. And this Adolf Hitler seems to have great plans for Germany.'

'What's his party called?'

'The National Socialists.'

'Perhaps they need a strong leader. It must have been dreadful for them at the end of the war.'

'Mm.' Trip didn't sound too sure as he read on. 'He sounds a bit of a fanatic, but he's certainly patriotic. You can't deny that.'

'Just so long as he sticks to helping his own country

and doesn't bother us, good luck to him, I say. Now, Trip, can you make sure Lewis goes round to Mrs Dugdale's before you leave for work? I really must get to Rockingham Street this morning.'

With the business of the day ahead filling her mind, all thoughts of Hitler and his plans for Germany were forgotten. But it wasn't long before Trip, an ardent follower of the political scene, both at home and abroad, began to feel uneasy about the new regime in Germany. In February 1933, when the German Reichstag burned down, he told Emily, 'Hitler's blaming the Communists and he's curtailing freedom of speech. He's becoming exactly what Hindenberg had originally feared, Emily. A dictator. I don't like the sound of it at all.'

'Mm.' Emily was hardly listening, her mind busy with her plans for one of the small retail shops in the city centre that was now hers. 'Trip, I've been thinking.'

'Oh dear,' Trip said, pretending foreboding. 'I don't like the sound of that, either.'

Emily grinned at him and carried on. 'The tenant at one of the little shops that Mr Hawke left me has given notice. Instead of advertising it for rental, why don't we turn it into a centre for cutlery, selling items of the very best quality right through to inexpensive household cutlery?'

'I'm glad you didn't say "cheap".'

'But what do you think?'

Trip wrinkled his forehead thoughtfully. 'It might be a bit of a limited market, if you only stocked cutlery. Think about it. Once households have got the cutlery they need, they won't be buying any more. I mean, it lasts for years. Well,' he added proudly, 'Sheffield-made cutlery does, anyway.'

'We-ell,' Emily said slowly, thinking aloud, 'I could make it a shop for general household goods, but with cutlery as the focal point. But I'd be putting myself in direct competition with the big stores.'

'You wouldn't have the overheads that the bigger shops and stores have got. Maybe you could undercut their prices.' Trip nodded. 'It does sound like a good idea. Who would you get to run it for you? We don't know anyone in the retail trade, do we?'

Emily shook her head. 'No, but I think I know the very person to manage it; I'll talk to your mother and George. Who that man doesn't know in Sheffield, isn't worth knowing.'

Trip laughed and with a fond kiss, he set out for work. He was still chuckling when he arrived at the factory in Creswick Street.

That same evening Trip arrived home late, carrying a wireless set into the house. 'I am determined not to miss any of the news and I thought you would like to listen to the entertainment programmes.'

Lewis bounced up and down in excitement as he watched his father install the square-shaped wooden box with a speaker in the top half and three dials and the programme finder on the bottom half.

'Can I listen to *Children's Hour*, Daddy? Samuel at school has a wireless and he says it's brilliant.'

'Of course you can, Lewis.'

That evening the three of them sat listening in

silence to the new invention that Trip had brought home. Lewis was so entranced with it that he was reluctant to go to bed until Trip took charge and turned it off. 'Off you go, young man. You can listen to it again tomorrow, I promise.'

Thirty-Seven

'Mrs Nicholson, how would you like to become manageress of one of the shops in the city that Mr Hawke left me?'

Ruth's mouth dropped open. 'Me? Oh – I – er – don't know. Aren't you happy with the work I'm doing now? I thought . . .'

'More than happy. But there are so many men out of work in the city, I thought I could employ one of them – one who can drive, of course – to do what you're doing. But a woman's touch would be best in a shop selling household goods. Don't you agree?'

'Well, yes, but I don't know anything about selling, Emily.'

Emily beamed. 'You can learn. And you're good with paperwork and figures. I saw that for myself when you were the buffer missus at Waterfall's.'

'It'd be rather nice, I have to admit.' Ruth was warming to the idea. 'And if I might make a suggestion . . . ?'

'What is it?'

'There's a nice young man who lives in the court now in your old home. He has a wife and two young children and they've hit hard times, Emily. He used to be a delivery driver, but he was laid off four months ago. Would you interview him?'

'Of course. I'll ask George to sit in with me. He's so good at weighing folk up very quickly.'

When the young man presented himself at Ryan's workshop in Rockingham Street, he was obviously very nervous. His jacket and trousers were shabby, the cuffs of his shirt frayed, but he was clean-shaven and his light brown hair was neatly cut.

'Please come into the office, Mr Wragg. This is Mr Bayes.'

Suddenly, Alan Wragg smiled. 'I know Mr Bayes. How are you, sir?' He held out his hand to George, who shook it and smiled broadly.

'Mrs Trippet didn't tell me the name of the applicant, so I didn't know it was you.' He turned to Emily. 'Alan's family lived next door but one to Muriel and me. I've known him since he was a nipper.'

'Ah . . . I see,' Emily said, and couldn't keep the note of doubt from her tone. She was not prepared to employ someone just because George had known him as a child.

Sensing her hesitation, George, ever tactful, said, 'Perhaps I should withdraw from the interview . . .'

'No, no,' Emily said swiftly, 'that won't be necessary, but I would like to know what you've done as a job, Mr Wragg, in recent years.'

So the three of them sat down and the interview, though searching, was more like a friendly chat. When the questions and answers came to a natural end, Emily said, 'Perhaps you'd wait outside whilst Mr Bayes and I have a little chat.'

As the door closed behind him, George said at once, 'I'm sorry, Emily, I didn't mean to put you in an awkward position. If you don't feel . . .'

'On the contrary, I think he'd be perfect. He has a pleasant, deferential manner that I'm sure will go down well with our customers. I don't want anyone too full of themselves. Actually, I think I've seen him before. I'm sure he and his wife and children have been to the soup kitchens.' She sighed. 'Poor things, they must be desperate. So, we'll employ him and there's something else we can do without hurting his feelings.'

Puzzled, George frowned. 'What's that?'

'We can say he needs a uniform with the name "Ryan's" on his jacket. That way, he'll look smart without having to provide his own clothes, which he obviously can't do at present.'

'Oh Emily,' George murmured softly, 'you really are the most extraordinary young woman.'

Emily brushed aside his compliment. 'I'm just thankful we've found someone without having to advertise. Did you hear about the firm that advertised for a warehouseman and over eighty men turned up to apply? It nearly caused a riot.'

George shook his head sadly. 'I don't know where it's all going to end.'

'Well,' she said with a smile, 'we'll just have to keep battling on, won't we?'

On Thursday, 11 May 1933, the same day that Emily opened her new shop in the city centre with Ruth

Nicholson in charge, news came through that on the previous night huge bonfires in Berlin and Munich had destroyed thousands of books which were considered by the Nazis, as Hitler's party was now being called, to be 'un-German'.

'They're even brain-washing children,' Trip said in disgust as he sat at the dinner table. They were holding a small dinner party to celebrate Emily's latest venture. Constance, George, Richard and his mother, Belle, were their guests. The day had been a great success, despite the economic depression that was still gripping the whole country.

'You're helping to give people a feeling of optimism,' Constance said, smiling at her daughter-in-law. She was very fond of Emily. 'People may not be able to buy very much at the moment, but women love to window-shop and plan what they'd like when they can afford it. And many of the things you're stocking are necessities with a few tempting luxuries thrown in for good measure.'

'Our takings were quite good, we thought, for the first day.'

'I bought a lovely tablecloth and matching napkins,' Belle said. 'You must all come to dinner so that I can have an excuse to use them. And I do like that wonderful canteen of cutlery you have as a centrepiece in your display, Emily. The one in the mahogany box and lined with red velvet. It's magnificent.'

George smiled fondly across the table at Emily. 'Mr Hawke would be very proud of you, my dear. You're using his generous legacy wisely.'

'Thank you, George. That means a lot to me.'

'I just hope,' he began and then he hesitated before adding, 'you haven't overstretched yourself. You're doing so much to help others, but I worry for you. This Depression doesn't seem likely to end in the near future.'

Trip reached out and touched Emily's hand. 'My wife is very shrewd and has even taught me the need for thriftiness.' He glanced at his mother. 'I was lucky enough to have been born into a wealthy family. I've never known real hardship, but Emily has and so, right from when she started her own buffing business, she's saved. We live in this nice – but modest – house. We have two cars, I know, but we need them for our separate businesses and, yes, we eat well, but no grand houses or expensive holidays for us. We've always saved for the proverbial rainy day and now that a few rainy days are here, well, we're all right at the moment.'

'Be sure to let me know if you're not, won't you?' Constance said. 'The hotel is doing very well considering the circumstances and making a modest profit. I think most of our clientele are those who will always have money no matter what happens. And, following Lizzie's wedding, we now offer the Riversdale Hotel as a venue for wedding receptions right from lavish affairs down to a modest event for those less well off. We have held several already and have more bookings.'

'We're holding our own at the factory,' Richard put in. 'Since we rented out a few of the unused workshops to little mesters or –' he smiled across the table at Emily – 'to enterprising women, we're holding our own. We haven't had to lay anyone else off yet.'

'How's Mr Arnold doing?'

Richard frowned. 'All right as far as his work is concerned. He was glad to accept the offer I made him, but I have my suspicions that he's a bit of an agitator amongst the employees. We'll have to keep an eye on him. I think all that's keeping him quiet is that he has reason to be grateful to the Trippet family on his own behalf and his daughter's. I don't think he would dare make waves – at least not at the moment. But it troubles me that he seems to admire what Hitler is doing in Germany. His favourite saying seems to be "they lost the war, but they'll come out on top".'

'Well, I certainly don't like what he's doing,' Trip said earnestly. 'I'm all for patriotism, but Hitler's taking it a bit far to my mind. Burning books you don't agree with and replacing them on the shelves with your own seems egotistical in the extreme to me.'

'What do you mean?' Emily asked.

'He wrote a book in the twenties called *Mein Kampf*, which means "my struggle", outlining his political ideology and plans for the future of Germany. Evidently, he started writing it whilst imprisoned for political crimes in the mid-twenties.'

Emily laughed. 'And that's what's replacing all the books being burned – his own?'

Solemnly, Trip nodded and then turned to Richard. 'Perhaps someone should tell Percy Arnold that Hitler's also trying to smash the trades union movement. His Storm Troopers have already seized files from their offices and arrested leaders.'

'It sounds as if he – Hitler, I mean – is trying to stifle free thinking.'

'He is.'

George shook his head. 'I'm sorry to cast gloom on what is a celebration tonight, but I'm very much afraid the problems in Germany could escalate into war.'

There were startled gasps around the table, but no one could think of an answer to refute his fears.

Suddenly, Emily jumped to her feet. 'Let's not think about it just now. And talking of extravagances, I bought a bottle of champagne for tonight. It's high time we opened it. Trip, will you do the honours?'

The evening ended merrily, but none of them forgot George's dire warning.

There were no such worries in Ashford-in-the-Water. Life went on happily. Josh thrived as the manager of Riversdale and with his mother as one of the cooks and Amy helping out front-of-house whenever she could, it was a real family affair. Even those employed there, who were not actually related to the Ryans, felt as if they were part of the family. And when Harry, at twelve, began pestering to help out in any way he could to earn pocket money, his father found him a part-time job after school and at weekends helping Kirkland in the garden at Riversdale Hotel.

'But you're to finish your schooling. Education's important to a lad – to anyone, if it come to that,' he added, thinking of his enterprising sister.

Harry laughed. 'You sound like Granny Ryan.'

Josh blinked and stared at the boy for a moment.

And then he had the grace to laugh. 'Aye, maybe she's right – sometimes.' Pausing for a moment, he put his hand on his son's shoulder. 'Whatever you want to do in life, I'll support you, Harry.'

'I want to join the RAF, Dad. I want to be a pilot.'

For a moment, the image of Harry's attic bedroom was in Josh's mind. The ceiling was strung with dangling model aeroplanes, lovingly and carefully crafted by Harry's own hands with a little help from his two grandfathers over the tricky bits. And any spare pocket money he'd earned was spent on aircraft magazines, all neatly stacked under his bed. He should have guessed, Josh thought. Harry's interest went much deeper than a boyish hobby.

'Aye, well, that's a long time off, lad. See how you feel when you're old enough, eh?'

Harry's face was solemn as he said quietly, 'I won't change my mind, Dad.'

Josh felt a tremor of apprehension. Though he said very little to his family, he followed the news as keenly as his brother-in-law, Trip, and if the newspapers were to be believed, the political situation in Europe was looking decidedly shaky. If there was to be another war, the last place he wanted his son was in the RAF.

Thirty-Eight

Unemployment and hardship were still rife in the city and when cuts in the unemployment assistance were announced in February 1935, there was a noisy and disorderly protest in the Town Hall Square by thousands of people. Over twenty arrests were made and several people, including members of the police force, were injured.

But the demonstration had an effect and only two days later the cuts were restored.

'Thank goodness Percy Sillitoe smashed the gangs. I daren't think what that protest would have turned into if he hadn't.'

'A nasty riot and street fighting for weeks,' Emily said bluntly, then added, 'I wonder how he's getting on in Glasgow.'

Four years earlier, his job done in Sheffield, Percy Sillitoe had been appointed Chief Constable of Glasgow, with the same brief that he had been given in Sheffield; to break up Glasgow's razor gangs.

'It might be a bit tougher there, but I hope he succeeds.'

'The next thing we need,' Trip said decidedly, when he heard that a new telephone exchange had been opened in the city in March, 'is the telephone. We need one at the factory and we should certainly have one here at home. What about you, Emily? You really ought to have one at each of your workshops. It might save you a lot of time running between them if you could just speak to your employees on the telephone, and you should definitely have one at the shop.'

'You're right, Trip.' And so telephones were installed in all their premises and the instruments certainly saved everyone a lot of time and effort.

'What are we going to do to celebrate the King's Silver Jubilee in May?' Emily asked. 'We ought to have a street party at the very least.'

'Mm.' Trip seemed preoccupied.

'Trip?'

He jabbed at the newspaper he was reading. 'It's starting, Emily. Hitler's making demands that Germany should have an air force on a par with ours, and a navy too. And he wants to build an army five times that which was permitted under the Treaty of Versailles at the end of the war. He's just ignoring that treaty.'

Emily pulled the paper out of his grasp. 'In the meantime, Trip, we'll just get on with our lives and not worry about Herr Hitler.'

'I'm sorry, but we should worry about him, Emily. He's a threat to our security. To the security of the whole of Europe, if only they could see it.'

Emily stood in front of him with her hands on her hips. 'So, what are you going to do about it? Become an MP?'

'D'you know, if I thought I could win a seat, I would.' He stood up suddenly, his sombre mood pushed aside. 'But you're right, Emily. I shouldn't be worrying about things over which I have no control – sadly. Now, what were you saying?'

'What are we going to do to celebrate the King's Silver Jubilee?'

'They'll be bringing out a commemorative medal with a red, white and blue ribbon, I've no doubt, but Richard and I have been working on a design for a special penknife.' He grinned. 'In fact, they'll be coming to your girls very soon. Oh, and how many would you like to order for your shop, Mrs Trippet?'

'What a marvellous idea! We'll take six dozen to start with.' Then she frowned. 'Will you be supplying Coles?'

Trip chuckled. 'No, Richard and I have agreed that you should have exclusive rights. No one else in the city will have them but you.'

'Oh Trip!' was all Emily could say.

The day of the Jubilee, 6 May, had been declared a public holiday and Emily was determined that her workers and their families should enjoy it. She was the prime mover – with Bess's help – in organizing a street party. On that sunny morning, it seemed as if everyone she had invited – and a few more besides – came to the party.

'It's like Armistice night,' Bess mused, glancing round at the children tucking into the sandwiches and cakes Emily had ordered from a caterer, at young couples dancing to music blaring from wireless sets that had been carried into the street, and at the older folk enjoying the fun and forgetting just for a few brief hours the struggles of their daily lives. 'Let's hope we never have to have another one of those.'

Emily smiled, but said nothing. Daily, she lived with Trip's gloomy predictions of the trouble brewing on the Continent and, whilst she hoped and prayed he was wrong, she had the awful premonition that he was not worrying unnecessarily and when, a few months later, Hitler stepped up his persecution of the German Jews by banning marriage between Jews and non-Jews and proclaiming that any 'friendships' would result in arrest, even Emily began to fear where it would all lead.

But by the Bank Holiday in August that year, Trip was more cheerful.

'D'you know, Emily,' Trip said, as they motored towards Skegness on the Saturday morning for a long weekend by the sea. Three excited boys took up the back seat; Lewis, Harry and Phil, who had come to stay with Emily and Trip for the first time. 'I really think things are starting to improve slowly.'

'Do you? What makes you say that?'

'The papers say that unemployment has fallen by about a third over the last three years and there is a feeling of optimism. We've a few more orders trickling in. Not vast amounts, but enough to mean that I don't have to lay any more of my own men off or put any of those who rent workshops in our premises in jeopardy. It's such a relief, Emily, I can't tell you. How are things with you?'

'I hardly dare say it, but all right, thanks. "Nell's girls", as we call all the recently trained ones, are doing really well.'

'So, your workshops are fully staffed now.'

Emily nodded. 'We've even had to encroach on Billy's territory but he doesn't seem to mind.'

'Of course he won't. What man would mind working alongside pretty girls?'

'They're not so pretty covered with black, oily sand.'

'I shouldn't think he even notices them with a lovely wife of his own. Any more than I do. Ah, here we are. This is Skegness. Now, where can we park?'

'I don't see the sea, Uncle Trip.'

'It's here somewhere, Phil. We'll find it, never fear.'

Trip parked the car in a side street and they walked until they neared the clock tower standing sentinel near the shore. It was a lovely day, warm and sunny, but there was a cool breeze blowing in from the sea. They strolled on the beach, paddled in the sea and then walked the full length of the pier until they felt as if they were standing in the sea with the waves lapping beneath them. The two younger boys had donkey rides; Harry and Trip had an impromptu game of football on the beach, whilst Emily sat on the sand watching them. It was a carefree day that they would all remember for, as the summer turned to autumn, new fears obsessed Trip. Italy's fascist dictator invaded Abyssinia.

'Hitler will be watching him,' he remarked dolefully. 'And emulating him, if it's a success.'

Thirty-Nine

1936 was proving to be a turbulent year. With the death of King George V in January, the country looked to its new handsome young king for leadership. The old king had been well liked and on the day of his funeral a huge crowd gathered in Town Hall Square as a mark of respect. Abroad, life was just as unsettled, but in Ashford, Harry had only one thing on his mind. His interest in aircraft and flying had not diminished and by the time he was nearly fifteen, he was determined to make it his career. Though he now worked at the hotel under his father's direction in any spare time he had, his ambition to join the RAF never wavered. For him, the job was just marking time until he could become a cadet.

'I'm going to apply, Dad, as soon as I'm old enough,' he told Josh at the beginning of March. 'I'll be fifteen in just over a week's time.'

'We want you to stay on at school, Harry, and besides, you'd need my consent.'

Harry gaped at him. 'Aw Dad, you wouldn't stand in my way, would you?'

Josh wrestled with his conscience. He remembered how his mother had ruled his life – had almost wrecked it when she had dragged him to the city and away from Amy. He'd vowed he would never do that to his own children. Now, he sighed heavily, 'No, Harry, I wouldn't, but think of your mother and how she would worry.'

'Mam said she'd never stop me doing whatever I wanted with my life.'

Josh nodded slowly. Amy too had suffered because of Martha Ryan's ambitions. She'd had to bear the shame of being an unmarried mother. Amy would keep her anxiety to herself and support Harry in his chosen career and Josh decided that he must do the same.

'When you're a little older, we'll talk about it, son.' He was about to turn away, but Harry pushed a magazine under his nose.

'Dad, have you seen this?'

Josh looked down at the magazine Harry was holding. 'It's a picture of the Vickers' Spitfire. It's a new plane on show at Eastleigh Aerodrome near Southampton. It's going on its maiden flight on Thursday. Can we go and see it?'

'Southampton? That's right down on the south coast. Have you any idea how far that is, Harry? No, we can't possibly go. Besides, we can't spare the time. We've a wedding a week on Saturday and I shall want you to work here as much as you can to help Mr Kirkland get the grounds looking nice.'

Harry turned away before his father saw the tears of disappointment in his eyes. He was almost fifteen; far too big a boy to be seen crying.

'Amy?' Josh shouted as he opened the back door. '*Amy?*'

Amy was standing at the kitchen table, her hands deep in a bowl of floury mixture as she made pastry.

'Whatever's the matter?' By the tone of his voice, she knew something was wrong. It had been only an hour since Josh had left for work at the hotel.

'Where's Harry? The headmaster has just rung through to the hotel to ask why he's not in school. He wants to know if he's ill? He's not, is he?'

'I'm sure he isn't, though –' Amy bit her lip – 'I have to admit, I haven't seen him this morning. You know he often gets up early, gets his own breakfast and then goes off to school.'

Josh gave a low groan and headed for the stairs, shouting as he went, 'Harry! *Harry!* Get yourself up this minute. You're late.'

But the boy's bed was neatly made and his bedroom immaculately tidy.

Josh stomped back down the stairs. 'He's not there, so where is he?'

'Are you sure he hasn't come to the hotel? He sometimes calls in before he goes to school and your mother often gives him breakfast in the kitchen there, if she's on duty. And this morning, she is.'

'Then why isn't he at school by now?'

Amy shrugged. 'I don't know.'

Then Bob spoke up from his chair by the fire. 'You won't find him at the hotel or at school.'

Josh and Amy stared at her father. 'What do you mean?'

The old man was smiling. 'He's gone to Southampton.'

'Whatever for?' Amy asked.

'Has he indeed?' Josh muttered, tight-lipped.

'He hasn't got the money for fares to get to Southampton.'

'I gave it to him,' Bob said calmly.

'You shouldn't have done that,' Josh said angrily, 'especially when I'd said he couldn't go.'

'And why did you say that, Josh?'

'Because I've too much work on. We've a big wedding next weekend and—'

'Aye, you've too much work on to have time for your family.'

As Josh opened his mouth to protest, Bob held up his hand. 'I don't deny you're doing a brilliant job there and we're all very proud of you, but don't let it take over your life, Josh. I agree you'll have to be there next weekend for the wedding, but if you'd got things organized, you could have taken the lad this week. If me legs hadn't been playing up, I'd have gone with him, but I'd have been more of a hindrance than a help.'

'But he's too young to go all that way on his own,' Amy said anxiously.

'No, he isn't, love. I was doing a man's job by the time I was his age and he's working now too, whenever he's not at school. And he's got a sensible head on his shoulders. He'll be fine.'

'He should have told us,' Josh muttered. 'He shouldn't have just – gone off.'

'If he had, you'd have stopped him going and, besides, he *has* told you – in a roundabout way. He's not left you anxious and worrying for two days. He asked me to tell you where he's gone.'

'Aye, when he was safely on his way.' Josh glowered.

Bob grinned. 'That's about the size of it.'

'When he gets back, he's in big trouble.'

'Josh, you're a good son-in-law, a wonderful husband and – most of the time – a brilliant father, but you have to realize your children are growing up. Harry needs to make his own decisions about his life. You, if anyone, should know all about that. And to do that, he has to get out and see the world a bit. He's gone to look at this new aeroplane Vickers have built. The Spitfire, I think it's called.'

'I know all about it. He told me last week and he also said he wants to be a pilot in the RAF.'

'What?' Amy's voice was a high-pitched, terrified squeak. 'Oh no, he's not going to do that. I won't let him.'

'I don't think you'll have much say in the matter, love,' her wise father said gently.

Forty

By the time Harry returned, both Josh and Amy had agreed not to be angry with him. Amy hugged him hard and asked him if he was all right and Josh ruffled his hair and said, 'Just don't go off again without telling us *before* you go?'

'You'd have stopped me.'

'Aye, well, maybe this time I would have, but I promise I won't another time as long as you tell us where you're going. All right?'

Harry nodded. He was surprised. He had expected tears and recriminations from his mother and anger from his father. Perhaps the broad wink from his grandfather Bob explained it all.

'So,' Josh went on, 'tell us all about it, then.'

And as the family sat down to supper around the kitchen table, Harry regaled them with his adventures, his younger brother and sister listening with growing admiration and envy.

'I saw the Vickers new long-range bomber, but I didn't like that much. But the Spitfire – it was like a bird . . .' He demonstrated as if his hands were a bird wheeling and diving through the sky. 'It's the fastest single-seater fighter aircraft in the world and flies at between three and four hundred miles per hour.'

'Can me and Sarah go too next time, Dad?' Phil asked, pleadingly.

'I don't know if there'll be a "next time" for Southampton, but I tell you what we will do. Now and again, we'll go out on some trips as a family.' His father-in-law's words had struck a nerve; Josh had been so wrapped up in his duties at the hotel that he wasn't paying enough attention to his wife and children.

'Maybe you could employ an under-manager,' Amy said softly.

Josh pulled a face. 'Mrs Bayes says we're holding our own, but only just. I wouldn't want to put any more strain on the modest profit we have got, but maybe, if I work things out, I could get a little more time off.'

'I'm sure you work far more hours than you're paid for.'

Josh smiled wryly. 'I can't deny that.'

When Constance heard that Josh was taking a Sunday off now and again to take his family on a bus trip or a train journey, she said, 'Why don't you use the Rolls, Josh?'

The black and yellow 1919 Silver Ghost Rolls-Royce that had belonged to her husband and had been under wraps since his long illness and subsequent death was now used to ferry guests to and from the station or sometimes to take them on a special outing.

'But that's for hotel use. I wouldn't want to—'

'Nonsense,' Constance said. 'You have every right

to use it and I'm sure you can work it out so that it doesn't clash with the needs of our guests. I hadn't realized just what long hours you've been working, Josh –' he wondered how she had found out, for he had said nothing to her, but her next words answered his question – 'until I had a little chat with your mother. Perhaps we should employ an under-manager. I think we could afford it. Our bookings seem pretty steady, despite these uncertain times. Let me think about it and talk it over with George. He is eminently sensible. We'll discuss it again on my next visit.'

The following week, Constance said, 'I've decided that we should look for an under-manager. Do you think Kirkland could do it? I know he's always been employed as a gardener, chauffeur, handyman – a jack of all trades – but he does seem very capable. What do you think?'

Josh wrinkled his brow. He had been grateful for the man's knowledge and common sense on many occasions since stepping into the role of manager. Kirkland had been a huge help. Slowly, Josh nodded. 'I think if you still continue to do all the paperwork, Mrs Bayes, as you do now, I think he'd cope.' He laughed. 'As you know, I'm no good with the paper-work. I'm a practical chap and I think Mr Kirkland is too.'

Constance chuckled. 'The only difficulty I shall have is remembering to call him *Mr* Kirkland after all these years.'

'I'm sure he won't mind that.'

When their idea was put to him, Ernest Kirkland was

overwhelmed. He stood uncomfortably before them, twisting his cap round and round through nervous fingers. 'I don't know what to say, ma'am. I've been with you a lot of years and always been loyal to you, but I don't know if I could handle such a position. It's a big responsibility.'

'I think that's how Josh felt when he took on the manager's role and look what a success he's made of it.'

'Often with your help, Ernest. You know that,' Josh put in generously.

Ernest Kirkland smiled weakly, but did not contradict him. Though he was a modest man, he knew that his advice on numerous occasions had helped the younger man. He took a deep breath. 'May I suggest a month's trial on both sides, ma'am? If I don't like the work, I'll tell you, and if you're not satisfied with me, you say so.'

Constance and Josh glanced at each other and then she nodded. 'That sounds very sensible, Kirkland – I mean, Mr Kirkland.'

Ernest laughed. 'Don't you worry about changing what you call me, ma'am.' Then he was serious again as he added, 'But there's just one thing. If I don't suit, I wouldn't want to end up without a job at all. If it doesn't work out, can I go back to my old job with no hard feelings?'

Without consulting each other this time, Constance and Josh chorused, 'Of course.'

Only one week later, as Josh arrived home at six o'clock in the evening, just in time for tea with the family, Amy said, 'You're home early. Is something wrong?'

Josh grinned. 'Just the opposite. Ernest's taken to his new position as if he'd been born to it, so it's looking likely that we'll have to make Mr Partridge permanent.' Grace's husband had worked on the land for most of his life and had been working part-time as the gardener in Ernest Kirkland's place. Now it already looked as if he would be needed for longer than a month.

'And guess what? We can have the Rolls tomorrow. I thought we'd go to Sheffield and see Emily.'

'What about me?' Harry asked. 'Can I come, or do I have to work?'

'No, you can have the day off. Maybe you can make up the time later. Tomorrow is a special treat for all of us.'

Harry grinned. He was wondering if he could see Lucy. He had never forgotten the pretty little girl he had met at Lizzie's wedding to Billy and the time that she and her mother had taken him to the pictures in Sheffield. But perhaps she wouldn't want to see him. She'd be a grown-up young woman now. Perhaps she would consider that, at fifteen, he was far too young for her.

Forty-One

'Aunty Emily, where does Lucy live?' Harry asked after they'd had dinner.

'Not far away. Walkley Street. It's about ten minutes away. Why?'

'I – um – I'd like to see her, but I've never been to her home.'

'Lucy is working now. She's started training to be a nurse at the Royal Hospital. She works all sorts of different shifts.'

'Even on a Sunday?'

Emily laughed. 'Yes, Harry, even on a Sunday. Poorly people need nursing on a Sunday too.'

'Do you think I could go round to her house? Just to see if she's at home?'

'If your dad says it's all right, then, yes, I'll tell you the way.'

After a moment's hesitation, Josh nodded. 'Mind you're back by five, though. We'll have to leave then. I must take over from Mr Kirkland.'

'Don't get lost,' Amy said nervously. The city frightened her. She couldn't understand why Emily had chosen to live here instead of coming back to Ashford. But, as he walked along the streets with the piece of paper on which Emily had written directions for him, he could understand his aunt's love of the city. There was excitement in the air, even on the Sabbath. It was a fine day, though cold, yet people – workers, he supposed – were out in the city's streets and parks, dressed in their finery and a group of girls walked along the pavements laughing and calling out to young men. One or two, who were not much older than he was, Harry thought, were coming towards him. They stopped in front of him and almost encircled him.

'Now, here's a handsome young man. What's your name, luv?'

'Harry.'

'That's a nice name. And how old are you, Harry?'

'Fifteen.'

The young woman asking the questions grimaced. 'Aw, that's a shame. You're a bit young for us, luv. Ne'er mind, eh? You'll grow and then I'll be watching out for you. Ta-ra, luv.'

Laughing, the group moved on. Harry watched them go with a heavy heart. No doubt Lucy would think just the same as they did. He wasn't quite sure of her age, but he thought Lucy was at least two years older than he was, if not more. Maybe she even had a boyfriend by now. He hesitated, wondering if he should turn around and go back home. Then he shook himself and laughed wryly. He'd hardly come a'courting. He just wanted to say "hello" to her, that was all. Squaring his shoulders, Harry glanced down at the piece of paper and set off again. But when he arrived at the address which Emily had written down, his nerve almost deserted him again.

There was a man painting the front window and when he turned round, Harry recognized Lucy's dad, Mr Henderson. The man stared at him for a moment and then smiled. 'Hello, there. It's Harry, isn't it? I almost didn't recognize you. You've grown a lot. What are you doing here?'

'We've come to visit Aunty Emily and I just thought I'd call round and say "hello". I hope that's all right.'

''Course it is.' Steve climbed down from the ladder, wiped his hands on a rag and led the way down the passageway between the terraced house and the next, opened the gate, then the back door of the house and ushered him inside.

'Nell, look who's here, all the way from Ashford. The family's visiting Emily and Harry's just called round to see us. You sit down, lad, and Nell will make you a cuppa. I'll just call Lucy down. I 'spect you'd like to see her. She's often talked about meeting you at Lizzie's wedding.'

'Hello, Harry. Come in, luv, and sit down.' Nell smiled at him. 'How's everyone in Ashford?'

'Fine, thanks, Mrs Henderson.'

'Are you working yet?'

Harry hesitated, but there was no use in even trying to bend the truth. Nell knew only too well exactly how old he was.

'I help out at the hotel after school and at weekends, but –' he grimaced – 'Mam and Dad are insisting I stay on at school.'

'Quite right too.' She glanced quickly at the door and then lowered her voice as she bent towards him. 'I'll let you into a little secret, Harry. I never learned to read and write until I met your aunty Emily. She taught me. You get all the learning you can, luv. It's never wasted, whatever you want to do in life.'

'Aunty Emily says you're the best buffer girl she's ever known.'

Nell smiled. 'She's right there. I'm never one for false modesty, but I wish I'd had a bit more education, you know. Just think what I might have done then. I'd have been a force to be reckoned with.'

Harry grinned. He liked Nell. 'I think you probably are anyway.'

Nell laughed loudly, throwing back her head and standing with her hands on her hips. 'You've been listening to too many tales from your aunty.' Then she glanced up as the door opened.

'What's all the noise going on in here?' Lucy said. 'Hello, Harry. How nice to see you.'

Harry got to his feet. She was even prettier than he remembered her and she looked so grown up dressed in her nurse's uniform. Her clear green eyes looked straight into his. With her auburn hair tucked neatly beneath her nurse's cap, she looked very smart and professional.

'I'm just off to report for duty at the hospital, but you can walk with me, if you like. I've not forgotten I promised to show you one or two places in the city when you came to visit again. Only you must remember your way back.'

'Let him drink his tea first,' Nell said, placing a cup and saucer in front of him. 'And you'd better have one before you go.'

The four of them sat around the table chatting until it was time for Lucy to leave.

When they parted at the hospital gates and Harry began to find his way back to Carr Road, the boy, on the threshold of becoming a young man, knew he had fallen in love. But he was honest enough to realize that he probably had no hope where Lucy Henderson was concerned. She was older than he was and the years between the fifteen-year-old and the young trainee nurse, who looked so grown up already, was a chasm. A pretty girl like her would soon have a string of suitors. He doubted she would wait for him to grow up.

The same weekend that Josh took his family to see Emily, Adolf Hitler, in deliberate defiance of the peace Treaty of Versailles, signed in 1919, marched into the Rhineland, but at the same time he offered a new treaty to guarantee peace for twenty-five years.

'If you believe that man, you'll believe anything,' Trip muttered over the breakfast table as he read the news on the Monday morning. 'One of the journalists in this paper says – and I quote – "He has merely re-occupied his own backyard." That's all very well, but it takes him about a hundred miles nearer France and consequently us too.'

'Trip, can you take Lewis to school today? Mrs Dugdale isn't well.'

Trip looked up, his thoughts about world affairs forgotten. 'Anything serious?'

'I hope not. Just a head cold at the moment, but

you know how it always goes to her chest. I'd rather she stayed in the warm.'

'What about Simon?'

'Could you pick him up from Nell's?'

'What about after school?' Usually, Bess took the two young boys to school each morning and collected them in the afternoon, keeping them at her house until their parents arrived home, though Lewis was beginning to protest that at nine, almost ten, he was able to walk to and from school on his own. Perhaps she was being a little over-protective, Emily thought, but the memory of Lucy's abduction on her way home from school could never quite be buried.

'She says she's all right to look after them,' Emily went on. 'If she's not, I'll let Lizzie off work early to collect the boys and take them home. She might as well take the rest of the day off and let her mother rest.'

'Right you are,' Trip said, folding his newspaper and getting up. The problems from overseas were forgotten in the demands of their daily lives.

But as the months went on it was impossible to ignore the news coming from across the Channel. In July, a civil war broke out in Spain, both sides of the conflict seeking aid from other countries. In August, the Berlin Olympics were used to glorify Adolf Hitler's Nazi regime. What echoed round the world perhaps more than anything was Hitler's deliberate snub to the black American, Jesse Owens, whilst personally congratulating German athletes on their success. At home, unemployment still caused great hardship and in October, two hundred Jarrow men undertook a long march to London carrying over eleven thousand signatures. They wanted the Government and the people in the south to understand the hardships they were facing in the North-east, where there was seventy per cent unemployment.

Trip rarely lost his temper, but on Tuesday evening, 6 October, he returned home fuming. 'D'you know what's happened, Emily?' he raved, pacing the hearth. 'About half my employees have taken leave without permission to join the marchers, without even asking or saying what they were planning to do. Evidently, they set off yesterday. I thought nothing of it then because I just accepted it as a 'Saint Monday', but when there were so many missing this morning, I started to ask questions. It's left the factory hardly able to operate. I've been too soft. I expect they think I'm a pushover. Well, not any more. I'll sack the lot of 'em. There're plenty of unemployed men in this city to take their place.'

'No, you won't, Trip. You won't do anything of the sort, but when they return, you need to call your whole workforce together and express your displeasure. Warn them that if anything like that ever happens again, they're out.'

'I'd have the unions on my back, if I did that,' Trip muttered. 'Richard thinks it was Percy Arnold who instigated the whole thing. And after all we've tried to do to help that family, that's the thanks I get.'

'You need to be calm, Trip, when you talk to them. It'll have far more effect than ranting at them. A steely calm – that's what you need.'

As his temper cooled, Trip saw the sense of Emily's reasoning and by the time the marchers returned, some of them now anxious when they realized what they'd done, he was composed and had prepared a calculated speech.

They assembled at his demand in the largest workshop.

'I understand why you joined the Jarrow lads and I do have sympathy with their cause. What I am angry about – very angry – is that you just took the time off without so much as telling us what you were doing.'

'You'd not have let us go, Mester Thomas, if we'd told you.'

Trip's gaze sought out the man at the back who'd spoken. He was not surprised to see that it was Percy Arnold. He paused a moment before saying steadily, 'Over the past few years, when times have been very difficult, I have laid off only a few men – a lot fewer than other factories in the city – and only when I really had no other choice. Some firms, as you well know, have closed down altogether, but we have struggled to keep going. And we have struggled. Some weeks, I haven't known if I'd have enough money at the end of the week to pay you all. But we've coped. I've kept most of you in employment, sometimes when I couldn't really afford to do so, but I have. Even my stepfather gave notice at his own suggestion, so that it left one of you in work.'

There was a murmuring amongst the men and Trip waited until it had died down again.

'Most of you here, but not all,' again his glance

found Percy, 'will remember the time of the General Strike. I *gave* you that time off willingly because I didn't want anyone running the gauntlet of the picket line, or being vilified for coming to work. And besides, I was on the side of the strikers, if truth be known. We weathered that together and, maybe, if you'd only spoken to me this time, I would have found a way to let some of you take time to show your solidarity for your fellow workmen from the North.'

He paused to let his statement sink in. Then his tone hardened. 'But I am not the soft touch perhaps you think I am. I *give* willingly, I help others where I can, but nobody – nobody – *takes* from me.'

He looked around the assembled company and already a few were hanging their heads, understanding that this time they had taken advantage of a generous man a step too far.

'If anything like this ever happens again, those taking part will be sacked without references.'

'T'unions'd have summat to say about that,' came the same voice from the back.

'I don't doubt that they would have, but I'll fight them, if I have to. Just remember,' Trip added, his tone frighteningly calm now. 'My brother and I own this factory. We can close it down any time we like and walk away without a backward glance. Just think on, eh?'

He stepped down from the box where he'd been standing to speak to them all and marched out of the room, leaving his workforce stunned and not quite able to understand what had actually happened. Had they still got a job or were they all sacked?

'What are we to do, Mester Richard?'

Richard hid his smile. 'I should get back to your work pretty quick and keep your heads down.'

The men literally scuttled back to their machines until there was only one man left standing in the middle of the workshop.

'What about me, Mester Richard?' Percy Arnold asked. 'I 'spect I'm on me bike, am I?'

Richard shrugged. 'He didn't say so, but I do think you're on a final warning, Mr Arnold. Like my brother said, we can shut the doors any time we like – unions or no unions.'

With that he, too, turned and left.

Later, when Trip recounted the whole incident to Emily, her reply was surprisingly harsh. 'We've done a lot to help that family, Trip. If he makes any more trouble for you, I'd get rid of him. Philanthropy only goes so far.'

Forty-Two

In November the citizens were intrigued by the appointment of Sheffield's first woman Lord Mayor.

'Do you realize,' Trip laughed, 'that she is likely to be the first woman ever to attend a Cutlers' Feast? I think you should get into local politics, Emily. You'd make a wonderful Lord Mayor and wouldn't I love to see you in pride of place at the Feast?'

Emily punched him playfully. 'I'm far too busy to get involved in all that and, besides, I'm holding my place quite nicely in a man's world, thank you.'

'Indeed, you are,' Trip said proudly, and kissed her forehead.

But during the final month of the year, the whole nation was shocked to read in their newspapers that their popular king was abdicating to marry the woman he loved, a twice-divorced American. The love affair had been common knowledge overseas, but the British press had suppressed the story.

'I'm backing the new king and his family,' Trip declared stoutly. 'He has two lovely little girls and the eldest is now heir to the throne.'

'That'll be interesting. A woman on the throne.'

'Some of our greatest monarchs have been women

309

– Elizabeth and Victoria, for instance – but let's hope it won't be for many years. She has to grow up first. By the way, do you want to go to London to see the Coronation next May?'

Emily's eyes lit up. 'Could we?'

'I don't see why not. We could see if Mother and George would like to go. And it would be good for Lewis to be present at a bit of history. And it'll be a special birthday present for him.'

On Lewis's eleventh birthday, they motored to London in the Rolls Royce and stayed at a hotel.

'This will be my treat,' Constance declared, 'though you will have to drive us there, Thomas. I really can't tackle London traffic. I've only just mastered driving in Sheffield. Besides, I can watch how a London hotel works.' She smiled broadly. 'I might pick up some tips.'

'I've never seen so many people,' Lewis said, as they weaved their way through the crowds the following morning. The day was cloudy but the rain seemed to be holding off. 'Is the whole country here?'

Trip laughed. 'Not quite, but I expect there are a lot of people who've come here especially. It's a great moment.'

'There will be a lot of people come from abroad too, just to say they were here,' Constance said, holding firmly on to Lewis's hand. She thought the boy might object to having his hand held at his age, but he seemed rather overawed by the crowds and clung to her gratefully.

'We want to find a spot in Trafalgar Square, if we can. The procession is sure to pass through there,' Trip said.

Just after ten-thirty, a murmur went through the crowd. 'They've left Buckingham Palace. They're on the way.'

It wasn't long before they heard the ripple of cheering getting closer and closer. A long procession preceded the royal couple, contingents from all parts of the Empire, massed bands and marching soldiers, sailors and airmen, prime ministers and dignitaries, members of the royal family and then, towards the end of the long procession, they saw it: the golden coach pulled by eight Windsor greys and flanked by grooms and Yeomen of the Guard walking on either side.

'Look at his beautiful robes,' Emily gasped. 'Ruby-red and white ermine. What a magnificent spectacle. I'm so glad we came, Trip. We'll remember the twelfth of May 1937 for ever.'

They waited until the procession returned after the ceremony and saw the King looking very solemn with the heavy crown on his head.

'D'you think we can get to Buckingham Palace? They say the family might come out onto the balcony,' Emily said.

'We can try,' Trip said. 'Come on. Stay close.'

They couldn't get to the railings, but in the far distance they were able to see the tiny figures on the palace balcony.

'It's been a wonderful day,' Emily said later, and

Constance agreed, 'And now we'll have one more night in the hotel and then home tomorrow.'

Not long after the excitement and pageantry of the coronation, the cloud of war hung over the country once more.

'Now, we've got Japan and China at war. You wouldn't believe it, would you? And Hitler and Mussolini are far too pally for my liking,' Trip remarked. 'Hitler's always bleating about needing "living space" for Germany. That can only mean one thing, can't it?'

'What – exactly?' Emily asked.

'He's going to overrun other countries to get it, isn't he?'

'But I thought they were both saying they want peace? Do they think they can just march into countries with no resistance?'

'He did with the Rhineland. They cheered him, didn't they?'

'Maybe so, but I can't see anyone else doing the same.'

But Trip was wrong. In March 1938, Hitler marched into Austria, to the sound of the church bells ringing in welcome.

'They're an independent nation.' Trip was mystified. 'Why on earth would they want to become just another part of Germany?'

'I really haven't the faintest idea, Trip,' Emily said. 'But I'll tell you one thing, he won't just march into Britain like that.'

'He might try,' Trip said gloomily.

Life carried on as normal on the surface, but

beneath the ordinariness of everyday life there was a growing fear. Various peace-keeping deals were made, but many mistrusted their validity and Trip was one of the doubters. 'These agreements aren't worth the paper they're written on,' he fumed. 'If anyone thinks either Hitler or Mussolini will keep their word, they're mad.'

And then, in Trip's mind, came the greatest betrayal of all. After an agreement between the French and the British in April to defend Czechoslovakia, in September it was agreed to hand over the Sudetenland to Germany and the British Prime Minister flew home waving a piece of paper, which bore Hitler's signature and which he declared promised 'peace for our time'.

On 5 October, Hitler walked into the Sudetenland, strangely hailed by the people as their liberator.

'That does it. There'll be war without a shadow of a doubt,' was Trip's view.

Forty-Three

Christmas 1938 was a strange one. Everyone tried to make merry as normal, but the threat of war hung over the whole country. Most tried not to believe it and to put faith in Mr Chamberlain's statement. Martha adamantly refused to speak of it.

'If you're going to talk about all that foolishness starting again, then I won't join you at Christmas lunch, even though I'm going to be helping to cook it at the hotel for all of us and the guests.'

Emily, understanding how her mother must feel, put her arm around her shoulders. 'Then we'll ban all talk of the impending war at the table, Mam.'

'What do you mean "the impending war"?' Martha said sharply. 'You talk as if it's going to happen.'

Emily sighed. 'Trip thinks it is.'

'He would, wouldn't he? If we have a war, he'll make a killing manufacturing armaments.'

'Mam!' Emily was shocked. 'Is that what you think of Trip? That it's all about money?'

Martha shrugged. 'It's what his father would have done.'

'Trip's not his father,' Emily snapped. 'And well you know it.'

Martha laughed wryly. 'Then more fool him

because –' and her mother's next words startled Emily – 'it's exactly what I would do in his place.'

The prospect of war was not mentioned, but there was an atmosphere of everyone trying studiously to avoid the subject, even though it was uppermost in their minds.

'Phew!' Trip muttered, as they drove home on Boxing Day morning, neither of them wanting to stay any longer. 'That was hard. I think I've actually bitten the end of my tongue off trying to steer clear of war talk.'

'Did you get a chance to speak to Harry?'

Trip shook his head. 'Not on his own, no, and I didn't like to broach the subject in front of his parents either. I suspect it's a touchy subject with them too. But he's always said he wants to go into the RAF. I can't imagine he's changed his mind, can you?'

Emily said nothing; there was nothing she could say, because she was uncomfortably aware that what Trip said was true.

The New Year brought no hope of lasting peace. In fact, when, at the end of February, the British Government decided to recognize General Franco's regime in Spain, it caused furious scenes in the House of Commons. And as Hitler entered Prague in March, the British Prime Minister pledged whole-heartedly to defend Poland against attack. Even he, it seemed, no longer had any faith in Hitler's signature on the famous piece of paper.

In May, Italy and Germany signed a military and political alliance and British farmers were being advised to increase food production as the threat of war came closer and closer.

Harry had stayed on at school into the sixth form, believing that his application to join the RAF would be helped by his Higher School Certificate. Early in July 1939, when his examinations had finished, he visited Emily and Trip in Sheffield.

'D'you think', he asked Emily hesitantly, 'Lucy would like to go to the theatre with me?'

Emily hid her smile. Harry was such a handsome and kindly young man, but he seemed to lack self-confidence where girls were concerned. 'I don't see why not. What makes you ask me?'

'I just wondered if she already had a boyfriend.'

'Not that I know of. Nell's never said anything.'

'She might think I'm too young for her.'

'Nonsense. Age has nothing to do with it. You're a young man now. Go and ask her, Harry. She can only say "no".'

Harry laughed. 'That's what I'm afraid of.'

But Lucy didn't say 'no' and she even suggested where they might go. 'The Palace Theatre in Attercliffe is opening a new theatre bar on Monday,' Lucy told him. 'I'd love to go.'

'Then we will. What's playing?'

'*The Crimes of Burke and Hare*,' Lucy chuckled. 'You can hold my hand if I get frightened.'

They had a wonderful evening and did indeed hold hands, but only as they walked home in the dark.

'Lucy, I want to tell you something, but please

keep it secret for the moment, won't you? I'm applying to join the RAF.'

'Not waiting for call-up?'

'No, because if I wait, I risk getting sent just anywhere. If I join now, I think I might have some choice.'

'You'll probably be recommended for a commission now you've got your Higher.'

'I haven't got it yet,' Harry said.

'No, but you will have.' Her faith in him touched Harry.

They walked along in silence until Lucy said, very softly, 'You will take care, Harry, won't you?'

'Of course I will. And will you – would you –' he hardly dared to ask the question – 'write to me?'

Lucy echoed his answer. 'Of course I will.'

Of all the agreements and alliances that were being made, the one that shocked the Western world was the Non-Aggression Pact between Germany and Russia signed in August. War was now thought to be inevitable.

'So, you really think there's going to be a war?' Emily asked Trip. Now he was not the only one to predict conflict. Ever since the Czech crisis, Sheffield had begun serious preparations. Gas masks had been distributed and anti-aircraft guns and searchlights had been installed around the city. Even a small supply of Anderson shelters had been built. 'If there is a war, what are we going to do?' Emily asked Trip. 'With the businesses, I mean?'

'Richard and I have talked about it and, if it does

happen, we think we'll change the works into a munitions factory. In fact, I've already written to the authorities. It's time we all started to plan for war and I'm not just being pessimistic. I've seen this coming for a long time, Emily.'

'I know you have.' Emily felt a little guilty about all the times she'd listened to Trip reading out the depressing news and had thought he was obsessed by the prospect of war. But now, she could see that he had been right all along. 'What do you think I should do with my buffing workshops?'

'A lot of your girls might go into munitions for the duration of the war. The pay will be much better for them. But you might find,' Trip went on, 'that there will be a demand for inexpensive cutlery to supply the forces. How about you make some enquiries?'

Emily was thoughtful. 'I wonder if I could design a range of cutlery and submit samples to the War Office, or whoever's responsible for that sort of thing?'

'Good idea and, if it comes about, maybe you could strike up a deal with several of the little mesters to supply you. I suggest the older men, who aren't likely to be called up. That way you could still keep your buffing workshops going and,' he added pointedly, 'you'd be helping the war effort too.'

'That's very good thinking.' She smiled. 'You know me so well, don't you? You know I'd want to feel I was "doing my bit".' Then her face clouded. 'Trip, I know Lewis is too young, but *you* won't be called up, will you?'

'I doubt it. I'm forty next year.'

'Thank goodness for that.'

'I do intend to offer my services for local defence in some form, though.' Trip moved across the room and put his arms around her. 'But you know who will be called up, don't you?'

Emily laid her cheek against his chest, her voice a muffled whisper. 'Yes. Harry's eighteen now. He'll go. There's no doubt about that. Sooner or later, he'll have to go.'

'Mam – Dad – I've volunteered for the RAF and I've been accepted. I'm going tomorrow.'

On a hot day in late August, Harry faced his shocked parents. Josh stared at his son, whilst Amy gave a little cry and pressed her hand over her mouth.

Harry rushed on, knowing how much he was hurting them. 'It's something I had to do. Please try to understand.'

Amy sank down into a chair whilst, beside the fire, her father stared into the flames in the grate, not speaking. So, he was thinking, the forebodings in the recent press had been justified. They – the powers that governed their country – were going to let it all happen again. Hadn't they learned the last time the horror war could bring? Weren't millions of dead on all sides of that conflict enough to show all those in a position of power the futility of such carnage? Some of the papers were saying that the last war had never really ended, that there had only been a twenty-year truce and that now it must be resolved once and for all. But why did it have to involve his beloved grandson Harry? And wasn't the sight of his other grandfather, Walter Ryan, so cruelly maimed by the last war, enough to deter him? The boy was so special to Bob Clark. When Josh had gone away, ignorant of the fact that he had left Amy pregnant, it had been her father and the good people of Ashford who had rallied round the girl and cared for her. When Josh had returned eighteen months or so later and had learned the truth, he had become a man overnight. He had stood up to his mother and returned to the village to marry Amy. Since then, there had been two more children and whilst Bob would never admit to having a favourite amongst his grandchildren, he could not deny that Harry was very special. Bob continued to stare into the fire as he strove to hide the tears that welled in his eyes.

'To be honest, son, I've been surprised you didn't go the minute you were eighteen.' Josh smiled thinly. 'I was expecting it.'

'I considered it, but I wanted to finish my education first. I appreciated you encouraging me to stay on at school but I didn't want to wait for call-up when I could be sent into any of the services. I've always wanted to go into the RAF to train as a fighter pilot – if I'm good enough.' Harry faced them, his firm chin set in determination, his blue eyes sparkling with ill-concealed excitement.

Josh ran his fingers distractedly through his hair. It was as if he were being catapulted back through time and he was a young boy again listening to the very same argument coming from his own father's lips at the outbreak of the Great War. 'I have to do this, Martha,' Walter had said, 'I don't want to be called a coward.'

'I do see, son. Really I do – and I understand, but . . .' Josh gestured helplessly towards Amy sitting huddled in the chair weeping quietly into her hand-kerchief. Harry knelt in front of his mother, looking up into her face. For several minutes, they stared at each other, saying nothing. The moment was too deep for words, but at last Amy put out a trembling hand and stroked her son's curly hair. 'You must promise me,' she said shakily, 'that you will write every week.'

'I will, Mam, I give you my word.'

'Then,' she whispered, 'you go with my blessing and my prayers.'

Beside them, Bob bowed his head and covered his face with his hand.

Later, when Josh arrived at the hotel, Martha, on duty that day in the kitchen, asked, 'What is it, son? There's something wrong. I can see it in your face.'

There was no point in trying to keep the news from her; she would find out soon enough and he'd already asked Harry to go next door and break the news to Walter.

'Be gentle with him, Harry,' he'd warned. 'It'll be hard for him to accept.'

'I will, Dad.' Though he was determined to follow his dream and become a pilot, Harry was a thoughtful young man and sensitive to the feelings of others, especially those whom he loved dearly.

But it had fallen to Josh to break the news to Martha. 'It's Harry. He's joined up.'

'Joined up?' Martha repeated. 'Volunteered, you mean? Going before he has to?'

Josh nodded, unable to speak.

'What's he want to go and do that for?' She gave an impatient 'tut'. 'Just like your fool of a father last time. I'll talk to him. I'll make him see sense.'

'It's done now, Mam. He's signed up for the RAF. There's nothing any of us can do, even if we wanted to.'

'What do you mean?' Martha snapped, her voice rising. She paused a moment before adding incredulously, 'You don't mean – you can't mean – that you *want* him to go?'

'Of course I don't, but I do want him to do what he wants.' He met his mother's gaze for a moment as he said steadily and pointedly, 'He's a man now and I want him to make his own decisions.' And the unspoken words lay between them – *just as I should have done at his age.* But Josh was not unkind. He would not rake up old sores and cast them at his mother. With the passage of time, he had come to understand that she had only wanted what she thought was the best for him. That city life and the work there had not been right for him was not her fault. Nor could she have possibly foreseen what disasters their life in Sheffield would bring. Out of it all, the one good thing was that Emily was making a huge success of her life there. He wondered how the coming war would affect her and Trip. And what would happen to him and the rest of his family? Would the hotel keep running as it did now? Though no doubt there would be an increase in the number of marriages taking place before the war started in earnest and young men were sent away, it was doubtful whether young couples would spend money on lavish receptions any more.

Constance arrived later that day in a flurry of excitement. 'Josh, I've been thinking . . .'

Josh's heart sank. 'Yes, I thought the news would affect us – as a hotel, I mean as well as—'

Though her head was full of plans, Constance was always sensitive to the feelings of others. 'What is it, Josh? Come into my office. We can talk privately there.'

As soon as the door closed behind them, Josh blurted out, 'Harry's volunteered for the RAF.'

Constance stared at him for a moment and then said, 'Good for him.'

Josh blinked in the face of her congratulations; it was not what he had expected. As if sensing what he was feeling, she said softly, 'I'm sorry, perhaps you don't feel the same.'

Josh shrugged. 'To be honest, I've got very mixed feelings. I'm proud of him, of course, but he wants to become a pilot – a fighter pilot.'

'Ah, then I understand your concerns, but he'd have to go anyway and probably soon. At least, this way, he's volunteered for what he wants. What does Amy say?'

'She shed a few tears, but she's given him her blessing.'

'She's a wonderful young woman, your Amy.'

'I know, but if anything happens to Harry . . .'

'That rather brings me to what I've been thinking

about. Josh, I want to turn this hotel into a convalescent home for the wounded. A lot of big houses did that in the last war and I want to do it this time round. I can't think of a better place for them to recuperate than here in the Derbyshire dales, can you? It wouldn't be for surgical or serious cases, just for their final recuperation.'

'Isn't it a little early to set up something like that? I mean, the war may be over quite quickly . . .' His voice trailed away.

'Sadly,' Constance said softly, 'I don't think that will be the case, Josh, and I want to be ready.'

Now he remained silent, wondering what his future would be if he was no longer required here as a hotel manager. But he said nothing; any such question would sound selfish.

Constance smiled as she said softly, 'All the staff will remain in place – if they're willing to – but they might find that their duties are somewhat different. I shall be bringing in qualified nursing staff and I have one person in mind already. Lucy Henderson. She might have qualified as a State Enrolled Nurse by now and I can't think of anyone better. Can you?'

Mesmerized by the speed at which all this was happening, Josh shook his head.

'And there's another thing. The villagers must be prepared to take evacuees from the cities. From Sheffield, certainly, but probably from Liverpool and Manchester too. I'll get Martha and Grace on to that.'

Josh thought quickly. 'Could – could we take Lewis and Nell's boy, Simon?'

'How old are they now? Remind me.'

'Lewis was thirteen in May and Simon – let me think – he must be eight now. The thing is, if I know my sister and brother-in-law, they will be in the thick of whatever the war effort demands. They certainly won't leave the city however bad it gets.'

'I don't see why not. Leave it with me.'

Forty-Four

Just after 11 a.m. on Sunday, 3 September, Trip, Emily, Constance and George gathered around the wireless set to listen to the declaration of war by Mr Chamberlain. Shortly afterwards the King spoke directly to his people.

'So, that's it, then,' Trip said as he switched off the wireless and turned to face the solemn faces of his family.

'Yes, that's it,' Constance said with new resolution in her tone. 'And we'd better get on with it. I understand a lot of children left on Friday for the country, but we've been a little tardy. I have spoken to Josh about Ashford village taking evacuees and, of course, he has suggested that Lewis and Nell's boy, Simon, should go there.' She turned to Emily. 'Has your mother said anything about Lewis going to them?'

Emily shook her head. 'We've not spoken much about the war, to be honest. I think the very mention of it holds bitter memories for her.'

'If you're happy to leave it with me, then I'll arrange it all.'

After Constance and George had left, Emily faced Trip with tears in her eyes. 'Must he go, Trip?'

Trip put his arms around her and held her close.

'Emily, darling, sad to say, this is going to be a war like we've never known before. All the big cities are going to be targets, especially those that will be manufacturing armaments. Sheffield is going to be one such city.'

Though her voice shook a little, Emily said defiantly, 'Then we'd better be prepared.'

Emily returned to the workshop in Rockingham Street late the following afternoon after a long and difficult day visiting customers. It was only natural that the talk was of nothing else but the war. And several were floundering in indecision; they hadn't thought that it would really come to this and were totally unprepared. Lizzie and the others were working normally, just as if nothing had happened, but she found Ruth Nicholson hovering near the small office. Her face was white, her eyes terror-stricken.

'Mrs Nicholson – whatever's the matter?'

'Billy's volunteered.'

'What?' Emily was shocked. 'No! Whatever has he done that for?' Then as realization sank in, she said, 'But – he can't. I mean – he's too old.' A pause and then, a little uncertainly, 'Isn't he?'

Ruth shrugged.

'Trip was enquiring into the rules and regulations about himself,' Emily went on. 'But because he's involved in engineering – and planning to turn his factory to manufacturing munitions anyway – he *should* be exempt.'

'What about his employees?'

'Once the factory's turned over to munitions, they

should be regarded as being in a reserved occupation too, surely.'

Ruth bit her lip. 'I really don't know. But none of that matters. Billy's volunteered and – and they've accepted him.'

'But – but . . .' Emily waved her hand in a gesture of helplessness. 'Didn't he think of you – of what you would feel? And Lizzie?'

Bitterly, Ruth said, 'Do men ever think of anyone except themselves and what they want to do? My husband and two sons went without even so much as a "what d'you think" to me. And, of course, they never came back. Killed on the first day of the Somme – all three of them. They're buried out there some-where. Side by side, a father and his two sons, so I've been told.'

'Oh Ruth, haven't you seen their graves?'

Ruth pressed her lips together and shook her head. Shakily, she said, 'I couldn't afford to make the trip and besides, what good would it do? It won't bring them back, will it?'

Emily couldn't think of an answer, but she felt for the woman. If it were Lewis buried out there – God forbid that would ever happen – she knew she would want to visit his grave, just to be near him for one last time. Lewis was far too young but, she thought suddenly, and the realization threatened to overwhelm her, Harry wasn't. She must go to Ashford at once. She must see Josh and they must stop Harry doing anything foolish. Perhaps they could stop him having to go at all. Trip would find him work in the factory and then . . .

But she voiced none of this to Ruth. The woman had enough worries of her own.

'Trip? Are you home?'

Emily burst in through the back door.

'Here,' he called from the living room.

'Billy's volunteered,' Emily said at once as she entered the room and sat down on the opposite side of the table. 'Can you do anything? Can you apply for an exemption for him?'

'You'd have to do that. He works for you, but I don't think the authorities are going to look upon cutlery manufacturing as war work, though I could be wrong. People still have to eat.'

'Can you give him a job at your factory?'

'Nothing's settled yet, Emily. There's a lot of red tape to go through, though I must admit, now we're actually at war, things are moving more quickly.' He put his head on one side as he looked at her. 'But I thought you said he'd volunteered?'

'He has.'

'Then I think it's too late. He can't back track now and besides, knowing Billy, I wouldn't think he'd want to.'

'But isn't he too old?' Emily was not prepared to give up just yet.

Trip shook his head. 'No, and neither am I. Parliament has passed an act that all males between eighteen and forty-one have to register for service. The medically unfit are exempt, of course, and certain jobs like mining, farming, shipbuilding and engineering will be classed as reserved occupations.'

Emily sighed. 'You can't call Billy unfit by any stretch of the imagination and he's not forty yet. So it looks as if there's no way out. His mother's distraught.'

'I bet she is,' Trip murmured sympathetically. 'I don't think he'd've been called up yet, but as he's volunteered, there's nothing we can do.'

Emily jumped up. 'Not about Billy, no. You're right, but there is someone I can stop going: Harry. I'll bring him to live with us and you can find him a job in your munitions factory. He won't get called up then.'

'But . . .' Trip began, but Emily had whirled around and was already on her way out of the front door towards her little car standing on the road outside their house. As he heard the engine start, he knew she was setting off for Ashford at once.

'Cold meat and pickles for my dinner tonight, then,' he murmured, but it was said without rancour.

He knew what a special place Harry occupied within the family. He was not only Josh and Amy's firstborn, but also the first grandson for both Bob Clark and the Ryans. Whilst the children who had followed were all loved just as much, of course, the circumstances of Harry's birth – being illegitimate at the outset – had brought Amy and her father even closer. And when the Ryans had moved back to Ashford, it had been the young's boy's influence on the war-damaged Walter that had aided his paternal grandfather's partial recovery. Patiently, the little boy had read to him, had encouraged him to speak again and the terrible shaking that had afflicted Walter had gradually lessened until now, twenty years later, it was scarcely noticeable. Only when Walter got upset, did it begin again. Trip sighed. Walter was going to be very upset if his beloved grandson went to war.

'Josh! Amy! Where are you?' Emily opened the back door of the smithy, but there was no answer, not even a sound coming from Bob Clark's anvil. It was obvious there was no one in the house, not even the children. She closed the door and went through the gap in the fence between the two cottages and glanced through the kitchen window. Inside, she could see her mother sitting at the table with Josh and Amy standing near her. Josh had his arm around Amy's shoulders and she was leaning into him. Walter was sitting beside the fire with his head bowed. There was no sign of Bob Clark at either house. Feeling as if she was intruding, Emily knocked softly on the door. After a few moments Amy opened it and Emily could see at once that she had been crying. Emily's heart seemed to leap in her chest. Had something happened to Amy's father? Is that why the house next door was so silent and the family were all gathered here in The Candle House? Had he had an accident? Had he . . . ? For what seemed a long moment the two women stared at each other. Amy blinked as if she suddenly recognized who was standing there. 'Emily. Sorry, do come in.'

Emily stepped into the kitchen and glanced around her at each one of them in turn. They looked like stone statues. Her gaze came to rest on her brother's face and there was a question in her eyes.

He moved towards her and kissed her cheek. 'Sorry, Em. We were just talking about Harry. He volunteered for the RAF at the beginning of the month – though he didn't tell us until last week.'

'Oh no! Then I'm too late.'

He blinked and looked down at her, mystified. 'I don't understand. Too late? For what?'

'To stop him going. To stop him being called up.'

Josh frowned. 'I don't understand. How do you think you could do that?'

Emily grasped his arms. 'He can come and work for Trip in the city.'

Josh shook his head slowly. 'I don't think working for Trip would count as a reserved occupation.'

'Yes, it would. Trip's turning his works into a small-arms factory. It would be – will be – classed as war effort.'

'I see.' Josh's voice was flat and quite hopeless. Then he nodded. 'But you're right, you are too late. He wants to be a fighter pilot and he's already left.'

'Oh no,' Emily breathed. 'Not that.'

The next thing that happened shocked Josh even more than the news that his son had volunteered. Emily began to cry. Emily rarely wept; Josh could count on the fingers of one hand the times he had seen his big sister shed tears. But now she pressed her face against his chest and clung to him. 'Josh, I'm sorry. I'm so sorry. It's all our fault.'

Josh put his arms around her and held her close. 'Shush, there, there,' he soothed, completely at a loss to understand. As her sobs subsided a little, he held her at arm's length and looked down into her face.

'Emily, what are you talking about? How can it possibly be your fault?'

'We took him to the air show in Sheffield. We took him on a flight. It's our fault he got so interested in aircraft and in flying.'

'Oh Em!' Again he hugged her close. 'Don't be silly. He was interested in aeroplanes from a little boy. Don't you remember Amy's dad – and our dad, if it comes to that – building model aircraft with him? You could hardly walk into his bedroom without banging your head on a Sopwith Camel or a Gipsy Moth dangling from the ceiling. It hasn't got anything to do with you taking him flying.'

Emily sniffed, a little comforted, but she still wasn't convinced. It was one thing to build model aircraft as a child but quite another to be taken on a flight, to feel the thrill of flying.

Josh forced a laugh and, trying to comfort his sister, he said, 'If anyone's to blame then it's both his grandfathers. Our dad for building model aeroplanes with him and Amy's dad for giving him the money to go to Southampton that time to see Amy Johnson's plane. Now, come on, Amy will make you a cup of tea and we want to hear all about Trip's grand ideas for his factory.'

The mood in the room, though still sombre, lightened a little, but no one noticed Walter's hands begin to shake.

Forty-Five

Evacuation of children and nursing mothers and their babies had begun on the first day of September, when war seemed inevitable. Two days after Mr Chamberlain's solemn declaration that Britain was at war with Germany, Constance drove Lewis to Ashford to live with Martha and Walter.

'We've enrolled you at the Lady Manners School in Bakewell but we've heard that the school is taking half the boys of a Manchester school,' Martha told them. 'So for the autumn term at least and possibly longer, the local lads will only be doing half-time. But we'll keep you occupied. You're a big lad. You can help at the hotel in the gardens with Mr Clark.'

In the days following the announcement there was a flurry of activity everywhere, none more so than in Emily's and Trip's lives. Missing their son, they threw themselves into work and making plans. They sent off numerous letters to various government departments detailing the ways in which they thought they could help the war effort and, at the same time, they kept all their workers fully informed of their actions. Constance, too, was very busy. She made an appointment with the matron of the Royal.

Sitting down opposite the severe-looking woman, she outlined her plans for Riversdale Hotel adding, 'I'm hoping to get the nurse who looked after my late husband in his final illness to run it, but she couldn't be expected to be on duty round the clock. So I need someone I like and trust to help her. I have someone in mind, but I'm afraid it's one of your nurses. Lucy Henderson.'

The matron smiled and her whole demeanour changed in an instant. Her features softened and there was an impish twinkle in her eyes. No doubt the stern manner had been deliberately cultivated to strike fear into the heart of every young nurse. Constance was in no doubt that it did so. 'Though still quite young, Mrs Bayes, she is one of my best nurses. I shall be sorry to lose her.'

'Perhaps you won't. I haven't asked her yet if she's willing to undertake the position. I needed to talk to you first. Is she capable of such work? I would need her to be in charge when Nurse Adams was off duty.'

'If that's all it's to be – just a convalescent home – I think she would be. I will have to make sure with the authorities, of course. But, as yours will be a private concern anyway, I can't see a problem.'

'I would want to comply with any regulations, Matron.'

'Of course, and I respect you for that. You wouldn't be carrying out operations there nor would you be sent severe medical cases. It would just be the wounded in the last stages of recuperation, but it would be a very useful type of premises. Hospitals,

I'm sorry to say, will soon be bursting at the seams. I was a young nurse in the last war and the sights I saw . . .' She shook her head sadly.

They went on to discuss how many patients Riversdale could take and the number of nurses required to care for that volume around the clock and when Constance left the matron's office, she knew exactly what she needed to do. But first, she must tell her family and then all her staff at Riversdale.

'It's a marvellous idea, Mother,' Trip said when Constance told him her plan. 'Have you asked Lucy yet?'

Constance shook her head. 'I'm going to call round to see if she's at home when I leave here.'

'Nell will be there,' Emily said. 'But you must eat with us first.'

'That would be lovely. I've been so busy today that I missed lunch.'

As they sat over the meal, Constance was delighted to hear of their plans. 'It's a marvellous idea, but you will find that if the war goes on for some time, women will be drafted into service too, though I think working in munitions and probably what you're planning too, Emily, will be regarded as valuable war work. My only advice is that you should keep in close communication with the authorities. Make sure you follow the regulations to the letter.'

Emily and Trip both nodded and, as they rose at the end of the meal, Trip added, 'I'll come to Nell's with you, Mother, and then see you home. I don't want you walking the streets after dark, especially now that there are no street lights.'

Nell was surprised when she opened the door. 'What's wrong?' she asked at once.

'Nothing, Nell. Don't worry,' Constance said hurriedly. 'Is Lucy at home? It's her we've come to see.'

'Lucy? Why, yes, she is. She's on day shift at the moment, so she's home in the evenings.' Nell was still mystified, but she invited them in and offered them tea.

'Not for me, thank you, Nell. I've just eaten with Thomas and Emily.'

'Then I'll call Lucy down. She's just changing. She hasn't been home long.'

A few minutes later Lucy entered the room, her expression as puzzled as her mother's.

Constance – as was her way – came straight to the point and explained the reason for their visit. After her first initial surprise, Lucy said, 'It sounds a wonderful idea. I'd be delighted if – if you think I could do it.'

Constance turned to Nell. 'How would you feel, Nell, because she would have to live in at Riversdale? It would mean her leaving home.'

Nell smiled. 'I'd miss her, of course I would, but to be honest, I'd be very relieved that she'd be away from the city. If anywhere's going to be a target for bombing, then it's Sheffield with all its industries.'

'Sadly, I think you're right.'

Nell bit her lip and, for a moment, looked uncharacteristically uncertain.

'What is it, Nell?' Constance asked gently.

The words came out in a rush. 'It's Simon. Steve said I should have let him go with the others being evacuated, but I didn't want him to go to strangers . . .'

'You wondered if he could come to Ashford?'

'He'd be with friends.'

'I'll see what I can do. Martha and Grace have taken on the job of billeting the children in the district, so I'll speak to them.'

'So,' Constance began as all the people who worked at the hotel sat in the residents' lounge and looked expectantly towards her as she stood in the window. George sat nearby. 'I expect you're all wondering why I've called you together. It's to explain what is going to be happening to the hotel during the war.'

Several of them glanced at each other, their faces sober; they were expecting the worst.

'We're turning the hotel into a convalescent home for wounded soldiers who are in the final stages of their recuperation. There won't be surgical cases or any with serious medical problems, but we shall still need a nursing staff. All of you –' she paused, relishing the good news she was about to deliver – 'will be kept on, though the actual work you do might be a little different from what you do now.' There was a unanimous look of relief on all their faces and a few murmurs of thankfulness. Jobs had been difficult enough to find in the countryside over the last few years and now that the nation was being plunged into war, the future was even more uncertain.

'Of course some of you – especially the younger ones – may be called up or obliged to do war work, but I might be able to apply for a dispensation for you. It might be regarded as a kind of war work you're doing here. But I can't be sure yet. Anyway –' she placed her hands together almost as if pleading with them to agree – 'are you all happy to stay?'

The swift chorus of 'yes, of course' left Constance in no doubt.

As they began to disperse, Constance said, 'Martha – Grace, can you stay a few moments, please.' As the others returned to their various duties, she said, 'How is the billeting of children going?'

Martha and Grace exchanged a glance. 'Very well, Mrs Bayes. Everyone's been very willing to help out and some of the farmers are delighted because they've been able to have one or two strong young lads who can lend a hand.'

'I've had a request from Nell Henderson, who works for Emily, that her young son Simon should come to Ashford. Can we do anything on a more personal level? His older sister will be coming here to Riversdale. She's a trained nurse. But I didn't want to take up valuable space here that could be used for patients. She will live in, as might one or two nurses, as we'll have to cover twenty-four-hour nursing care. I'm intending to convert the old stables at the back of the house into accommodation for staff. That way, I think we should be able to take about ten patients.'

'Simon can come to us,' Martha said swiftly. 'Lewis

is already with us and though he's a good bit older, he's a kindly boy. Him and Philip – being the same age – are great pals now. They'll keep an eye on young Simon.'

Constance beamed. 'I was hoping one of you would agree to take him. Nell doesn't want him to go to strangers, but if he's with you, Martha, that will be perfect. And he can see his sister whenever he wants to.'

'I could take a couple of the nurses, if you need billets in the village,' Grace offered. 'They'd have to look after themselves when I'm working here, but we've the room.'

'That'd be ideal, Grace. Are you sure your husband won't mind?'

Grace chuckled. 'What? Mind having a couple of pretty lasses living with us? I very much doubt it, else I don't know my Dan as well as I thought I did.'

The three women laughed together. 'Then I'll see Nell and bring Simon to you as soon as I can, Martha.'

It didn't take long for Trippets' to be turned into a small-arms factory making bullet casings. Lathes, drilling machines and other machinery required was soon installed and the training of existing workers and the employment and training of women to work the machinery followed. Trippets' was one of the first factories in the city to turn their premises into the manufacture of munitions. There had been such factories in Sheffield during the Great War, so it didn't take long for other firms to follow Trip's lead.

'We've lost so many of the young men to the forces,' Trip said. 'We're only left with old men and women now.'

Steve grinned. 'You speak for yourself. I don't consider myself old. I've had to register, but I'm hoping I won't get called up, 'specially if I'm on your payroll. Trip, can I work for you now? You can use my workshop for whatever you like for the duration.'

'Do you mean it? That'd be great. We're already short of space.'

'Do you think you'll get called up?'

Trip shook his head. 'No. I think it'll be a while before they get to the forty-year-olds and besides, I think I am now in a reserved occupation.'

'What about Richard? He's younger than you and not married, either.'

'He's applied for exemption on the same grounds, but it also seems he might not be fit enough. A recent medical revealed he's got a slight problem with his heart. Nothing serious, but enough to keep him out of the forces. And as regards his marital status . . .' Trip grinned. 'He has a string of girlfriends, so I hear, but no wedding bells yet.'

'What about you? Your fitness, I mean?'

'Me? I'm fit as a flea. I passed A1, but, like I say, I think I'll be more valuable running this place, don't you?'

'Absolutely. Now, what do you want to do with my workshop?'

'Let's go and take a look at it. D'you know, it's at times like these I miss George still working for us.

With his experience and memory of what's gone on in the past, he'd be able to advise us in a flash.'

'You could still ask him. He is your stepfather now, after all.'

Constance called at Nell's house the following Saturday morning to pick up Simon and take him to Ashford. He had fair hair and blue eyes like his father and a cheeky grin, but this morning the boy was white-faced and solemn. Nell's mother, Dora, had struggled to the door to see him off, tears streaming down her face. Constance felt impatient with the woman. It was bad enough for the eight-year-old – and for Nell – without Dora crying over everyone. Briskly, Constance took hold of his suitcase and held out her hand. Smiling down at him, she said, 'At least you don't have to have a luggage label tied to your jacket like the children who went on the train did. Come along, Simon. I've got a real treat in store for you when we get there. Mrs Ryan is making ice cream especially for you and Lewis. And you know Lewis, don't you?'

The boy nodded. After succumbing to another tearful hug from his grandmother and a brisk no-nonsense ruffle of his hair from his mother, Simon followed Constance out to her car. When he saw it, his face brightened considerably. 'Are we going in that?'

'We most certainly are.'

'Wow!' the boy said and he clambered aboard, his mother and grandmother, standing in the doorway to wave him off, completely forgotten.

With a wink at Nell and a cheerful wave, Constance climbed in behind the wheel.

As they drove up the hill out of the city and into the countryside the boy bounced up and down on the seat beside her. 'Look look, Mrs Bayes, real cows. Will I be able to watch them being milked, d'you think?'

Constance laughed at his innocent excitement and promised herself that whenever she visited Ashford, she would make time to take the children out into the hills and fields.

Forty-Six

'Here we are,' Constance said, ushering the boy into Martha Ryan's home. It was still known as The Candle House.

'Hello, Simon, come in. Lewis, take Simon upstairs and show him where he'll be sleeping. You'll have to share,' Martha added, turning back to the new arrival, 'but you won't mind that, will you?'

Lewis grinned at the younger boy. 'Come on, I'll show you round and then we'll go out.'

'Now, just be careful,' Martha warned. 'He's a city lad, not used to country ways.'

Lewis laughed. 'He soon will be once he's been here a while.'

'How long am I staying here?'

The two women heard Simon's piping voice as the two boys climbed the stairs. 'Till the war's over, I should think,' was Lewis's reply and Constance and Martha glanced at each other. 'I'll make us some tea. Sit down, do, Constance. How are things in the city?'

Constance seated herself and drew off her gloves. 'We're waiting in trepidation.'

'Eh?' Startled, Martha stared at her.

Constance smiled thinly. 'For the bombing to start. It's bound to come. We're such a well-known city

344

for industry and many of the factories are turning to manufacturing products for the war. Even Thomas.'

'What about Emily and her businesses?'

Constance hid her smile. Martha and her ambitions! 'If she gets approval from the authorities, she's planning to make cutlery for the War Office. She'll employ the little mesters and then use her own buffers. It's an awful thing to say, but the war often makes businessmen.'

Martha said nothing. After a pause, Constance asked, 'How's Walter?'

'Surprisingly, he's doing very well. Him and Bob potter about in the garden up at Riversdale and do odd jobs and they'll be on hand to chat to the patients a lot when they start arriving. They won't charge for that, mind,' she added swiftly.

Constance laughed. 'I wouldn't really mind if they did. It'll be good for them – both sides, I shouldn't wonder.'

'You're a very generous woman, Constance,' Martha murmured pensively, silently wishing that she had been blessed with a more charitable nature.

'Oh, I don't know about that,' Constance said modestly and hastily changed the subject. 'I'm glad to hear that this war hasn't upset Walter.'

'It did at first, especially when Harry went, but I think being able to go up there –' she nodded her head towards Riversdale – 'is a huge help. He'll still feel he's "doing his bit".'

'I think we all are.'

'I don't feel as if I'm doing much.'

'You're giving a home to evacuees and still cooking

at Riversdale and so is Grace and I'm running about like a scalded cat, though that might soon be curtailed as petrol gets harder to get.'

'How's George?'

Martha couldn't help noticing how Constance's eyes lit up at the mere mention of his name. How good it was that this lovely woman had found happiness in her life, albeit a little late in life.

'He's fine. Trip has asked him to be in charge of organizing the changeover to munitions production. So he's back working at the factory again. He's in his element. It's amazing how this war is not only bringing out the best in most folks, but is also making everyone pull together too.'

'You're right, Constance, but I just wish it wasn't taking all our fine young men away from us.'

Constance nodded and though she said nothing, she knew both their minds were thinking of Harry.

Harry was loving every aspect of his life in the RAF. Over the first few weeks and months after the declaration of war, his letters kept them informed of his progress. In every line his excitement was obvious:

I don't know how much of this letter will get through the Censor (if they've started with censorship yet, which, no doubt, they will very soon). I don't think I should tell you where I am in a letter (we get lectures about what we can and can't write). I've been kitted out and I've had my hair cut very, very short. I don't think you'd recognize me at the moment, but

*the good thing about it is – it will grow again.
There are lots of rules and regulations and the
discipline takes a bit of getting used to. I've
already had an hour's punishment drill for
what I'd consider a very minor offence!
Beware of the sergeant, I've been warned. One
good thing is that we're allowed out of camp
when we've done hours and hours of square
bashing. And we all have to be able to swim,
so thank goodness for those childhood romps
in the river, though my technique evidently
leaves a lot to be desired. The regime is pretty
strict. Up early, beds made and kit laid out,
breakfast and then on parade ground for seven
a.m. followed by lectures, PT, route marches,
cross-country runs. I've never been so fit – or
so exhausted. I'll probably be here for a month
or so . . .*

*I'm now at Initial Training School and likely
to be here for about eight weeks. And then I'll
be going on to Elementary Flying School for
about ten weeks . . .*

*Best of all – which makes all that strenuous
physical activity worthwhile – we've started to
learn the rudiments of flying – just in the
classroom at the moment. I can't wait to climb
into an aircraft. Doesn't look like we'll get leave
while we're here, but your letters are getting
through, so please keep writing. Aunty Emily
writes regularly, so I'm getting all the city news
too . . .*

Bess, with no young children to care for now since the evacuation, felt lost.

'I need to be busy, Emily,' she confided. 'I'm missing those little rascals more than you can imagine.'

'I know what you mean. The house is so quiet without Lewis. I still listen for him when I get home and then I realize he's not there.'

'I'll still housekeep for you, Emily, if you want me to, because I reckon you're going to be busier than ever. But I still need more to do. Lizzie's out a lot and, with Billy gone, there's only so much I can cook and bake.' She pulled a wry face. 'And that won't get any easier with the rationing that's bound to start sooner or later. I feel I want to *do* something, Emily, but I don't know what. I think I'm a bit old for working in a factory now.'

'Why don't you join the WVS? They did a fantastic job with the evacuation of the children at the beginning of September and there'll be so much more they'll be able to do.'

Bess's face brightened. 'Now, that *is* a good idea, Emily luv. I hadn't thought of that. Thank you. I'll make enquiries straight away.'

Bess was not the only one who was restless; Lizzie was missing Billy more than she would have believed possible.

'Jane,' she said one night as they left work, 'd'you fancy a night on the town?'

'I don't know. Me dad . . .'

'Tell him you're with me. I'm a married woman.' She pulled a wry face. 'I can't get up to much mischief, now can I?'

Jane giggled. 'Oh, I don't know.' Lizzie laughed with her, but persisted. 'So, what do you say?'

The theatres and cinemas had closed briefly on the declaration of war, but when no serious bombing started, they had gradually reopened. It was soon realized that entertainment would be a great morale booster and also a way of getting news to the people and so, many had reopened.

'And there's dancing,' Lizzie wheedled. 'We could go dancing. Billy's not much of a dancer and never wanted to go.'

'I don't think I dare . . .' Jane was so frightened that her father would throw her out of her home again, that she hardly dared to go out at all now. 'I mean, we'd be dancing with men. Me dad—'

'Never mind your dad. I'm not asking him to come out with us. Just think, Jane, all those lovely soldiers home on leave or awaiting posting. They've already sent thousands to France, you know.'

'Has Billy gone?'

Lizzie shook her head. 'I don't think so. I think he's still training somewhere.'

'Don't you hear from him?'

'About every two weeks and I write back, but there's not much to say. Do come, Jane. We can have a bit of harmless fun. Mam's out all the time now with this WVS.'

Surprisingly, Percy Arnold said very little. Jane told him she was going out with Lizzie. Lizzie and her mother were close to the Trippet family and he owed the return of his daughter to say nothing of his present livelihood to that family. So, Percy decided to hold his tongue, though he worried.

'I hate to say it,' Trip said, 'but this war's revived the economy.'

'Maybe so, but what will happen when it's all over? We'll be in even more debt as a nation then.'

'We'll worry about that when we've got this little job done, Emily. By the way, what are we doing for Christmas this year? It'll be a strange one.'

'I don't know if we can go to the hotel now that it's been transformed. Your mother was telling me they've had their first patients.'

'Have they really? Who?'

Emily's face sobered. 'A couple of soldiers and a pilot, who'd been doing a reconnaissance flight over France and had engine trouble. He got back over England, but then crash landed and broke his leg.'

They exchanged a glance, both thinking of Harry, but neither said anything.

'I'll have a word with Mother. See what they want us to do. We could always go and stay in one of the other hotels just so we can see a bit more of Lewis.'

'What about inviting Nell and Steve to join us? I'm sure they'd like to spend Christmas with Simon.'

'How would we get round the expense of a hotel? They're too proud to let us pay for them.'

Emily was thoughtful for a moment. 'Do you give any of your employees a Christmas bonus? I mean, Steve is working for you now, isn't he?'

Trip's eyes twinkled. 'No, but I could. And they needn't all be given the same amount. I'm sure they wouldn't compare notes as to what anyone else received, but I'll have a word with Mother first.'

'I'd been thinking about that too,' Constance said when he broached the subject, 'but I'm sorry, Trip. It really isn't convenient for anyone to stay as a guest now. All the rooms have been equipped for patients and, as you know, we have three installed already.'

And so it was discreetly and tactfully arranged that they would stay in a hotel in the village, close to the Ryans. Martha was in her element, insisting that everyone should come to The Candle House for Christmas lunch. 'Though how I'll fit you all in, I don't know.'

But the crowded feeling would only add to the enjoyment, and Amy insisted that they should go to the smithy for a late tea. 'It's no good having it early, if my mother-in-law is providing lunch,' she laughed, 'everyone will be FRUTB.'

'What's that mean, Aunty Amy?' Lewis asked and Amy tweaked his nose playfully.

'Full Right Up To Busting.'

Then her face sobered. 'I just wish Harry could get home. Lucy's coming down for an hour or two in the afternoon and, if he came, we'd have everyone here.'

Forty-Seven

But Harry would not get home for Christmas. At the beginning of December he had been been posted to Elementary Flying Training School. He sent apologetic letters that he would not get leave, but there was no hiding his excitement.

> *Guess what, I've actually flown a Tiger Moth, but I won't be allowed to go solo until my instructor thinks I'm ready . . . They're a great bunch of lads here. I hope one or two of us get a posting together. We're likely to go to Service Flying Training School about February. That'll be a sixteen-week stint!*

The letter addressed to Amy, Josh and the rest of the family was read out as they all lingered over mince pies at the end of Christmas Day lunch.

'What a shame it wasn't a Gipsy Moth, that would have been very special for him,' Emily said and Josh and Amy exchanged a smile. 'How much longer will his training be? Do you know?'

Josh shook his head. 'Several weeks, I should think. He might not even pass out to be a pilot.'

There were mixed feelings and no one dared to

say anything, except Amy, who said quietly, 'I hope he gets to do whatever he wants. We'll just have to accept it, won't we?'

Her quiet courage in accepting what her son would have to face was an example to them all.

George cleared his throat. 'Did you read about the *Graf Spee* being scuttled last week by its crew on direct orders from Hitler because she was trapped in Montevideo harbour by three of our cruisers? At the moment, it seems most of the action is taking place at sea.'

'Let's hope,' Josh said, getting up to help his mother clear the table, 'that we can take command of the sea and prevent a battle in the air.'

'I hope you've all enjoyed your lunch,' Martha said, as she began to stack the plates together. 'Because I hear rationing is to start in the New Year and then the queuing will begin. It's doubtful we'll get a feast like this again for years.'

Harry wrote spasmodically during the first months of the year, but then, at the end of May, he wrote:

I've got my wings and I'll be going to an Operational Training Unit for about a month or so . . .

His family were not sure that they could share his enthusiasm when, at the same time as they received his news, the evacuation of Dunkirk took place and the focus changed to the battle in the air. Now, they all feared for his safety. But Harry was in his element when, a month later, he wrote to say he'd been posted down south to an operational station.

Although keen to meet his fellow officers and men, he had first to report his arrival. He stood smartly to attention in front of the adjutant's desk in an office just outside the commanding officer's room. The flight lieutenant was older than Harry had expected. His dark hair was thinning now, but his eyes were a steely blue and set close together. His nose was hooked, but what drew attention to his face was the jagged scar down his left cheek. Harry waited patiently, trying to avert his gaze from the man's face. He seemed to be taking a long time to study the paper-work. At last he looked up and scrutinized Harry with a piercing look. 'From Derbyshire, are you, lad?'

'Yes, sir.' Emboldened by hearing a northern twang in the man's accent, Harry said, 'And you're from Yorkshire, somewhere in the Sheffield area, if I'm not mistaken.'

Flight Lieutenant Hartley's expression hardened and it was a moment before he said curtly, 'Aye, I was, but I left there years ago.'

'You never quite lose the accent, though, do you, sir?'

The man fingered the jagged scar down the left-hand side of his face and murmured, 'Apparently not.' After a moment's pause, he became brisk once more and issued several orders. A few minutes later, Harry saluted smartly and marched out of the office to seek the hut he would be sleeping in.

He did not see the flight lieutenant's gaze following his progress across the parade ground, the tightening of the man's mouth or the years of resentment glittering in his narrowed eyes.

'Harry Ryan,' Hartley murmured to the empty room. 'Well, well, well.'

Harry soon settled in. He enjoyed the banter and relaxing with a drink in the mess and he enjoyed the flying, even the dangerous times. He learned how to fly in formation until they encountered the enemy and then it seemed to be every man for himself. He was not a dare-devil and respected the rules and regulations not only of flying, but also of the life on the station too. Of course, he was no prude and enjoyed the nights out of the camp in the nearest town as much as any of the young men thrown together in such unusual circumstances, but there was always a figure at the back of his mind that kept him from getting too close to any of the girls he met.

He made a close friend of his room-mate, Barney Lingard, who teased him mercilessly. 'Can't have this. We've got to get you fitted up with one of the local beauties, Harry, old boy.'

Good naturedly, Harry shook his head and made the excuse, 'I've got a girlfriend back home.' If only that were true, he thought.

'Ah well, in that case, we can't have too many unfaithful types like me, now can we? What's her name? Is she pretty?'

'Very,' Harry said, thinking of Lucy. 'But there's no way I'm telling you her name.'

'Oho, frightened I'd steal her away,' Barney

guffawed. 'You're probably right. I'm known as a bit of a ladies' man.'

Harry smiled. He liked Barney's gung-ho attitude, but there was no way he was ever going to let him anywhere near Lucy, if he could help it.

'*Now we'll get at 'em* . . .' he wrote, but this time, only to Lucy.

> *This is where all the action is. We're only about twenty minutes from the south coast and a mate of mine has a little sports car, so if we get a few hours off, that's where we go. The airfield has recently been enlarged and a lot of the villagers have left and we are billeted in their houses. Seems so unfair but there you are. That's war, I suppose . . .*

'*Do you think you'll get a long enough leave soon to get home?*' she wrote back, but his reply was: '*Doesn't look like it. Things'll soon hot up down here . . .*'

'Harry doesn't say where he is or what he's doing now. When he was training, his letters were so newsy and interesting,' Amy said, standing in the middle of the kitchen with her son's most recent letter in her hand.

Josh put his arm around her. 'My darling, of course he can't tell us anything now. If he did, he'd be in trouble and you wouldn't receive his letter at all.'

Amy sighed heavily. 'It's just – it's just that I'd like to know where he is. I do hope he's not down south involved in this "battle for the skies", as the papers keep calling it.'

The evacuation of over 380,000 soldiers from the beaches of Dunkirk had shocked the nation and now they knew, as Mr Churchill had told them, their hopes for salvation lay in the hands of young men like Harry.

Josh sighed and let his arm slip from her shoulders. He wished he could reassure her, but he was not going to lie. 'He trained to be a pilot – a fighter pilot. You know that, so it's quite possible that that is exactly where he is.'

Amy gave a little sob and covered her mouth with her hand. Josh enfolded her in his embrace once more and, though she did not actually shed tears, he could feel her trembling against his chest.

'Come, it's time we went to work. There are hungry patients to feed.'

Amy nodded and drew back from him. 'I'm sorry. I'm being silly. There are countless parents all over the country in exactly the same position as us. I'm being selfish.' Bravely, she smiled up at him. 'Come on, then. Let's get those lads fed. At least we're doing our bit, aren't we?'

As they walked hand in hand along the road towards Riversdale, Josh said, 'And I'll tell you who else is certainly doing her bit. Lucy.'

Amy was thoughtful for a moment before murmuring, 'I know Nurse Adams is in charge, but it's Lucy who organizes everything. I've seen her. Do you think there's anything between her and Harry? She says she gets letters regularly from him.'

Josh wrinkled his brow. 'I don't know, love, but it'd be nice, wouldn't it? She's a lovely girl.'

Harry was flying high above the clouds in his Hurricane. The sun was glinting on the wings and he could just have been out for a joy ride, but he kept his attention focussed, glancing at the skies above and below and all around him. And then they were on him. Two Messerschmitts were bearing down on him out of the sun. The formation scattered and Harry banked to his left, but one of the enemy planes was on his tail. He twisted and dived, trying to shake his attacker off and then he saw another Hurricane on the tail of the German aircraft and the enemy gave up on Harry now as he concentrated on keeping out of trouble himself. Harry turned and followed the fight until he saw a burst of flame and the wing of the Messerschmitt blew off. The plane tumbled out of the sky, spiralling down and down until it was lost from Harry's sight.

The Hurricane pilot who had come to his aid was now in trouble himself and it was Harry's turn to try to help him. The rattle of gunfire left his guns and hit the enemy's aircraft. It wheeled away and flew off. The dogfight went on until the remaining enemy aircraft withdrew to fly back across the Channel.

Landing back at the aerodrome, Harry climbed out of his aircraft and found that his legs were shaking. Barney was running across the airfield towards him. 'You all right, old boy? I got the bastard who was trying to down you and then you saved my bacon. I reckon that's a kill for you. Is it your first? I say, Harry, you look a bit green. Here, let's get to debriefing and then we'll go into the village for a pint. We're not on ops tomorrow, so tonight we can get well and truly plastered. Come on, stick with Uncle Barney. He'll look after you.'

This was the pattern for the next few weeks, though sometimes there was no trip to the local pub because they were flying every day. Harry was only too glad to throw himself on his bed and sleep and sleep.

But despite the tiredness and the danger, Harry still loved flying. He couldn't wait for the order to scramble as they waited near the dispersal hut, dressed ready in their flying gear. It only took a moment when the bell clanged to run across the grass and climb into his aircraft. Up above the clouds, he felt free, without a care in the world – until he saw an enemy aircraft, which he was obliged to attack. Harry was not, by nature, a violent young man. He didn't really relish this war as some did – like Barney did, if truth be told – but he had a strong sense of duty and patriotism. If they didn't win this battle of the air, then an invasion of his beloved England was almost a certainty. But if they won and he survived – and such was the confidence of youth that it never really entered his mind that he would not – he planned to stay in the RAF. Compared to this, flying in peacetime would be magical.

Often when the order came, within minutes of being in the air he was involved in a dogfight over the Channel. Wheeling and diving, turning and twisting out of the way of the enemy's guns and then fortune would turn and it was he who was the aggressor. And then, as fuel began to run low, they would land back at base, almost fall out of their aircraft and stagger towards the truck taking them to debriefing, their faces ashen, their eyes wide with fatigue and hardly daring look around them to count how many had made it back. Every time they went out, it seemed as if at least one or two did not return. On the rare occasion that everyone got back, it was cause for a celebration in the mess that night.

Letters arrived from home regularly, from his parents, from Emily and from Lucy. All of Harry's letters had been opened and resealed and at first he thought this was the normal procedure until he noticed one day that Barney had not had his envelope opened.

'Hey, why do mine get opened?' Harry asked him.

Barney looked up. 'Your letters, you mean? I think they open a few at random, just to check up on what's being written to us. I've had a couple opened before now.'

'But *all* mine have been opened. Every one of them. Look.'

He held out the envelope, which he had yet to open himself, but it was obvious that someone had already read his letter and crudely resealed it.

Barney shrugged. 'You're unlucky, mate, that's all I can say. Why don't you ask Hartley about it? All the mail comes through his office.'

Harry gazed at his letter, thinking. 'I don't reckon that bloke likes me for some reason. I can't think why. Still, not to worry. Next time I get leave, I'll tell them all to mind what they're writing.'

'Don't forget they'll also read outgoing mail, probably even more thoroughly than that coming in.'

'Mm, that's a point, Barney. Thanks.'

Forty-Eight

The Battle of Britain, as it became called, raged through the summer and autumn of 1940, but by October, things were a little calmer, though for Harry there had been little let up. There had been no leave for weeks so at the end of October he applied for a pass.

'I'm sorry, I can't grant you leave just now,' Hartley told him.

Harry opened his mouth to argue; Barney and several of the other aircrew had recently had leave.

'Sir!' he said tightly, saluted and marched from the office.

'That man seems to have it in for me,' he moaned to Barney. 'I wonder if he's behind me not getting any letters at all now. I haven't had one from anyone for three weeks.'

'You're getting paranoid, old boy. Why don't you wait till he's on leave himself and then ask the CO,' Barney advised.

'Does Hartley ever go on leave?'

'Oh yes, he disappears off up to the Smoke every few weeks. Haven't you noticed?'

Harry shook his head, but now he watched and waited for Flight Lieutenant Hartley to take a day or two off. He applied for and was granted seventy-two hours.

'Harry!' Amy squealed with joy as her son, handsome in his blue uniform, walked in through the back door.

'Hello, Mam.' He picked her up and swung her round.

'Why didn't you let us know you were coming?'

'Didn't want to disappoint you in case all leave was cancelled at the last minute. It does happen sometimes. Where's Dad?'

'At Riversdale, of course. And your Granddad Bob is there too. He helps in the garden.'

'And the youngsters?'

Amy pulled a face. 'Not so young any more. This war's made them grow up so fast. Too fast for my liking. Sarah's already talking about joining one of the women's forces, though your dad's not too keen. He's trying to persuade her to become a nurse like Lucy. She idolizes Lucy and is up at Riversdale helping out whenever she can.'

With deliberate casualness, Harry asked, 'How is Lucy, by the way?'

Amy glanced at him archly. 'As pretty as ever. Why don't you go up and see her?'

Harry laughed. 'There's no getting anything past you, is there, Mam?'

'Not much, no.'

'What about the boys?'

'They're good pals. They're both getting on well at school, though we don't like them only getting half-time education just now. It's hard to make them do any work at home, though your granddads both try.'

'They'll be fine.'

'I just hope this war's over before they're old enough to be called up.'

Harry grinned. 'I'm doing my best, Mam.'

'So, Miss Lucy Henderson, do they ever let you have any time off, then?'

Lucy's eyes sparkled with mischief. 'Since it's me who writes the duty roster, it's my own fault if I don't have time off. Nurse Adams usually covers for me when I have leave. And we've a couple of younger nurses billeted with Mrs Partridge.'

'And when have you next allowed yourself an evening off?'

'Tomorrow, actually.'

'Right, I'll book a table at the Rutland Arms in Bakewell . . .'

'Would you mind if we just went down to the Devonshire Arms at the end of the road?'

'Mrs Bayes's rivals,' Harry laughed.

Lucy joined in his laughter. 'Hardly, just now.'

'But why do you want to go somewhere so close? It'll not feel like an evening out.'

'Oh it will, but . . .' She hesitated and added, 'Don't laugh at me, Harry, but I just can't bear to be very far away from Riversdale.'

'I understand, Lucy,' he said solemnly, 'and I admire your dedication. I'll book at the Devonshire Arms. I'll walk up for you about seven. Is that all right?'

'Perfect. I'm off duty at six.'

He chuckled, the laughter lines round his eyes crinkling. 'Are you sure you'll really be "off duty"?'

She pulled an apologetic face, but knew he understood.

They had a lovely meal, tucked away in a corner, and no one arrived in a fluster to ask for Lucy.

As it grew late, they walked along Church Street towards Sheep Wash Bridge and leaned on the parapet to look down into the dark water.

'Do you remember when you first brought me here?'

'I do. It was after Lizzie's and Billy's wedding, but I didn't think *you* would. I thought you'd think I was just a little boy.'

She turned to look at him through the gloom. 'I've never thought that about you, Harry. I know you're a bit younger than me, but you've always seemed the same age. That's how I've always thought of you, anyway.'

The thought warmed him and, greatly daring, he put his arm about her waist. Joy flooded through him when she did not protest or shrug it off.

'How are things down south? You can tell me, you know. I'm good at keeping secrets.'

Solemnly, he said, 'Yes, I expect you are. It's – tiring. Very tiring, but exhilarating at the same time.'

'We get a lot of pilots – fighter and bomber – here to recuperate.' She forbore to tell him that many of them woke up screaming in the night after dreadful nightmares and he didn't tell her that he had to shut out the fact that he was hunting down aircraft with another human being inside whom he was intent on destroying. It was a case of kill or be killed and he must never forget that. He had a job to do. He had to help win freedom from tyranny for his family, for his country, but, perhaps most of all, for this lovely girl by his side.

'What's going to happen to us all, Harry?'

'I wish I knew,' he said and then added swiftly, 'though perhaps I don't. I think it's better we don't know.'

They stood quietly side by side until with a little sigh, Lucy said, 'I'll have to go in.'

'Who's going to tell you off for being late in?'

'No one, but I must set a good example. Sorry, Harry.' To his delight, she sounded regretful.

As they walked up the short driveway and round to the rear of the building, Harry said, 'I'll be leaving in the morning. Keep writing to me, Lucy. Please? I haven't been getting any letters recently. I think they must be getting lost.'

'Really? That's strange. I've been writing every two weeks,' she said at once. 'But I haven't had many from you either. I expect you're right. It must be very difficult just now for the postal service. Some letters are bound to go astray.'

'I'm sure you're right.' He squeezed her hand and kissed her chastely on the cheek. He was still grinning as he walked home. He felt he could win the war single-handedly if it meant Lucy would be waiting for him at the end of it all.

What a girl! he was thinking. *What a courageous, dedicated, wonderful girl!*

Forty-Nine

When Harry returned to duty, it was to find that his squadron had been equipped with Spitfires. The first time Harry flew one, he knew he had 'come home'. The aircraft was much more manoeuvrable than the Hurricane.

'She's a beaut,' Barney enthused, after they'd all had a practice flight. 'Now we'll get 'em. Good leave, old boy?'

'The best.' Harry grinned.

'Oho, do I hear wedding bells?'

'Hey, steady on. Early days yet. Now, are we down the pub or . . . ?'

Barney was shaking his head. 'Not tonight, nor probably for a few nights. Whilst you've been gallivanting, things have been hotting up down here. I reckon it's a good job you got your spot of leave in when you did, because all leave's been cancelled for the next week or so anyway.'

'Trip, you'll never guess what.'

Trip smiled indulgently at his excited wife. Her eyes were shining and she was smiling broadly.

'You've got some special plans for Christmas?'

She shook her head, so he put his arm around her. 'Then tell me.'

'You know that line of cutlery I designed, targeting the authorities? I've won a contract to supply the NAAFI with cutlery, so my girls will be fully employed for the duration.'

'That's wonderful. What a lovely Christmas present for them all when you tell them.'

He was silent for a moment, before Emily prompted gently, 'I can see you're pleased for me, but there's something bothering you, I know.'

Trip sighed. 'I'm just concerned that my munitions factory might be enticing women away from you. The pay is much better than you can afford to pay them. And I've also got a contract to make parachute buckles. I'm setting Steve on to organize that in a separate workshop.'

To his surprise, Emily was smiling. 'Don't worry about my buffer girls. I still have Nell and those young girls she trained up before the war – the ones straight from school – are still too young to work in your munitions factory, aren't they?'

'Probably, yes.'

'A few of them might leave, but I'll be better placed to pay them more now I've got this new contract. I shall put them all on piece work as soon as they're good enough and it'll be up to them and I'll be able to keep them as long as they want to stay.'

But Trip still seemed hesitant. 'There's something else.'

'Go on.'

'Steve told me that Lizzie's been seen out most

nights at The Marples Hotel and – er – she seems to be seeing rather a lot of one particular airman.'

'How long's this been going on?'

'Ever since just after Billy went.'

Emily pursed her mouth. 'Does Nell know?'

'I don't know. Steve said he hadn't told her because he was afraid there might be an almighty row.'

'I guarantee it,' Emily said firmly. 'But not between Nell and Lizzie.'

'Oh now, Emily, do you think you should interfere?'

'Lizzie's my friend and my employee. If she's making a fool of herself and risking her marriage, then, yes, I should interfere. But I will,' she added, making a slight concession, 'talk it over with Nell first.'

The following morning, Emily arrived at work earlier than usual. Since Trip now needed the whole of his factory space, Emily now had only the three workshops, the two in Rockingham Street and the one in Broad Lane. Her workshop in Creswick Street and those of the little mesters there had been incorporated into Trippets' munitions factory.

'Nell, I need a word in the office.' Nell was in the main workshop today as they had a big order to complete.

'T'lasses'll be all right on their own for a day or two,' she'd told Emily, referring to the trainees under her supervision. 'They're all coming on nicely.'

Nell, who was just about to don her buff brat and start up her machine, raised her eyebrows.

'Right you are. Be with you in a moment. Maisie –' Nell addressed the errand lass who had been working for them for two weeks. Winifred had now learned enough to start work as a proper buffer girl and so another errand lass had been set on. Straight out of school, she was mesmerized by the work and still needed instruction and guidance. 'Get the fire lit and make us some tea. And mind you have our dinner hot by midday. That's when the girls like to eat. And then, this afternoon, I'll show you how to cut out brown paper aprons. Oh, and by the way, I'll want some shopping doing this afternoon. I've to work late tonight and won't have time . . .'

Then she stepped into the office.

'Just shut the door for a minute, will you?'

'This is sounding ominous. Am I on the carpet, Emily?'

Emily smiled thinly. 'Not you, no, but Lizzie might well be. I've heard that she's been going to the pub most nights and keeping company with an airman.'

Nell was shocked. 'Oh 'eck.'

'You hadn't heard anything?'

Nell shook her head and Emily knew she'd been right to keep Steve's name out of the conversation. Nell would likely give him a hard time if she learned that he hadn't told her first. Luckily, she didn't seem interested in how Emily had found out, only about how they could put a stop to it.

'Does her mam know?'

'She must know she goes out. Lizzie's still living with her.'

'So what are we going to do?'

'Catch her at it, that's what. Are you up for coming with me?'

'Of course. Poor old Billy. I hope he doesn't find out. A nicer bloke you couldn't wish to meet. The little tyke, her. He doesn't deserve that. I'm with you all the way, Emily. We'll put a stop to this. We'll go tonight. I'll not work late like I'd planned and I'll call for you about a quarter to seven.'

That evening, when normally she would have been working late or catching up on her household chores, Nell arrived at Emily's home all dressed up for a night on the town.

Trip opened the door. 'Hello, Nell. My, you look smart.' Used to seeing the young woman in her working – and it had to be said – dirty clothes, Trip was always surprised by the transformation on the few occasions he had seen Nell in her finery. 'Where are you two off to, then?'

'We have a job to do, Trip,' Nell said, stepping over the threshold. 'Is Emily ready?'

'She's upstairs. She shouldn't be long.'

He waited, the unspoken question hanging in the air, but Nell made no further comment.

Trip laughed, 'All I can say is he must be a very important customer for you both to be going to see him dressed to kill and in the evening, too.'

Still, Nell said nothing. She just smiled weakly and glanced impatiently towards the staircase as if willing Emily to appear. Then they heard the bedroom door close and her footsteps on the stairs. Trip was sure he heard Nell breathe a sigh of relief.

'Right, we're off, then, Trip. Don't wait up.'

'Oho, like that, is it?' he teased. 'Maybe I should come with you.'

Alarm crossed both their faces and Trip laughed. He wasn't worried – only perhaps about their safety in the blackout – as long as they stayed together. Nell was well known in the city, as was her connection to Steve Henderson. Although he had changed his way of life, the memories of what he could do if crossed were still sharp. His bright blue eyes and his cheeky grin could change to thunder in a trice. Only Mick Dugdale had ever been foolish enough to endanger Nell and incur Steve's wrath. And though Trip was curious to know exactly what it was they were going to do, he had a shrewd suspicion that it had to do with what he had told Emily about Lizzie.

The two women set off, arm in arm.

'Do you know where she's going?'

'The Marples Hotel.'

'Blimey! She doesn't do things by halves, does she?'

The hotel was one of the most popular venues in the city for entertainment. It was seven storeys high and boasted a concert hall as well as a number of bars.

'I've heard that Joe Davis is due to give an exhibition billiards match there tonight,' Nell said. 'Steve was going, but he's decided not to. I'm surprised. He enjoys his billiards.'

Emily said nothing; she knew why Steve had changed his mind. He knew that his wife and Emily would be going there tonight and didn't want to interfere with their mission.

'I'm surprised that Lizzie goes there. It's very popular with folks calling in after they've been to the cinema, to say nothing of its own entertainments. There are bound to be people see her there who know her. *And* who know Billy too.'

As they walked towards Fitzalan Square, the sirens started to wail.

'Ought we to find a shelter?'

'Nah, it'll only be a false alarm. Besides, if we get to The Marples, it's got the safest underground cellars I know.'

They entered one of the hotel's bars; it was crowded with soldiers and airmen grabbing a few hours' leave. Emily was reminded poignantly of Harry, but she pushed the thoughts away and concentrated on finding Lizzie.

Nell touched her arm. 'There she is. Over there, in the corner. Just look at her, Emily, laughing and talking and pawing that young pilot. She's nearly old enough to be his mother.'

'That's half the trouble, I reckon. If only she'd had children . . . Come on.'

'Let's get a drink first. I think we're going to need one.'

When they'd been served after quite a wait, they weaved their way through the throng and stood in front of the small round table. Lizzie looked up and a variety of expressions flitted across her face. Surprise, anger and then a kind of sheepishness. But then defiance came to the surface as Emily, with her hands on her hips, asked, 'Lizzie, what d'you think you're playing at?'

Lizzie lifted her chin, but she avoided meeting Emily's eyes; eyes that flashed with anger and disapproval. 'What's it look like I'm doing? Having a bit of fun, that's all. Where's the harm in that?'

Emily leaned towards her. 'Plenty, when you've a husband away fighting for his country.'

'Eh? What was that?' The young pilot at her side spoke up, his speech a little slurred. 'A husband, you say.' He turned reproachful eyes on Lizzie. 'You didn't say you was married.' He stood up suddenly, knocking the table and spilling Lizzie's drink. He turned towards Emily, 'Thanks for that. I'm not getting involved with anyone who's married. I thought she was fair game. She's a bit long in the tooth, but she's a looker all right.'

As he lurched away, Emily and Nell sat down, one on either side of Lizzie.

'Thanks for nothing,' Lizzie muttered bitterly.

'Is he the one you've been seeing for some time?'

'Got your spies out on me, have you?' Lizzie snarled. 'What's it got to do with you anyway?'

'Nothing. Absolutely nothing. But what about Billy?'

'He's not here.'

'Precisely. He's away fighting and could be killed at any minute.'

'No, he won't be. He's still in this country. And don't tell me he could be sent abroad, because where would they send him? We got pushed out of France at Dunkirk, didn't we? It's been up to the RAF boys since then. Lads like him –' she nodded towards the young man she'd been sitting with – 'they're the ones in danger. They're the ones who could be killed any minute. Like your Harry. Wouldn't you like some nice girl to sit with him and laugh and joke for a few hours, if he's going to get killed tomorrow?'

Emily winced as Lizzie's voice grew louder. One or two drinkers glanced round at her, but she was beyond caring. 'And who d'you think you are to tell me what I can and can't do? The high an' mighty Missus Trippet with her business empire. A business that should have been mine. We started it together, the three of us, but you stole it away from me. You wanted it for yourself . . .'

'Eh, hang on a minute, Lizzie,' Nell butted in. 'That's not fair and you know it. It was your brother that was to blame for all that. If he'd let well alone and let us manage things for ourselves, it might have been different, but he had to come the big I am and threaten poor Mr Hawke into renting us his workshop and getting machinery. I shouldn't wonder if he didn't threaten others into putting work our way.'

'Well, it was *your* brother that was the cause of all the trouble.' Lizzie prodded her finger into Emily's shoulder. 'Don't *you* forget *that*.' She was shouting now, so that the whole of the crowded bar could hear her. 'I was never in love with Billy. It was Josh I loved.'

Emily turned white, shocked beyond belief that Lizzie could still believe herself in love with Josh. Crossly, she said, 'Don't start all that nonsense again, Lizzie. It was infatuation, pure and simple.'

'No, it wasn't.' Lizzie thumped the table and the glasses rattled. 'I truly loved him, Emily, but don't worry, your precious brother's quite safe.' Tears sprang to her eyes. 'He never wanted me – just that whey-faced Amy and her brood of brats.' She laughed hysterically. 'See, I couldn't even get pregnant with Billy, could I?'

'I think I'll go and find you a nice strong cup of coffee,' Emily said. 'We'll never get you home like this.'

'You can get me another drink, though, Emily,' Nell asked. 'I need it.'

They sat beside Lizzie whilst she drank the coffee, pulling a face at its taste. 'This isn't coffee. Ugh!'

'There is a war on, you know,' Emily said, trying to lighten the tension between them but, at that moment, there were thunderous crashes in the square and people were rushing into the hotel from the street.

'Incendiaries are dropping in t'Square. There're fires everywhere.'

'Come on, we're getting out of here,' Nell said, standing up and grasping Lizzie's arm roughly. 'And you're coming with us, m'girl.'

'No, I'm not. I'm staying here. They've got a good cellar here. It's the safest place to be.'

'I said, we're going. Emily, get her other arm.'

They dragged Lizzie towards the door into the street.

'Let me go, let me go,' she cried, struggling and kicking out at Nell, but the two women were stronger than she was. Briefly, Emily was aware of the young RAF pilot watching them go. She saw him put down his drink and start to push his way through the crowd to follow them.

But once they were in the street, people were still running towards the hotel and Emily lost sight of him. The siren still wailed as they half dragged, half carried Lizzie between them. Suddenly, as they heard the noise of more aircraft overhead, she stopped fighting them and the three of them ran down the street.

'Where shall we go?' Nell panted. 'It's too far to get home.'

'Just keep running . . .'

Fifty

As they ran, all Emily could think was, 'Thank goodness we sent the children away.'

'We're nearer the workshops than our homes,' Nell
shouted. 'Let's go there.' Without even waiting for
an answer from the other two, she veered off to her
left. 'Come on.'

Lizzie seemed to have given up trying to argue as
she and Emily ran after Nell.

'Have you – got a key?' Emily gasped.

'Always carry it,' Nell said shortly. 'You never
know –' she turned the corner into Rockingham Street
and ran on ahead – 'when you might need it,' she
finished as the other two caught up with her. She
opened the door, but for a few seconds, just before
they entered, Emily turned back to look at what they
had left behind. 'My God! It looks as if the whole
city's on fire.'

The sky was alight with the flames leaping into
the air. And overhead, the shadows of bombers still
lurked.

'Ne'er mind sight-seeing, Emily. Get inside.' Nell
pushed her roughly through the door. 'Quick – under
the stairs.'

Afraid to put on any kind of light, they felt their

way across the darkened workshop. As soon as war had become a certainty, Trip had insisted that Emily have a reinforced air-raid shelter constructed under the staircase at all three workshops. It was something he'd done at his factory and he wanted to be sure the girls were as safe as they could be.

'It'll be a squeeze for all the workforce to get in there, but it'll be better than nothing,' Trip had said and now Emily had cause to be thankful for her husband's foresight. Once inside with the door shut, Emily took the small torch from her pocket. 'I brought this in case we were late getting home.'

Lizzie sat down, huddled against the wall, her knees drawn up, her head buried against them. Nell was still standing, her hands pressed against her sides as she tried to regain her breath. She appeared to be listening intently.

'I think they're going. I can't hear the planes now.'

'You won't in here, will you?' Lizzie said morosely.

'Sit down, Nell. Let's get as comfortable as we can. I think there's a box of emergency rations somewhere. I asked Maisie to keep it stocked up and to check it every day.' She shone her torch around until she saw a hamper basket tucked away in one corner. 'Ah, here we are. I don't know about you two, but I'm famished. Hold the torch, Nell, will you?'

Whilst Nell shone the torch into the basket, Emily pulled out various packages of biscuits and bottles of water.

'Here, Lizzie, have something to eat.'

'I don't want anything from you, Emily Trippet, not ever again.'

Emily sighed. 'Suit yourself, then.'

'Oh, I will, don't you worry about that. I'm giving you my notice right now. I don't want to work for the wealthy Mrs Trippet any more, thank you very much. And I expect I'll have to leave town now, because by tomorrow everyone will know about me, won't they?'

'Not from us, they won't, but I can't guarantee what the folks in The Marples might say. There were plenty of people overheard you in the bar, Lizzie, and I suspect it's likely that one or two of them know Billy.' There was silence between them until Emily added softly, 'So, what about Billy and that RAF lad too? You're not being fair to either of them.'

'Huh! He's gone now, hasn't he? You've seen to that.'

Emily decided not to say that she thought she'd seen the young airman trying to follow them. Better that Lizzie thought he'd deserted her. 'Maybe – maybe not,' she said carefully. 'I hope he has, for his sake as well as yours.'

'Thanks – for nothing.'

'What about Billy?' Nell asked bluntly. 'I hope you're not going to do anything stupid like writing him a "Dear John" letter.'

There was silence for some time before Lizzie said huskily, 'No, I wouldn't do that. Besides, I'm not planning on leaving Billy. I'm – I *was* – just having a bit of fun. It's so awful here now, what with the rationing, the blackout and the constant fear of being bombed. Look at us now. Huddled together in a dark, damp place like rats in a trap, just waiting to be killed. I'm not standing for any more of it. Tomorrow, I'm off. I'll volunteer for war work. The land army or something. All I know is, I'm not staying here. There's nothing to keep me here. Though what I'm going to tell Jane, I don't know.'

'Jane? What's she got to do with it?'

'We've been going out together. See, I'm not so wicked as you're trying to make out. We look after each other.'

'Was she with you tonight?' Emily asked in alarm. 'Why on earth didn't you say? Oh my, we haven't left her there, have we?'

'No, her dad wouldn't let her come out tonight.'

'So you were out on your own,' Nell persisted and gave a sniff of disapproval. 'And besides, I don't think Jane can be held up as an example of virtue, do you?'

In the dim light from the torch, Lizzie glared at her mutinously for a moment, and then dropped her gaze.

'What about your mother?' Emily said. 'You wouldn't leave her on her own, would you?'

'She can do what she likes.'

'You really don't care about anyone else but yourself, do you, Lizzie?' Nell said softly. 'You're more like that brother of yours than you realize.'

'Don't you dare compare me with him. I've never been involved in his scams.'

'Mm,' was all Nell said, but there was no mistaking the note of doubt in her tone. There was a pause and then she added, 'Did you mean it about always being in love with Josh and not Billy?'

'Eh?' Lizzie was startled. 'What are you talking about?'

'Back there, in the bar, that's what you said and loud enough for everyone there to hear.'

'I didn't say anything of the sort,' she denied Nell's accusation, but then uncertainty crept into her voice. 'Did I?'

''Fraid so, Lizzie, but,' Emily added kindly, 'I expect it was the drink talking.'

'They always say,' Nell murmured, 'that you get the truth from a drunk.'

They sat there for hours.

'We ought to try to get home,' Emily fretted. 'Our families will be worried sick.'

'We're not going until the All Clear sounds. They'll know we'd've had the sense to get into a shelter.'

'We should have gone into the cellars at the Marples,' Lizzie said. 'They're huge.'

The All Clear didn't sound until four in the morning, by which time the three women were cramped and stiff with cold. They left the workshop and stepped out into the street. Their quickest route home was not past Fitzalan Square, but they saw plenty of bomb damage on their way. Houses reduced to a pile of rubble, some half gone, with the interiors showing. They could see people's possessions strewn in the roadways and folks climbing over what remained of their homes, trying to find their precious belongings.

Firemen were still damping down and the homeless were wandering about with dazed expressions on their white faces. And the grim task of searching the ruins for bodies had already begun.

The three of them said nothing though they were each thinking the same thing; just let our families be safe.

They parted where they took different directions to get home. Trip was standing in the doorway and as he heard her footsteps, he came out into the street and held his arms wide. 'Thank God, you're all right,' he said holding her tight, not caring if anyone saw them. 'I'm never letting you out of my sight again. Where have you been?'

For a moment Emily clung to him, grateful to be home and even more thankful that Trip was unharmed too. Even the house was untouched.

'Oh Trip, we've seen some terrible sights. Let's get inside and I'll tell you.'

'Steve came round about one o'clock this morning. He'd not been to bed and neither have I,' he told her as they went inside and closed the door. 'He wasn't sure where Nell was going except that she was coming round here.'

'He hasn't gone looking for her, has he?'

Trip shook his head. 'No, we decided – since we had no idea where you'd gone – it'd be foolish to try to roam the streets in an air raid. All we could do was pray that you'd found a shelter.'

'We were in The Marples and everyone was going down to the cellar there. It's reckoned to be one of the safest places to be, but we decided to make a dash for it before the bombing started in earnest, but then it got a bit hairy so we went to the workshop.'

She smiled up at him. 'Thanks to you, we were in the shelter under the stairs.' There was a pause as she stared at Trip. He had turned white and his hands were shaking. 'What? What is it, Trip?'

Haltingly, he said, 'When Steve came round he told me that he – he'd heard that The Marples had taken a direct hit.' Once more he held her close. 'I could have lost you. We could have lost both of you.'

'The three of us,' Emily murmured against his chest. 'Lizzie was with us too.'

No more was said about Lizzie. The dreadful shock that awaited them when more news came through about the night's tragedies left them stunned and appalled. The loss of life had been horrific. All but seven people in the hotel had been killed and throughout the city there had been more deaths. A lot of the city centre had been destroyed. 'Why,' folk asked, 'did they go for the city centre?'

But there were quiet acts of unsung heroism too. 'Did you hear about the brave clippie girl whose tram was hit on High Street?' Trip said. 'She got all her passengers to safety before she even thought of herself.'

But Emily's mind was, as always, on the welfare of those who had been left homeless. 'We must do whatever we can to help. I'll talk to Mrs Dugdale. She'll have contacts in the WVS.'

Trip and Emily were fortunate; none of their workplaces were damaged and work could proceed more or less normally, though the transport in the city was at a standstill.

Lizzie did not arrive at work the day after the air

raid, but the following morning, the Saturday, when she knew they'd be working to catch up on the backlog, she appeared at the workshop in Rockingham Street.

Her face was mutinous. 'I meant it – I'm going. I'm not having the pair of you trying to run my life. Me mam's bad enough. Besides, there're more useful things I can be doing to help the war effort than polishing knives and forks.'

'Oh aye,' Nell said sarcastically, 'being a comforter for the troops.'

Lizzie raised her right hand as if to slap Nell across the side of her face, but Nell was quicker than she was. She grabbed her wrist mid-air. 'Don't you dare, Lizzie Nicholson. And just remember what your name is now. Nicholson. You're married to a decent guy who volunteered to fight for his country when he needn't have done. You'd do well to remember that.'

'What are you going to do, Lizzie?' Emily hated to see her band of workers being broken up. She thought they'd all been a happy team.

'What's it to you?'

'I – I just want to know you're going to be all right.'

'I'm going to work in munitions.'

'Then maybe Trip could—'

'I don't want any help from any of the Trippet family, thank you very much. And besides, I've got a job.' Her glance went to Jane standing meekly at the back of the room. 'I s'pect you haven't told them.'

Jane flushed and hung her head.

'Me and Jane went together yesterday. The air raid

did a lot of damage in the city, but surprisingly, a lot of the factories weren't touched. Me and Jane are going to be lady welders. The pay's better, for starters.'

Emily turned questioning eyes towards Jane.

'I'm sorry, missus. I should have told you. Me dad never stops going on at me at home about – well, you can guess, can't you? I can't stand it any longer. I'm leaving home and going into lodgings with Lizzie.'

'You're going to live with Mrs Dugdale and Lizzie?'

Jane shook her head. 'No, me and Lizzie are finding lodgings together on the other side of town, nearer where we'll be working.'

Nell gave an unladylike snort of derision. 'Aye, so you're well away from anyone who might know you.' She turned away in disgust. 'You'd better both get on with it, then. But don't come running to me when you need help. Nor Emily. She's done more than enough to help the pair of you and this is how you repay her. Right, Flo, let's get on with our work. If we're two down, we'll be here all night.' She glanced briefly over her shoulder. 'Oh, and by the way, two of the girls I trained up, Emily, might like to come here. Beryl and Phyllis. I'll tell them to come and see you, shall I?'

'Er – oh – yes,' Emily said hesitantly. Her head was still reeling. 'Lizzie – please don't do this. If you want to work in munitions, then fine. I can under-stand that. But please don't leave home. Think about your mam. Maybe she would have Jane as a lodger.'

But Lizzie shook her head adamantly. 'No, we're going.'

*   *   *

That evening Bess came round to Emily's in tears. 'She's gone, Emily. She's packed her bags and gone.'

'Come in, Mrs Dugdale. I'll make us some tea.'

'Do you have any idea why she's done it? All she would say is that she's given you notice and that she's signed up for war work. Well, I don't mind her doing that, but there's plenty of other war work she can do here in the city. She doesn't need to go away.'

'I don't think she's left Sheffield, but her and Jane have both gone to train to be lady welders.'

'They don't need to leave home to do that.'

'Jane's not happy at home.'

'Then they could both stay with me. I wouldn't mind having a lodger.'

'I think they want to be nearer where they're going to work.' It sounded a lame excuse, even to her own ears.

Bess dried her tears and seemed to regain some composure as she asked, 'Emily, what's been going on and don't say "nothing", because I know there's summat. Have you had a falling out?'

Emily set two cups of tea on the table and sat down with a sigh. Avoiding a direct answer, she said, 'I think Lizzie's very unsettled. Maybe she feels she's not doing enough to help the war effort.'

'But she is. You've got a contract, haven't you, to supply cutlery? She's involved in that, isn't she?'

'Well, yes, but . . .' Bess was putting Emily in a very awkward position. She didn't want to tell tales on Lizzie. 'But maybe she feels it isn't enough when Billy's away fighting.'

Bess frowned. 'I reckon there's summat you're not

telling me, Emily Trippet, but I can guess. She's been going out almost every night for weeks now, dressed up to the nines. I warned her, but she wouldn't listen.'

Emily glanced down at her teacup and said nothing.

'Aye, I thought as much. Your face says it all.' She gave a wry laugh. 'Do you know, Emily, you're a very bad liar. All right, I'm not asking you to tell me what's been going on. I take it you tried to put a stop to it an' all. She did let one thing out, though. She said the three of you – you, her and Nell – were out together the night the air raid happened and that you were at The Marples. That frightened her, I can tell you. She said she'd wanted to go down to their cellar, but that you and Nell dragged her – dragged her, she said – out of there and tried to get home. Well, if that's what happened, then I've even more reason to be grateful to you than I had before, because you've saved her life, Emily.'

She heaved herself up and stood for a moment. 'Whatever's been going on, Emily, I just hope it's finished, that's all. I respect your loyalty and I won't ask you any more except this: is she staying with Billy?'

Emily looked up at her. 'She says so. That's all I can tell you.'

'Ah, well. So be it.'

Fifty-One

The following night, the enemy bombers returned again and this time their target was the East End of Sheffield. Several steelworks were hit, but the damage was miraculously not serious enough to affect production.

'We've been incredibly lucky, Emily,' Trip said. 'All our premises are unscathed. I can hardly believe it.'

On the Monday morning, Emily told the other women about Lizzie. 'She's left home without even giving her mother her new address. It seems she wants to cut herself off entirely from everyone.'

'She's up to no good, that one,' Nell remarked. 'And I expect Jane is no better. Anyway, Emily, have you seen those two lasses I told you about?'

'I have, Nell. I saw them early this morning before I came into work. They're starting next week.'

'Aren't you going to try them out on a wheel first?'

Emily laughed. 'No need, Nell. If you trained them, they'll be fine.'

The two girls fitted in well, but Emily missed Lizzie. They'd had their ups and downs, but their lives were intertwined, or so she'd thought.

Bess, living alone now, threw herself even more into her WVS work, but although her days were again fully occupied, she found it hard to live alone. She missed not being able to cook for someone else other than herself so she spent much of her spare time at Emily's home on the pretext of cleaning, cooking and washing for them for longer than was strictly necessary. The house gleamed, all their clothes were washed and ironed almost before they needed them and they had more than enough to eat with Bess's ingenious ways with the rationing.

'I still don't understand why Lizzie left home. I suppose I used to remark about her going out at night and she didn't like it. I can't get used to the fact that she's a grown woman, you see, and has the right to do whatever she likes.' Bess smiled wryly. 'Even if I don't approve. Now, I've lost them both, Emily. I know the boys are gone – and you and Nell must be missing them dreadfully – but at least you both know they're safe. I dread to think what might have happened last week if they'd been here.'

Sheffield slowly recovered from the two dreadful nights of bombing, but things would never be quite the same again.

'You can rebuild houses and shops and factories,' Emily said sadly to Trip, 'but you can't restore people's shattered lives. All those poor folk who lost loved ones. It's a miracle we haven't lost someone close to us.'

The following weekend Billy came home on compassionate leave. He had not been posted abroad and so was able to request a forty-eight-hour pass.

'They let me come because of last week's bombing,'

he told Bess, as he dropped his kitbag on the floor in the narrow hallway. 'Where's Lizzie? Still at work? I'll go and meet her. Give her a nice surprise.'

'Oh Billy, lad. I'm afraid it's you who's in for the surprise and it's not a very nice one at that.'

'You – you don't mean she was injured in the bombing or . . . ? Oh no, don't tell me . . .'

'No, no, nothing like that. As far as I know, she's fine.'

'What d'you mean – as far as you know?'

'Come and sit down. I'll mash tea.' Bess turned and led the way into the kitchen. Billy followed but said, 'I don't want to sit down. I want to see Lizzie. Where is she?'

'That's just it, Billy. I don't know.'

'D'you mean she's missing? Since the bombing?'

'No – no. She *was* out the first night . . .' She tempered it by adding, 'With Nell and Emily, but they got home safely.' Bess bit her lip. She was on the verge of telling lies. Already she was deliberately misleading him.

They were standing in the kitchen and Billy glanced at the mantelpiece. He pointed with a finger that shook slightly towards a letter tucked behind the clock. 'Is that my last letter to her?'

Bess nodded. 'She's left home, Billy, and that arrived after she'd gone.'

Billy ran his hand over his short-cropped red hair. Flatly, he said, 'You mean she's gone off with someone else.'

Nervously, Bess plucked at the corner of her apron, but said stoutly, 'No, I don't mean that at all. She's gone to be a lady welder and wanted to live closer to the work. That's what Emily told me, anyway.'

'Emily? Emily told you this, not Lizzie herself?'

'Yes, I'm guessing it's somewhere the other side of town. She and Jane went together. But I don't know where they are.' Sadly, she added, 'Lizzie didn't even bother to leave me a note to say "goodbye".'

'When did she go?'

'Last Saturday.'

'Before the second raid?'

Bess nodded.

'So – you don't really know if – if she's all right?'

Bess stared at him, suddenly anxious. 'I'd've heard. Wouldn't I?'

Billy shrugged and then said, grimly, 'I'd better see Emily. I'll get it out of her.'

Bess caught hold of his arm. 'Don't be too hard on Emily. It's not her fault. In fact –' she paused and then the words came out in a rush – 'Emily and Nell might well have saved Lizzie's life.'

'How?'

'They were in The Marples that night and Lizzie wanted to go down into the cellars there, but the other two insisted on trying to get home. They didn't make it here, as it happened, but took shelter in the workshop where Trip had had a shelter built under the stairs.'

Now Billy turned white and sat down suddenly in a nearby chair. He'd heard all about the hotel.

'So, please, Billy, be careful what you say to Emily. I don't think she knows any more than I do about where Lizzie's gone.' Mentally, Bess crossed her fingers. She believed that Emily didn't know where Lizzie was now, but she did think that the young woman knew a little more than she was saying about *why* her daughter had left so suddenly.

'I'll have that cup of tea now, Ma-in-law, if I may, and then I'll go and find Emily.'

When Billy stepped through the door of the main workshop in Rockingham Street, Emily's heart sank. She guessed why he had come to find her. She greeted him with a bright smile that she hoped hid her anxiety. 'How lovely to see you, Billy. Are you well?'

'I'm fine, thanks, but disappointed not to find Lizzie still here. Where's she gone, Emily?'

He glanced around the workshop to see the other girls working at their machines and, above the noise, he could hear Nell singing. He wondered if she'd noticed him come in and was studiously avoiding looking at him.

'Come into the office,' Emily said. 'We can't talk out here. Would you like a cup of tea?'

'Why the hell does everyone keep offering me cups of tea when all I want to know is where my wife is?' He snatched his cap from his head and ran his hand over his hair. 'I'm sorry, Emily. I shouldn't snap at you, but I'm that worried.'

'I understand,' Emily murmured, knowing that the questioning would start now. She'd expected this to happen at some point and decided to get in first.

'We were out that night – the first night of the bombing – having a drink in The Marples. It's where a lot of folks go when they've been to the cinema.'

Without actually saying so, she was implying that that was where the three of them had been. 'When the sirens went, we decided to make a dash for it, but the planes came overhead quicker than we thought and we made a dash for here. We hid under the stairs. At Trip's suggestion at the start of the war, we had it reinforced and made into a kind of air-raid shelter. It was a blessing we did, because – well – I expect you know what happened to the hotel. It was dreadful.'

'That's what Ma-in-law said. That – that you probably saved Lizzie's life by leaving.'

Emily shrugged and murmured, 'It's the luck of the draw, isn't it?'

'So you don't know where she's gone either?'

Emily repeated exactly what Bess had told him.

'What about Nell? Does she know any more?'

'Sorry – no. None of us do.'

'And Jane went with her?'

'Yes. The pay is better in munitions, Billy. I couldn't blame them.'

He frowned. 'But it's so odd her not even letting her mother know where she is.'

'Working in munitions can be very secretive, Billy. At some places they're actually told not to tell their families anything about their work.'

He sighed heavily. 'I wish I'd more time, but I never thought when I requested a forty-eight that I'd have to scour the city looking for her. I must catch the early train tomorrow. I was lucky to be allowed to come at all. Mind you, now I almost wish I hadn't. I'm even more anxious.'

'Try not to worry, Billy. These are difficult times for all of us.'

He smiled thinly and said stiffly, 'I'm sorry I've bothered you. I'll be off.' He pulled on his cap and turned to leave.

'It's no bother, Billy. I'm sorry I can't tell you any more.'

He glanced back briefly and said over his shoulder, 'Can't – or won't?'

With that, he marched from her office and out of the workshop without looking back.

Emily watched him go with a heavy heart. In a surprising spurt of bad temper, Emily muttered, 'Damn you, Lizzie Nicholson. Damn and blast you.'

It was two months into the New Year before Lizzie came home to visit her mother. Bess had done a lot of thinking since her daughter had left home and she had promised herself that if and when Lizzie chose to visit, she would not 'go on at her'. So when she opened the door to her one Sunday afternoon, she managed to smile a welcome and not immediately bombard her with questions or recriminations.

'It's lovely to see you, luv. How are you? Come on, I'll make you some tea. And guess what, I've even made rabbit pie from a recipe Martha Ryan gave me. Would you like a bit? I still like to keep me hand in at a bit of baking, even though it's so hard to get the ingredients now. I do a lot of cooking for Emily and Trip now they're busier than ever.' She was chattering nervously, she knew it, but she was anxious to let Lizzie know from the start that she wasn't going to interrogate her. But there was one thing she couldn't avoid telling her. Better get it over with straight away.

'There are three letters behind the clock on the mantelpiece from Billy.'

She desperately wanted to ask all sorts of questions, especially, 'Have you written to your husband?' But Bess literally clamped her teeth on her tongue to stop herself. Instead, she busied herself making tea and warming the pie in the oven.

'Are you orreight, Mam?' Lizzie managed to say when at last Bess fell silent.

'I'm fine. I'm keeping very busy what with all I do for Emily and at the WVS. They're a nice bunch of women and, despite all the worry, we have a laugh. Can't do owt else, really, can you?' Again she had to bite back the natural questions – 'How are things with you?' 'Where are you living?' 'What's the work like?' 'Are you being fed properly?' – but she couldn't hold back on one thing.

'Billy came home a few weeks back. Soon after you'd gone. He'd got compassionate leave because of the bombing we'd had. He was very upset you weren't here and angry when I couldn't tell him anything. I'm not sure he believed me when I said I didn't know where you were. And he was even madder at Emily because she wouldn't say owt either.'

'That's a surprise,' Lizzie murmured softly. She reached for his letters from the mantelpiece and pushed them into her pocket, promising, 'I'll write to him and explain.'

'I wish you'd explain to me.' The words were out

of Bess's mouth before she could stop them. 'Sorry, luv. I vowed I wouldn't ask questions.'

At last Lizzie sighed and then said, 'Go on, Mam, ask whatever you like.'

Bess chuckled. 'You know me too well, Lizzie. That's the trouble.'

'We've found nice lodgings with an elderly lady who lost her husband in the last war and now her two sons are away in the forces, so she's glad of the company. She cooks lovely meals,' Lizzie grinned impishly, 'though not as good as yours, Mam.'

'Away with yer flannel, our Lizzie. Go on.'

'I can't tell you much about the work we're doing.' Lizzie was serious now. ''Cos we're not supposed to talk about it, either what we do or even where we are.'

'I understand that.'

'All I can tell you, Mam,' Lizzie laughed, 'is that it's just as mucky a job as buffing.'

They laughed together and talked a while longer until Lizzie said she had to go.

As she waved her off at the front door, Bess kissed her cheek and said, 'It's been lovely to see you. Come again, when you can.'

As Bess closed the door behind her, she realized that Lizzie had not asked one question about Emily or Nell.

The rift between the former friends went even deeper than Bess had known.

Fifty-Two

Sheffield was slowly getting back to normal, or as normal as it was going to be after the devastation wrought on the city. The weeks and months passed as folk everywhere struggled to cope with the hardships of wartime.

In May, they read of the dreadful night of intensive bombing on London.

'Poor folks,' Trip murmured, as they listened to the wireless. 'They've had nine months of the Blitz.'

The report said that the moonlit night had helped the enemy planes, but it must also have helped the British fighter pilots who'd shot down twenty-nine German bombers.

'I hope Harry wasn't one of them,' Emily murmured, her thoughts never far from her beloved nephew.

Trip would have liked to have been able to soothe her fears, but he couldn't. They had no idea where Harry actually was now; just that he was down south somewhere.

At the end of May, Trip was jubilant as he read of the *Bismarck* being sunk. 'That's hit their morale.' But at the end of June, he was mystified by the actions of the Fuhrer. 'Is he mad?'

'Of course he is. We've always said that. What's he done now?'

'Attacked Russia.'

'No! Really? But I thought they had a mutual non-aggression agreement?'

'They did – at the beginning of the war.'

'Will it take the heat off us? He can't fight on two fronts, can he?'

'There's no knowing what that megalomaniac believes he can do.'

Over the coming months, whilst Emily struggled with rationing and keeping her employees fully occupied, Trip followed the news even more avidly, bending close to the wireless set to listen to the bulletins.

'You know, America has said it won't get involved in our war and yet, besides providing us with much-needed aid, their troops have landed in Iceland to stop the Germans occupying it.'

'Mm. Trip, can we go to Ashford on Sunday and take Nell and Steve to see the boys and Lucy? Have you got enough petrol?'

'I think so. Yes, it would be nice to get away from it all even for a day.'

By September, the Nazis were attacking Leningrad and in Germany a law was passed forcing Jews to wear the yellow star of David.

'How dreadful for them,' Emily said, touched by their plight. 'Can you imagine that happening here?'

'I expect it will be enforced everywhere that Germany occupies.'

By October, Hitler was celebrating as he neared Moscow.

'You know the Russians have one great advantage on their side.'

'What's that, because I can't see anything that's going to stop him?'

'The Russian weather. That could be his downfall, like it was for Napoleon. You wait and see.'

'Put the wireless on, Trip, but please no more war news. Not tonight. Let's listen to ITMA. I like Tommy Handley.'

With a smile, Trip turned the dial and music and laughter filled the room.

Another Christmas loomed and still there was no more news from Lizzie. Emily invited Bess to join them for Christmas, and took her, Nell and Steve to Ashford to a local hotel. But it was a very subdued festive occasion this year. Each of them had their own worries, none more so than Amy and Josh, who hadn't heard from Harry in weeks.

'But we've got real hope now,' Trip said, trying to instil some cheer into the gathering. 'Now America's really with us.'

The surprise attack on Pearl Harbor at the beginning of December had brought America into the war and Trip was quick to realize the strength of Britain's most recent ally. 'They've helped us since the beginning, but now we'll really have their might with us.'

And George nodded. 'I really think we're going to win now.'

Just days into the New Year of 1942, Emily opened her front door to Bess's frantic knocking.

'She's really gone now. She's left Sheffield. She's written me a letter, but she still won't tell me where she's going. Says she's been told it's top secret and even her family mustn't know.'

Emily was shocked. 'Hasn't she even given you an address you can write to?'

'A post office in Wetherby. That's all.'

'Wetherby? Oh, right. I'll see what I can find out.'

Lizzie and Jane had gone to work at the Royal Ordnance Factory No. 8, a Filling Factory at Thorp Arch, near Wetherby in Yorkshire. Work on its construction had started in May 1940 on 642 acres of land near the River Wharfe. Materials and workers were brought by the LNER's lines to Harrogate and Leeds. A connecting line was built by the railway company in June 1940 to join up to the newly constructed sidings near the factory. Although it was still not quite complete, the site had been officially opened by King George VI the previous year and certain sections were already being used. The whole site would be completed very soon now. The work was extremely dangerous and there were all sorts of rules and regulations that had to be strictly adhered to for the safety of everyone on the huge site.

They'd been given the opportunity to work there, having proved themselves as hard workers and discreet too. Both girls had leapt at the chance.

'I don't care what the work is,' Lizzie had said. 'I just want to get out of the city – right away from everything – and this sounds like the answer.'

'Me too. Let's do it, Lizzie.'

They'd arrived on the train from Sheffield and reported to a hostel at Wetherby and the following morning they'd boarded the train that had brought them directly to the site.

'Oh my,' Lizzie had gasped as she and Jane stepped off the train. 'I didn't realize it would be so big.'

'It's massive,' Jane murmured. 'D'you think they've built this railway line 'specially?'

'Yes, they have,' a voice piped up beside them. There stood a blonde girl, with bright lipstick and a cheery grin. 'I'm from Bradford and I can get here on t'train. They built a special single track that goes reet round t'site, so trains drop workers off and then wait in the sidings to pick them up.' She glanced up and down at Lizzie and Jane. 'I'm Angela. Where a'thee from?'

'Sheffield,' the two girls chorused and introduced themselves. 'We're staying at one of the hostels near Wetherby,' Lizzie told her. The three girls walked into the site together.

'You need to report to t'admin block there.' Angela waved her hand towards a long, single-storey building. 'I'll sithee later.'

'See you later,' Lizzie chuckled and as the girl moved away, she added, 'I like her. I hope all the women are like that.'

The administration block had been built some distance from the production buildings for safety and was also close to the station. Here, they met up with several other new girls reporting for work. They spent the first day being given the uniforms they would have to wear: white cotton jackets and trousers or skirts, with a coloured headscarf.

'Not much different to buff brats, is it?' Lizzie murmured to Jane.

'The colour of your headgear,' their instructor, a Mrs Giles, told them, 'denotes what shift you're on. Now, you girls are all staying at the hostels, aren't you?'

There was a ripple of assent through the room, crowded with about twenty-five girls and young women. Glancing around, Lizzie felt she must be one of the oldest there.

'Your train journey to work will be paid for by the company and you will find a weekly train ticket in your wage packet. The shift pattern is mornings, afternoons and nights, and when you arrive at the beginning of your shift, you will report to what we call the shifting house, where you will have to leave your personal possessions, matches, cigarette lighters and anything made of metal that might cause a spark including all items of jewellery. Even your wedding and engagement rings, I'm afraid.' There was a murmur of disappointment, but the instructor, a severe-faced, thin woman, was adamant. 'Nor are you allowed to take in any food. You can collect all your belongings at the end of your shift.'

They were divided up and told where they would be working. Mrs Giles picked out Lizzie, Jane and two other girls. 'You'll be working in Group Two, where you'll be making fuse magazine pellets using TNT and Tetryl – highly explosive materials, so it is vital you obey all the regulations. This is one place where rules are NOT made to be broken.'

'She's a bit of a tartar, isn't she?' Lizzie muttered, as they were led away to the series of buildings where they would work.

'I think she has to be,' Jane murmured. 'It all sounds a bit dangerous, Lizzie. Are you sure we've done the right thing?'

''Course we have. Just think of all that lovely money in your pay packet at the end of the week.'

'As long as we're still alive to spend it.'

The rest of the day was spent watching how to paste and wrap the pellets. It was a dirty job and at the end of the shift their hands were yellow.

'It's a bit monotonous, isn't it?' Jane remarked, as they climbed aboard the train at the end of their shift. 'There's not even the variety we had welding and certainly not when we were buffing.'

'We've just swapped black dust for yellow dust,' Lizzie said dryly.

But there were compensations; life in the hostel was merry.

'They're a great bunch of girls here, aren't they?' Lizzie said at the end of their first week and Jane agreed.

'The best part for me is that no one knows me. Except you, of course, and I can trust you.'

Lizzie chuckled. 'You certainly can. I'm no angel either, Jane, and I expect there are a few more here who've got a colourful past, if only we knew.'

By degrees, they got to know all the girls in their hostel, some later than others because they were on different shifts. In their free time, they chatted and laughed and exchanged stories, though Lizzie was careful not to say too much about her life back in Sheffield. She'd hidden the fact that she was married from the time she had worked as a welder in the city and she wasn't sure whether she would have been allowed to come here if the authorities had known. She'd been careful to give her name as Elizabeth Dugdale so that it matched with her birth certificate, in case she was asked to produce it. She knew she could rely on Jane not to give her away; Jane had secrets too.

If they had enough time off, they would go into one of the bigger towns or cities to the theatre or the cinema, but mostly they made their own entertainment in the hostel. Occasionally, they would organize an outing to the seaside, but a trip to Bridlington in April disheartened them when they saw the pillboxes in the sand hills and the anti-tank blocks in close formation on the beach. It seemed to bring the war even closer to them than the work they were doing every day.

'I shan't go on another outing there,' Lizzie declared. 'It depresses me.'

Fifty-Three

In Sheffield, Lizzie's whereabouts were still shrouded in mystery and when Billy came home on leave in May, there was very little any of them could tell him. He'd got a seventy-two-hour pass this time with the hope of being able to track down his wife.

Stepping into the house at Emily's invitation, he thrust a bunch of flowers at her. 'I'm sorry about last time, Emily. I was out of order saying what I did. You're not to blame for whatever she's done. I know that. But please,' he glanced at both Emily and Trip, 'I'm begging you, have you any idea where she's gone? She hasn't even bothered to write to me. I'm half out of me mind with worry.'

'Sit down, Billy. We do know a little bit more now than we did before, but not much. The only thing we knew last time was that she hadn't left Sheffield. This time, she wrote to her mother and left an address. The Post Office in Wetherby.'

'Ah, right. I haven't seen Ma-in-law yet. She's out.'

'I expect she's at the WVS. She spends a lot of her time there now.'

Hesitantly, Trip said, 'I have been able to find out a bit of something, Billy, but it's very hush-hush and you mustn't breathe a word.'

'I'm used to that, Trip. "Careless talk", and all that. Go on.'

'Well, this is serious. If the enemy got to know of this location, it would be disastrous.' He took a deep breath. 'There's a filling factory near Wetherby at Thorp Arch.'

'What's that when it's at home?'

'It's the most dangerous of all the Royal Ordnance Factories. It's where they fill the bomb and shell casings with explosives. That's why they're located in rural areas. You couldn't have one of those in a city or even a town.'

'And my Lizzie's gone there?' Billy was shocked.

'I'm sorry to say it, Billy,' Trip said slowly, 'but I think it's possible. I've heard that there are several girls from Sheffield who've gone there.'

Billy turned to Emily. 'I only have one day's leave left, so can I ask a big favour?'

'Of course, Billy. What is it?'

'Will you take me to this place near Wetherby?'

'I don't know if we should. If it's so secret, it's very likely they won't let us in.'

'Probably not, but the workers will have to come out sometime, won't they? I just want to see if I can see her.'

Emily sighed. 'I don't think it's a good idea, Billy, but yes, if you really want to go, I'll take you.'

Billy didn't know that Emily's reluctance was because she was very afraid of what they might find when they got there. It had nothing to do with the dangerous work that Lizzie might be involved in now, but more to do with what she might be up to in her free time.

They set off early the following morning. 'She'll be working shifts, I expect,' Emily said, 'so we might not see her and they certainly won't let us into the premises.'

'It's worth a try,' was all Billy would say.

And, sadly, 'a try' was all it was.

They managed to gain admittance to the administration block, where a man took their details and requested, very formally, the nature of their business there.

Billy kept his temper in check. 'I would like to see my wife, if you please. Mrs Lizzie – Elizabeth, that is – Nicholson.'

The man stared at him. 'Your wife, sir? There are no married women here, I can assure you.'

'She might have said she wasn't married,' Emily put in, smiling pleadingly at him. 'But we think she's working here. Please can you check if you have anyone working here of that name?'

The man was obviously reluctant, but he couldn't resist Emily's lovely smile.

'I'll try and find out for you.'

He was gone for twenty minutes whilst Billy paced up and down impatiently.

'I'm sorry,' he said, when he came back. 'There's no one of that name here.'

'We must have got it wrong,' Billy muttered. Then he asked, 'Are there any other munitions factories near here or anywhere doing war manufacturing?

She trained as a welder. She might be doing something in that line.'

'I really can't say, sir,' the man said primly.

Billy was very tempted to give the man the same response that he had to Emily months previously, but he held his tongue. Antagonizing those in any kind of authority was not a good idea!

'I just wanted to see her,' Billy murmured, as they were forced to give up and drive away. 'Surely they could have let me see her?'

'Billy, if she is working there, I don't think she's supposed to be married. That man was positively shocked when you said you were looking for your wife.'

'I don't reckon he believed me – that I was married to her, I mean.'

'Perhaps we've got it wrong. Maybe she's not there at all.'

'Then where the hell is she? And why hasn't she been writing to me? I haven't had a letter from her in weeks.'

'Neither has her mother.'

'Do you think something's happened to her, Emily? I couldn't bear it if – if . . .'

'No, I don't. We'd have been informed if it had. I think the fact is that it's so top secret, the workers are probably told not to communicate with family more than necessary.'

'But surely it's "necessary" that she should at least be able to let us know that she's all right, even if she can't tell us much else.'

Emily sighed. 'I'm so sorry, Billy, but I really don't

know.' For once Emily was able to be completely truthful; she really didn't know where Lizzie was or what she was doing.

Billy was obliged to leave the following morning without having seen Lizzie or even having heard anything about her. Emily was desperately sorry for him, but there was nothing else she could do except promise him that if she heard anything, she would write to him at once.

Three months after Billy's visit, there was an urgent knocking on Emily's front door in the middle of the night.

She sat up suddenly in bed. 'What on earth is that? Is it an air raid? I didn't hear the sirens. Trip, wake up. Someone's banging on our door.'

Trip roused himself sleepily. 'Drunks, I expect, on their way home from the pub.'

'It's a bit late for that. It's gone midnight.'

She scrambled out of bed and pulled on her dressing gown.

'Stay here, Emily. I'll go.' Trip pushed his feet into his slippers and reached for his own dressing gown. 'I don't want you answering the door at this time of night. There's no knowing who it might be.'

'I'm coming down with you.'

When Trip opened the door, she was shocked to hear him say, 'Mrs Dugdale and – Good Lord – Jane? What's happened? Come in, come in.'

'We're sorry to bother you, Trip, but I didn't know who else to turn to.' Bess was in tears. 'It's Lizzie. Jane's come all the way home to tell me. There's been an accident where they work and Lizzie's badly injured.'

'Oh no! Emily – Emily,' Trip called. Come quickly . . .'

'I'm here. I heard.' She put her arms around the older woman. 'What can we do? Here, sit down – both of you. Jane, tell us what's happened.'

'I can't say much – you know that. But she's been burned all down her left arm and the left side of her face.'

'Her face! Oh, her lovely face,' Bess moaned. 'She'll be scarred for life.'

'Maybe it's not as bad as that,' Emily began, but Jane shook her head. 'It is, Mrs Trippet. One girl was killed outright and three more injured like Lizzie.'

'Where is she?' Trip asked. 'We'll take you to her.'

'Leeds. They've taken them all to a Leeds hospital,' Jane said. 'I think they said the St James.'

'Right, Mrs Dugdale,' the ever-practical Trip said. 'You go home and get yourself ready. I'll take you to Leeds right now.'

'In the dark, Trip?'

'Yes, my car's fitted with the headlight adaptors, but we'll have to go rather slowly, I'm afraid.'

'Can you take me back, Mr Trippet?' Jane asked. 'I'm on afternoons tomorrow and there'll be hell to pay if I don't turn up.'

'Is the place still working, then?'

'Yes, the explosion was only in one section. It's a huge site . . .' Jane clapped her hand over her mouth. 'Oh my – I shouldn't have told you that. Please – please don't say anything to anyone.'

Trip put his arm around the frightened girl. The accident to her friend had shaken her badly, yet she knew she must go back and do her duty.

'Don't worry. We know all about secrecy when involved in government work.'

It wasn't long before the four of them were in Trip's car and heading out of the city. Emily sat beside him in the front passenger seat to help watch the road in the darkness. It seemed a long time before they reached the outskirts of Leeds.

'Do you know where the hospital is, Jane?'

'No, sorry.'

'Look, Trip, there's an Air Raid Warden. Pull up. We can ask him.'

The man insisted they all show him their identity cards before he would give them directions. 'Visiting someone there, are you, sir?'

Trip indicated Bess sitting in the back of the car. 'We've come from Sheffield. We've just heard that Mrs Dugdale's daughter's been injured in an accident where she works, except that we don't actually know *where* she works. It all seems very hush-hush.'

'Oh-ah.' The man said no more, but from the tone of his voice it sounded as if he had a shrewd idea of exactly what had happened. In the back seat, Jane kept her head down.

'It'll be difficult for you to find it in the blackout,' the warden said. 'If you hang on a minute, I've got my motorcycle over there. I'll lead the way.'

'That's very good of you.'

They followed the dim back light of the motorcycle through the unfamiliar streets. As they pulled up in front of the hospital, Trip said, 'That was a piece of luck finding him. We'd never have found this place in the blackout.'

The warden was standing his machine up and coming back to the car. 'I'll take you in, if you like. We might be able to cut down a bit on the formalities if I'm with you.'

A night porter admitted them. 'I've already checked their identity cards, Jim,' the warden greeted the porter. 'I think they're here about one of the lasses brought in today. They've come from Sheffield.'

Trip saw him wink and the porter nodded. 'Aye, come this way, folks. I'll find the sister on night duty for you.' He showed them into a small waiting room. 'And I'll see if I can rustle up some tea.'

They were drinking the tea when a sister in a dark blue dress beneath a starched white apron bustled in, carrying a sheaf of papers.

'I understand you're looking for your daughter?' Her eyes alighted on Bess as she was the oldest woman there.

Bess nodded, but found she couldn't speak.

'Her name is . . . ?'

'Mrs Elizabeth Nicholson,' Emily spoke up.

The sister consulted her notes. 'I don't have anyone by that name here.'

Bess's face contorted with anxiety and disappointment.

'I'm sure it was St James they said,' Jane murmured. 'Oh Mrs Dugdale, I'm so sorry, I must have got it wrong. What can we do now?' She glanced helplessly at Trip as if, being the man of the group, he would have some suggestion. He turned towards the sister to ask about the other city hospitals, but she was staring at Bess.

'Did you say "Mrs Dugdale"?'

'Yes,' Bess answered, her voice shaking. 'It's my daughter Lizzie we're looking for.'

'We do have an Elizabeth Dugdale,' the sister said.

Emily gasped. 'That's her,' and added under her breath, 'No wonder we couldn't find her. She gave her maiden name.'

But the sister's sharp ears had caught Emily's murmured words. She glanced at Emily and asked, rather curtly, 'Is she married?'

'Yes, her husband's away in the army.'

'I – see.' The sister paused, then said, 'Do you know the place where she was working?'

'Don't answer her,' Jane said shrilly. 'I'll get into trouble.'

The sister's face softened. She could see that the young woman was very agitated and distressed. She glanced at her watch and then sat down beside them. At once, her manner seemed gentler. 'Look, you've nothing to fear from me, my dear. We all know about secrecy and, from her injuries, I have a good idea where she was working. Two other girls were brought in at the same time, so it's rather obvious to anyone living in this area. I'll have a guess, shall I, and then if you don't deny it, I'll know, but you won't have told me anything. All right?'

After a moment's hesitation, Jane nodded.

'Thorp Arch?'

Jane hung her head and did not reply.

'Don't worry, love. It's rather a big site to hide away completely. The only thing none of us must do is say what goes on there. I certainly don't know, nor do I want to. I just help pick up the pieces when there's an accident.' She turned to Bess. 'Your daughter has been badly burned. We're doing all we can for her at the moment, but we have sedated her just now. The pain is unbearable for her. I can't let you see her yet and, besides, she won't know you're there and it will distress you . . .'

'I want to see her,' Bess said but, as she stood up, she swayed and at once Emily guided her back down into the chair. 'Don't pass out on me, Mrs Dugdale. Put your head between your knees.'

'I'll get you some water,' the sister said. 'You've had a nasty shock and I expect you haven't had anything to eat for several hours. I'll see what I can do.'

They sat there – all four of them – until the dawn light filtered through the windows and the hospital began to come alive. And still they waited. Outpatients came and went. They watched others being attended to, saw a few walk out with bandaged heads or arms in slings. A few limped away, but at least they were going home.

'You ought to go home,' Bess said at last. 'And you'd better get yourself a bit of rest, Jane, before you have to go to work.'

Though still worried half out of her mind, Bess was beginning to realize just how much the others had put themselves out to help her.

'You should get back to the factory, Trip,' Emily

said. 'I promise I'll let you know as soon as we hear anything about Lizzie, but I must stay here with Mrs Dugdale.'

'Perhaps you're right. But Richard's there. I'll telephone him now, though he'll know there's a good reason why I haven't gone in.'

'So will Nell, but could you call her too and ask her to take charge? And Mrs Nicholson too, could you . . . ? Oh my goodness,' she said as another thought struck her. 'We ought to get word to Billy as soon as possible.'

'Yes – yes, you're right. I should go back, and I'll see about getting in touch with the authorities to inform Billy. But you promise you'll let me know any news?'

'Of course I will. I'll telephone either home or your factory.'

As he stood up to leave, he touched Bess's shoulder gently, but could think of nothing to say. He kissed Emily's cheek.

'Right, Jane, I'll drop you wherever you are living. Like Mrs Dugdale says, you should get some rest before your shift starts this afternoon.'

After they'd left, Emily and Bess continued to sit in the waiting room, side by side, saying little to each other; there was nothing they could think of to say. About mid-morning, a doctor came to find them.

'You've been told of your daughter's injuries, I understand. She is still very poorly, Mrs Dugdale.'

'Will she – live?' Bess asked, her voice shaking.

'The next twenty-four hours will be critical – it's

the shock to her body, you understand – but if she comes through that, then, yes, I think she will.'

'May I see her?'

'Not yet. Maybe tonight. I would advise you to go home and get some rest. Come back this evening and we'll see then.'

'We don't live here, doctor,' Emily said. 'We're from Sheffield.'

'Ah, that makes it a little more awkward. I can't offer you accommodation within the hospital, I'm afraid. We're fully stretched.'

'I'll find us a hotel for the night,' Emily said. 'We can have a rest this afternoon and come back tonight . . .'

But Bess shook her head firmly. 'No, I'll stay right here, doctor, if I won't be in the way.'

'You won't be in the way, no, but I don't think anyone will have time to make you cups of tea or feed you.' He sighed sadly. 'We're all going to be very busy today.' He smiled ruefully. 'But then we always are.'

'I'll look after her,' Emily said.

'You should go back home, Emily luv,' Bess said, when the doctor had left them.

'They'll all cope. Nell will take charge.'

Just as she was about to say more, two women were shown into the waiting room, an older woman, who was in tears, and a younger one supporting her.

'Let me get you some tea,' Emily said, getting up.

'Please don't trouble,' the younger of the two women said.

'No trouble,' Emily said, smiling sympathetically at

them both. It was obvious they had similar worries. She went in search of a nurse, who showed her to the kitchens where the staff kindly allowed her to make cups of tea. She carried a tray with four cups on it back to the waiting room.

'There,' she said, handing them round.

'This lady's daughter's been hurt too,' Bess said. Obviously they'd been talking in Emily's absence. 'We reckon at the same place – probably in the same accident.'

'Our Phyllis is burned, they say,' the younger woman said. Then she explained, 'This is her mam and I'm her sister, but we can't seem to find much out and they won't let us see her yet. Not before this evening, they said.'

'It's the same for us.' Bess nodded. 'It's the waiting that gets you, isn't it?'

The older woman nodded, 'The not knowing is the worst.'

For the rest of the morning and the whole of the afternoon, Emily tried to help in any way she could. She found it impossible to sit in the waiting room. She fetched and carried drinks and food to the other three women and, soon, she was not only making copious cups of tea in the hospital's kitchen, but she was also acting as a porter, wheeling patients to wherever they needed to be. By early evening, she was exhausted, but adrenalin kept her going.

When she took a brief respite and sat down next to Bess, she said softly, 'I popped out earlier. There's a hotel not far away. I've booked us in for the night.'

As Bess opened her mouth to argue, Emily said, 'And I won't take "no" for an answer.'

'Thank you, Emily. I'll accept, then, 'cos I don't want to leave till I've seen her. Do you think Trip will have sent word to Billy?'

'I'm sure he will have.'

It was eight o'clock in the evening before a nurse came to fetch Bess into the small room where Lizzie was. 'There are only three patients in the room, all of them seriously injured,' she told them, 'so we're just letting relatives in two at a time for five minutes. Come with me.'

Bess nodded and reached out to clasp Emily's hand. 'Come with me, Emily. I'm so afraid of what I'm going to see.'

The sister paused at the door of the room and turned to say gently, 'We are trying a new method of treatment for burns here, recommended by Mr Archibald McIndoe and therefore she is not bandaged as she would have been in the past. It'll be upsetting for you but she is heavily sedated with morphine and is in no pain at the moment. We shall do our best to keep her out of pain as much as we can.'

When she saw the horrific injuries, Bess put her hand over her mouth and sobbed. She stood for several minutes looking down at her beautiful daughter and tears ran down her face. 'She was so lovely, Emily. What's she going to do now?'

'We'll all still love her, Mrs Dugdale. It makes no difference.'

'But will Billy?'

'Billy?' Despite the seriousness of the moment,

Emily almost laughed aloud. 'Billy will love her no matter what. You should know that.'

'I just hope . . .' Bess began and then stopped. Emily didn't press her to continue for she guessed what the older woman had been about to say.

Fifty-Four

By the time Billy had got compassionate leave and arrived home, Lizzie had made it through that first long night and the next few days. She was still in the Leeds hospital, though there was a promise of her being transferred to Sheffield as soon as she was fit enough to travel.

'We'll hire a private ambulance, if necessary,' Emily promised Bess, 'and I'll settle any hospital bills. You mustn't worry about a thing.'

Bess wiped her eyes. 'You're very good to us, Emily luv.'

Although Emily had to return to Sheffield, she arranged for Bess to stay at the hotel in Leeds for a week, at the end of which she planned to bring her home. But she was willing to take her back any time she wanted to go until Lizzie could be transferred. Bess was at her daughter's bedside each day for as long as the hospital would allow. But now Lizzie was out of danger, her visitors were restricted to the regulation hours.

'Though we'll bend the rules for her husband when he gets here,' the sister told them. 'We do a lot of rule-bending for the armed forces,' she added, with a smile.

Emily had had little chance to speak to Lizzie alone, but on one of her visits when Bess left them briefly, Lizzie grasped Emily's hand and whispered urgently. 'He came.'

'Who, love? Who came?' She wondered if Lizzie was slightly delirious. She was often drowsy from the sedative.

'Andrew – the – the RAF lad. I didn't know he'd survived the bombing that night. I – I thought he must have been killed.'

Emily said nothing; she didn't want to admit to Lizzie that she'd thought she'd seen him follow them out of the hotel.

'I don't know how on earth he found out about my accident, but he just turned up here.' Tears filled Lizzie's eyes. 'He never said a word. He didn't even speak to me. He just took one look at me, turned and left the room. He's not been back.'

'Good,' Emily said stoutly. 'Good riddance, I say. The man who really loves you is on his way home, Lizzie. He should be here tomorrow.'

Now the tears ran down her cheek. 'I'll have to tell him.'

Emily was thoughtful for a moment. Though she couldn't ever imagine being unfaithful to Trip, she tried to imagine what she would do in Lizzie's place, and she decided that, yes, she would confess.

When Billy arrived the following morning, it was outside normal visiting hours, but he was allowed in to see his wife briefly.

422

He kissed her uninjured cheek gently and sat close to the bedside, holding her hand.

'Thank God you're alive,' he said huskily. 'Don't worry about a thing, darling. Just get better.'

'I'm so sorry, Billy. I don't know how you're going to forgive me.'

'Don't be silly. It's not your fault. I admired you for going into munitions, but you must have known the risk? I just wish you'd let me know where you were, though, and that you'd written to me a bit more.'

'No – no, it's not that. It's – it's something else. Billy – while you've been away—'

'Don't, Lizzie. Please, don't say any more. Whatever it is, I don't want to hear it.'

Already Billy had guessed what it was Lizzie was about to tell him. When he had arrived at the hospital, a young nurse had taken his name and said, in a surprised tone, 'Oh, *you*'re her husband. But I thought ...' Then the girl had stopped suddenly, turned bright red and had led him swiftly to Lizzie's room, scuttling away in embarrassment. But it had been enough – more than enough – for Billy to guess that there had already been another visitor.

He leaned closer and whispered, 'Just tell me it's over, Lizzie.'

When she nodded, he patted her hand and smiled. 'Just remember I love you with all my heart, Lizzie. I always have and I always will.'

'But my face. I'll be scarred for life.'

'Not to me,' Billy said, bravely. 'To me you'll

always be beautiful.' But inside his heart was breaking for her.

After a whole week's compassionate leave, Billy went back to Sheffield before he had to return to duty. He called in to Emily's home one evening. 'I have to go back tomorrow, Emily. I don't have to ask you to look out for Lizzie and her mam, 'cos I know you will. They're transferring her back here next week, they think, but it's when she's out of hospital that I'm worried about. Her wounds are healing remarkably well, but . . .' He stopped and bit his lip. There was obviously something else bothering him and Emily had a shrewd suspicion she knew what it was. She was unsure just how much Lizzie had told him and she didn't want to make matters worse.

So she just said, 'As soon as she's well enough, I'll see what I can find for her to do. She won't be able to go back to munitions or to the buffing. For one thing, they don't know if her arm will heal completely yet, do they?'

Billy shook his head.

'And she mustn't get any dirt in her facial wound either, so I'll see what I can find for her. Maybe she could help out in the shop with your mother.'

'Maybe, but she's so upset about her face. I don't reckon she'll want to go out in public. She – she seems so depressed – I'm afraid she—' He stopped, unable or afraid to put his terrible fear into words.

Emily touched his arm and said softly, 'I'll look after her. We all will. I'll talk to your mam when Lizzie's feeling better. See what we can come up with.'

424

He frowned. 'I don't know if she'll be able to work and Bess is getting on in years. I send my pay home, of course, but . . .'

'Now, you really needn't worry about that, Billy. We've been through some tough times before and come through them. We'll look after both of them, you have my word.'

His worried expression lightened and as he stood up to go, he hugged her swiftly. 'Thanks, Emily. I don't know what we'd do without you. Your strength and courage keep us all going.'

The following week, Lizzie was brought to a Sheffield hospital but it was another two weeks before she came home. She was still weak and sunk in gloom. Bess fussed around her, but it wasn't until Emily went to see her in the evening that Lizzie brightened up.

'Mam's driving me mad,' the girl confided in a low whisper. 'Fuss, fuss, fuss. She won't let me lift a finger.'

'Well, it's high time you did. And it's time you came out for a little walk each day or you'll never get stronger.'

'I can't go out, Emily. I couldn't bear the stares and the pointing fingers.'

Emily put her head on one side and regarded her friend thoughtfully. 'And why would they do that, pray?'

Lizzie laughed wryly, but tears filled her eyes. 'Look at me! I'll have kids following me in the street, shouting "Quasimodo" after me or worse.'

'He was a hunchback.'

425

'And ugly. Like I am now.'

Emily stood up suddenly. 'Well, if you're going to sit here and drown in self-pity, Lizzie, I'm going. I've better things to do and other people to help.'

'Don't go, Emily. *Please* don't go. No one else comes to see me.'

Emily frowned as she sat down slowly. 'What do you mean? You've had a stream of visitors. Mrs Bayes has been several times and Nell's called, I know that.'

Emily saw the surprise in her eyes. 'I have? I – I didn't know. Mam must have stopped them coming in.'

Emily pursed her lips and said, 'Mm.'

For the first time since the accident, Lizzie smiled, though her smile was a little lopsided. 'Oo-er. I know that look and the ominous "Mm". I wouldn't be in Mam's shoes.'

Emily laughed. 'I'll go easy on her. She only wants what's best for you, but hiding yourself away, Lizzie, isn't the best thing.' She leaned forward. 'Don't you think our lovely city is scarred after all the bombing and a lot of folk have been injured? And what about the ones who've been killed? Don't you think their families would give anything for them still to be alive, even if they were maimed? Sadly, you're not the only one, love.'

'I know, but it doesn't make it any easier.'

'No, I know that.' Emily took her friend's right hand in hers and squeezed it. 'But what I'm trying to say is that people understand. They won't laugh, because, sadly, they're getting used to seeing wounded folk just like you.'

Lizzie gave a heavy sigh. 'You're right, Emily. Of course you are and I will try. Maybe tomorrow . . .'

As Emily left the house, she found Bess busy in the kitchen. She put her arm around the older woman's shoulders. 'Let visitors in to see her, Mrs Dugdale, there's a love. It'll do her the world of good.'

Bess wiped her eyes with the corner of her apron. 'I can't bear for them to see her like that. She was so pretty, Emily. I can hardly bring myself to look at her, ne'er mind strangers.'

'We're not strangers. And, like I've just said to her, there are countless folk in our city in the same boat. Soldiers wounded in the war, civilians injured in the bombing and in accidents like the explosion where she worked. And there're a lot worse than Lizzie. One of those girls alongside her had lost her leg. At least they managed to save Lizzie's arm and she's getting the use of her hand back, isn't she?'

Bess nodded. 'But her face. What about her face?'

'She'll have to be very brave – and so will you. She's going to go out tomorrow and start to face the world again.'

But tomorrow turned into two days, then three and, a week later, Lizzie had still not ventured out.

In the south of England, Harry continued to fly his Spitfire. The Battle of Britain was deemed to be over, but fighter pilots were still fully occupied with various duties. After a particular tiring tour, Harry requested permission to see the Commanding Officer. But first he had to get past the CO's watchdog; Flight Lieutenant Hartley.

'And this is about?' Hartley asked him as he stood smartly to attention in front of the man.

'I'd like to request permission to go home for a few days.'

'Why?'

'A close family friend has been injured in her place of work. I don't know details – it's all very hush-hush – but Lizzie has been badly hurt. Burned, so I understand.'

Hartley was staring up at him and his next words came out in a strangled whisper. He cleared his throat and repeated his question. 'Who is this Lizzie exactly?'

'Lizzie Nicholson. She's been friends with my Aunt Emily for years.'

'Is she – married?'

'Yes, sir.'

'And – where is her husband?'

'He's in the army, sir.'

There was a long silence whilst Hartley shuffled his papers. Then he cleared his throat again and said, 'It's not really policy to allow you to go home for the illness or – or injury – of a friend. However, if it had been a member of your family, that would have been different – even if it had been your Aunt Emily – we would have considered it, but I'm afraid it's out of the question.' As if relenting a little and making a generous gesture, the flight lieutenant motioned towards the telephone on his desk. 'But I could allow you to telephone home and make enquiries, if you like.'

'That's very good of you, sir. I would like to. I

can phone my uncle at his works. He'll likely have the latest news.'

'If you know the number, then help yourself.'

Harry hesitated a moment as the man made no move to leave him alone in the office to make his private call, but then he moved forward and picked up the receiver.

Fifty-Five

'Do you think Lizzie would benefit from a week or so at Riversdale?' Constance asked Emily. 'Lucy would look after her.'

'I'm not sure it would be a very good idea, Mother.' From the time of their marriage Emily had called Trip's mother 'Mother'.

Constance had been the one to suggest it, saying, 'Mother-in-law is a bit of a mouthful. You call your own mother "Mam", don't you? Why don't you call me "Mother"?'

'I'd worry about her seeing all the injured soldiers. It might make things worse for her, not better. But if she fancied a little holiday,' Emily went on, 'I'm sure she could stay with my parents.'

'Have they room? With the boys there, I thought their house would be bursting at the seams. Besides, I don't want to put any more work on your mother's shoulders. She's still cooking at Riversdale. By the way, how are the boys? Are they well settled there? They always seem in high spirits whenever I see them on my visits.'

Emily laughed. 'They're fine. Loving the freedom of the countryside. We go to see them as often as petrol will allow and we write every week. And we take Nell with us too.' Now Emily sighed as her thoughts returned to the thorny problem of how best to help Lizzie. 'If she wants to go, I'm sure we could find somewhere in the village.'

But when Emily broached the subject, Lizzie was adamant. 'No, I'm not going anywhere, 'specially to a lot of strangers. They'll not be used to seeing injured folk.'

'That's where you're wrong. The soldiers convalescing at Riversdale mingle freely with the villagers – those that are mobile, that is. And even the ones who can't get about are visited by the locals.'

'Very magnanimous of them, I'm sure.'

Emily shook her head and gave up – for the moment.

'I just don't know what to do next,' Emily confided in Ruth when she visited the shop one morning.

'I've been thinking.' Ruth, too, had heard the whispers about her wayward daughter-in-law but had said nothing to her son. She had guessed, from something he'd said when he was home on compassionate leave, that he'd an inkling about what had been going on in his absence but had decided to ignore it. Ruth could do no less. 'She could help out here in the back of the shop, if she really doesn't feel able to face people yet. Some of the cutlery we're getting now – and it's no one's fault because there is a war on –' She paused and the two women exchanged a smile. It was a favourite remark when someone was trying to make an excuse for something. Ruth went on. 'It isn't quite up to the standard we'd like. Now, I know

Lizzie can't use a buffing wheel because of her wounds, but she could inspect everything that comes in and return it for further work if it is really unsaleable.'

'But you do that already, don't you?' Emily asked.

'Of course, but I have so much to do. There's all the paperwork, though I don't think Lizzie likes that, does she?'

'She always refused to get involved with it and during the time she was trying to run the business on her own – when we fell out that time –'

Ruth nodded. She remembered it well.

'– she didn't do very well with the paperwork and they lost custom,' Emily went on. 'That was really why they had to close.'

Ruth was thoughtful for a moment before saying, 'If she was prepared to work in the evenings, she could help with the displays after the shop was shut.'

Emily's face brightened. 'Now that is a good idea. Have I your permission to say that you really could do with the help? She won't like it if we're creating a job for her just because we're sorry for her.'

'You most certainly can say that, Emily, because it happens to be the truth.'

'Oh, I don't know, Emily,' Lizzie said, but Bess, standing beside her, said. 'It's perfect, Lizzie. Do give it a try, luv.'

'But I'll have to go out to get there. I'll have to pass people in the street.'

'To start with – but not for ever – I'll take you and fetch you home in the car,' Emily said. 'You're

432

not the only one, Lizzie, to have been injured. You could have been killed.'

'Perhaps it would have been better if I had been.'

'Now, I don't want to hear talk like that. Billy loves you and your mother loves you and needs you.' Her tone softened as she added, 'Her son is lost to her, Lizzie, don't forget that. You're all she has now.'

'If only I'd had children, Emily, it would have been different. I wouldn't have been tempted to stray if I'd had little ones.'

Emily forbore to say that even if Lizzie had had children, they would probably have been evacuated anyway. They wouldn't have still been in Sheffield. But instead she said firmly, 'We're not going to talk about that any more, Lizzie. You made a mistake, but it's over. Now, you must rebuild your life, starting today. Come on, get dressed. I'm taking you to the shop.'

'Oh Emily, I—'

Emily stood over her, her arms folded. 'It's no good you arguing because I'm going to stay here until you get dressed and then we're going. So, come on, look lively.'

Half an hour later, Lizzie stepped into the shop. She had put on a broad-brimmed hat with a black veil. It was one her mother always used for funerals.

'Hello, Lizzie,' Ruth greeted her. 'Come through, luv. I've got a lot of work waiting for you.'

Once in the back of the shop, Lizzie removed her hat. She was now only with people who'd already seen her.

'There's this delivery of cutlery needs inspecting.

I haven't had time to do it. I know you don't like paperwork, Lizzie, so I won't ask you to do that, but there is one thing you can do to save me a bit of time. You can open the mail each day and sort it into piles. Invoices, payments and miscellaneous. Then you can keep me supplied with cups of tea through the day . . .'

On and on the list went and Emily smiled inwardly. All the tasks which Ruth was giving Lizzie were genuine and the young woman couldn't possibly believe that Ruth and Emily were creating work for her.

'And,' Ruth finished, 'if you could keep this back office a lot tidier than it is now, that'd be a godsend. Are you up for doing a bit of filing?' Without waiting for Lizzie's agreement, Ruth went on, 'I've devised a system, which I'll show you, but keeping it up to date is a nightmare.'

For the first time since the accident, Lizzie smiled. 'I can see you do need a bit of help, so, yes, I think this is something I can do. Thanks . . .' Her glance included them both. She sat down at the table and pulled the box of cutlery towards her. 'Some of these look a bit of a mess. It's a pity I can't use a wheel, I'd have these looking good in a jiffy.'

'I'll leave you to it, then,' Emily said. 'What time shall I pick you up tonight?'

'It's all right, Emily. I won't trouble you. As long as I've got my hat and veil, I'll walk home.'

'My,' Emily whispered as they returned to the front of the shop. 'I didn't expect an improvement quite so quickly. Thank you, Ruth.'

'I really do need her help – as no doubt you can see.'

Lizzie settled in well, but she would only scurry between the shop and her home. She adamantly refused to go elsewhere in the city and a trip to the cinema or the theatre was out of the question.

'My next project,' Emily told Bess when they were alone, 'is to get her to go to Ashford for a little holiday.'

'Right, old boy,' Barney said cheerfully. 'It's foggy today, so we've orders to go on a "rhubarb".'

Harry grinned and threw down the magazine he'd been reading. 'I'm with you.'

The two fighters took off through the mist and climbed until they were above the clouds. Once over the Channel they flew down, searching through the mist for a likely target.

'There! See it. A railway.'

They flew lower, firing at the line and leaving it damaged enough to disrupt the enemy transport for a few days whilst repairs were done.

'Same again tomorrow?' Barney asked as they climbed out of their aircraft back at base. 'The weather forecast says it's going to be like this for several days.'

'You're on.' Harry grinned. He enjoyed these little skirmishes with just him and Barney alone against the enemy and, because they were carrying out surprise attacks, they had very little trouble from enemy aircraft or from flak. They'd come and gone before the enemy had time to realize they were there.

Harry was on his way home after another rhubarb run, but not with Barney this time. Another pilot from his flight was beside him. They'd attacked a fuel dump and left it on fire, the flames leaping into the sky. Then they'd turned for home. Just a few more miles and he'd be over the enemy coast, Harry mused. Sleep and a seventy-two-hour pass awaited him. Though he wouldn't be surprised if the latter was cancelled at the last minute. He'd become suspicious that Flight Lieutenant Hartley was putting a stop on his leave requests. He hadn't been home since he'd heard about Lizzie's accident, though, strangely, Hartley had enquired after her health and had even wanted to know the details.

'It seems there was a nasty accident where she was working – an explosion of some sort,' Harry had told him.

'Where did she work?'

'I don't know. She used to be a buffer girl and worked for my aunt, but I don't think there's anything that could have burned her in that job. Maybe she was doing war work. I don't think it happened in Sheffield. Now, if it had been when the bombing happened, I could have understood it, but they all escaped that, thank goodness.'

'They were lucky, then,' the flight lieutenant had said, but there was a tightness about his mouth and, somehow, his words didn't sound genuine.

But Harry had ceased to worry about Flight

Lieutenant Hartley. All the chaps agreed that he was 'a strange bloke'. He was something of a mystery. All they knew was that he'd been in the RAF for some years before the war had started and no one knew much about his personal life or his background.

'I don't think the chap's got one,' Barney had joked.

'He goes up to London regularly when he's on leave,' one of the others had said.

'And I wonder what he finds to do there?' Barney had remarked sarcastically and the others had laughed.

Harry was thinking about the flight lieutenant as he flew home. Perhaps he could be a little crafty and say he wanted to find out more about Lizzie. He could say he wanted to go and see her. Then he'd be able to find out what happened. He felt his aircraft jolt and out of nowhere there was an Me 109 on his tail. There was a rattle all down the side of his plane and the engine began to make a strange noise. The aircraft was losing height rapidly . . . down and down it plunged as Harry fought to check his parachute, open the aircraft's canopy and throw himself out into the sky . . .

'Hello, love?' Josh greeted Amy. 'What are you doing here? You're not due until six this evening, are you?' He stood up and came around the desk in the little room that was used as an office. It was from there that Josh ran Riversdale and where Constance still came to do all the necessary paperwork that Josh couldn't handle.

And then he noticed his wife's white face and her

quivering mouth. His glance dropped to the envelope she was carrying in her hand. At least, he thought briefly, it wasn't a yellow telegram, but her face indicated that whatever it was certainly did not hold good news. He put his arms around her and drew her close. 'What is it, Amy?'

Her words were punctured by sobs. 'It's Harry. It's a personal letter from his commanding officer. He's been posted – missing –' her voice dropped to a strangled whisper – 'believed killed.'

Josh's arms tightened around her and he groaned. 'Oh no! No!'

They stood like that for a long time, unwilling to leave the safety of the little room, unable, for the moment, to impart the dreadful news to others. At last, they drew slowly apart, as if letting go of one another made it all the harder. 'How – how are we going to tell everyone?' she whispered. 'Your parents, my dad – Lucy?'

'And everyone in Sheffield. I'll have to go there in person. I must tell Emily face to face. She adores her nephew.' He was thoughtful for a moment. 'I'll come home with you now and we'll tell the family, then I'll come back here and break the news to Lucy.'

'Mrs Bayes is due to come today, isn't she? Maybe she'd take you back with her. You – you could stay a night, if you wanted.' Amy was making a brave gesture, but Josh could tell from the hesitancy in her voice that she didn't want him to stay away from her. She needed his strength by her side to face this terrible news.

'I'll try to get back if I can,' was all he could

promise her. He didn't want to put on Constance, though he was sure she would do the double journey in a day, if necessary. He was confident she would bring him whenever he asked her.

Amy took a deep breath. 'No, no, stay a night with Emily. I'll be all right.'

They walked down the road towards their home. Their feet felt like lead and they clung to each other's hands.

They told Amy's father first. He said nothing, just stared at them for a long moment, the colour draining from his face. Then turned away and went into the smithy. Though the workshop was hardly used now, it remained the place that Bob liked to be. He still did a few small jobs now and again. 'Just to keep my hand in,' he would tell them. Moments later, they heard his hammer striking the anvil.

Josh sighed. 'Now, we'd better go and tell my mam and dad.'

Martha shrieked, sank into a chair and covered her face with her apron and Walter began to shake, just as he had when he'd first come back from the Great War. He'd been better since their return from Sheffield, but now it looked as if all the horrors of his war had come flooding back.

'Do you think we should call the doctor?' Amy whispered, her anxious glance going from Martha, rocking and moaning in her chair, to Walter and his shaking hands.

'Might be an idea,' Josh said grimly. 'It's the shock. I ought to stay here.'

'No, no, you go back. I'll pack an overnight bag

for you and bring it up later. You must go and see Emily.'

Though her heart felt as if it was breaking, Amy had a quiet inner strength that always came to the fore in times of trouble. She didn't want Josh to leave her, but she knew he had to go. 'I'll look after my dad and your parents.' She gave him a gentle push towards the door. 'Go on, before I change my mind. And – and you must tell Lucy. I'll break the news to Lewis and Simon when they come home.'

Josh walked slowly back to Riversdale. He didn't know which he was dreading the most, telling his sister or Lucy. He was sure that Lucy and Harry had fallen in love. Seeing them together on Harry's last leave, he had seen the light of love in their eyes when they'd looked at each other and, walking home late on that last night, he had seem them standing close together on Sheep Wash Bridge.

When Josh arrived back at Riversdale, he went in search of Lucy to find that, as usual, she was bustling about as busy as ever. 'Mr Ryan, there you are. We have three new patients arriving this afternoon, but two of our patients are going home today. Isn't that wonderful? I know you like to say goodbye to them, so—'

'Lucy, could I have a word in private?'

She blinked and, catching the seriousness of his tone, she nodded and followed him to his office.

'Sit down, love,' Josh said and then he knelt down in front of her and took her hands. 'It's Harry,' he said, coming straight to the point. 'We've received a letter from his commanding officer saying that he has been posted missing, believed – believed killed.'

Tears sprang into her eyes and she gripped his hands tightly, clinging to them for a moment. She closed her eyes for several moments, her face briefly contorted with grief but then she took a deep breath to steady herself, opened her eyes and nodded.

Shakily, she said, 'Thank you for telling me.' She stood up suddenly, almost causing Josh to over-balance. Then she held out her hand to help him up. 'I must get on. Work is the best thing, you know. Keeping busy. At least –' her voice shook a little – 'I can carry on helping those who have come back. I can do it for Harry.'

'Of course. You're right. We're not the only ones to receive such news but . . .'

'It doesn't make it any easier, does it?' she said softly as she turned towards the door and left the room, leaving Josh staring after her. What a brave girl, he was thinking, and now he must go and tell another courageous woman the same dreadful news.

If ever, he thought, anyone deserved the title of Daughter of Courage, then it was his sister Emily. And it seemed to him now that perhaps Lucy was out of the same mould.

Fifty-Six

Josh arrived in the city in the early evening. Constance had been shocked by the news and had wanted to take Josh straight to Sheffield there and then to see Emily, but Josh had shaken his head. 'No, no, this afternoon will be fine. You do whatever you have to do here and then we'll go.'

'I'll bring you back tonight of course . . .'

'There's no need. Amy has agreed that I should stay the night with Emily.'

'Yes, of course, but you must let me drive you back tomorrow – or whenever you're ready. You know I can get extra petrol because of running this place as a convalescent home.'

'Thank you. I will accept that kind offer.' He smiled at her, but the smile did not reach his eyes, so deep was his sadness.

Trip opened the door to his knock. 'Josh – what a nice surprise. Come in, come in. Emily's in the—' He stopped as he saw Josh's face. 'Ah, there's something wrong, isn't there? Is it Harry?'

Wordlessly, Josh nodded.

'Come through and tell us both.'

He opened the door into the living room. Emily

was sitting darning socks by the fire. As soon as she glanced up, the smile of welcome faded from her face. She laid her sewing aside and stood up, going at once to put her arms around her brother.

'It's Harry, isn't it? Sit down and tell us.'

When he had explained – however many times was he going to have to repeat the awful words – Emily asked, 'How are they all?'

Josh sighed heavily and told them how each member of the family – and Lucy – had reacted to the news.

Emily wiped the tears from her eyes. She rarely cried; but this was the worst news she'd ever had in her life. Even her father's return from the Great War hadn't been as bad as this. At least he'd come back, even though he was terribly injured. And he had been much better since the family had gone back to Ashford, but now . . .

'How's Dad?' Emily asked, her voice shaking.

'Not good, nor is Amy's dad. They've taken it very hard. We all have.'

'Is there anything we can do?'

Constance had asked the same question as she had dropped Josh outside Emily's house, but what was there that anyone could do? Their beloved Harry was gone.

Sadly, Josh shook his head. 'Amy is clinging to the wording "missing" and if that's the way she can deal with it, then who am I to argue? We – we've each got to come to terms with it in our own time and in our own way.'

'Just let us know, Josh, if there's anything – anything at all – that we can do,' Trip said.

'Could I stay the night? I was wondering if I should see Lizzie while I'm here.'

Emily bit her lip. She could hardly tell them of her fears that, if she saw him again, Lizzie might rekindle the flame she'd held for Josh.

As he saw his sister hesitate, Josh smiled wryly. 'Amy knows. I wouldn't go behind her back, Em.'

Emily smiled weakly and nodded. 'I'll take you to see her after I've found you something to eat. She's working with Ruth Nicholson at the shop, though she refuses to serve customers. The left-hand side of her face is badly scarred, Josh. It might shock you, but please don't let it show on your face when you see her.'

'I won't. I'm used to such sights at Riversdale.'

Emily stared at him for a moment and then murmured, 'Of course you are. Now, I wonder . . .'

The two men exchanged a glance. 'What's buzzing through that busy little head of yours this time?' Trip asked.

'I was just wondering if it really would do Lizzie good to visit Riversdale. Your mother suggested it before, Trip, but I'd thought of it as just a holiday, you know, to get her away from the city, but now I can see that it might do her good to meet some of the soldiers and see how they cope with their injuries.'

'Would she agree to go there, though?' Trip ventured. 'It's taken you long enough to get her to go to the shop, and even then she hides herself away in the back and refuses to meet anyone.'

'It's not Lizzie I'd be concerned about, it's the

wounded. I wouldn't want them to think we were treating them like – guinea pigs.'

Despite the terrible news they had just received, Josh laughed. 'You needn't worry about that, Em. That's what Archie McIndoe calls all his boys. "The Guinea Pig Club". They're all proud to be members.'

'I'm sure the sister at the hospital in Leeds mentioned him, but to be honest, I was so worried about Lizzie that I didn't really take in what she was saying, only that it was about some kind of new treatment they were using. Who is he?'

'A brilliant man,' Josh said. 'A lot of our lads have been operated on by him and have come to us to recuperate. Those who still have to have more operations stay at his hospital in East Grinstead, but once he's done all he can for them, they come to homes like Riversdale to heal. He's doing some marvellous work. He's a real pioneer.'

'And you think this great man might help Lizzie?'

'I don't see why not. She's a war casualty just the same as the RAF lads who've been burned in their planes—' He stopped suddenly and stared at Emily before whispering hoarsely. 'Oh my God, don't say that's what happened to Harry.'

Emily enfolded him in her embrace. 'Keep the faith, Josh. Be like Amy and believe what they've said. "Missing". We must all cling to that.'

Emily was a little fearful as they stepped into the shop.

'You remember my brother, Josh, don't you, Ruth?'

Ruth smiled and held out her hand. 'I do indeed. How are you, Josh? It must be twenty years since

I've seen you.' She searched the man's face. He'd altered in the intervening years. He was no longer the fresh-faced, slightly diffident young man, who had relied so much on his sister's strength of character back then. Now, he had confidence. He was broad and tall, but he was just beginning to show signs of his forty years. His hair was thinning and he was starting to have a double chin and a slight paunch. He was a nice-looking man with a kind face, but he was no longer the handsome young feller with whom Lizzie had been infatuated.

'And what brings you to the big bad city?'

'He—' Emily began and then faltered. Josh put his arm around her and faced Ruth. 'Sadly, I've had to come to see Em and Trip with some bad news. Harry is missing.'

Ruth's face contorted. 'Oh Josh, I'm so sorry. So very sorry.' She, more than anyone else they knew, understood what it meant to receive such heart-breaking news. She wiped her eyes and then said, 'I'll tell her you're here. I don't know if she'll see you though, Josh.'

But moments later, Ruth came back and said, 'Go through, both of you.'

As they stepped into the back room, Lizzie kept the left-hand side of her face turned away from them, but Josh went towards her with his arms outstretched wide and bent to kiss her forehead. He would have liked to have made a point of kissing her scarred cheek but, although the wound was healing well, he didn't want to cause infection. Tears welled in Lizzie's eyes as she looked up at him.

'I'm not the pretty girl you knew, Josh. Not any longer.'

He smiled down at her. 'Of course you are.' Gently, he took her by the shoulders and turned her to face him. Watching, Emily held her breath. 'You'll always be beautiful, Lizzie,' Josh murmured and then added, more strongly, 'I want you to come to Riversdale. There are people there I'd like you to meet.'

'Oh Josh, I can't. I – I don't go out – except to come to work.'

'Mrs Bayes will bring you to Ashford if I ask her.'

'Who – who is it you want me to meet?'

Josh tapped the end of her nose playfully. 'That's a secret. You'll see.'

Fifty-Seven

'It's very kind of you to take me, Mrs Bayes,' Lizzie said as she climbed into Constance's car the following Sunday morning. She'd taken some persuading. 'But I'm not at all sure about this.'

Today, she was wearing one of Constance's pretty hats with a pink veil tied beneath her chin, one that Constance had always worn when driving her open-topped car. The veil, cleverly positioned, hid the left side of Lizzie's face.

'It'll be fine. They're very brave young men, who've had all sorts of injuries, but Riversdale is a happy place. You'll be surprised.'

'I'm not very brave,' Lizzie said in a small voice.

'I think you're very courageous,' Constance said, telling what she thought of as a little white lie to try to boost the girl's confidence. Constance was honest enough to admit that had the same thing happened to her, she didn't know how she would have coped.

When she ushered a hesitant Lizzie in through the front door, both Josh and Amy were there to greet her. Amy moved forward and, for a brief moment, the two women stared at each other, then Amy put her arms round Lizzie and held her.

'I'm so, so sorry to hear about your boy, Amy,' Lizzie whispered.

'Thank you, Lizzie,' Amy said softly and then with forced brightness she added, 'Now, we've afternoon tea laid out in the patients' lounge.'

'Amy will look after you now, Lizzie,' Josh said gently. 'Mrs Bayes,' Josh turned to Constance, 'might I have a word?'

The two moved away towards the office.

'Will – will patients be there?' Lizzie asked nervously.

'One or two. They know you're coming and are waiting to meet you.'

As Amy led Lizzie to the room that had once been Constance's morning room, Lizzie heard loud laughter greeting them. As they stepped through the door, she saw that there were three young men sitting there. All of them had scars on their faces. One had lost his left arm, for his empty sleeve was tucked into the pocket of his jacket, but they all stood up politely.

'Hello,' they chorused and shook her hand in turn.

'This is Roland,' Amy said, introducing them, 'William and Bernard.'

'Here, sit by me,' Roland said. 'We'll let Amy be mother today and pour the tea, shall we?'

'You're quite capable, Roland, even with one hand,' Amy laughed, 'but, yes, as we have a visitor, I'll pour.'

Lizzie glanced round at them all again and then, slowly, she took off her hat and veil. For the first time since the accident she didn't feel embarrassed, not even when the three of them all leaned closer to inspect her injury.

'I reckon Archie'd make a marvellous job of that, don't you, chaps?' Roland said.

'It doesn't look like it's gone too deep. I reckon one op, or two at the most, would do it.'

Lizzie looked round at them all. They were all smiling at her. 'What? What are you talking about?'

'We've all been treated by Archibald McIndoe at the Queen Victoria Hospital in East Grinstead,' William explained. 'He's fast becoming an expert in the treatment of burns. It's happening quite a lot to pilots.'

Lizzie couldn't help glancing at Amy. How could she cope with meeting these airmen every day and wondering if that was what had happened to her son?

'It's called plastic surgery, but it's skin grafts really.'

'Don't tell her where they take the skin from,' the one called William teased. 'Let's just say that sitting down was a bit uncomfortable for a week or two.'

'And it'll give me a heck of a kick when my mother-in-law kisses my cheek.'

The three men laughed uproariously at their own banter and Lizzie wasn't sure if they were joking or not.

Now Roland leaned towards her and examined her face closely. 'I really think he could help you, Lizzie.' His tone was serious now, the joking and the teasing over for the moment. They could see how nervous and lacking in confidence the young woman now was. They could also see how beautiful she'd been.

'Do you?' she asked tentatively.

'Sure of it,' Bernard, the quieter one of the three, said. 'He'd need to see you first, of course.'

'But – would he do it? I mean, I'm not even in the services.'

'Not exactly, but you were injured whilst doing valuable war work, weren't you?'

It seemed they'd been told all about her – or at least as much as they were allowed to know.

'I suppose so, but . . .'

'No "buts". William will write to him straight away and ask if there's anything he can do.'

'That's very kind of you,' Lizzie murmured and, for the first time, she had real hope.

'And now,' Roland said, holding out his arm to her, 'let me show you around Riversdale and you can meet some of the others. Of course, they're not all burns patients. They've all sorts of injuries and have come here because they're well on the mend. Some of them will go back to their units when they're fully fit.'

To her surprise, Lizzie enjoyed her visit. All of the patients, without exception, were cheerful, exchanging merry banter with each other and with the staff, even – to Lizzie's astonishment – with Constance when she came to speak to them all.

As they climbed back into her car for the return journey, Lizzie said, 'I can't thank you enough for bringing me today, Mrs Bayes. I didn't want to come, but it's given me real hope. I must write and tell Billy when I get home.'

'I'm glad, my dear,' Constance murmured. She was heartened on two counts, though Lizzie would not realize it. She was happy to hear that the girl had a newfound confidence, but she was also relieved to hear that Lizzie's first thought was to write to her husband.

As Constance was about to start the engine, Lizzie put her hand on the woman's arm. 'Can I tell you something in confidence?'

'Of course.'

'Normally, I would tell Emily, but I – I can't. Not about this.'

'Go on.'

Lizzie took a deep breath. 'I expect you know all about my silliness over Josh and – and even about my more recent –' Lizzie ran her tongue nervously around her lips – 'stupidity.' When Constance remained silent, Lizzie went on, 'I just want you to know that for the first time ever I could look at Josh today and see him just as a friend. I'm no longer imagining myself in love with him, Mrs Bayes. And I – I feel released. Is that a strange thing to say?'

'No, I don't think so, my dear, and I'm so glad to hear it.'

'I know now that it's Billy I love. He's been so good to me. So understanding and – and forgiving.'

'So he knows about . . . ?'

Lizzie shook her head. 'Not really. I tried to tell him when he came to the hospital, but he stopped me – said he didn't want to hear. I suppose he suspected something, but he just asked me if it was over and, when I said "yes", he said we'd never speak of it again.'

'Then you mustn't – not to him, but I do think

you should tell Emily how you feel about Josh now. I think it would set her mind at rest.'

Lizzie was thoughtful for a moment. 'I expect you're right. I just feel so sorry for them – Josh and Amy – to think that they have lost their son.'

With that, Constance started the engine and they drove home, each busy with her own thoughts.

Fifty-Eight

When Emily arrived to pick her up the following morning because it was raining heavily, Lizzie said, 'Tomorrow, Emily, if it's fine, I'll walk to work. And –' she smiled – 'I won't even wear a veil, though Mrs Bayes has kindly given me the pink hat I wore yesterday to use when I go somewhere amongst strangers who might stare.'

Emily blinked and then smiled. 'So – the visit to Riversdale helped, did it?'

Lizzie nodded. 'Enormously. They've not only made me realize that I needn't hide myself away, but they've given me hope that something can be done to make it look – if not perfect – then a whole lot better.' And she went on to tell Emily about Archie McIndoe, ending, 'Constance has been so kind. She's offered to help me in any way I need. Even financially.'

'She's a wonderful woman and I give thanks every day that she's found happiness. No one deserves it more than she does.'

'William – one of the airmen at Riversdale – said he would write to him. There were three of them there who'd been treated by Mr McIndoe, so they feel they know him. But Mrs Bayes has said she's going to get in touch with him too. I'm no good at writing that sort of letter.'

Constance did everything she could. When she heard that the surgeon was willing to see Lizzie, she took her to East Grinstead and offered to pay whatever fee he charged.

The kindly surgeon smiled at Lizzie. 'We'll soon have that little blemish looking a whole lot better and you'll have your pretty face back. Trust me.'

And, along with the members of the Guinea Pig Club – the airmen who had been so badly damaged in their burning aircraft – Lizzie did trust him implicitly.

Her trust was well founded. After two operations there was only slight scarring that Mr McIndoe told her she would be able to cover with cosmetics once the wound was fully healed. So, after a few weeks of recuperation, Lizzie returned to work in the shop alongside her mother-in-law full-time and, bravely, she now faced all the customers.

It took a long time for Lizzie to pluck up the courage to talk to Emily about the other matter, which she had discussed with Constance, but one evening in April when she knew Trip was out, she walked the short distance to Emily's home and knocked on the door.

Emily smiled a welcome, but Lizzie was still hesitant. 'If you're busy, I can come back another time.' She almost hoped Emily would say 'Yes'.

'No, no, come in. I'll be glad of the company. If you don't mind staying in the kitchen. I'm just doing a bit of baking, though I'm not much good at it. Not like your mam – or mine. You make us both a cup of tea while I finish making this vegetable pie.'

'I thought Mam baked for you?'

'She does. But I don't want to forget how to cook and bake altogether. Besides, I quite like doing it now and again. I find it restful.'

When Emily's pie was in the oven and they were both seated, Lizzie couldn't put the moment off any longer. She took a deep breath. 'I just wanted to tell you about seeing Josh again when I went to Riversdale.' She paused and expected an outburst from Emily, but none came. She was silent, watching Lizzie's face and waiting for her to explain.

'I – I realized that I no longer think I'm in love with him, Emily. It was a girlish infatuation. I see that now. Do you remember that film that was all the rage not long after the war started? Everyone was talking about it.'

'Oh, I remember. *Gone with the Wind*, you mean?'

Lizzie nodded. 'Do you remember Scarlett's passion for Ashley Wilkes and how it blinded her to the man she should have loved? Rhett?'

Emily nodded.

'Well, that was me. I was infatuated with Josh and, if at the beginning he'd liked me too, then I think we might have ended up together, but he was always in love with Amy, wasn't he? Just like Ashley Wilkes was always in love with Melanie.'

'My word, you have remembered the story and the names,' Emily laughed.

But Lizzie was very serious. 'I didn't get to see the

film – I wish I had – but I was so intrigued by what the girls were saying at work – always quoting what Rhett Butler said as he left her at the end of the film – that I got the book and read it. In fact, I read it twice. Well, I'm luckier than Scarlett. The man I *should* love isn't going to walk away from me like Rhett did at the end of the book. Billy does give a "damn" about me – a lot more than a "damn" – and now I know that I love him. Oh Emily, if only he comes home safely, I vow I'll spend the rest of my life proving it to him.'

Emily covered Lizzie's hand with her own. 'He will, I'm sure of it. And I'm so glad you told me all this. Thank you, Lizzie. It can't have been easy for you.'

As 1944 dawned, a feeling of optimism pervaded the country. It was as if something very exciting, though very hush-hush, was going to happen.

'I think they're preparing to get a foothold back in Europe,' said Trip, who not only read all the newspapers avidly and listened to the wireless every night, but was also adept at 'reading between the lines'. He seemed to have an uncanny feel for what was happening.

'Mm,' Emily said, her head bent over her mending, her mind not really concentrating on what Trip was saying.

He switched off the wireless, put down his paper and leaned forward, his elbows resting on his knees. 'Come on, Emily Trippet. Out with it.'

She looked up, a pensive smile on her mouth. 'Out with what?'

'I know you too well, my darling. Something's bothering you. Tell me what it is. Maybe I can help.'

She lay down her sewing on her lap and her voice trembled a little as she said, 'Lewis will be eighteen in May. I know we persuaded him to stay on into the sixth form at school with the hope that he might go to university . . . we really thought the war would be over by now, didn't we?'

'We certainly hoped it would be, yes.'

'If he does well and applies to go to university and is accepted, do you think his call up would be deferred?'

'I really can't say, but even if it was, I wouldn't be surprised at him wanting to volunteer.'

Emily stared at him, then she sighed and said flatly, 'I thought that too. What about Philip? He's still working on the land, so he should be all right, shouldn't he? I couldn't bear it if Josh and Amy had another son to worry about.'

'He's worked on the land since he was fourteen, so, yes, I think he'll be in a reserved occupation.'

'Thank goodness for that. But what about Lewis?'

Trip's face was solemn. That was a question he could not answer.

'Hartley – Hartley, ah, there you are.'

The CO, Nigel Price, came in through the office doorway like a whirlwind. Michael Hartley stood up from putting another log on the fire in the outer office where he had his desk and did all the paper-work for the station's CO.

'Word's just come through that Harry Ryan is

alive. He's a prisoner of war. I don't know why on earth we haven't heard before this, but never mind. I want you to write a letter to his family immediately. It isn't often we can send such good news. Type it up and I will sign it.'

When Price had disappeared into his office, Michael, grim faced, inserted a sheet of paper and began to type. He wrote the bare minimum of words and, when he handed it across Price's desk for signature, his superior said, 'That's a bit bald, Hartley. Show a little more enthusiasm for the fact that he's survived. It'll mean the world to his family.'

Tight-lipped, Hartley retyped the letter. 'That's better.' Price smiled and signed it with a flourish. 'See that it catches today's post, will you? And now I must be on my way. A big meeting at Area HQ. I've no idea what time I'll be back – probably not until tomorrow.'

As Hartley listened for the engine of the CO's car to start up and move away from its parking bay beneath the office window, he smiled grimly to himself. He rose from his chair, crossed the room towards the fire that was burning brightly now and tossed the letter, which he had just written and which Price had signed, into the flames.

'I'll be damned if I let them know he's safe,' he muttered. 'Let them suffer.'

Lewis was called up in the summer of 1944, when the country was in a state of high excitement after the victories of the D-Day landings. In a combined effort of American and British forces, troops had

landed on the beaches of Normandy and had begun
to drive the enemy back. But the celebrations were
tempered by the V-1 flying bombs being unleashed
on London and the South of England.

'Those poor folks. As if they haven't been through
enough at the start of the war. And where else will
they send them – the bombs, I mean?'

'I think their range might only reach to the south,'
Trip said, scouring the paper for news. But a shroud
of secrecy surrounded the new weapons and the
newspapers were not allowed to reveal the exact
locations where the bombs had fallen.

'They are saying that anti-aircraft guns are virtually useless against them, and the RAF are trying to
find new methods of interception.'

'I expect Harry would have been—' Emily began
and then stopped as thoughts of her nephew threatened to choke her.

'I know, love,' Trip said solemnly.

'And where is Lewis? I know he's still training,
but will he be sent down there or – or across the
Channel? I'm glad he went into the army and not
the RAF, but he could still be in danger, couldn't he?'

Trip nodded and folded his newspaper. 'I see
they're evacuating children from London again with
these wretched doodlebugs, as they're being called.'

Emily sighed. 'I'd offer to have some of them here,
but Sheffield might not be much safer.'

'Tell you what. Let's go to the pictures tonight.
Get our mind off things.'

Emily pulled a face then smiled. 'All right. It'll be
fine – until the newsreels come on!'

Although the Allies were back on French soil, there was still a long way to go. The Russians advanced on Poland and by August, the French regained Paris. But the bitter fighting continued and whilst the Nazis were being driven back, there was still fierce resistance and it wasn't until March the following year that the Allies finally crossed the Rhine and only at the end of April, when Mussolini was shot and Hitler committed suicide, that people could really begin to believe that the war might soon be over.

'But there'll be someone to take his place, won't there?' Emily asked worriedly.

'I expect so, but with him gone, maybe they'll come to their senses,' Trip said. He was far more optimistic now. With the many allied victories, he could see the Third Reich crumbling and the picture of the Russians and Americans meeting up in Berlin seemed to herald the end.

'There's one good thing,' Emily said, her mind, as always, on those close to her, 'Lewis is still in this country. Maybe it'll all be over before he has to go abroad.'

And though she didn't voice it aloud, her thoughts, as they always did, turned to her brother and the rest of the family in Ashford. Perhaps, once it was all over, they might find out what had happened to Harry. At least it would be a comfort to know.

Soon, Emily hoped, the war would be over and they could all begin to rebuild their lives. There had been more bombing raids, but none so severe as the Sheffield Blitz, as it came to be known, of December

461

1940. That industry had not been more severely damaged was a miracle to all those who lived and worked in the city.

Fifty-Nine

The back door to the smithy flew open and Lucy called out even before she'd stepped over the threshold.

'Aunty Amy – Aunty Amy!' When she'd first got to know the Ryans as a young girl, they'd been Lucy's 'adopted' aunty and uncle. Her nurse's cap was awry, her hair flying free, her eyes wide. 'He's come back. He's here. He's home.'

'Lucy! Whatever's the matter? You look as if you've seen a ghost.' Amy guided the girl to a chair. The usually composed and utterly professional nurse was laughing and crying at the same time. She flopped into the chair near the range opposite to where Bob now spent most of his time. Though his brain was sharp and active, his back caused him a lot of pain. 'Too much bending and wielding a heavy hammer,' he would say wryly. 'But I'm luckier than a lot of folks,' he would always add, casting a fond glance at Amy.

'I thought I had, Aunty Amy. But it's no ghost. It's him all right.'

For a moment, Amy stared at her and then she whispered, 'Harry!'

Lucy sat forward, looked up into Amy's face, grasped both her hands and said, 'Yes, he's alive.

463

He's here at Riversdale. You must come and see him right away.'

The colour drained from Amy's face and she might have fainted if Lucy hadn't jumped to her feet and steered Amy to the seat she'd just vacated.

'I knew it all along. I knew he wasn't dead,' Amy murmured and closed her eyes in thankfulness. But then they flew open again as she asked hesitantly, almost afraid to hear the answer, 'Is he – is he – all right?'

'He is now, but –' Lucy sat down on a low stool at Amy's feet and took her hand, chafing it to bring back the warmth – 'his leg was broken when he bailed out.'

'Was he captured?' Bob asked, his voice husky. He could hardly take in the wonderful news. He'd not had Amy's faith.

'Yes. He was in a prisoner-of-war camp for quite a while. He said he was medically well looked after, though, and when he was better, he tried two attempts to escape, both of which failed. So he was transferred from camp to camp, each time the security getting tighter and tighter. But then he tried again and succeeded. He was picked up by the French Resistance and sent down their escape route. And so, here he is in our very own convalescent home. That's all I know. I wanted to come to tell you straightaway.'

'Why didn't he come here?' Amy asked.

'The RAF brought him. He's very thin and under-nourished so he needs nursing care for a while.'

'I could look after him . . .' Amy began, anxious to have her son back home.

'Let Lucy care for him, Amy love,' Bob said gently. 'You'll be able to see him whenever you want, but Harry must obey the RAF's procedures.'

'Please let me look after him, Aunty Amy,' Lucy said softly and Amy could see the girl's love for Harry in her eyes.

'Of course you can, my dear, but I'm afraid I shall make a nuisance of myself visiting him.'

The two women hugged each other.

'Eeh, I don't know when I felt so happy,' Bob said, grinning. 'Wait till I tell Walter and Martha. I'll go right now. I presume Josh knows already?'

'Yes, it was Josh who met the three new arrivals at the door and saw that Harry was one of them. He wanted to rush home to tell you all, but he had to see that they were comfortable first. I said I'd come instead. Nurse Adams is looking after them. We didn't want to keep you in the dark a moment longer than we had to.'

'When can I see him?' Amy asked.

'Now – this minute.'

'We'll all come,' Bob declared, the news giving him a new vigour, 'though we won't all go in at once,' he added quickly.

'It'll be all right. He's up and about. You can see him in the patients' lounge. We only restrict the number of visitors when it's necessary either for a patient or others around them. No, you all come. He can't wait to see you, though he's mystified as to why you'd not heard that he's alive. That's what's upset him more than anything.'

'You're sure he wasn't badly injured?'

465

Lucy shook her head. 'He'll be fine. Though officially,' she winked and tapped the side of her nose, 'it's going to take him a good while to be fully fit enough to return to duty.'

Amy stared at her for a moment and then made a gurgling sound that was somewhere between laughter and tears.

At last it was all over and VE Day brought celebrations throughout the country. Trip and Emily drove to Ashford to celebrate with both sides of their family and – because Billy was not yet home – they invited Lizzie and Bess to go with them. Riversdale was still busy. Casualties had occurred right up until the fighting had stopped and patients were still filtering through from the hospitals.

'I think we shall be a convalescent home for a while longer,' Constance said.

Lucy had scheduled herself to be on duty that day. So many of the other members of staff deserved a day off. She would have Harry all to herself that night when everyone else had gone, for he was still a patient there. He was in no hurry to leave, even though his home was only just down the road.

'I'll have to kick you out if we need your bed, though,' Lucy teased him.

The number of visitors for each patient was relaxed for this day only and Riversdale heaved with patients and their families. Grace and Mrs Froggatt kept everyone supplied with drinks and snacks.

'You go and celebrate with your family, Martha,'

Elsie Froggatt declared. 'We can have any old day off.'

And so the Trippets, the Ryans and the Clarks, and Constance and George were all sitting together in the residents' lounge. Even Nell and Steve were there too. They had come to take Simon home for the first time in six years. In that time, he had grown from a little boy into a young man of fourteen and no one knew – not even Simon himself – how he was going to settle back into life in the city.

'Billy's coming home on leave again next week,' Lizzie said, 'but he doesn't know when he'll get demobbed.'

'I expect it will be those who've served abroad who'll get first chance.'

'No, I think it's more to do with length of service,' Trip said. 'Those who went in first will get home first. There's a chart somewhere that tells everyone on what date they'll be demobbed.'

'I'll tell Billy. Thanks, Trip. I'm so glad everyone's coming home safely, well, comparatively safely,' she said, glancing at Harry. 'We all had a worrying time when you were posted missing. I still don't understand why your family didn't hear that you were a POW. Surely, the authorities must have known?'

A voice spoke from the doorway. 'Can anyone join the party?'

'Barney! What are you doing here?' Harry struggled to his feet and slapped the newcomer on the back. 'This is Barney Lingard,' he introduced him. 'My very good friend from camp. How are you?'

'In the pink, old boy. How about you? And where,

might I ask, is the lovely lady who's going to be Mrs Ryan? I really must meet her.' He held up his hand in a mock promise. 'And I promise not to exert my charm on her. She is here, I presume.'

He glanced round at everyone and his eyes alighted on Sarah. 'Ah, is this . . . ?'

'That's my sister,' Harry laughed. 'So be careful.'

But Barney was not to be denied the chance to flirt. He took Sarah's hand and kissed it. 'I am very glad to meet you, Harry's pretty sister.'

Sarah, always shy, blushed whilst Harry introduced everyone to his friend.

At that moment, Lucy came into the room wheeling a medicine trolley. 'Sorry, folks, routine still has to go on, even today.'

Barney caught the look that passed between Harry and Lucy. 'Aha, now I think I have found the future Mrs Ryan, have I not?' He stepped towards Lucy and would have kissed her hand too, if Lucy hadn't chuckled and said, 'And you must be the infamous Barney. I've heard all about you.'

Barney grinned. 'All dreadful, I hope.'

'Indeed,' Lucy said, but she was still smiling.

'So? When's the big day?'

It seemed as if the whole family was holding its breath.

'He hasn't asked me yet.'

Barney glanced at Harry and winked broadly. 'Harry, you're slipping. Haven't you learned anything from your uncle Barney? Well, I won't embarrass you any further, old boy. But I should get a move on, if I were you. Just as I suspected, she's a lovely girl.

Some old reprobate like me will steal her away from you, if you're not careful.'

Lucy picked up two pills and a glass of water and moved to Harry's side. For a moment, they exchanged a long look that everyone could see, before Lucy said, 'Not a snowball's chance in hell – *old boy*.'

Everyone laughed, Barney the loudest of all.

When Lucy had administered the medication to Harry and to the other two patients in the room, she left and Barney sat down beside Sarah. He glanced round at the family. 'You must have all been so relieved to receive the letter telling you he was a POW.' For once Barney was quite serious now. 'It must have been an anxious time for you all.'

There was a moment's silence until Josh said, 'We didn't get a letter. We didn't know he was alive until he turned up here at Riversdale.'

'Didn't hear?' The ebullient young man was obviously shocked. 'But we knew at camp months ago. The CO told us when he heard. He'd told old scarface to write to you.'

'Don't call him that,' Harry said, and added, 'The flight lieutenant, who was the adjutant and the CO's right-hand man in the office, had a nasty scar down the left-hand side of his face, poor chap.'

'All right, then. He told *Flight Lieutenant Hartley* to write to Harry's family.'

There was a strange moaning sound and everyone turned to see Bess with her hand clamped over her mouth, her eyes wide, staring at Barney.

'Mam, what is it?' Lizzie, sitting beside her mother, was concerned. 'Are you all right? Sarah . . .'

'I'll get Lucy.' The girl, though training to be a nurse, didn't want to take the responsibility.

'Hartley?' Bess's question came out in a strangled gasp. 'You said his name was Hartley?'

Everyone was looking at her, puzzled, except perhaps Lizzie. She looked at Barney and then at Harry. Softly, she asked, 'Do you happen to know his Christian name?'

The two men glanced at each other, mystified. Barney shrugged and then said, 'I think it was Michael.'

Bess gave a groan and would have slipped sideways in her chair, if Lizzie hadn't been supporting her. At that moment Lucy came hurrying into the room. She bent over Bess. 'What is it, Mrs Dugdale? Are you ill?'

'It's all right, luv. I've just had a bit of a shock. At least – I think I have.'

'Would you like to come and lie down?'

'No – no, I'm all right. I've got to hear this. Please.' She turned to Harry. 'How old do you think he was?'

'In his early forties, wouldn't you say, Barney? He worked as the CO's right-hand man. He wasn't a flier or anything.'

'He'd been in the RAF for several years, I think,' Barney said.

'And he had a Sheffield accent,' Harry said. 'I did notice that.'

Bess glanced round the room and then explained. 'Mick's middle name was Hartley, after my dad.'

There was a murmur amongst the family. They didn't quite know what to say. Michael Hartley

470

Dugdale had caused several of them a great deal of heartache, and yet they felt for Bess. Steve fidgeted uncomfortably in his chair and Nell bit her lip.

'Do you think this man was your son, Mrs Dugdale?' Lucy asked gently. She had vague memories of the man who'd kidnapped her. And she remembered the scar. She would never forget the frightening scar.

'What I can't understand,' Bess said slowly, 'is how he could have got into the RAF, specially calling himself a different name.' She glanced round the room. 'Wouldn't he have had to produce his birth certificate?'

Before anyone else could answer her, Lizzie laughed wryly. 'You think a little thing like that would've stopped our Mick? With his contacts in the Smoke, he could have got any false documents he wanted.'

'It's possible, I suppose,' Bess mused, 'but I expect I'll never know for sure, 'cos he'll never come back to Sheffield, will he?'

No one answered her.

'Perhaps you could write to him, Mam, at this camp where he is.'

Barney looked embarrassed and cleared his throat. 'There's something you should know. If you do think he's who you say, er – Hartley used to go up to London whenever he had leave. None of us knew why. In fact, we knew very little about him. But on one of his jaunts, the hotel where he was staying was hit by one of those dreadful doodlebugs. I'm sorry, Mrs Dugdale, but he was killed. The CO got word at camp.'

Bess stared at him for a moment and the tears ran down her face.

'I think you should come with me for a moment,' Lucy said firmly now. Bess struggled to her feet and, leaning heavily against the young nurse, allowed herself to be led from the room.

Lizzie wiped her eyes. Though she was saddened by the news, she was not quite as devastated as Bess.

'It's an awful thing to say,' she said, her voice trembling a little, 'but maybe he's better off where he is. He was a bad lot and if what you're saying is true, Barney, he must have had something to do with Josh and Amy not getting a letter about Harry. Vengeful to the last, eh? I'm sorry if that's the case, Josh – Amy.'

Amy knelt beside her at once. 'It's not your fault, Lizzie, or your mam's. We all love you both. But I'm sorry for your loss. Whatever he did, he was still your brother and Mrs Dugdale's son.'

With Bess out of the room for a few moments, they could all speak more freely.

'I still don't understand how he could have whee-dled his way into the RAF. They don't just take anyone, you know,' Barney said bluntly.

'He was very clever,' Trip said. 'The sad thing was that he used that intelligence in the early days for criminal purposes.' He glanced at Lizzie, trying to bring her a little comfort. 'Perhaps he tried to redeem himself by finding a worthwhile career.'

'I doubt it,' Lizzie said tartly, no longer blind to her brother's wickedness. 'More likely he thought the authorities would never think of looking for him there. Like us, they'd think he could never have been accepted.'

The news had put a damper on the celebrations and soon after that the party broke up.

As the sun set in the western sky, Harry and Lucy stood on Sheep Wash Bridge, gazing at the gurgling water below them. The river curved between the trees on its way to Bakewell and was lost to sight.

Harry put his arm around her waist and took hold of her left hand. 'Do you realize that this is the very spot where I fell in love with you? I was nine years old.'

Lucy chuckled softly. 'After Lizzie's wedding? I do remember standing here with you and talking and I promised to show you around Sheffield, if you ever came to the city.'

'And you did.' Harry paused and then asked, 'When the convalescent home closes, will you go back to the city?'

'I don't know. I love it here. What will you do?'

'Probably stay in the RAF, if they'll have me. I signed on as a regular, not just for the duration of the war.'

'Will it still be – dangerous?'

'There shouldn't be anyone shooting at us now,' Harry laughed, 'but I suppose there's always an element of danger when you're several thousand feet up in the clouds, relying on one engine and a tank full of flammable fuel.'

'Life's all about risks, isn't it? It was a dreadful time when we thought you'd been killed. We've been very lucky that you've come back and Billy and Lewis will soon be home too.'

'So, Lucy Henderson, are you willing to take a risk? Will you marry me?'

Lucy touched his cheek with gentle fingers and whispered, 'I thought you'd never ask.'

On a warm September day, the members of the families, whose lives had been intertwined for over twenty-five years, met again in Ashford-in-the-Water to celebrate the marriage of Lucy and Harry. They were all there again and a great deal of reminiscing went on. Even Barney was there as Harry's best man. After the ceremony, when they all returned to Riversdale for the reception, Emily pulled Lizzie to one side. 'Are you all right, Lizzie? You looked a bit pale in church and I saw Billy take you outside while they were signing the register.'

'I had a bit of a shock yesterday, Emily, I don't mind admitting.'

'Oh dear, not bad news, I hope.'

Lizzie shook her head. 'No – no – it's good news, but it was a surprise.' She bit her lip and added, 'I didn't want to say anything today. This is Lucy's and Harry's day, so please, if I tell you, keep it to yourself.'

'Of course I will. Go on.'

'I haven't been feeling too well recently, so I went to the doctor and – and I'm pregnant.'

Emily's mouth fell open – she couldn't help it – and for several seconds she just stared at Lizzie. 'That's wonderful news. Lizzie, I'm so happy for you and Billy. I wondered why he was grinning broadly, like the proverbial cat that's got the cream.'

'I'm a bit old for having a baby,' Lizzie said and Emily heard the anxiety in her voice.

'Lots of women with large families are your age by the time they have their last babies.'

'Possibly, but not their first baby.'

'You'll be well looked after, Lizzie. We'll make sure of that. We'll mind your baby's not born in the back of the car like poor Lewis was.'

They both laughed. Lizzie linked her arm through Emily's and together they walked into the house to take their places at the table for the wedding breakfast.

'I'll keep my promise, Lizzie,' Emily whispered. 'I won't say anything to anyone today, but this is the start of a whole new life for couples like Harry and Lucy, for you and Billy, embarking on parenthood, and for all of us now the war is finally over.'

Lizzie hugged Emily's arm to her side. 'And the most wonderful thing is, Emily, through all the ups and downs, you and I are still friends.'

'The best, Lizzie. The very best.'

The Buffer Girls
Margaret Dickinson

Putting the shine back into Sheffield
in the aftermath of war

It is 1920 in the Derbyshire dales. The Ryan family are adjusting to life now that the war is over. Walter has returned home a broken man and so it falls to his son and daughter, Josh and Emily, to keep the family business going.

The Ryan children grew up with Amy Clark, daughter of the village blacksmith, and Thomas 'Trip' Trippet, whose father owns a cutlery manufacturing company in Sheffield. The four are still close and as romance blossoms for Josh and Amy, Emily falls in love with Trip – but is unsure if the feeling is mutual.

Martha Ryan is fiercely ambitious for her son and so she uproots her family to Sheffield, where she feels Josh will have more opportunities. But all Josh wants is to continue his father's candle making business and marry Amy. As the Ryans do their best to adapt to city life, their friendly next-door neighbour Lizzie helps the newcomers settle in. She even finds Emily employment as a Buffer Girl for the cutlery industry; though her attraction to Josh worries Emily.

Though her mother cannot recognize it, it is Emily who is best equipped to forge a career, while Josh's ambitions lie in a different direction. And as time goes on, problems and even dangers arise that the Ryan family could not possibly have foreseen.

Read the opening chapters here . . .

One

'You're not serious, Mam.'

Emily Ryan stood with her hands on her hips, her curly blond hair flying free, wild and untamed, and her blue eyes icy with temper. She was tall and slim, with a figure that had all the young men eyeing her longingly as she strode through her young life. Her lovely face, with its perfectly shaped nose and strong chin, was the epitome of determination. Nothing and no one would stop Emily Ryan doing exactly what she wanted with her life, except maybe one person: her mother, Martha.

'I'm deadly serious,' Martha said firmly, folding her arms across her ample bosom. She knew she had a battle royal on her hands as she faced her daughter. Emily resembled her mother, but the older woman's hair was now grey and drawn back into a bun and her once lithe figure had thickened with age and child bearing. Her face was lined with the anxieties life had brought her; her eyes were still bright but they turned cold when she was angry. And she was ready now. Battle lines were being drawn but Martha knew she would win in the end. She always did.

'But this is our home. You can't take us away from

1

all this.' Emily swept her arm in a wide arc to encompass the small, friendly Derbyshire village where they lived, and the surrounding fields and hills. 'It's Dad's life. He was born here in this cottage. His parents and grandparents are buried in the churchyard. You can't drag him to live in a *city*.' She spat out the word. 'He'd hate it. 'Specially now.' Her voice dropped as she thought about her beloved father, sitting huddled by the kitchen range where he now sat every day, so cruelly maimed by the Great War that he could no longer work. He'd been the village candle maker, working in the front room of their cottage and supplying the local village shop and several others in the district. And he'd always served those who came knocking on the front door. It had earned him a modest income and the family had been content, until the war had come and taken away the tall, strong man with a ready smile and a gentle manner. Now he was unbearably thin, his shoulders hunched. His hands shook uncontrollably and any exertion left him gasping for breath. His two children – Emily and Josh – had taken on the work and were trying to keep his small cottage industry going, but it wasn't the same without their talented father at the helm.

'He'd no need to volunteer,' Martha said quietly, her thoughts still on the carnage that had robbed her of the man Walter had been. 'He could at least have waited until he was called up.' Her mouth curled. 'He'd no need to be a hero.'

'Oh really,' Emily said, her tone laced with sarcasm, 'and have everyone around here brand him a coward? Handing him a white feather every time he set foot in Bakewell Market?'

'He could have found work in a reserved occupation and appealed against his call-up whenever it came,'

Martha snapped. 'But he didn't even wait to find out if he was to be conscripted. Off he went to answer the country's call as if Kitchener had been pointing his finger directly at him.'

'The ones who stayed were lads too young to go or old men,' Emily argued. 'The ones like Dad – fit and strong and healthy –' tears smarted at the back of her eyes as she thought about the proud, upright man her father had been before he'd marched away to fight for his country. But she kept her voice steady, silently vowing not to cry in front of her mother. Later, alone, perhaps she would allow the tears to fall. But not now. This was one battle she had to win, for her father, for her younger brother and for herself too – 'they all went and such a lot of them never came home. At least, Dad came back.'

For a long moment, Martha stared at her. Then she glanced away and murmured flatly, 'Aye, he did.' The unspoken words lay heavily between them. Perhaps it would have been better for all of them – including Walter himself – if he had not survived to be the broken wreck he now was.

Walter Ryan had been injured on 1 July 1916, the first day of the battle of the Somme, when thousands of his comrades had been mown down by enemy gunfire and blown to smithereens by their shells. It was a miracle he had not been killed and even more amazing that he had survived his terrible injuries to make it home to Blighty. The shrapnel in his leg had been removed and the wound had healed, but an earlier exposure to a gas attack and the constant pounding of the guns had left him gasping for breath, shell shocked and unable to speak.

Martha and Emily were standing in their small back

garden, which Josh and Emily had planted with rows of vegetables. They were well out of Walter's hearing and Josh was at work in the front room. There was no one to overhear the quarrel.

'What I don't understand, Mam, is why? We're happy here, aren't we? Josh and I are doing our best with the candle making. I make the wicks –' the braiding of the fine cotton threads required nimble fingers – 'and Josh makes the candles. He's got some exciting ideas. He wants to try making coloured candles and scented ones too. He's already carving some of the bigger ones and he showed them to Mrs Trippet at the big house. She said they were wonderful and she placed an order there and then. Oh, I know we're not as good at it as Dad, but we're getting better. And everyone around here helps us with Dad, if we need it. Mr Clark and Mrs Partridge have been wonderful. They come and sit with him and talk to him, even though he never answers them. Who's going to be on hand in the city?'

Martha bit her lip; this was where it would get really difficult. 'It's for Josh's sake. I've got to think of his future. There's nothing for him here.'

'What do you mean? Not many lads of seventeen have their own little business ready made for them.'

'Josh will be eighteen next month,' Martha said, 'and besides, he won't have much of a business soon. The demand for candles is decreasing with every day. You know yourself it is.'

'Ah,' Emily said slowly. 'Now I understand. It's always about Josh, isn't it? You want to uproot the whole family and take us to Sheffield – all for Josh.'

'Of course it's all for Josh,' Martha snapped, not even attempting to be apologetic. 'He's a man and he's got to make his way in the world.'

4

'And what about me?' Emily asked softly. 'Do I really count so little with you, Mam?'

'Don't be silly, Emily. Of course you *count*. But you'll get married. You don't need a career. Not like a man does. Not like Josh does. And you tell me –' Martha prodded her finger towards her daughter – 'what else there is around here for him that would make him a good living – that would make him someone – because if you know of something, then I'd like to hear it.'

Emily couldn't answer her. There was nothing locally that could offer Josh the opportunities he would find in the city. But she was not about to be beaten yet.

'What about Amy?' she said, trying a different tack. 'She and Josh are walking out together now.'

Martha's eyes narrowed. 'Are they indeed? And when did that start?'

Emily shrugged, wishing she hadn't said anything. It was not her secret to tell, but it was done now. 'They've always been friends, but just lately – well, they've got closer. Or are you thinking that she'll come with us?'

Martha shook her head. 'No, she wouldn't leave her dad.'

The village blacksmith, Robert Clark, who lived next door, had been a widower since his wife had died shortly after giving birth to Amy. In the early years, Robert had paid a kindly woman, Mrs Grace Partridge, who lived in one of the cottages further up the lane, to care for the infant whilst he worked. But at all other times, father and daughter had been – and still were – inseparable and so it had brought Robert peace of mind when Josh Ryan had begun courting Amy. Whatever happened, he would still have his daughter close by. Perhaps they could even live with him, he had daydreamed, and, in time, maybe another little one would bring joy to his life.

5

Emily stared at Martha. 'So, you don't care about tearing them apart? I thought you liked Amy.'

'I do. She's a sweet girl, but Josh can do better for himself. If he marries, he needs someone who'll help him achieve his ambitions.'

'*Your* ambitions, Mam. Let's be honest about this. Josh is quite content to stay here, make candles, marry Amy and raise a family. But that's not good enough for you, is it? What do you want him to be? The owner of a steel works and live in a mansion?'

Martha shrugged. 'Maybe one day. If he would only apply himself, work hard and—'

'Mam, have you taken leave of your senses?'

'Don't you talk to me like that, Emily Ryan, else you'll feel the back of my hand.' Martha raised her arm as if to carry out her threat.

Emily faced her unflinchingly and smiled grimly. 'I've felt it often enough. One more time won't make any difference.' But Martha dropped her hand and turned away, saying over her shoulder, 'And don't you go telling Josh. I'll be the one to tell him tonight.'

Through narrowed eyes, Emily watched her mother go into the cottage by the back door, but even though she knew her father would need attention, the girl made no move to help. Her mind was working feverishly. Not for the first time in her young life, she was about to disobey her mother.

Two

The Ryans lived in the picturesque village of Ashford-in-the-Water in Greaves Lane. Stone cottages and houses lay beside the River Wye as it meandered towards Bakewell, just over a mile away. The village had, in its time, boasted several small industries; the quarrying, cutting and polishing of black marble; lead mining; and cottage industries of stocking making and candle making. A member of the Ryan family had been the village's chandler for at least four generations. No one was quite sure when the small business had begun, but the Ryans knew that Walter's grandfather, Luke, had certainly been the first in their family to take it on in the mid-1800s. Since then, each successive generation had continued with the profession. Now it had fallen to a very young Josh to carry it on. And it was what he wanted to do. He loved the work; he even gloried in the strong-smelling tallow, rendered from animal fat, though now he experimented with a refined form called stearin, which gave off a more pleasant odour. Special candles for the church or for the wealthy houses in the district were made from beeswax and Josh still made these too. But the young man was full of other ideas to move the business into the twentieth century. Next door to The Candle House was the village smithy, with its wide door open to the street whenever Bob Clark was working at his anvil with the glowing coals of the forge behind him. And next to that, on the corner of the lane, was the building that had once been a beer house.

After the confrontation with her mother, Emily walked through the cottage, passing her father still sitting in his rocking chair by the kitchen range. She didn't even glance at him, so afraid was she that he might see the anger in her eyes. She entered the front room, which their great-grandfather had made into a workshop for the candle making, on the right-hand side of the cottage's front door. In that way, customers could visit the small workshop without disturbing the rest of the family. Emily sat down beside Josh. He glanced up at her with a swift grin before carrying on with the intricate carving of a large, thick candle with a thin-bladed tool.

'I'm still working on it, Em, but I'll get it right one day. I'm getting better at it.' It was something new that Josh was trying and one of several ordered by Mrs Trippet, the lady in the big house near the Sheep Wash Bridge over the River Wye that flowed beside Ashford.

Emily glanced at her brother, resisting the impulse to ruffle his tousled hair. She loved him dearly, even though she'd always been aware that he was their mother's favourite – a fact Martha had never even tried to hide. He was a good-looking boy, who was swiftly growing into manhood. He was thin, but deceptively strong and would grow taller and broaden out. Soon, he would look very like their father had once done, with light brown hair, hazel eyes and a merry face that always seemed to be smiling. But Emily knew that the news he would receive this day would wipe the smile from his face. The thought brought a lump to her throat and her voice was a little husky as she said softly, 'Josh,

Mam is going to tell you something tonight so you must promise to act all surprised when she does.'

With a sigh, Josh laid aside the tiny knife, stretched his shoulders, yawned and then turned towards her with a wide grin. 'What is it, Em? Out with it.'

Emily licked her dry lips. 'She's planning to move us, lock, stock and barrel, to Sheffield.'

'Eh?' Josh dropped his arms, the smile disappearing from his face. 'What did you say?'

'She's planning to move us to Sheffield.'

For a stunned moment, he stared at her. 'Whatever for?'

'She doesn't think there are enough opportunities here for you to go up in the world.'

'But I don't want to go up in the world. I'm perfectly happy here. I like making candles and I like the villagers dropping in to buy them and have a natter. And I've a regular order for plain candles and tapers from Mr Osborne at the corner shop.' He nodded his head towards the window to the shop across the road. 'And besides, there's Amy. I'm not leaving Amy and she wouldn't come because she won't leave her dad. So that's it.' He picked up his knife again. 'We're not going.'

Emily sighed. There were going to be ructions in this house tonight and no mistake.

'I've made your favourite for tea, Josh,' Martha smiled at him as she placed a plate of steaming food in front of him, 'stew and dumplings.'

Josh breathed in deeply. 'Smells wonderful, Mam.' He picked up his knife and fork and began to eat hungrily whilst, by the range, Emily gently spooned stew into her father's mouth. There was nothing she could do to prevent Walter hearing Martha's plans and, whilst he could not speak, she knew he would understand. Just occasionally, she could see a look of comprehension in his eyes or a faint smile on his lips. She smiled at him tenderly, knowing that in a few moments his whole world, such as it was now, was going to be shattered.

Martha sat down at the table, but she was not eating. She faced her son across the snowy tablecloth and took a deep breath.

'I've been talking to Mr Trippet.' Martha cleaned at the Trippets' home, Riversdale House, two days a week. It was unusual – but not unknown – for her to talk to the master.

Josh looked up and Emily, glancing briefly towards him, marvelled at his acting prowess. 'Oh, he's home at the moment, is he? Is Trip here too?'

Thomas Trippet – 'Trip' to his friends – was the son of Arthur Trippet, who owned a cutlery-manufacturing business in Sheffield but lived the life of a country gentleman in Ashford. At nineteen, nearly twenty, Trip was only a few months older than Emily and almost two years older than Josh. The four children, for they'd always included Amy Clark, had been friends since childhood, running wild and free through the village and roaming the hills and dales close to their home. They loved to stand on Sheep Wash Bridge, near to Trip's home, watching the farmers, who still used the river to wash the sheep before shearing.

'Oh, look at the poor lambs,' tender-hearted, six-year-old Amy had cried the first time the children had seen the old custom. 'They're crying for their mothers. Why are they being penned on the opposite bank?'

'To make the ewes swim across to them,' Josh, two months older and so much wiser, had laughed. 'That

10

way they'll be all nice and clean when they scramble out the other side. Come on, I'll race you home. Your dad will be watching out for you.' And then he'd taken her hand and they'd run down the road towards their two homes that stood side by side. Two years older, Trip and Emily had lingered by the bridge until dusk forced them home too.

At other times, the four of them would fish from the bridge with home-made rods and lines or throw sticks into the flowing water and then run to the other side to see whose stick emerged from beneath the bridge first, to be declared the winner. Often, they would beg chopped vegetable scraps from the cook at Riversdale House or birdseed from Mrs Partridge, who kept a bird table in her garden, to feed the ducks that always gathered around the bridge. One of their favourite spots was Monsal Head, where they looked down on the viaduct and watched the trains passing between Rowsley and Buxton. A rare treat for the children had been to catch the train at the little station halfway up the hillside of Monsal Dale and ride to Buxton, the two girls clutching each other as they travelled through the dark tunnels on the journey. One of their favourite times of the year – and one in which the children would all be involved – was the thanksgiving for water celebrated on Trinity Sunday and accompanied by the dressing of five wells dotted about the village.

Grace Partridge would always be the one to dress the well in Greaves Lane and each year she would say to Amy, 'I need you to help me. Your dad and Uncle Dan –' Grace referred to her husband, Dan Partridge – 'have got the bed of clay ready for me and now we must pick the flowers and press the petals into the clay to make a picture. What shall we do this year? A picture of the church, d'you think? We could use seeds to make the walls and cones for the trees. We can use anything we like, Amy, as long as it grows naturally.'

Sadly, since the Great War, the custom had ceased.

'I reckon folks don't feel like merrymaking just now,' Grace had said wisely. 'But I expect they'll revive the tradition one day. I do hope so.'

And with the end of the dreadful war that had left so many grieving, those idyllic childhood days were gone and now, since leaving boarding school, Trip had left the village to work in his father's factory in Sheffield. Arthur Trippet was a strict disciplinarian and had made his son start at the very bottom and work his way up in the business. There were no privileges of position for young Thomas Trippet. He even had to stay in lodgings in the city rather than travel home each night in his father's grand car.

Trippets' made penknives and pocketknives. Trip was first put to work as a grinder. It was a dirty job, sitting astride a seat as if he were riding a horse, with the wheel rotating away from him in a trough of water. The cutlery industry had originally developed in Sheffield because of the waterpower available from the city's fast-flowing rivers for the forges and grinding wheels. The tradition of the 'little mester', often working alone with treadle-operated machines, but sometimes employing one or two men and apprentices, has always been an important part of the city's famous trade. With the coming of steam power, which could operate a line-shaft system to drive several machines at once, large factories were built, although these were still made up of individual workshops rented out. Trippets' factory, built for one owner by Arthur's grandfather in the nineteenth century, was a rare phenomenon at that time.

'I'll not have you treated any differently from my other employees,' Arthur had told his son. 'You'll work your way up in the firm just like anyone else and, if you prove yourself, one day you'll take over, but only if you've earned it, mind.'

Now, hearing his name mentioned, Emily's heart skipped a beat. She'd been in love with Trip from the age of twelve. It had been then that she'd realized he meant more to her than the other village lads. As she'd grown up, they'd become even closer. Emily believed they were soulmates and would never be separated. But they had been, for Trip had been sent away, first to boarding school and then to Sheffield. Hearing her mother's plans now, Emily felt torn. She didn't want to leave Ashford and she dreaded the thought of what such a move would do to her poor father – and to Josh. But if there was a chance of being nearer to Trip . . .

Her wandering thoughts were brought back to what her mother was saying. 'Never mind about Thomas just now. This is about you. About your future.'

With a supreme effort, Josh kept a puzzled look on his face. 'My future, Mam? What has Mr Trippet got to do with my future?' Then his face brightened and Emily stifled her laughter. Oh, this was better than going to the theatre in Buxton. What a star performer Josh was!

'You mean,' her brother was saying with feigned innocence, 'he's placed a huge order for candles for Riversdale House?'

'No, I do *not* mean that, Josh,' Martha snapped, her patience wearing thin. 'Will you just listen to me? I've been asking Mr Trippet's advice and he says that although he has no vacancies in his factory at the moment, he has business colleagues in the city and he's

13

willing to put in a good word for you.' As Josh opened his mouth to speak, Martha rushed on. 'He was the Master Cutler of The Company of Cutlers in Hallamshire for a year, you know, a while back. I expect his name is listed on a brass plaque somewhere in Cutlers' Hall in the city. Now, wouldn't that be something if one day your name was up there too?'

Josh blinked. Now, there was no more need to pretend ignorance. 'You mean you want me to go and work in Sheffield?'

'We'll all go. We'll move there. Emily will soon find a job of some sort.' Emily was amused to hear how she was brushed aside as if she were of little or no importance. 'And your dad will be nearer a hospital, so it'd be better for him.' This was something Emily had not heard before; her mother must have come up with that persuasive argument since they'd spoken in the garden. But it was all designed to bend Josh to her bidding. 'And I'm sure I could find cleaning work to keep us going until you earn a proper wage. I expect there'll be some sort of apprenticeship you'll have to do.'

'Aye, about seven years, I shouldn't wonder, and an apprentice lad's wage would be paltry, Mam. It would be years before I could hope to earn decent money.'

'But it'd be worth it.' Martha leaned across the table, pressing home her point. 'In the end. Don't you see?'

Josh shook his head. 'No, I don't. We're doing all right here. I'd rather be a big fish in a little pond than a sprat in a river. I'm a country bumpkin, Mam, not a streetwise city lad. I'd be eaten alive.'

Martha sighed and shook her head in exasperation. 'No ambition, that's your trouble, Josh.'

'It's hard work, Trip was telling me the last time he was home for a weekend.'

Emily wiped her father's dribbling mouth as she remembered that glorious June Sunday when the four of them had walked from Ashford following the river's twists and turns until they had come to Monsal Dale and, this time, had walked beneath the viaduct to watch the fast-flowing water tumbling over the weir. They'd laughed and joked and had such fun. That had been a few weeks ago and she hadn't seen Trip since. But he would come back, she consoled herself. This was his home. He'd always come back to Ashford. But would it be to see her?

Thomas Trippet was a handsome young man in anyone's eyes, not only in Emily's. He was tall with black hair and warm brown eyes. His skin was lightly tanned from roaming the hills and dales near his home – he loved the outdoor life – and the lines around his eyes crinkled when he laughed. And he laughed often, for he was forever teasing and joking. Emily knew the friendship between the four of them was strong, but did Trip feel as much for her as she now knew she did for him? It was a question she often asked herself, but one she could not answer. When he'd left that weekend, he'd hugged her and kissed her cheek but there'd been no promise to meet again, not a hint that he wanted her to be 'his girl'.

Her thoughts were brought back to the present with a jolt. Suddenly, Josh jumped up from the table, sending his chair crashing to the floor behind him, making them all jump and agitating Walter. His shaking was suddenly worse and he clasped Emily's hand, his eyes wide and pleading. 'It's all right, Dad,' she whispered, trying to reassure him, but she couldn't make her voice sound convincing.

'I'm not going, Mam.' Josh was shouting now. 'You

do what you like, but I'm staying here, making my candles and marrying Amy – if she'll have me.'

'She'll have you right enough,' his mother snorted. 'She knows a good catch when she sees it. And I expect her father's pushing for the two of you to get wed, just so's he can keep her close by and looking after him. He'll want you moving in there with them, I shouldn't wonder.'

Josh bit his lip. The matter had already been talked about between them when Josh had asked Amy to marry him on the day when the four of them had walked to the viaduct. Falling behind Emily and Trip, he and Amy had paused beneath the shadow of the arches. He'd kissed her and asked her to be his wife.

'Oh Josh, yes.'

'Let's keep it our secret for a while, shall we?' he'd whispered. 'I've got to get my mother used to the idea first.'

Amy, a pretty girl with delicate china-doll looks that belied an inner strength, had giggled and shaken back her fair hair. 'Well, there's no need to worry about my dad. He can't wait to walk me down the aisle and he's already said we can live with him.'

'That's settled, then.' Josh had hugged her again. 'And how do you feel about a spring wedding in the village church?'

'It's what I've always dreamed of.'

'Marrying me, I hope,' he'd teased her, but Amy had been solemn as she'd said, 'Of course. There's never been anyone else for me, Josh.'

He'd kissed her again, his kisses becoming urgent with desire now that they were promised to each other. Since that day, they'd met often, just the two of them.

With Trip gone, Emily didn't seem to want to go with them.

'I'm not playing gooseberry,' she'd laughed.

Though nothing had been said, Emily could see the love between her brother and Amy blossoming and she wasn't going to stand in their way. But now it seemed as if all Josh's plans lay in ruins as he stood glaring at his mother across the table.

'I'm not going,' he declared again. 'I'm not leaving Ashford – or Amy – and that's final.'

Three

Martha lay in her single bed, her eyes wide open and staring towards the ceiling in the darkness. She and Walter had separate beds now for his constant restlessness disturbed her sleep. But tonight it was not Walter who was keeping her awake far into the night; it was her guilty conscience. Martha couldn't remember ever having told lies in her life, except perhaps a little white one when Mrs Partridge had bought a new hat and asked Martha's opinion. Of course, she'd said it was lovely and most appropriate for the woman with a surname like hers. The hat had been swathed in flowers with a tiny bird nestling in the crown. But it had been like a creation a music hall star might have worn! But tonight, even the memory of that moment could not bring a smile to Martha's lips as it normally did. Her lie to her family had been a whopper. She had, indeed, spoken to Mr Trippet as she had told them but his reaction had not been one of kindness and a promise to help Josh find work in the cutlery manufacturing trade for which Sheffield was justifiably famous. His answer had been the opposite. Arthur Trippet was a large man, overweight through years of good living and self-indulgence. Although his sleek hair was thinning, he sported a well-trimmed moustache. His heavy jowls were speckled with tiny red veins and his blue eyes were cold and calculating, yet he always dressed like a smart

Edwardian gentleman in morning coat and striped trousers, a waistcoat and white, wing-collared shirt and bow tie. The motorcar he drove to and from the city each day was more up to date than his mode of dress; it was a black and yellow 1919 Silver Ghost Rolls-Royce, complete with the flying lady emblem on the bonnet. It was the object of admiration or envy when it passed through the village.

Leaning back in the swivel chair in the room set aside in Riversdale House as his study and puffing on a huge cigar, Arthur Trippet had pursed his thick lips and shaken his head. 'Oh no, Mrs Ryan. I don't think it's the kind of thing your son would take to. Besides, he's doing very nicely with his own little cottage industry.' The words – and his tone – were condescending. 'And what about your poor husband? Here, he has friends and neighbours to help you should you need it.'

This was true and Emily had touched upon the same thing. Walter was well known and respected in the village. He had been born here, in the very house they still lived in, for whilst it was rented accommodation, the tenancy had passed down the generations to him and would one day likely pass to Josh. But Martha was not willing to see Josh as the next generation of chandlers. She had visions of his name being on one of the panels in the Cutlers' Hall in Sheffield and of him living in a big house like the Trippets.

Martha had no intention of taking Arthur Trippet's advice. He's jealous, that's what it is, she told herself. Just because his lad has had to start at the bottom in the business – not bright enough to be given a decent position from the off, I expect – he doesn't want my Josh outshining his own son.

19

Thomas Trippet was a nice boy, a good boy, and Martha had been pleased enough that he was a friend of both Josh and Emily. She had seen it as a way for Josh to go up in the world. For her son to be friends with the offspring of the wealthiest man in the village had been a feather in her cap.

'Master Thomas is coming to tea with us tonight,' she would say loftily to Mr Osborne, who ran the corner shop just opposite the Ryans' home. 'A nice piece of your best cooked ham, if you please. Yours is so much nicer than I can cook myself,' she would add with a smile that was almost coquettish, hoping her flattery would earn her a few coppers' discount.

But they saw little of Trip now and it was not only Josh and Emily who lamented his absence; their mother, too, was frustrated at the severing of ties between the two families. She took it as a personal affront, believing that Arthur Trippet thought the Ryans were not good enough company for his son. Martha's ambitious nature had been thwarted when she was young. She had been brought up in a large family, one of nine children, none of whom, in her words, 'had amounted to much'. Being the eldest girl, she had often been obliged to stay home from school to help her mother with the younger children. As soon as she was old enough, she'd been sent from Over Haddon where she lived to Ashford to work in a small stocking mill there and that was how she'd met Walter Ryan, son and heir to the village candle maker. To Martha's young mind, Walter, with his own business, would hold a respected position in the village. Pretty and vivacious, she had set her cap at Walter, sweeping aside any competition from the village girls and ensnaring him almost before he had realized what was happening. She had been a good wife and mother

– no one could deny that – but from the day that her son had been born, she had become a boastful mother and soon the locals grew tired of hearing about how Josh had walked and talked earlier than any other child, how he could read even before he started school and knew his times tables by the time he was seven. Even then, she had firmly believed that her boy was going up in the world.

We'll show Arthur Trippet, she told herself softly in the darkness. Josh will prove he's ten times the man Thomas is. One day Josh will be 'someone' and where will young Trip be then? Nowhere, that's where. But how am I ever to persuade Josh to move?

She lay there for a long time, twisting and turning as she thought over the problem. Sleep was impossible until she— and then she thought of something; something with which Josh could not possibly argue.

Her determination strengthened as she turned over onto her side, closed her eyes and pushed away her guilty thoughts. It would all be worthwhile in the end. What was the saying she'd heard? 'The end justified the means.' Yes, that was it. Well, the end of all this would be that her Josh would rise in the world. He would rise so high that he'd leave all the Thomas Trippets on this earth wallowing in the mud at his feet. But first, they were all moving to Sheffield and now she knew how she was going to bring it about.

Her decision made, Martha slept.

The argument raged on for days and into weeks. Emily watched as Martha launched a tirade of reasons why the whole family should move to Sheffield. She hardly dared to look at her father, whose ravaged body seemed to shrink even more. He hadn't spoken since the day

21

he had come home from France, but Emily was sure he understood every word that was spoken in his hearing.

'Just think of the opportunities you'd have in the city,' Martha persisted, trying to wear Josh down. 'You'd have a skill and a job for life.'

'I've got a skill now,' Josh muttered, his normal happy-go-lucky smile wiped from his face.

'Pah! Makin' candles! And how long d'you think folks are going to want them? We're moving into a new age of inventions that folk like us have never dreamed of. Candles will be a thing of the past, but cutlery and the like will always be wanted.'

'You sure, Mam? Maybe some clever feller will invent something that feeds us without us having to use knives and forks.'

'None of your sarcastic lip, my lad,' Martha snapped. 'I'm only thinking of you and your future.'

'Candle making is the family business, Mam, a business that our Great-granddad Ryan took on and Granddad and then Dad continued. Doesn't that mean anything to you?'

'Not much, no. Not when it's your future at stake.'

And then, Josh blurted out the news that he had been trying to keep secret, but now found impossible. 'I've asked Amy to marry me and she's said yes. We're going to be married in the spring.'

Emily's head jerked up. For a moment she gaped at Josh and then her attention focused on her mother. What would she do now? To her surprise, Martha was smiling smugly.

'Has she now?' Martha said slowly. 'Josh, you're seventeen and so is she. What do you think her father's going to say to that?'

Josh shrugged. 'I'm eighteen in three weeks' time.

Besides, her father's all for it. He's even said we can live with him.'

Martha nodded slowly. 'Of course he's for it. It'll keep her at home, won't it? Looking after him. Oh, you're the perfect match for her as far as he's concerned.'

'I'm the perfect match for Amy, an' all.'

'Of course you are,' Martha said again. 'Nice little business already going—'

'Exactly. Now you've said it yourself.'

'And how d'you think that *little* business is going to support two families?'

Josh stared at her for a moment and then was forced to look away. The income from candle making wasn't vast by any means and some weeks the Ryan family only just managed to scrape by. If he married Amy, he would obviously be expected to contribute to their household expenses too.

Emily rose from her chair beside her father where she'd been sitting holding his hand and patting it absently as she listened to the quarrel. She'd kept silent until now. Pushing aside her own secretly held reasons for wanting to move to the city to be nearer Trip, she said, 'We can increase output. I could have a stall in Bakewell Market on a Monday. We used to do that years ago. You ran it yourself, Mam, before – before the war.'

'You keep out of this, miss. It's none of your business.'

'Yes, it is,' Emily said hotly, 'if I'm to go to Sheffield too. And what sort of job can I get? I only know candle making, like Josh.'

Martha rounded on her. 'You can pick up a job anywhere.'

'Doing what?'

'*I* don't know,' Martha snapped impatiently. 'But

there'll be plenty of jobs in the city.' She turned her attention back to Josh and Emily knew that she was forgotten.

'Listen to me, Josh.' Martha's tone took on a gentle, almost pleading tone. 'Don't you think I have your best interests at heart?'

At the expense of everyone else, Emily thought, but now she said nothing.

'I know that, Mam, but I don't want to go "up in the world". I just want to be happy. And I will be – with Amy.'

'She's not the right wife for you. She's no drive, no ambition. You could do far better for yourself.'

'I love Amy and she loves me.'

'And when did all this happen, might I ask?'

There was a moment's pause before Josh muttered, 'We've been walking out together for over two months.'

'And you never thought to say anything? You left it to your sister to tell me and that was only yesterday.'

Slowly, Josh raised his head. 'I – we wanted to keep it to ourselves.'

'Because –' Martha nodded knowingly – 'you knew that I wouldn't agree to it.'

'No – that wasn't the reason. I didn't know you wouldn't be happy for us. I thought you liked Amy.'

'I do like her. She's a nice girl, but she's not good enough for you.'

Josh gaped at Martha and gasped. 'That's a horrid thing to say. Who on earth do you think *we* are to be so high and mighty?'

'Nobody – yet,' Martha said, 'but you're going to change all that.'

Josh shook his head. 'No – no, I'm not. I am staying here and—'

'You are *not*. You are moving to Sheffield and one day you're going to make even the likes of Arthur Trippet sit up and take notice.'

'You can't make me.' Josh was showing stubbornness that none of them had ever seen in him before and whilst it frustrated Martha, it filled Emily with pride and admiration. She'd thought she was the only one who ever stood head to head and argued with their mother. Now she was a mere bystander as Josh remained adamant.

But Martha had a trump card up her sleeve and now she played it.

'You're not of age yet, Josh. You're not even eighteen. You need my consent to get married before you're twenty-one.'

Josh stared at her, dumbstruck now in the face of her declaration, which he knew to be no idle threat.

'You – you wouldn't?'

Martha smiled as she said softly, 'Oh yes, I would, Josh. It's for your own good. I'm not letting you throw yourself away on the likes of Amy Clark when you can do so much better for yourself. Do you think Arthur Trippet would let his son marry Emily? Of course he wouldn't and I'm not going to let you marry beneath you either.'

At her mother's words, Emily's heart constricted. It was like a physical pain in her chest. She'd never stopped to think for one moment that Trip's family would be against their friendship, but now her mother was voicing it.

'I shouldn't wonder if that's not why he's sent young Thomas away to work – and live – in the city. To get him away from the village and prepare him for his rightful place in the world.'

25

Emily felt her legs weak beneath her and she sank back down into the chair beside her father. To her surprise, Walter reached out a shaking hand and put it over hers. She turned to face him with tears in her eyes and though he did not speak she could see his features working with emotion and the anguish in his eyes broke her heart. She knew that he understood every word that was being said, but was helpless to do anything about it. Though his hand trembled against hers, his touch and his obvious understanding comforted Emily, even though, in that moment, hope died within her. Emily loved and respected her mother, but she had always idolized Walter. He had always been a kind and loving father, never too busy to mend a broken toy, to join in a childish game or to bathe a scraped knee. Martha had been the one to discipline their children, to teach them right from wrong and instil in them the right values and morals – a good code of life – but it had been Walter who had brought fun into their lives. Sadly, now he could only sit and listen to the raging argument, unable to voice his point of view, at the mercy of Martha's sharp tongue.

Josh was still not ready to capitulate. 'Dad would sign for me. I know he would.'

'No doubt,' Martha said tartly. 'But, even if he could still sign his name properly, which I doubt, who is going to take the word of a broken man against mine?'

Now Josh had no answers left – and neither, sadly, had Emily.

FOR MORE ON

MARGARET DICKINSON

sign up to receive our

SAGA NEWSLETTER

Packed with **features, competitions, authors'
and readers' letters** and **news of exclusive events,**
it's a must-read for every Margaret Dickinson fan!

Simply fill in your details below and tick to confirm that you would
like to receive saga-related news and promotions and return to us at
Pan Macmillan, Saga Newsletter, 20 New Wharf Road, London, NI 9RR.

NAME

ADDRESS

POSTCODE

EMAIL

I would like to receive saga-related news and promotions (please tick)

*You can unsubscribe at any time in writing or through our website where you can also see
our privacy policy which explains how we will store and use your data.*